DARKLIGHT
COMMANDO, INC.

DARKLIGHT

Commando, Inc.

C.J. Daniels

ABSOLUTELY AMA⚡ING eBOOKS

ABSOLUTELY AMAZING eBOOKS

Published by Whiz Bang LLC, 926 Truman Avenue, Key West, Florida 33040, USA.

For information contact:
Publisher@AbsolutelyAmazingEbooks.com
ISBN-13: 978-1945772252 (Absolutely Amazing Ebooks)
ISBN-10: 1945772255

I want to dedicate this to my wife Janice, for without you and the need for your "new outfit" none of this would ever be possible. Keep on pushing me.

DARKLIGHT
Commando, Inc.

CHAPTER 1

Firestorms blazed across a blood-red sky. Illuminated in their fury, there stood a lone structure. Its two stone towers, decaying and in ruin, reached upward from the surrounding wasteland, seemingly in a gesture of defiance. The castle resembled a dark, nightmarish fairytale, but there was no beautiful princess inside, no damsel; there was only distress, only lingering horror and death.

A wall of stone, weathered and beaten, surrounded and sheltered all within, as a shroud protecting a morbid corpse. From the vantage point of the small volcanic ridges that ringed the valley from almost a kilometer away, the towers rose above the high wall like the fangs of some inverted serpent.

Inside, within a large dimly lit chamber, a malevolent form paced, dark thoughts of hate clouding its mind. The time was almost at hand, and they would be made to pay. The universe would crawl before him, just as it had done more than millennia ago.

Long ago, his march of conquest had been stopped, his minions forced back to their own planet. *The audacity of those creatures,* he silently fumed, *forcing me – me! – to seek shelter in my own city. The fools!*

After all he had done to them, they would not kill him. Instead, they exiled him to that cold, dark world, sealed behind an impenetrable dimensional lock. He was painfully aware that his prison was inescapable. All attempts to re-create the portal on his side had been met with failure, only providing an entrance with no exit. The swirling chaos beneath the small arch he had created had been a great disappointment. The same conditions that kept them trapped had distorted the dimensional warp generated by the arch, and there was no way to tell where the portal would transport those who dared to go through it. He had tried, more than once. Many of his minions had been sent through, but the last he heard from them were their screams of terror as they disappeared. Now, he could only remain there indefinitely, trapped inside those walls, until someone activated the machinery of the arch within the old city.

For anyone else, the world they had been provided would have seemed a paradise, but for them, it was a nightmarish world, teeming with bright colors and living things. It took but a little time to correct that problem.

The planet had paid dearly for his failed attempts at escape. Unstable in nature, the portal had disrupted the frail ecological balance, causing global disaster. The magnetic poles, altered by the energies released by the portal, caused the firestorms in the upper atmosphere, and those continued even now. The intense heat ravaged coastal areas, melting polar ice fields. Floods produced tidal waves 200 meters high, washing away animal and vegetable life wherever they touched. Those areas that survived the flooding were subjected to incredible heat. Whole forests were reduced to burning ash, and aboveground water supplies dried up under the continuous onslaught. The former inhabitants had died by the millions; heat and dehydration had left nothing but their bleach-white bones. It made no difference though; he would have happily killed an entire galaxy of planets to escape. Eventually, an ecological balance was found, and the violent intensity reduced to something more endurable for those remaining.

Stepping over to the open balcony that connected to his private chambers, he faced his many subjects. They were his children. Experiments, some successful and others not so much, could be seen here. The world was no longer beautiful, and neither were its inhabitants. All was now in his image. Where there were once great forests with trees reaching to a blue sky, now there was only barren wilderness. Nothing grew nor lived without his allowance. Tentacled feelers quivered with almost orgasmic delight as he faced those who would willingly give up their worthless lives for their god.

They were ready. After an eternity of preparation and planning, the opportunity to escape was nigh, about to present itself. The fools had trampled into his city, and soon they would find the sacred chamber. Once the great machines were activated, he and his army would sweep out and destroy the intruders. They would leave this insignificant speck of a planet and bring chaos again to the galaxy.

As he moved out to the balcony, an area ghostly lit at best, his large body seemed to radiate the power of the heavens. To those dimwitted creatures below, he must have resembled nothing less than a god. With his clawed tentacles spread, he bellowed to his minions, "My people, listen closely! The time is near. For millennia, we have been imprisoned. Now, vengeance shall be ours! We will swarm through the galaxy. Those who stand in our way will feel the bite of your jaws on their soft, weak flesh. I promise, you my children, that you will be nourished by their blood. You will feel their strength become your own. You will teach them fear and terror – the terror that can only come from prey who has nowhere left to run. We will take that which should have been ours so long ago. We will conquer and rule, as is our right!"

A chant began to rise from the assembled, a chant that quickly spread: "Donar! Donar! Donar!"

The speaker smiled, knowing they were ready, that they would willingly and eagerly kill anything or anyone who stood in their way. Donar opened his mouth into a horrible grin. His reptilian head moved from side to side, his sharp teeth flashing to his bloodthirsty audience.

Down below, his werewolf guard patrolled the inside of the great wall. They circulated amongst the others, always keeping a wary canine eye out for any sign of disloyalty, which was punishable by death; the sentence would be served immediately by the overzealous guard, rarely leaving a morsel of the traitor to dispose of. The mutant wolves loved their work. After all, they had no other game to hunt, so it fulfilled their daily minimum nutritional requirements. Under their dark fur, their skin was a hard, armored shell, capable of withstanding extreme physical punishment. Loyal, bloodthirsty, and almost indestructible, they would be the foundation of Donar's hideous army. However, he was not a fool; he knew the werewolves were ambitious by nature and had to be watched closely.

Donar thought briefly about the others who were cheering below. He would take some with him, but others would have to remain. In spite of their loyalty to him, many had come from weaker stock or were living products of failed experiments. The predatory wolves he had mutated would serve as his warrior guard, while the others would serve as nothing more than simple cannon fodder.

The werewolves were the successful culmination of the experiments he'd been performing since first being stranded there. The others, results of earlier, haphazard experiments, were the evolutionary equivalent of insects. They varied greatly from each other, with one exception: a shared hate that radiated stronger than a thousand suns. They were all hideous parodies of the life scattered throughout the planet, genetic monstrosities seemingly put together without thought, like a badly woven quilt. They were the perfect army, all created with an inherent and overwhelming desire to kill and to enjoy it. They were truly his children.

Suddenly, a voice came from behind, one that typically brought dread and often death to all but a few who heard it. "My Lord, we are ready."

Donar turned to face his war chief. Modok was a horror, even to his own. Primate in form but with huge, crustacean-like claws at the end of muscular arms, he struck fear and terror in even his own troops.

"Good, Modok. Time is short," Donar said as he walked back into the chamber.

"My Lord," Modok asked hesitantly, "what of the old man?"

Donar turned quickly. His harsh gaze drilled into the mutant creature, down to the depths of his dark soul. "I still have need of him. We will leave him his little helpers, but he must remain here, alive and unharmed."

"But, Lord, if you already have the knowledge, why must he be kept alive?" Modok realized his mistake as soon as he finished the question, but even that was a fraction too late.

Wrapping a long tentacle around Modok's muscular neck, Donar pulled him up, level to his long, scaly muzzle and the sharp teeth therein. "You will not discuss Atlo with me again. Do you understand?"

"Yes," Modok whispered hoarsely, using as much air as Donar would allow him.

His point made, Donar cast him roughly down to the hard stone floor.

Modok, rubbing his bruised throat, stood slowly and walked back to his master, keeping his head down like a scolded puppy.

Donar decided right then and there that the next time Modok brought the subject of the old man up, he would kill him. If his creations discovered that he was not omnipotent, his own life might be in jeopardy. The old human had taught him almost all of his many secrets, save one. Even after being subjected to the most brutal kind of torture, elderly and stubborn Atlo would still not reveal the final mystery that would make render Donar all-powerful. He was confident, though, that in time, the man would relent. The only question was how many had to die before Atlo would talk. His confession would not ultimately save any of them, but the wrinkled one didn't know that, and Donar intended to play that little fact to his cruel advantage.

Donar stepped to the far wall, where he laid a tentacled arm on a small inset console. The wall quietly slid aside to reveal an assortment of deadly weapons.

Modok lumbered over and chose a huge battleaxe. He hefted it over his huge, misshapen head and grinned in anticipation of what was to come. He and his master had gone through such a routine a number of times in the past, and he looked forward to it each time.

Donar moved to the other side of the long inner chamber, where he picked up a strange, silvery, metallic object. It seemed to be comprised of three tubes of varying lengths, welded together to form one unit. "A very good choice, my friend," Donar said.

A bell sounded as he pushed a small button on the side of the console. In answer to the signal, an emaciated, young, humanoid female walked in, carrying a serving tray. Dressed in frayed rags, the elflike servant turned toward Donar, with her head bowed, her eyes pointed to the floor.

What most would have considered her beauty repulsed her master. She was, after all, a genetic misfit, an early experiment of Atlo's, and she was a failure without many uses, save one.

Donar pointed the metallic at the servant, who was standing just outside the weapons chamber. "Child, come to me," he said, more of a fatherly-sounding request than a demand.

The servant moved closer and turned to face her master. "Yes, My Lord?" Her voice quivered in fear as she approached.

A beam of blinding light leapt out of the collection of tubes and struck her. The spear of intense energy pierced the young girl's body, nearly cutting her in half. Her high-pitched scream filled the chamber, spurning Modok to jump up and down, howling in glee.

"You see, times have changed, and we must adapt." Insane laughter filled the chamber as Donar turned and snarled at his war chief. "Fool! Bring me the sorcerer. There is still much to do. And before you go, dispose of that," he said, pointing a tentacle pointing at the nearly severed body.

"Yes, My Lord," Modok said, fear looming in his voice as he hung the huge axe back on its bracket on the wall and quickly grabbed hold of the small creature before he left the chamber.

Donar still held the energy weapon, its upper barrel aglow with the incredible power it had just released. Nevertheless, even with all the powerful weapons at his disposal, he still needed the old sorcerer for his plans to succeed. A narrow line separated his science from the others' black skills. He had been a useful convert before his exile and had used his imprisonment to perfect his craft. The creature seemed to possess a power that transcended the normal bounds of science. How Snatak accomplished some of the things he did, Donar didn't know, but if Snatak proved useless to him, he would again use the resources of his laboratory deep within the bowels of the old castle. Donar sealed the weapons chamber and moved back to the window to once again bathe in the chants of his adoring entourage far below.

Minutes later, he heard a light knock on the door of his chamber. Sitting, he rested his energy weapon in his lap. "Enter."

An ancient elfin figure entered. Resembling a two-legged rat with long, pointy ears and a whiskered snout, the old sorcerer stood before his king, his tattered brown robe clinging to his frail and withered body. "You wished to see me, My Lord?" the sorcerer asked, his head bowed.

"Yes, Snatak. Sit, for we have much to discuss."

The sorcerer obediently sat by Donar's side.

Donar looked over at him intently. They had failed in the past, but that was no longer an option. *This time, all will succeed.*

CHAPTER 2

By all rights, the planet should not have existed. Alone, it orbited a small yellow sun at the far edge of Orion's belt. Solo, a fitting name indeed, had always been merely a large, unremarkable chunk of rock, until now. It was a planet of mysteries, and the Alliance Science Academy had commissioned a survey ship to investigate further.

A dark, cloud-shrouded sky and barren landscape greeted the science team upon their entry into the geo-synchronous orbit. Long-range sensor scans discovered no signs of life, though they did reveal a city and a vast network of roads. The city was like no other, and the ruins seemed to stretch across the wasteland for hundreds of kilometers. Still, in spite of the evidence of an advanced civilization, no living thing was found.

Selecting a landing site within close proximity to the ruined city, the survey ship settled down just long enough to offload the science and archeology teams and their equipment before lifting and leaving orbit. Fifteen scientists, of the various races that comprised the Alliance, immediately began to investigate the ruins, cataloging any artifacts found. Fleet headquarters had also provided a small contingent of guards to ensure security.

In the security shack that was set up in one of the many vacant rooms on the outer boundary of the city, Lieutenant Ank contemplated his post. For over a year, nothing had happened, and a general malaise and mind-numbing boredom had set in. *A disease,* he thought, *robbing a warrior of his edge.* The scientists had gone into the city every day, sometimes remaining there longer than either he or his squad could appreciate. Thus far, the only real discovery had been made by a human, Dr. Clarkson, a chamber that contained some very strange machinery. Despite the apparent age of the ruins, the machinery appeared untouched by time. Ank told his men that Clarkson and the others were allowed to go wherever they pleased, so long as a security officer accompanied them to any newly discovered chambers. Once established, they set up cameras so he could monitor everything on the viewscreens that now sat before him.

Ank watched as scientists scurried around the chamber like little mice; that thought brought a bemused expression to his dark muzzle. Ank was a felinoid from Cada III, a descendant of the carnivorous cats that had roamed the tropical planet long ago. At almost seven feet tall, Ank was an imposing figure, even to his own people, warriors and hunters. Now, he and his men were nothing more than highly trained babysitters.

The supply ship was due in the morning and with it his replacement. Ank hoped that whoever was replacing him either enjoyed boredom or was in a semi-permanent coma. The planet was so far off the usual galactic trade routes that other than the occasional military cruiser sent to bring supplies or crew replacements, they had no visitors.

Noting that his shift was ending, Ank put a large, furry paw on the comm panel to call his relief. "Corporal Anderson, report to security immediately," Ank growled into the communicator. Sitting and monitoring in the small confining security office was tiring enough, but having to remain any longer than necessary would certainly do little to brighten his gloomy disposition; tardiness was not a trait to be tolerated by someone in his command.

"On the way, sir," the voice came back over speaker.

Ank enjoyed the effect he had on some of the humans, and he looked forward to chewing Ank out. After all, he had to take his enjoyment where it came. Before Anderson's arrival, Ank made a final sweep of the video screens that monitored the chamber where Clarkson and his people were currently working.

In the large chamber, dominated at one end by strange, alien machinery and on the other by a huge, hemispherical arch, Dr. Peter Clarkson watched with keen interest the progress of his team. The chamber had been discovered through the use of high-frequency sensor scans. There seemed to be no way in, but a small, explosive charge had been used. The blast excavated a perfect entrance through which he and his people could enter.

When Clarkson entered, a strange chill descended. He didn't understand why, but there was a malevolent feeling in the room. Lights were quickly set up, and at that point, he noticed that his assistant, Dr. Paul Michaels, was trying to get his attention. "Yes, Paul?" Clarkson asked, noticing that Michaels was staring intently at some drawings on the wall.

Michaels was his special projects assistant. Ten years his junior, Michaels had that youthful enthusiasm that he, himself, was now lacking. "Peter, come take a look at this. What do you make of it?"

Clarkson peered at the drawings on the wall and was inwardly repulsed by them. "This is...amazing," said

11

Clarkson.

The drawings were hideous, depicting chaos in its purest form. Death and destruction seemed to be the running theme, creatures of undeniable cruelty marching out of some sort of circular structure.

"Paul, get pictures of this. I want it all on sensor tape."

Michaels ran his scanner along the drawings, cataloging every image. "Peter, could these represent the creatures that lived in this city?"

Clarkson shrugged. "I don't know. Gimme a hand over here, would ya?"

Clarkson examined the console to his right. He knew the city was incredibly old, but the machinery seemed to be untouched. Neither Clarkson, Michaels, nor any of the others could find any operating surfaces on the silvery metal: no buttons, switches, or any other recognizable controls.

Clarkson gently laid his hand on top of the closest console and felt a surge of power jump across his hand. As he quickly and instinctively jerked his hand away, the machinery seemed to come alive. The arch began to glow a bright, incandescent yellow. Some kind of power was feeding the machinery, as bank after bank became active.

Michaels looked at the arch in surprise. Obviously, Clarkson had somehow accidentally activated the console. It was as if it had been waiting for the touch of another living being all that time. *But what have we done now?* Michaels wondered. Turning to Clarkson, he saw that the doctor was transfixed by the sight of the glowing arch. "Peter, are you all right? Should I, uh...get the others?"

There was no response from Clarkson at first, but after

what felt like a very long second, he turned to the younger man and nodded. He had, after all, only done as the voice in his head commanded.

Below the arch, Clarkson could see the rear of the lab, beginning to quiver as if it was suffering under the intense desert heat. As if in a trance, Clarkson moved his hands over the glowing unit. Power levels began to increase, as the arch glowed more intensely.

"Dr. Clarkson...Peter, what are you doing?" Michaels called out. He had already signaled the other researchers and hoped they would hurry. He cautiously moved over to where Clarkson was standing, trying desperately to separate him from the glowing control unit.

The power levels increased, and an image seemed to be forming under the arch. Something like a desert mirage, the image seemed to waver.

Seemingly possessed, Clarkson shoved Michaels away from the console and moved his hands over its seemingly blank surface. "We must increase the power!" Clarkson called out. "Donar must be free!"

The others finally arrived in the chamber, but there was little they could do but stare helplessly at the arch as the image of an angelic figure began to appear.

"Look!" screamed an Antarean scientist.

Almost Christlike, the figure seemed to reach out of the arch.

"Who are you?"

Every eye turned to Clarkson, who seemed to be close to losing his sanity.

"*What* are you?"

The image smiled, and the voice that followed boomed

through the cavernous chamber: "Who do you say that I am? I am God, of course!"

"Oh shit," Michaels said softly as his hand went to a small communicator on his belt. He brought the small device up and activated the frequency for the security station. "Security, this is Dr. Michaels in Chamber 102. We have an emergency! Security, come quick! Please!" he finally screamed, giving in to his terror. He glanced up at the security monitors on the wall and hoped his plea for help had been heard.

The angel laughed at the futile attempt, an evil cackle that filled the chamber. As it neared the horrified and confused onlookers, its features began to change, morphing into something far more hideous. Large, sharp teeth quickly appeared, and the face took on a reptilian shape, with frightening features.

From the arch, other figures soon emerged. It seemed as if the very gates of Hell had opened, for beasts and monsters poured out of the glowing portal. The hideous paintings on the wall came alive, and each awful being clutched a strange, metallic device. Without warning, the devices lashed out, striking the startled scientists with harsh beams of intense energy.

Michaels made a desperate lunge for the door but came up short as a shaft of light speared through his body. He was dead before his charred corpse hit the cold floor. The last thing Dr. Peter Clarkson and his thirteen colleagues heard was the wailing agony of their own final screams.

In the security shack, Ank reacted with amazing speed for a being his size. After witnessing the incredible inhuman massacre of the entire science team, he had signaled a red alert. Alarms sounded as he slid over to the comm panel. Frantically, he activated the unit and cried, "Attention! All security teams report to Chamber 102. I repeat, we have an emergency. Aliens with heavy weapons are firing on the scientists in Chamber 102. All security teams report there immediately!" Ank turned and saw Anderson finally entering the shack.

"What's up, Boss?" Anderson asked, noticing that the emergency was clearly out of hand, for he had never seen Ank so unsettled before.

"Something got into the chamber with the scientists. Look!" Ank pointed at the main monitor.

What Anderson saw sent a chill down his spine. Blood was everywhere, splattered all over the chamber walls. Bodies, limbs, and chunks of flesh littered the large room. When Ank rotated the camera to scan in a 180-degree arc, the room appeared to be empty, except for one large, simian figure, holding something round in its huge, pincer-like claws. Ank adjusted the magnification as the creature turned and held its prize in front of the camera, the blood-dripping, decapitated head of Dr. Peter Clarkson.

Ank reached again for the comm panel. "Security report. Donaldson, Noel, Ganth, answer me, damn it!" he growled into the console, looking again at the grotesque scene on the monitor.

The homicidal thing was aware that it was being watched, as it turned and faced the camera, baring its blood-red teeth and letting out an unearthly howl. The bloodcurdling noise soon turned into insane laughter as it hurled the unseeing head of Peter Clarkson. Ank flinched as the head hit the camera and the monitor went dead.

Anderson looked over to Ank, wearing an expression Ank had seen before; the terror in his eyes was apparent. Anderson began to pace nervously across the small room, his voice quiet as spoke to himself. His voice grew louder as his pacing progressed. "Dead. They're all dead – just...dead. Dead, dead, dead," he repeated over and over again, like a man gone mad

Ank reached over and grabbed Anderson's blue duty uniform in a tight grip. With very little effort, he threw the human roughly into the closest wall he could find. Ank held him by the throat, pinning him to the reinforced metal wall. "Listen to me. You will do as I say. Do you understand me, Corporal?" he growled in a commanding voice that he hoped would terrorize Anderson almost as much as what they'd just seen.

Anderson nodded weakly as he was gently lowered to the floor.

Ank moved over to a cabinet by the side of the door. He quickly entered a code sequence into the lock, causing a panel to slide open to reveal a collection of lethal-looking weapons. He handed a powerful laser rifle to Anderson and took one for himself. "I want you to load the emergency rations into the land skimmer. I'm going to warn the supply ship, destroy the equipment, then get both of us the hell outta here." Ank then turned back to the communications console to carry on with his plans.

Anderson obediently and silently left the room, still wide-eyed, and the door slid back into place behind him.

There wasn't much time left as he activated the circuits to the hyperspace transmitter. Ank adjusted the transmitter frequency as the door behind him slid open. "Anderson, that skimmer had better be loaded," he said, adjusting the communicator without bothering to look behind him, "because I'm almost finished here."

"You are correct, my friend. "You *are* finished," answered a voice that most certainly did not belong to Corporal Anderson.

Ank turned quickly and saw a massive, robed, two-legged reptile peering at him in an almost mocking way, holding some sort of weapon in its tentacled arms. By the reptile's side stood a large, wolfish creature. Standing upright, the creature held the same tri-barreled weapon in its paws that the lizard held.

"You will not be sending a message," Donar said, pointing the strange artillery at Ank's chest.

"Where's Anderson?" Ank growled, his anger swelling by the second.

"I need your supply ship to carry me to other worlds," Donar replied, ignoring the question, his tone softening in its intent. "I have so much to teach, but you are correct. We mustn't discuss this without your friend." Donar then turned to the corridor and called to his war chief, "Modok, bring the pathetic creature here."

To Ank, Corporal Anderson seemed to glide through the door, his feet barely moving, with the simian he had seen on the monitor following only a few feet behind him. Anger and disgust boiled in him as Ank realized that a huge axe was buried deep in Anderson's back; Modok was walking him in with a handle, like a puppet.

Modok turned to his evil lord and smiled. "See, Master? The old ways are effective too." After a nod of approval from Donar, Modok pulled Anderson closer to him and sank his powerful jaws deep into the human's neck. Blood spurted from severed arteries, coating Modok's face and chest in a crimson spray. Finally, the tendons and bone severed, and Anderson's head fell to the floor, coming to a rest at Ank's feet, causing a smile to break across the murderous creature's bloody face.

"No!" Ank screamed. The rage building within him pushed him to action. Faster than Donar believed possible for such a lesser creature, Ank swung his rifle up and fired from the hip. The beam of intense blue light sliced through the air.

Donar quickly snaked a tentacled arm around the werewolf standing at his side, pulling the foul creature to him. The beam of energy struck the hideous living shield, melting a sizable hole through his chest armor. At close range, not even the werewolf's hard, natural plating could protect him from the intense laser blast. Donar then threw the dead creature to the ground and fired his own weapon. The beam sliced through the communications console, the force of the explosion throwing Ank like a broken doll against the weapons cabinet, stunning him. Modok moved toward the security chief, his claws held out in front of him, but Donar stopped him with a long tentacle.

"Leave him, Modok. We must prepare for our transportation." Donar could see that Modok was greatly disappointed, but his underling still obeyed his instructions. "After all, our friend isn't going anywhere."

Ank's ears were assaulted by their sinister laughter as they faded from his sight. Consumed by thoughts of failure and extreme embarrassment, he soon fell unconsciousness.

CHAPTER 3

Several light years away, an old man stood by the view port of his office, gazing out at the asteroids and stars that seemed just beyond his reach. Clayton Brooks, former Alliance Fleet admiral, was currently the head of Commando, Inc.

After a moment, Brooks walked back to his desk and picked up the communications report that had just been placed there. He looked at the message again, reading it word for word. In a fit of anger, he crumbled the printout into a small ball and tossed it at the innocent little fern that resided in the corner of his office. *I've got enough on my mind*, he thought, *without having to worry about receiving that stupid buffoon from Fleet headquarters.*

Two days before, a special request had come from Admiral Olstad at Fleet Operations on Earth. One of their military transports had gone missing on its way back from a supply run to a group of scientists doing an archeological survey on some newly discovered planet.

Unfortunately, that planet fell outside Alliance jurisdiction, but it was well within the area claimed by the Dreedan Empire. While the Dreedan Imperial Council had reluctantly allowed the Alliance to send a small science team to investigate the mysterious planet, Solo, there was still an extremely tentative truce between the military establishments of both governments. Brooks wasn't surprised to see that the agreement guaranteed a share in whatever was discovered. It was believed that the appearance of an Alliance battlecruiser in the area might provoke a military response from the Dreedans, thus damaging the already fragile truce. Because of this, Olstad wanted his people to look into the disappearance of the missing cruiser and science team. Again, unfortunately for Olstad, the team was already on a case.

Brooks looked again at the crumbled ball of paper sitting very quietly alongside his fern. The communication represented the third attempt by that idiot to pay them a visit. He had ignored the other two and would have treated that one the same way if he'd had the choice. Brooks sat back down and wondered quietly, *Just what have I done to deserve this?*

Taking a deep breath into his sixty-nine-year-old lungs, he reluctantly reached out and flipped a switch on his comm panel. "Griffin, get in here...and bring a current status report with you," he bellowed.

Griffin was his executive assistant and personal verbal punching bag. He was also his old second-in-command from the years before Commando, Inc. Needless to say, and despite the abuse he always inflicted on him, he trusted Griffin with his life.

"Coming, Admiral," responded the voice through the speaker. Even though Griffin knew there was no need for titles and protocol, Brooks would always be an admiral to him.

A few minutes later, the door slid open, and Griffin entered. He was in his early forties, with a very sparse head of hair and a waistline that seemed ready to consume him. Other than those flaws, he was immaculate in his

Commando, Inc.-issue white duty uniform. A deep blue stripe ran down each sleeve, and there was a patch over the left breast, sporting the Commando logo: an Earth eagle with twin bolts of lightning grasped in each claw.

Brooks was sitting with his chair facing the view port. "Sit down, Griffin, and give me the bad news," he said.

"Yes, sir," Griffin said as he took the seat facing the desk to fill the admiral in on the current state of affairs. "Shall I start with anything in particular?"

"Might as well get the nonsense out of the way first." Brooks was still facing away from Griffin, but his disgust for the inevitable conversation was apparent.

"Olstad, sir?" Griffin guessed.

"Right. First him, then current mission status," Brooks said, obviously looking forward to moving on to the next topic.

"We've already received a confirmation from Olstad's ship. His ETA to the belt is four hours, twelve minutes," he said, glancing at the chronometer on his wrist.

"That pompous idiot doesn't seem to take no for an answer." Brooks shook his head from side to side in disgust at the thought that the man was one of the few trusted with the security of the Alliance and its worlds. "Griffin, just let me know when he enters the perimeter. Next."

"Very well. Carson seems to have made progress in locating Senator Weltman's daughter. His latest report, logged in at 08:00 today, states that they've just entered orbit around Tanda IV and will advise upon completion of the mission."

"Very good," Brooks said, still looking aimlessly out the view port. "Keep me appraised, but please get out for now.

I've got a lot of thinking to do."

"Yes, sir." Griffin stood from the chair, did a perfect about-face, and marched out of the spacious office.

Brooks thought of his team out in the field and the mission they were currently engaged in. Senator Frank Weltman had called him seventy-two hours prior, pleading for help to locate his missing daughter. On a vacation to Utopia, a tropical paradise and the in spot for the rich jetsetters of the galaxy, her ship had been stopped. Whoever stopped them had killed the crew and her male companion onboard. The freighter that found them reported no sign of the senator's daughter, just the bodies of the crew. Brooks had suggested to the senator that the matter be handled by Alliance Security, but Weltman wanted the matter resolved quietly and discreetly. The most important fact, though, was that Frank Weltman had been a very good friend through the years and would, therefore, be granted all the help Commando, Inc. could provide. Since his team had a rare moment between assignments, the case would not interfere with any of their other duties.

Brooks figured that if anyone could find the missing woman, it would be Mark Carson. He and the others had handled more dangerous assignments in the past, so Brooks tried to tell himself not to worry. It was hard, though, for they were all like the children he'd never had time to have.

Brooks closed his eyes, hoping to find some answers in the quiet and solitude would clear his mind enough for him to drum up some answers. Only one thought really came to mind: *I am too old for this.* Only a few short years earlier, such a thought would never have crossed his mind. When the idea for his organization first took root in his mind,

Brooks was still an admiral in the Alliance Star Fleet. As an admiral, he noticed the never-ending bureaucracy that went along with any critical decision. By the time those decisions were finally made, though, it was usually too late to help anyone.

His breaking point had occurred when terrorists hijacked a starliner with its crew and passengers, 162 people. He had watched with amazement as negotiations for their release had failed. A strike team was eventually sent in, but by then, ninety-six of the hostages had been killed, and the terrorists were gone. Among the dead was the daughter of Dolan Wilson, one of the wealthiest Alliance arms manufacturers.

Dolan was a man with the drive as well as the resources to make his vision come true. Brooks had gone to him with his proposition shortly after the funeral. Dolan, a powerful man, seemed helpless after his daughter's death. The terrorists had disappeared, and Alliance forces seemed in no real hurry to locate the wrongdoers. Brooks remembered the meeting with Dolan Wilson as if it was yesterday...

* * *

On a chilly, fall day almost three years earlier, Brooks entered the offices of Wilson Industries. After taking the computerized lift to the main office level, Brooks introduced himself to the pretty redheaded receptionist. "Excuse me. I'm Admiral Clayton Brooks. I have an appointment with Mr. Wilson."

"Of course, sir. Please have a seat. I'll let him know you're here."

Brooks appreciated the fact that Wilson employed people rather than the impersonal machines that seemed to be quickly becoming the standard in the business community. He smiled at the redhead and took a seat as he was asked.

"Admiral Brooks," the pretty receptionist called from her desk.

Brooks checked his chronograph and saw, to his relief, that he had only been sitting for a few minutes.

"Mr. Wilson will see you now. Please come this way." She led him to a set of double-doors that pneumatically and silently slid aside.

"Thank you very much for your assistance, my dear."

The redhead smiled and ushered him into the office.

Wilson was sitting behind an antique wood desk, with a large pile of documents resting off to the side, seemingly awaiting a signature that he was in no hurry to make. "Come in and have a seat, Admiral. Tell me, what can I do for you?" Wilson stood and held his hand out as Brooks approached the desk.

"Thank you, Mr. Wilson. I won't take up much of your time," Brooks said as the two men shook hands and sat down.

Brooks didn't hold back; he excitedly told Wilson his entire vision: the creation of an organization to battle the horrors of galactic terrorism, an organization that would be there to help when no other would. He had already drawn up the proposal, so he handed Wilson a printout of what would be needed and how much it would cost to finance an undertaking of such proportions. By the time he finished his sales pitch, he felt as if he'd aged by years in only the last few minutes.

Wilson just sat there with the proposal on his desk, his

eyes taking in every small detail. After a few more minutes that had also somehow seemingly stretched into hours, Wilson looked up at Brooks and spoke those fateful words: "Admiral, I want you to know that if we do this, we have to do it right." He glanced back down at the proposal and continued, "If we begin immediately, how soon do you estimate completion?"

Brooks could not believe his ears. "Uh, I...well, if I start making the arrangements now, probably about eight months to a year, working around the clock."

"Admiral, in that case, we have a deal. I trust you will take care of all the details. And, Admiral, from now on, please call me 'Dolan.'"

After that, they stayed up for thirty-six straight hours, laying the groundwork for the organization that would later become Commando, Inc.

After leaving the meeting, with Wilson's blank check and well-wishes, Brooks went back to Fleet Headquarters and promptly submitted his resignation. He knew all his attention would be needed for such an ambitious project, and he needed to sever all connections with his past if Commando, Inc. was to have any real chance at success.

An asteroid of immense size was selected to be the home of his dream. Alliance engineers spent six months hollowing out the mineral-laden ball of rock and another four to build the complex structure within it. When finished, the base would consist of a massive docking bay, facilities for weapons control, communications, the most sophisticated laboratory complex in the Alliance, as well as living quarters for 1,000 men and women. Security was simple: placing state-of-the-art sensor array, as well as energy weapons on neighboring asteroids that could detect and destroy anything within the perimeter of the asteroid belt.

Next, a ship was built. Drawn from Brooks's own specifications and built by the greatest minds in the galaxy, the ship would be one of the fastest, most powerful starships in space. Equipped with a powerful sentient computer and the most advanced weapons system money could buy, the vessel would carry his field team wherever they were needed. All that was left for consideration was the recruitment of the team itself, and that, too, had been accomplished in time.

* * *

Now, Brooks sat with the immenseness of the universe behind him, staring at the holographic picture of his special operations team that he kept on his desk. In the couple years while they'd been working together, Brooks had truly come to think of them as family.

First, there was Dr. Joshua Grant. The tall, wiry black man had been with him ever since the beginning. Brooks had known Grant since he was a child, and he eventually drafted the young man right out of the Alliance Science Academy. Grant was one of the first members of the startup team, and a great many of the design innovations incorporated within *Pulsar* were his. The sentient computer, dubbed "Ernie" by the development team, was also the brainchild of Joshua Grant. With the immense size and sophistication of *Pulsar*, Ernie had the capability to monitor and control all the ship systems. Even more impressive than that, Grant had made a name for himself by helping settlers on Arton III ward off an attack by Dreedan raiders. He was, for all intents and purposes, the perfect combination of brains and courage.

Standing next to him in the photo was a beautiful, graceful woman. Her hair was so long and blonde that it could melt any man from any galaxy. Her deep blue eyes were equipped to stare deeply into the soul. Melanie Patula was a petite woman, but she had achieved one of the highest PSI ratings the Science Academy had ever tested. While she could not read minds, she could receive psychic impressions from any object she handled, a skill of utmost important in the areas they explored; they had found more than one missing person with her help, though interpretations of the impressions could sometimes make things difficult. She was also capable of taking care of herself, something any man who knew her would swear to.

Melanie was from Planet Helos, in the Vega star system, where life was hard for a woman. The continuous civil war had reduced a once-great civilization to barbarism, and vicious gangs had overtaken the streets, making rape and brutality a fact of life for the people of Helos. In fact, the life expectancy of the average citizen was not very long at all, depending on one's gang affiliation. Melanie had grown up in the streets, eking out her own survival long enough for an Alliance exploration team to land on her war-wrecked planet.

The team found her on the outskirts of one of the devastated cities and became her first real friends in a world where friendship and trust were alien concepts. When members of that exploration team were captured by one of the more savage gangs, Melanie somehow engineered an escape back to the ship, and the captain offered to whisk her off the planet. She quickly accepted and returned with the survivors of the crew. That captain's name was Clayton Brooks. In the fifteen years since her escape from Helos, Melanie had refined her skills and discovered new ones. In the process, she had also become a first-rate doctor and now doubled as the team medic.

Brooks's eyes drifted over to the third member of the team, perhaps the one he felt the closest kinship to. Mark Carson, the team leader, was a darkly handsome man of thirty-five. Brooks had been a close friend of Mark's father's and had followed the younger Carson's career in military intelligence with a keen interest. Mark had grown up on Earth and had been ushered into the Fleet Academy at an early age by his father. Thomas Carson, Mark's father, had been part of the Fleet Appropriations Committee and a councilmember, making it quite easy for him to secure an Academy vacancy for his son. For Mark, this only put extra pressure on him to succeed, but succeed he did. In fact, Mark became an expert at almost every known weapon, from the blade to the laser.

Rising quickly through the ranks, Mark was given command of a Special Forces unit that quickly gained glory during the Alliance/Dreedan conflict of a decade ago. Carson led a team of three behind the Dreedan Imperial lines and successfully destroyed an important sensor network, allowing Alliance cruisers to enter what was, at the time, Dreedan space to rescue an Alliance diplomat and his family. After the conflict, Mark was recruited into a special covert Intelligence Department of Fleet operations. The training he'd gone through before seemed easy compared to the hell he was put through for his new duties. Mark was taught to kill, and his body and mind were trained as never before. If the situation called for it, Mark was very capable of killing with his bare hands or anything else he could obtain on the spur of the moment. Simple objects, he was told, could be transformed into something lethal. Mark learned, and, as in everything he'd studied before, he became an expert.

Brooks continued to follow the career of Mark Carson, even though a great deal of it was classified. Intelligence had sent Carson to every nook and cranny of the galaxy, for various missions. Brooks never knew the details of any individual mission, and Carson would never tell him, but Mark seemed to come back a little changed each time, though always successful. His exploits were considered almost legendary, until his last mission. As an admiral, Brooks was privy to some of the details of that final assignment.

Alliance Intelligence had received word that terrorists were planning an assassination attempt on the Dreedan delegate to the Alliance/Dreedan Peace Conference. If they had succeeded, war would have certainly followed. Though most of the details were sketchy, Brooks discovered that Carson was sent, in part, to coordinate security for the conference and, to a greater extent, find the assassin and put a halt to the attempt. The only other information that was available to Brooks was that the mission was a success. After that, Mark returned to Earth. He submitted his resignation from the service and disappeared.

Brooks didn't know the full story until months later. Using all the resources at his disposal, he traced Carson back to Earth. He found him sitting on a beach in southern California, gazing out at the sunset, with a container of dark liquid by his side; it wasn't hard to figure out what he was drinking. Now, Brooks thought back to that meeting, when they sat on the cooling sand and stared at the horizon, painted in the setting sun's orange and violet hues...

* * *

"Hello, Mark. How are you feeling?" He looked over at Carson and could see that retirement wasn't going well. The man was withering away and had lost a lot of weight since they'd last seen each other, and the drinking didn't help.

"Hi, Admiral," Carson said aimlessly, his eyes still glued to the sun going down in the distance. "What do you want?"

The admiral took another look at Carson, unable to fathom that it was the man he knew. "I've been worried about you, son." Brooks took the bottle from Carson's hand and looked at the label. "Hmm. I thought you had better taste than this."

Carson took the bottle back and took a long swig. "So times have changed." He then got to his feet, surprisingly agile, and started to walk away.

Brooks stood, forcing the blood back into his legs as he started off after him. He stuck out his hand and grabbed Carson's arm. When Carson stopped short, just for a moment, Brooks thought the younger man might strike him. "Mark, what happened to you?"

"What do you care?" he asked, slumping as if a great weight sat atop his shoulders. Carson looked at Brooks, and his expression seemed to soften, Then he tensed again as he spoke, "All right." Sounding uncharacteristically defeated, he pointed to an outcrop of rock, gesturing for the admiral to accompany him. "Pull up a rock, Admiral...and I'll be giving you a pop quiz on this after I'm done."

Carson then proceeded to fill Brooks in on the details of the mission, his arrival on Rigel IV and his search for the assassin. During his time on the planet, he had fallen in love with a member of the Dreedan security team. Dandi was beautiful, a humanoid female with blazing red hair and deep blue skin, and they seemed to share a strong attraction from the moment they met. They enjoyed long walks and wonderful conversation and, after a while, a long bout of passionate lovemaking in his quarters.

The night before the conference was to begin, Mark woke to find that Dandi was gone. Wondering where she had taken off to in the middle of the night and why, he dressed quickly and walked over to Dandi's quarters, hoping to find her there. When he found her room empty, he began to worry. Mark decided that while looking for her, he might as well run through his security checks. He looked all through the complex, but if she was outside, there would be nothing he could do till morning.

Before returning to his quarters, he decided to stop for one last check of the conference chamber before the meetings would begin in just a few short hours. When the door slid open, he saw a sight that both confused and angered him. There was Dandi, on the floor beneath the conference table, finishing up the wiring on what appeared to be some kind of explosive.

As Carson continued the story, Brooks could see that it was getting more and more difficult for his friend to control himself. Dandi, the one he loved, had turned out to be the assassin, a member of a fraction of the Dreedan society that didn't want peace. She saw him standing at the door and pulled out a small blaster from her belt. She told him how sorry she was, but said it was something she had to do. Carson said she seemed sad, as if she was wrestling with a decision she didn't want to make.

Nevertheless, she pointed her gun at him, telling him it was just business and nothing personal. He saw her finger tighten on the trigger, and in one swift motion, he sent a small, formerly well-concealed dagger flying in her direction. Reflexes, conditioned by years of combat and training, threw him clear of the beam from the gun. The dagger though flew true, slamming into the middle of her chest. With a soft sigh, Dandi collapsed weakly to the floor.

"I-I went over to her and held her in my arms as she died."

Brooks could see the tears streaming down Mark's face; clearly, Carson was having a problem finishing his story.

"Do you know what she said to me just before she died?"

Brooks shook his head, though he did have his suspicions.

"She said she loved me and that she was sorry...and then she just...died. I-I had to kill her. I didn't want to, but I had to." With that confession of the grim reality, Carson turned his head and put forth great effort to keep his tears at bay. He had long ago shed all the tears he could bear to weep for Dandi, but it was a relief to finally tell someone. Somewhat calmer, he raised his head and faced Brooks. "After that, I realized I'd had enough of the killing and the lies, so I ran. I took the next ship back to Earth, submitted my resignation, and became a drunk. So here I am. A nice little happy ending, don't you think?"

The former admiral's angry expression was not lost on Carson. He turned to Mark and said sternly, "Listen to me,

Carson. This self-pity nonsense ends here. I need you for something important, so I don't wanna hear any more of your bullshit." Once he was sure he had Carson's attention, he continued, "Now, we're gonna get you cleaned up, and then you're going to listen to the proposition I have for you."

Carson could only nod as Brooks led him off, and what he later heard sobered him up quite quickly.

* * *

Brooks reflected as he sat at his desk on that conversation he'd had with Mark Carson more than two years earlier. Mark had come around, but in many ways, he was still an introvert.

Wondering how Carson and the others were doing, Brooks reached for over to his comm panel and called Griffin, hoping there'd been some word from Carson.

Griffin entered and handed Brooks a comp tape containing the current status update.

"Griffin, I don't have time for this," the admiral said, his expression betraying his impatience. "Just tell me what's going on."

"Well, sir..." Griffin seemed confused as to where he should begin, but seeing Brooks's impatience change to annoyance, he continued, "Admiral Olstad's ship just entered the perimeter. He should be here in about twenty minutes."

At the sound of that wonderful news, Brooks gently cradled his head in his hands, trying to ward off an intense headache that was burning right between his eyes. In a gaze that seemed to plead for better news, he looked up at Griffin. "What about Carson?"

"I queried Ernie. He said Carson and the others are

meeting a suspected raider."

Brooks looked at Griffin curiously, noticing that something else seemed to be bothering him. "And? What else?" he asked as Griffin twisted uncomfortably in his chair.

"It's Ernie, sir," Griffin said slowly.

"What about Ernie?" Brooks asked, not sure he wanted to hear the answer. To make matters worse, having to pull the information out of his assistant was beginning to get on his nerves. "Out with it, Griffin."

"Well, uh...he asked me not to call him back, at least not until the mission is over," Griffin stammered out.

"He what!?" Brooks shook his head, not quite believing what he was hearing.

"Ernie said that while he was coordinating the mission from *Pulsar,* my constant interruptions were...becoming an annoyance." The embarrassment of the situation was evident in the redness spreading across Griffin's face.

Brooks shook his head, unable to take much more. "Griffin..." he said quietly, almost a whisper.

"Yes, sir?" Griffin asked, gleefully anticipating the orders that would allow him the joy of doing a complete overhaul on the disrespectful computer. *I can't wait to show that Ernie who's boss. Damn machine sassing me all the time just for doing my job,* he silently seethed.

"Griffin," Brooks continued in that same low tone, "please prepare the landing bay for Olstad's ship. I'll be there shortly." Brooks then stood and pointed a wrinkled finger at the door. He spoke two words loud enough that people outside the door wondered if the incoming ship could hear him: "Get out!"

It wasn't exactly what he was prepared to hear, but

Griffin bolted for the door.

Exhausted, Brooks sat back down. He didn't have the heart to tell Griffin that Ernie wasn't the only one who shared that opinion. Reaching over, Brooks pushed a small touchpad by his desk. A small door slid aside, revealing a monitor on the wall. Sitting back in his chair, Brooks keyed in the channel for the landing bay and watch as Admiral Olstad's ship came in, the large, shell-shaped doors closing behind it. He wasn't at all looking forward to the meeting, but he rose from his chair and headed for the door, then to the landing bay to welcome his guest. He only hoped Carson was having better day than he was.

CHAPTER 4

Carson sat in the corner of the bar, waiting for Regar Weent, his contact, who was supposed to meet him there at midnight. Weent was a mercenary, a soldier of fortune with deep connections to the raiders, as well as certain other terrorist organizations with bases operating on the planet. Tanda IV was positioned just outside Alliance jurisdiction, a place where many came to seek their fortunes, most in an illegal manner. While some succeeded, the majority ended up dead; the cost of operating on Tanda IV was very high.

Finding Weent had been the wildest stroke of luck. Between clues discovered in the kidnapped girl's ship and what Melanie was able to pick up with her psychic abilities, the trail had led them to Tanda IV. To Joshua Grant and Melanie Patula, the fact they were headed to Tanda IV didn't seem too significant, but to Mark Carson, former intelligence agent, Tanda IV seemed to be the most likely place for the raiders to be holding the girl.

A frontier planet, Tanda IV had first been settled as a mining colony. It was abandoned quickly once it was stripped of all its mineral wealth. The planet shared system boundaries with several different cultures, making it a United Nations, of sorts, for the criminal world. It was the only place in the known galaxy where beings of any race could interact with any other, in spite of their governmental status, conducting all forms of business, legal or otherwise.

It wasn't easy to violate the law on Tanda IV since there really wasn't one. Few actually resided there, and those who did had a short life expectancy. On Tanda IV, real estate was cheap, but so was life.

The two main industries were trade and recruitment. Women, weapons, the newest designer drugs, or simply information: Anything could be acquired for the right price. A new identity could be easily purchased, even a new face or a cybernetic weapons system implanted in the body. The price for such services was certainly high, but for anyone with the right resources, anything was possible.

The second industry was recruitment. The planet was a virtual employment agency for the freelancers of the galaxy. Mercenaries from all parts of the galaxy landed on Tanda IV, hoping to align themselves with one criminal organization or another. Regar Weent, ex-mercenary, was one such recruiter.

After landing *Pulsar* at the Tanda spaceport, Carson had decided to do the initial reconnaissance himself, leaving Josh, Melanie, and Ernie to monitor from the ship. Despite the overlapping abilities of his team, this was still his specialty. He had been to the planet before and had more of an understanding of its violent nature than either of his comrades.

The spaceport seemed similar to any number of others throughout the galaxy. Constructed over a century earlier by the company that had operated the original mining colony, the spaceport had seen its better days. Blaster holes could be seen in many of the spaceport walls, a testament to the danger that awaited unwary visitors. Carson, dressed in a plain, unmarked, light blue flightsuit, made his way to the main terminal. He at least had one comforting thought on his mind: Josh had wired him so he could be tracked from the ship.

Carson spotted Weent at the terminal arrival area. He seemed to be waiting for someone and was desperately looking at the chronometer on his wrist, as if it could somehow speed up time. As he watched the muscular man pace nervously, a plan began to form in Carson's mind. He walked over to Weent and stopped about three meters from him.

Weent turned and stared for a moment before a look of recognition crossed his face. Weent would have been a handsome man if not for the gruesome scar that crossed from above his left eye diagonally across his face to just below his mouth. His lips pulled into a wicked but slight grin, and he walked slowly to where Carson was standing. "Carson? What the hell are you doing here?" Weent said, the sinister grin growing bigger with every word.

Carson knew the big man, as he'd served with his Special Forces team during the Alliance/Dreedan conflict. From what Carson could tell, Weent had enjoyed the work. The only problem was that Weent eventually decided there was more money to be made hiring himself out. Carson hadn't seen him since he'd left the service.

"Good to see you to, Regar," Carson answered slowly, "and to answer your question, I'm looking for a job."

Weent looked at him as if he'd grown a third eye. "No shit? Word has been that you retired from the service a couple years ago. What's the matter, Carson? Retirement benefits not too good?"

Carson stared at Weent as the big man chuckled at his

own joke, finding it far more funny than Carson did. "I'm serious, Regar," he interrupted, his tone deadly. "I want back in the business. I want to make a profit, for me this time."

Weent gave Carson a long, hard look. Carson was keenly and painfully aware that his reputation had spread even to that backwater planet. His problem now was to convince the usually suspicious Weent that he was on the level, and Weent seemed to be having a problem deciding. Carson didn't find that too unusual, though, since there were brands of mouthwash with a higher IQ than Weent's.

"Okay, Carson." Weent stuck his large hand into his jacket and pulled out a card. "Take this. I'll meet you at that address tonight, around midnight."

"I'll be there," he said, gazing down at the address of a dingy little club on the other side of the small town. Carson stuck the holographic plastic card into an outer pocket of his flightsuit and headed back to *Pulsar* to brief the others on his plan.

Now, Carson ordered another drink out of sheer boredom and frustration; Weent was already thirty minutes late. Josh and Melanie were sitting at a table in a darkened corner, about seven meters away, serving as his backup and ready to follow him to wherever Weent would take him, hopefully to the place where the senator's daughter was being held. From that point on, they would have to play it by ear, one step at a time.

Carson checked the transmitter Josh had inserted just behind his throat. He was confident that if anyone happened to look his way, they would just think he was talking to himself – not at all odd behavior for the half-crazed beings that landed on Tanda IV. "Keep alert. I'm sure he's still coming."

The waitress brought him his drink. Scantily dressed and looking as used up as everything else on that godforsaken planet, she placed his water down on a napkin in front of him. "Anything else?" she asked.

Carson knew the offer was very broad, including anything from another drink to bedding her. "Uh...no thanks," he answered.

Realizing she was going to get no further business from him, in bed or otherwise, she simply turned and sashayed her way back to the bar.

As Carson lifted the drink to lips, he finally saw Weent heading for his table. "Showtime, folks," he whispered into the clandestine communicator.

"Carson, come with me," Weent said, standing beside Carson's table.

"Where are we going?" Carson asked, slowly rising from his chair.

"Just get up. I'm taking you to the people you wanna see."

Carson noticed that Weent looked a little nervous, and he realized that could mean problems. Weent gestured to the rear of the bar. "After you, Carson."

Without further hesitation, Carson led the way to the exit door at the rear of the bar. The door slid aside, and they stepped out into a dark, ominous alley. Awaiting them there was a skimmer, its engine warm and running. Weent activated the driver-side door, and the gull wing shape rose slowly in the warm, humid air. From the grinding sound the door made as it ascended, Carson could only assume the humidity was wreaking havoc on the old, rusty metal hinges.

The alley was full of garbage, and the skimmer fit right in.

"Get in and drive where I tell ya," Weent ordered, gesturing for Carson to sit in front of the control board.

Carson stifled what would have been an inappropriate laugh; The large man was acting like a scheming used skimmer salesman looking for a quick sale.

Weent entered on the passenger side and pulled a small gun from inside his jacket.

"What's going on, Regar? Why the gun?"

The gun was definitely not part of Carson's plan. He only hoped that wherever Weent was taking him, Josh and Melanie weren't far behind.

"Just insurance. Now drive," Weent demanded, holding the small but deadly weapon on Carson. The needler fired small, poison-coated darts, making it a potentially fatal piece, particularly in such close quarters. Such a weapon was typically used onboard ships, as the darts could not penetrate a hull but had no trouble entering a body and dosing the receiver with a quick-acting poison or tranquilizer. Knowing Weent, Carson was rather certain the darts were the most lethal dose.

They drove out of town, into the mountains. Since the skimmer operated on a cushion of air, the rugged terrain wasn't a problem. After about an hour, Weent instructed Carson to pull off the narrow main road and onto a small trail that seemingly led to an old miners' settlement.

"Pull the skimmer in over there and kill the engine." Weent gestured with the gun to a small outcrop by the side of the larger of the two small structures.

Carson did as he was told and shut down the skimmer drive, the whine of turbo fan engines reducing to a low whisper as the craft settled gently on the rocky ground.

"Now get out." Weent held the gun out of Carson's reach as they opened their doors and stood by the side of the small vehicle.

"What's going on, Regar?" Carson asked. He certainly didn't feel too good about things, as the situation had all the makings of a setup.

Regar moved to the wooden door and banged his large fist against it. "It's Weent. I'm back."

The door opened, and three figures piled out, two humans and one Luto, an insect-like biped. The Luto had a second-to-none reputation for violence throughout the galaxy. That, along with their almost instinctive need for money made them perfect mercenaries.

"Take him where he'll never be found again," Weent said to the three killers. He then walked back over to sit in the skimmer.

Carson had the sudden feeling that his friendship with Regar had somehow taken a turn for the worse.

"Carson, you didn't think I'd really believe that bullshit story of yours, did ya?" Weent started the turbine engine, lifting the vehicle up on its cushion of air.

"Weent!" Carson called as the Luto prodded him in the back with its blaster.

The skimmer came to a stop, and Weent looked back at Carson and smiled. "What is it, Carson?"

"I hope your mercenary insurance plan has good benefits, because you're gonna need them by the time I'm done with you," Carson said calmly.

Weent laughed as he waved goodbye. The raiders who had hired him didn't trust Carson and wanted him dead. It was a shame, for the two of them had undeniably made a great team in the past. Weent had paid his mercenaries well, and he was confident they would take care of the Carson problem. Still, as he drove away, he wondered why he suddenly felt a chill crawling up his spine.

The four marched to a drill hole. The carbon-scoring around the hole had been made nearly a century before. It was about an hour before the twin sunrise, so it was quite difficult to see how deep the hole actually was, but Carson guessed it was nearly bottomless. They continued walking until Carson was standing just in front of the dark abyss.

"L'ucto, burn him," one of the humans said to the Luto.

As the Luto raised his blaster-toting appendage, a beam of bright yellow light seared from out of the darkness, striking the oversized insect in the head. Black, viscous fluid erupted from carcass as it fell.

Seeing that the two human assassins were distracted by the stream of black fluid pumping from L'ucto's body, Carson dived at the closest target. He quickly delivered a flying kick to the chest of the startled man, causing the gun to drop from his hand and fall down the endless drill hole. The other man turned to fire, but the same type of yellow blast that had struck the Luto hit the man's arm, sending the gun and the hand holding it hurtling to the ground. Grabbing the seared stump, the man ran off into the darkness howling in pain.

Meanwhile, the fight did not seem to be going well for Carson. The other man outweighed him by about 200 pounds, with nearly twice his strength. The assailant grabbed Carson by the throat and lifted him off the ground with ease, like a ragdoll. With all the strength he had left,

Carson slammed his fists into both sides of the man's bald head, momentarily stunning him. Carson dropped from his grasp and rolled slowly to his feet. The bull of a man stood and charged, showing no signs of injury. Carson agilely stepped to the side and watched as the man, unable to stop his forward momentum in time, fell headfirst down the drill hole, releasing a chilling scream that seemed to echo on for far too long.

"Mark, are you all right?" Melanie asked, still cradling her trusty blaster rifle in her arms.

"Fine. Your timing was great," Carson said, grateful to see her. "Where's Josh?"

"I just wish we coulda kept one of them alive to talk," Melanie said, gazing down the hole.

"We did!"

Carson turned at the sound of the voice coming from the darkness.

Josh Grant lumbered closer, pulling a large shape behind him. "Here, Carson. Thought you might like one of these for your birthday." He shoved the raider with the missing hand in Carson's direction.

"Josh, I'm flattered. How'd you ever guess?" Carson said, smiling victoriously at the man on the ground. He was obviously in pain and not at all in a good mood. "Melanie, c'mere. I think it's time you and I have a little chat with our new friend. I need you to give me a hand," he said, then held his hand over his mouth in mock humiliation. "Oh. Sorry about that," he said sarcastically, nodding at the bloody stump where the raider's hand had been only a few minutes prior.

"Pssh. I ain't gonna tell you shit," the raider snapped

arrogantly.

"Where are you holding Senator Weltman's daughter?" Carson asked, though he wasn't expecting an answer.

"Kiss my ass, you son-of-a-bitch!" the raider answered smugly in return.

Melanie walked over and laid her hands on the raider's remaining hand.

"What's going on? Get your hands off me, you crazy bitch!"

Ignoring him, Melanie closed her eyes and began to receive impressions from her physical contact with the raider. "I see...mountains," she began. "Twin peaks in the distance." Concentrating deeper than ever before, Melanie tried to pull as much information out of the disgruntled criminal as she could. "There's...a path leading to a cave, with men inside."

They all looked at her questioningly, and the raider's eyes were wide with amazement.

Carson could see the strain on Melanie's face; the necessary concentration was very taxing. "Melanie, do you see any other landmarks?" he asked, trying to get it over with as quickly as possible so it didn't take too much out of her.

"In the distance, there's... It's a crater, I think. That's about all I can get," Melanie finished, collapsing to her knees. She looked exhausted and drained, as if she needed to recharge.

"I think I know where it is. Let's go," Carson said, and they all stood to leave.

"What about me?" The raider asked.

"What about you?" Josh answered.

"You can't just leave me here. You cut off my damn hand! I am in need of medical attention," the raider pleaded.

"Medical attention?" Josh asked in disbelief. "Look, mister, what you're in need of is a trip down that hole like your buddy!" he said.

Melanie rolled her eyes at Josh, then walked over to the enemy with her medical kit. "Let me have a look at that," she said, picking up his truncated forearm. She sprayed the wound with antiseptic and attached a pressure bandage, ignoring his whining and wailing. "You guys go on and head to the skimmer. I'll catch up. This won't take long."

Carson and Josh shrugged and started for the skimmer, leaving Melanie alone with her patient.

The raider looked up at her. "They trust you with me, little girl? Ha! Those fools."

"You'll live...unfortunately," Melanie said, then turned and started walking in the direction her friends had gone. After about five meters, she stopped, turned around, and walked slowly back to the raider.

"Couldn't get enough of me, huh?" The raider grinned at her, revealing darkly stained teeth.

"Actually, I could live a full life without you," Melanie said, delivering a strong kick to his groin.

In intense pain, he doubled over and rolled on the ground.

"And by the way, don't ever call me a bitch again." She then strolled casually off after her friends, smiling all the way.

* * *

The land skimmer headed back to the city at maximum speed. The occupants were already planning their next move in what had turned into a complicated situation.

"What took you so long back there, Mel?" Josh asked from his seat in the rear of the skimmer.

"He, uh...required a little more than standard medical care. I don't think he liked my bedside manner much though," she said, obviously quite pleased with herself.

"What'd you do to the guy anyway?" Josh asked.

"Josh, what the lady is trying to tell you is that she left him alive but in...a whole other kind of pain," Carson said, smiling knowingly at Melanie. "Now call Ernie and have him prep *Pulsar* for launch as soon as we get to the spaceport."

"Right, Carson." Josh activated his wrist comm unit and sent a signal to the sentient computer. "Ernie, this is Josh. Do you read? Over."

The signal from *Pulsar* came back almost immediately. "This is *Pulsar*. I am receiving you loud and clear, Josh." Even though Ernie was a computer, his synaptic circuits equipped him with all the personality of a living being. Thus, they had no trouble treating him like one. The others treated Ernie as if he was a true member of the team, so the computer responded in kind. "How's the skipper?"

"He's fine, Ernie. We're comin' in hot, though, so get the ship ready for an immediate launch. We'll fill you in when we arrive," Josh said.

"Roger, Josh," Ernie responded through the comm unit small speaker. "I'll have everything ready by the time you get here."

"Right, Ernie. Out," Josh signaled, then severed the connection. He knew if Ernie said everything would be ready by the time they arrived, it most certainly would be ready.

They arrived at the spaceport just as the twin suns rose.

They parked the skimmer outside the main terminal and entered the building. The three Commando, Inc. agents moved quickly to the docking area where *Pulsar* was waiting. Carson could see several aliens taking more than a casual interest near *Pulsar*'s docking entrance. Two Dreedan warriors and a Luto were there, all armed to the teeth. They had managed to get the spaceport seal opened and were now attempting to force their way into the starship beyond. The Luto, with a translator hanging from its neck, seemed to be working the lock while the Dreedans stood guard, their blaster pistols clutched tightly in their blue hands. Except for the three trying to break into their ship, the terminal was empty, as it should have been that early in the morning. Carson crouched behind a ticket dispenser and motioned for Melanie and Josh to do the same.

"Aw. A welcome party just for us," Melanie said. "How thoughtful." Melanie said.

Josh and Carson each looked at her as if she'd lost her mind. They each had a hand blaster, and Melanie was still armed with her blaster rifle.

"Josh, check with Ernie. Ask him about our guests," Carson said, a plan already forming in his mind.

"Ernie, gimme a status report," Josh whispered into his comm unit.

"Everything's okay here, Josh," Ernie reported. "All security systems are functional, and drive systems are up. We can leave as soon as you're aboard."

Josh closed the communications circuit to the ship and turned to Carson. "Ernie reports no problems. All systems are operational."

Carson studied the scene before him quite carefully.

When he turned back to Josh and Melanie, the look on his face was enough to frighten both of them; they had seen that expression before, and it usually meant trouble. "Josh, when I give you the signal, have Ernie crack open the hatch about a foot," Carson said quickly. "Hopefully, the distraction will give us time to act." He then turned to Melanie and held out his hand. "Give me two hypos from the med kit, and set them on their heaviest tranquilizer setting."

Melanie reached in and handed Carson the two cylindrical hypo-injectors.

"Now listen closely. I want this done as quietly as possible, just in case there are more of them around. We can't afford a prolonged firefight. When the hatch opens, I'll take out the two Dreedans. One of you will have to play exterminator and handle the Luto." Carson withdrew the small throwing dagger from its strap on his wrist and held it out to Josh.

"Don't look at me, man. I'd probably cut my own throat with that thing," Josh said, looking at the blade as if it was a poisonous snake.

Melanie stuck out her hand and took the weapon from Carson. "Oh, give it here," she said, rolling her eyes at Josh as she often did, as if she was slightly pissed off.

"Okay, Josh," Carson said, feeling his muscles tense as he prepared to leap forward. "Now!"

Josh sent his already prearranged signal to Ernie. The outer hatch slid opened slowly, stopping after about a foot.

The Luto looked up at the partially opened hatch in amazement. "It is opening. Help me!" the bug croaked. The translator around his neck quickly converted its words to Galactic Standard, but he still spoke in a thick, raspy voice.

The two Dreedans holstered their weapons and turned to help the Luto open the hatch the rest of the way.

Seeing his chance, Carson took off like a sprinter heading toward the finish line, his two hypo-injectors held in front of him. The two Dreedans heard him just a fraction too late. As they turned and reached for their sidearms, Carson barreled into them like a human cannonball. Dazed as they were from the impact, Carson was able to place the injectors at the base of their necks and press the triggers.

The drug worked quickly, and they both fell unconscious almost immediately. The insect-like Luto, though, was another problem entirely. The two Dreedans had collapsed on top of Carson, pinning him down under their dead weight, leaving him helpless as the Luto pulled his blaster and pointed it right at his head.

Seeing that Carson was in trouble, Melanie rose quickly from the ticket dispenser and threw the dagger with all the strength she could muster. The blade flew through the narrow corridor and punctured the Luto just above his large right eye. The deadly beam of energy fired upward, blowing a hole in the ceiling, another conversation piece to the already blaster-marked terminal. The creature howled in pain as he grabbed for the sharp object, dropping the gun in the process.

Knowing the sound of the Luto's missed shot was sure to bring trouble, Carson quickly drew his own weapon and fired at close range into the upper thorax of the insect. The blast from the weapon left a sizeable, smoking hole in the center of the creature, toppling him off his feet. Carson struggled to get up off the floor, then retrieved the dagger from the Luto's head, wiping the black fluid from his blade onto the tunic of the dead alien. "Josh, Melanie, get to the ship. Company's coming!" he then screamed to the others.

Ernie, monitoring everything outside, opened the hatch to allow Melanie and Josh access.

Carson ran toward the opened hatch as trouble in the form of Regar Weent and five human raiders came running down the corridor. Carson pointed his blaster and, with a smile on his face, sent a volley of shots at his pursuers. He intentionally aimed high, and none of the shots hit anyone, but the raiders were forced to dive for cover.

Carson saw Regar Weent staring at him from behind the very same ticket dispenser he and his friends had hidden behind a few short minutes before. Releasing a laugh loud enough for Weent to hear, he turned, went inside the ship, and shut the hatch behind them. Less than thirty seconds later, the sleek starship climbed into the air, pivoted to the northwest, and sped quickly away.

CHAPTER 5

With the information provided by Melanie's psychic vision, Ernie quickly cross-referenced local geographical landmarks and pinpointed the exact location of the raider base. They all hoped the senator's daughter would still be there when they arrived. Carson would have preferred a night rescue, but word of their abrupt departure from the spaceport had made a quick rescue imperative.

Ernie drove *Pulsar* low over the hilly terrain, hoping to avoid any sensor scans that might attempt to track them. It was a rough ride for the three human crewmembers as *Pulsar* maintained a constant twenty tree-scraping meters above the ground. Despite this, preparations were being made for their eventual arrival.

It took only minutes for *Pulsar* to complete its 1,200-kilometer journey, as Ernie brought the ship to a soft landing in a small clearing barely a mile from their destination.

Josh and Melanie sat at their stations on the bridge of the small starship as Carson accessed tactical data from Ernie's memory banks.

"Ernie, gimme a tactical view of the area from an altitude of 300 meters," Carson said, then watched as Ernie processed his request. The forward viewscreen illuminated almost immediately with the requested high-angle view.

"How's this, Skipper?" Ernie asked enthusiastically.

Carson studied the graphic representation of the area,

noting that Ernie had placed a small flashing beacon in the lower right portion of the screen to represent their present position. "Thank you, Ernie," he said. Carson continued to study the screen as both Josh and Melanie stared at him.

"Well?" Melanie said, her patience quickly waning. "Are you gonna tell us the plan or what?"

Carson turned to his friends and finally noticed their stares. "The plan, Melanie, is very simple," he began. "I'm gonna leave the ship in about five minutes. Give me about an hour. If you haven't heard from me by then, come in blasting. Either way, I'll need you guys to serve as a diversion so I can get out."

Josh squirmed a bit in his seat, as if something about the plan made him uncomfortable. "Are you sure you don't need any help, Carson?"

"Thanks, Josh, but I've made this type of penetration before." Carson glanced over at Melanie and noticed the evident concern on her face. "What's on your mind, Melanie?"

"Why can't we go with you? Ernie can run the diversion and the pickup without our help."

Carson stared into her eyes, his voice warm but stern as he said, "If this plan of mine doesn't work, I'll be the only one who pays for it. Besides, you know I work better alone."

Melanie couldn't argue with that. Both she and Josh were aware of large portions of Carson's past, and they now faced the exact type of situation he'd spent most of his life training for. Even though they were also highly trained, they would only slow Carson down or, even worse, perhaps get them all killed.

Carson had ways of operating that neither Melanie nor

Josh could even pretend to understand. The violence and killing didn't particularly bother her, but she and Josh were clumsy amateurs compared to Carson. Of the three, he was the only one who had the skill to enter that base silently, remove any obstacles, and rescue the girl without being discovered. He was a professional, and that was just what the mission called for.

"You're right. Just be careful." As Melanie finished her statement, she realized how ridiculous it sounded.

"Yes, Mother," Carson said, smiling at the wonderful shade of red on her cheeks. He then turned quickly for the hatch.

She heaved a small electronic clipboard at him. "Oh, just get going already!" The clipboard hit the door as it closed behind him, as if to punctuate the end of her statement.

Josh turned to Melanie, grinning from ear to ear like the proverbial cat who'd eaten the proverbial canary. "Oh, Mark, be careful," Josh mimicked in mocking impersonation of Melanie's voice to the closed door, finally throwing a few phantom kisses for effect.

Melanie turned quickly to Josh, her eyes burning into him, nearly searing his brain. "Shut up," she said, quietly but threateningly, and then she stormed out of the bridge.

Josh leaned back in his chair and let a soft sigh escape his lips.

"Josh, I don't think Melanie liked that," Ernie observed via the bridge comm system.

"Ernie, my friend, I think you just might be right. If looks could kill..." he muttered, knowing that if the old cliché was true, he would have been dissolved to a pile of smoking ash.

Carson stood by the weapons locker and took inventory of what he should take with him. In a shoulder holster, he carried his small, short-range needler. Similar to the one Regar Weent had used earlier, the silent weapon could hold a clip of only ten darts.

Before loading two clips of extra ammo on his belt, he checked to make sure the darts he was carrying would only tranquilize; he did not want to kill anyone unless he was forced to, but if that turned out to be the case, he was still otherwise prepared. Another holster on his belt was home to a very lethal-looking hand blaster. If he was discovered, the choice of weapon would change immediately. On the belt of his holster, Carson attached two very small but powerful explosive charges, each with its own electronic timer. He also carried, as always, two small but deadly daggers, with quick-release mechanisms attached to each wrist.

As he made his final checks, a voice from behind caused him to turn: "Everything check out okay?" Melanie asked.

"Seems so. You all right?" he asked, noticing that Melanie seemed to have something else on her mind.

"Yeah. Look, Mark, what I said on the bridge...well, you know..."

"You mean about me being careful?"

Melanie nodded.

Carson walked over to her and placed a finger on her chin, then raised her face to meet his. His lips gently but passionately brushed hers in what Melanie considered far too short of a kiss. Carson then broke free and activated the hatch release.

As the outer hatch slid open, a fresh cool breeze blew past the both of them.

"I'll be back," he said, then turned to the open portal and quickly leapt out of the ship.

Melanie just stood there, dumbfounded. For the first time in her life, she was absolutely speechless as she watched the hatch shut and seal with a whispered sigh. *Damn him,* she thought as she turned from the hatch and headed back to the bridge of the starship. *He'd better come back in one piece, or someone's gonna pay.*

* * *

Melanie was the last thing on the mind of Mark Carson as he made his way up the rugged, rocky path to the cave entrance at the base of the twin peaks that towered high above him. All of his concentration had to be focused on the task at hand if he had any hope of reaching his destination without being discovered.

Glancing at his chronometer, Carson saw that he'd used up about twenty-five minutes of his allotted hour, but the cave entrance was about fifty meters ahead of him. Security on Tanda IV was almost nonexistent. A strange code existed there. *Honor among thieves,* he mused silently.

Getting that far had been the easy part. Carson saw armed guards standing by the entrance, more alert than he had expected; he knew they were on the lookout for him. The word of his escape had spread, and his reputation made the raiders nervous in general, probably Regar Weent in particular.

Running out of time, he decided it best to scout around for an alternative entrance. In Ernie's high-altitude view of the area, he'd noticed a small ventilation screen that the raiders must have built into the side of the mountain, providing necessary cooling for the fusion reactors they used to power their equipment.

It was a short hike to the vent, leaving Carson just twenty-three precious minutes to get in, find the girl, and get out before *Pulsar* started its devastating distraction. The vent, constructed of one-inch-thick titanium, was solidly affixed to the rock face of the mountain with heavy bolts. Carson couldn't take the time to cut all four of the corner ones, He had to risk using one of the small explosive charges from his belt, but he hoped the noise wouldn't echo too loudly through either the cave or the surrounding hills. If he was discovered before *Pulsar* arrived, he would never get the girl out, and he likely wouldn't get out himself either. Carson smiled to himself. *Melanie sure wouldn't like that, would she? Especially after that goodbye I left her with.*

He placed the charge in the center of the vent grating and set the timer for thirty seconds, then quickly took cover behind a small pile of rock. He counted off the seconds as the charge blew the vent inward, making a sound Carson hoped would be carried off by the strong winds swirling around the peaks.

Carson climbed through the jagged hole in the side of the mountain, pausing just a few seconds to allow his eyes to adjust to the darkness. He could see that the vent fed the cooling mountain winds through a large fan, thus circulating fresh air through the entire cavern. The fan wasn't soundproofed, and the *hum* of the motor was loud; he hoped the noise of the explosion had been camouflaged by the deafening roar of the heavy machinery and the metallic whirring of the huge fan.

Moving deeper into the dark cavern, Carson passed the powerful fusion reactor. He stopped near the main power conduit, a large, crystalline box with fiber-optic wires feeding out of it. He carefully withdrew his other explosive charge and placed it squarely on the junction of the cobweb of wires, then set the timer with all the time he had left. Praying that eleven minutes would be enough, he tried to scout out the areas where the raiders might hold a captive.

As stealthily as possible in an unfamiliar, dark labyrinth, Carson made his way down a pitch-black corridor that he hoped would carry him farther into the catacombs of the mountain base.

Soon, a brightly lit area drew his attention. When he took a brief detour to get a closer look, he came upon a landing that overlooked an enormous open cavern, apparently a makeshift garage or docking bay. Raider space vessels of all shapes and sizes were there, fueling up for what Carson presumed would be yet another campaign of terror – one that would likely result in far too many deaths. Unfortunately, Carson knew he didn't have the time to do anything about it. At the moment, the only lives he could focus on saving belonged to the senator's daughter and to him.

While he knelt, looking down at the raiders' preparations, Carson failed to notice trouble coming from behind. As he rose from his concealed spot, a large, muscular arm slipped around his neck, the grip tightening until it was nearly impossible for him to breathe.

"Well, well. Look who we have here."

The voice sounded somewhat familiar to Carson, but when he smelled the man's vile breath, he knew for sure who had him – the same man who had tried to have him killed less than twelve hours earlier. He knew he didn't have long to break free of Weent's hold, for the creature was strong enough to break him in two if he gave him half a chance.

"Well," Weent said, pulling a knife out with his other hand, "this is it, Carson. To think, I was actually beginning to worry."

On the verge of unconsciousness, Carson took the only chance he had left. After activating the release of the small daggers with the twitch of a wrist muscle, Carson slammed them into Weent's upper thighs. As the raider screamed in pain, Carson felt the grip on his throat release. Weent instinctively moved his hands down to the small knife handle jutting out of his legs. Moving quickly, Carson swung a roundhouse blow against the side of Weent's head, knocking the large man down to the ground. Dazed, Weent tried to rise but was put down again as Carson kicked him hard in the ribs.

As Weent went down with a *thud*, Carson caught a glimpse of two guards quickly rounding the corner, weapons drawn. Faster than either raider could follow, Carson drew his needler and fired three shots in rapid succession, all of which found their mark. Both guards were dropped in their tracks, unconscious but alive.

Carson knelt by the unconscious Weent and decided he would have to do things the hard way after all. He grabbed a handful of the man's greasy hair and shook Weent's head until he heard a low moan escape his former friend's lips. "Morning, Regar. Nice to see you up."

Weent seemed to be regaining consciousness quickly, but he was certainly not in a very good mood. "Carson, I'm gonna kill you, you lousy son-of-a — "

"Language, Regar. You should start hanging out with a

higher class of scum." Carson smiled and leaned closer, his grin vanishing as quickly as it had appeared. "I wish I had time for a chat, but I don't, so I'll just ask you one question. If I don't get the answer I'm looking for...well, let's just say you're not gonna be a happy camper. Tell me where to find Senator Weltman's daughter, my friend...and I suggest you tell me now."

"Screw you and that little bitch!" replied Weent in disgust.

Carson ripped a small strip from Weent's tunic and stuck it in his open mouth, making an effective gag. He then grabbed the handles of the two daggers that were still deeply embedded in Weent's legs and viciously twisted them from side to side. "No more games. Tell me where she is," he demanded, knowing by the look on Weent's face that the pain was beginning to wear him down. Besides the moans, Carson could see that Weent's eyes had already rolled up into his head. "Weent, you either tell me, or I swear I'll rip your heart out and stuff it down your throat. You know me. I'm a man of my word, and I can and will do it." Once he had Weent's full, wide-eyed attention, Carson said, "If you're ready to talk, nod."

Weent quickly nodded in agreement.

Carson carefully removed the gag from the raider's mouth and waited for his answer.

With tears streaming down his filthy, sweaty face, Weent said, "She's in the level just beneath this one. That's where the detention cells are."

Carson knew the injured man had told him the truth; he would have been a fool not to. "All right, I believe you." He stood, took out his needler, and pointed it at Weent. "Now that wasn't so hard, was it?"

Weent's eyes almost bulged out of his head in fright when he gazed at the weapon pointed at him. "I thought you said you weren't gonna kill me if I talked!"

"So I lied," Carson said with a shrug, then fired the tranquilizer dart into a shocked Weent's chest. *Boy, he's in for quite a surprise when he wakes up alive,* Carson jested to himself. He then leaned over and pulled his daggers out of the two bloody legs, wiped them off on the unconscious man's tunic, and carefully placed them back in the special releases under his sleeves. He had done Weent a favor by pulling the daggers out after he was unconscious. *For old time's sake,* he thought to himself.

Carson replaced the dart clip in his needler with a fresh one and ran down toward the level where Weent had said the detention cells were. A quick look at his chronometer showed that he had about three minutes before the explosive charge would go off on the power conduit and *Pulsar* made its attack run. He was having a good run of luck, as most of the raiders seemed to be busy in the staging area, preparing their ships. The corridors were clear, and he hoped it would stay that way.

When he reached the lower detention level, Carson saw two Luto standing guard by the cell doors. He knew his trusty needler would not be as effective on the insect-like creatures as it had been on Weent and the other human raiders, for something about their metabolism burned the drug out of their system before it could take effect. He looked down at his chronometer again; there were only seconds to go till the blast would take out the power conduit and all hell would break loose.

"Well," Carson said quietly to himself as the blast rocked the whole mountain, "so much for stealth." He removed the blaster from his holster and, in the confusion of flickering lights and falling rocks, stepped out in the open and fired two quick shots, each striking a Luto guard in the midsection. The weapon, set on full, almost cut them in half.

Carson then moved quickly down to each of the cells. All were empty save one, which held an attractive brunette, sitting on the floor in the corner. Her clothes, probably expensive and glamorous when she'd first put them on, now looked like a beggar's rags.

"Miss Weltman, my name is Carson. I'm here to get you out."

She stood and slowly moved to the front of the cell, her hands smoothing out the wrinkles in her tattered gown. Even after all she'd been through, she was still a very attractive young woman. "Thanks. They planned to kill me before they leave," she said arrogantly, trying to speak up over the explosions tearing through

Pulsar was already making its run, and Carson knew it was time to go. "Move to the back of the cell. There's no time to find a key."

When she realized he was aiming his blaster at the lock, she obediently shuffled to the back of the cell and plugged her ears with her fingers, then closed her eyes.

Carson fired, and the lock exploded in a shower of broken metal. He then kicked the door open and pulled the frightened young woman out of her confinement. "Let's get outta here!"

Carson dragged the woman along with one hand and held his blaster with the other. In all the confusion, he tried to lead them back the way he had come, through the blown-open vent grating, but a Dreedan warrior suddenly stepped in his way, a blaster rifle clutched in his large, blue hands. As the Dreedan took aim, Carson roughly shoved the small brunette to one side as he dived to the other. The blast sliced through the air where they'd been standing only seconds before. Carson reached for his gun, but it had slipped out of his hand during his dive. The Dreedan raider moved closer, lifting the rifle to deliver its fatal blast.

As Carson waited out his final seconds, ashamed by his failed mission, a beam of energy lashed out from his right, catching the alien and throwing him to the ground in a smoking heap. Carson turned to see the senator's little girl standing there, with his own blaster held tightly in her hand. He reached over and took the blaster from the woman, though her small hands were a bit reluctant to give up their prize. "Nice shooting, Ms. Weltman," Carson said, prying the weapon from her and placing it back in his holster.

For a moment, she just stared at the body of the large blue warrior, her body tense. "Bastard," she said to the corpse, then lashed out with a strong kick at the dead alien's head while walking by. "Please call me 'Sabrina.' Weltman is my father's name."

"Right," Carson said, pulling her behind him.

When they finally reached the power conduit, Carson couldn't believe the extent of the damage his explosion had caused. He looked at the power gauges on the fusion reactor and saw that the core reactor had overloaded. It was only a matter of time, perhaps mere minutes, before the entire mountain would blow. "C'mon!" he said, tugging Sabrina along.

They increased their pace, as time was now their enemy, the raiders more obstacle than foe. When they reached the circulating fan, Carson saw light coming in through the hole he had blown earlier.

"This way, Ms. Weltman," he said.

She stared at him as if he was some vile creature spouting a dirty word at a fancy society event.

Having no time to argue about manners and political correctness, Carson snapped, "Sorry. This way, *Sabrina*."

She nodded her approval at the use of her first name, then crawled through the grating and out onto the windy ledge.

Carson activated his comm unit and put in an emergency call to *Pulsar*.

"*Pulsar*, this is Carson, do you read, over."

The return came almost immediately as Melanie's voice came back through the small speaker. "Mark, are you all right? Where are you?"

"Melanie, listen closely. I've got the senator's daughter." Again, he caught her staring somewhat disapprovingly at him, but this time he ignored her. "We're on the north face of the peak. Get down here fast. The whole place is gonna blow."

Inside the starship, Melanie was almost frantic. "Ernie, Josh, find them fast."

"I have him on my sensors," Ernie reported calmly. "I'm adjusting course to intercept."

Josh activated the viewscreen and quickly located the two figures standing on the north side of the peak. "Look, Melanie. There they are." Melanie joined him by the viewscreen as Josh stood and headed for the hatch. "I'm heading aft. This has to be done fast. Stand by!" Josh called to her as he disappeared through the sliding doors.

Carson saw the ship coming in with its rear hatch open and Josh standing by to help. He also heard the ominous rumbling coming from the cavern below him. *Won't be long now,* he thought as the ship lowered to almost within arm's reach.

"Carson, hurry!" Josh called, sticking out his hand out.

"Here. Take the girl." Carson shoved Sabrina Weltman up by a part of her anatomy that would never be brought up at a polite dinner party.

Once she was safely inside the ship, Josh stuck out his hand again.

Carson leapt with all the strength in his legs and grabbed successfully for Josh's hand.

Josh pulled him into the airlock and quickly shut the hatch. "Gotcha," he said with a smile.

Carson pulled himself to the comm panel on the wall and quickly punched the button that would connect him to the bridge. "Ernie, hit it! Full power ascent...now!"

The full power of the *Pulsar* fusion engines kicked in as the starship thundered spaceward. Gravitational forces pressed them against the deck as the artificial gravity systems tried to compensate for the quickly increasing g-force.

On the bridge, Ernie's sensors detected a massive nuclear ground detonation below them. As fast as they were traveling, the blast wave traveled faster, slamming into the ship and increasing their upward velocity. Eventually, the shockwave receded, and *Pulsar* cruised out of the atmosphere and into planetary orbit.

As soon as the ship stabilized, Melanie raced back to the airlock. "Are you all..." she began but stopped short when she saw Sabrina Weltman clinging to Carson's chest for dear life.

Carson noticed her disappointed stare and quickly moved away from where Sabrina was lying.

Without another word, Melanie glared at him, then stormed off in a rage.

"Josh, keep an eye on Ms. Weltman. I'll be back." Then, without waiting for a reply, Carson walked through the door and headed for the bridge. When he got there, he found Melanie sitting in his command chair, wearing an annoyed look on her face.

"Pretty, huh?" Melanie said as she swiveled her chair in quick circles.

"Melanie, take it easy. Ernie?"

"Yes, Skipper?"

"Set a course to the nearest Alliance base. We have a guest to drop off."

Melanie said nothing and continued to stare at him.

"Oh, and Ernie?"

"Yes, Skipper?"

"For all our sakes, please give 'er all the speed you can muster." Carson looked at Melanie and was happy to see a contented grin flash across her pretty face.

"You got it," Ernie replied, and the ship thundered out of orbit and into hyperspace.

CHAPTER 6

Time passed slowly for Ank as he stood in the dark, dank cell. Chains bound both his legs and wrists to a cold wall in what had to have been, for lack of a better term, a torture chamber. Dusty shelves lined the decaying walls. Strange metallic devices, their uses unknown to Ank, sat malevolently, waiting to be put to use. From the increasing activity he heard beyond the door, he knew it wouldn't be long before these creatures left Solo.

Donar and Modok had taunted him when he'd first come to, with his head throbbing in pain. He'd only been unconscious for a few hours following the explosion in the security shack when the door of his cell swung open. Donar and his grotesque stooge had come to tell him about the imminent arrival of the supply transport. Ank remembered the fetid breath as it reached his sensitive whiskered muzzle. The lizard-thing had leaned close to him, grinning to the other creature as if they were sharing in the dark humor of some depraved private joke.

"Lieutenant Ank, how nice to see you back with us," Donar said, turning to look around at the chamber. "I hope you find the accommodations...suitable."

Ank picked up his head and defiantly glared at Donar. "The accommodations are fine. It's you I don't really care for."

Modok, angered by the remark, stepped over to the chained felinoid and grabbed Ank's throat in his large claw.

"You will pay for that remark, cat," the mad creature said with a growl.

"You seem to have upset Modok. That was not a smart move."

Ank didn't even bother with a sarcastic retort; every breath was already enough of a challenge.

"Are you aware, little kitty-cat, that I could snap your head off with one squeeze?" Modok threatened, looking quite happy about the opportunity.

As the mutated simian added more pressure to the hold, Ank began to black out.

"Modok, release him," Donar said calmly to his war chief.

Modok either had other plans or was too caught up in the moment to hear his dark lord, because the violent lust to kill gripped the twisted creature's mind.

Knowing that he was not going to stop until Ank was dead, Donar swung a tentacled arm at the simian's head, finally getting his attention.

"Why must you stop me, Lord?" Modok asked, slightly confused.

"Because we may still have use of the good lieutenant," Donar said, somewhat relieved to see that Ank was beginning to stir again. Turning abruptly, he transfixed the chained security officer with a cold stare. "Ank, the reason I am here is to tell you that your precious transport ship will arrive shortly. I am offering you a chance to help me take the ship, in return for your life."

Ank's reaction started as a small chuckle, then rose to the full crescendo of a laugh, which only angered his hosts. Modok's incredible rage was only controlled by the thought that Donar didn't want him killed yet, and Donar just looked blankly at him, the grin wiped off his long snout.

Donar peered closely at Ank, then reached a tentacled arm out and encircled his throat, though not as tightly as Modok had before. "What do you find so humorous?"

Ank looked at the lizard king, the tears from the laughter finally drying on his furry cheek. He could feel Donar losing control, and the tentacle began to grip tighter. His laughter ceased as he stared into Donar's eyes, a piercing stare that threatened to tear right through the reptilian head. "The thought of helping you," he said coldly.

Donar stared back at him, finally loosening his grip. He stepped back and grinned himself. "Do you know why you're still alive?"

Ank thought it over but couldn't come up with an answer. He looked at Donar and answered honestly, "No."

"Because, believe it or not, I like you. More than that, I respect your courage," Donar said to the chained Ank. "Unfortunately for you, I don't really need you."

Ank didn't believe the former statement for a moment, but he certainly believed the latter. He knew that as soon as Donar tired of him, he was as good as dead.

There was still a grin on Donar's face, but something was different. Something was happening; he seemed to be changing. His snout grew smaller, and his tentacles began to absorb back into Donar's body. Fur quickly sprouted all over his previously scaly form, and a tail jutted out of his rear.

The amusement of the past moment quickly turned to terror as Ank realized what the lizard had transformed himself into. He shuddered against his chains, overcome for the first time there by absolute fear. He stared at the figure before him, the spitting image of his very self. So complete was the transformation that Ank doubted even his mate could tell the difference.

The doppelganger turned to him and spoke to him in Ank's own voice. "Well? What do you think?"

Ank couldn't answer. If he could have conjured up any kind of reply, it would have been frozen somewhere deep in his throat. He stared at the copy of himself and heard the sounds of laughter. Ank realized it was his own, and he hoped he wasn't starting to lose his grip on his sanity.

"My Lord, the ship is due very soon."

"You are quite right, Modok," Donar said as they turned to leave the chamber. Stopping at the door, Donar turned once again and grinned. "Oh, Ank, before I go, please promise me that you'll hang around just a little longer."

They laughed at him again as the chamber door swung shut, once again sealing him in.

That grim scene had occurred two days ago, and Ank had not seen Donar or Modok since, but the activity outside his small cell had certainly increased. He had no way of knowing what had happened to the crew of the ship, but he was certain they had not faced happy fates. To make matters worse, deprived of food and water for two days, his own mind and body were quickly weakening.

Hope? Pssh, Ank thought. *I surely don't have much of that at this point, do I?* The best he felt he could hope for was a reasonably quick death, but he doubted Modok would afford him that. For now, all he could do was wait and see, then try to act at the right time. "If I'm doomed to die here," he said to the cold stone wall, "at least maybe I can take a few of those damnable things with me."

CHAPTER 7

The large transport ship was parked just outside the crumbling stone walls of the city. All remnants of the battle just forty-eight hours prior were now gone, replaced by the drone-like activity of Donar's servants.

Machinery of all types, as well as weapons, were loaded into the large cargo bays. Supplies that had been meant for the science team were discarded, considered unnecessary; all crates marked "Alliance Science Academy" were simply dumped to the side.

The survivors of the attack were held behind the force field generated bars of the ship brig. So caught off guard they'd been that of the 157 crewmembers, only 28 remained alive. These were only allowed to live because of what they knew about starship operations. Not only that, but their bodies would also provide the raw materials Snatak claimed he required for his experiments.

Donar sat on the bridge of the transport. On the large viewscreen in front of the captain's chair, he could monitor the flow of his equipment into the cargo bays. It had been two days since they had taken the transport, and if they weren't ready to leave soon, he would make an example of some of his lazy subjects in order to motivate the others to work at a faster pace. Using one of his long tentacles, Donar activated the communications link to the main cargo bay. "Modok, you fool, how long until everything is loaded?"

Modok's face appeared on the main viewscreen. He

knew the wrong answer to his master's question might cost him his life, despite the value he put on his own clawed hide. "My Lord, loading should be completed within the hour."

Donar seemed almost dangerously quiet at the other end before he said, "Good. We shall finally leave this dead rock."

"Where will we go?"

"That is not for you to question, fool. Just advise me when the loading is completed."

"Yes, My Lord, I will personally " Modok began, but without warning, Donar severed the connection from the bridge. As the screen went blank, the rage again built up in the simian-thing. Knowing that he couldn't take his rage out on Donar, Modok did the next best thing. "Slave, put that down and come here!" he demanded of the nearest humanoid servant.

The elfin one put his burden down on the deck and slowly walked over to the huge war chief, his head bowed. "Yes, My Lord?"

Without hesitation, Modok swung his large, clawed arm and connected with the side of the unaware servant's head. The force of the blow sent the servant hurtling into the bulkhead by the open cargo hatch.

Modok turned at the sight of one of his warriors entering, searching for the cause of the commotion. "You, warrior!"

"Yes, My Lord?" replied the armored werewolf, its blaster weapon gripped tightly in its paws. Donar had been able to mutate the wolflike creature, giving it natural armor plating, while he and most of the others wore theirs.

"If the slave is still alive," Modok said, pointing at the figure lying prone on the deck, "put him back to work when he awakes."

"And if he is dead, Lord?"

Modok thought for a very short second before turning back to the wolf with a smile. "If so, throw him to the others."

"Yes, My Lord!" The werewolf turned and walked to the open hatch.

Modok smiled at the saliva dripping from the wolf's fangs. *Yes*, he thought, *things are working out just fine.*

* * *

Donar sat on the bridge, contemplating his next move. With the loading of his equipment nearing completion, he needed to decide upon a destination, and for that, he needed input from Snatak. "Snatak, on the bridge...now!" he snapped into the comm port built into the side of the command chair.

"Coming, My Lord," came from the attached speaker.

The rat had better come, Donar thought to himself, *and he had better come prepared.*

Moments later, the bridge doors opened, and the little scientist scurried over to his master's side. The robe he was wearing did little to hide his long, rat-like snout and pointy ears.

"Snatak, you better have good news for me."

"I do, My Lord."

"Then don't just stand there, rat! Tell me!"

Donar was growing visibly impatient, and Snatak was sorely aware that it might be dangerous to his continued good health. "My Lord, we need two humans, preferably at least one officer, to be delivered to my laboratory."

Donar once again activated the small communications

port on his command chair. "Brig, bring the captain and another of the humans to the sorcerer's laboratory. We will join you there."

"Yes, My Lord," the reply crackled over the speaker.

Donar stood from the command chair and motioned for Snatak to follow him. The doors whooshed closed behind them as they passed through.

Moments later, they entered what was once the transport gymnasium, now converted into Snatak's master laboratory. The walls of the large compartment were lined with machinery of all types and sizes. To one side, attached to a featureless console and fed by many wires, were five tubes, each about two meters in height. Those tubes fed an even larger one. Five glowing cables, each pulsating with power, came together in a single conduit, connected in turn to the top of a tube nearly twice the height and diameter of the others. Other machines sat powerless but malevolent in their intent, seemingly awaiting their command to come to life.

The ship captain and first officer were each tied to an examination table that had recently been liberated from sickbay. Three of his armored werewolf guards stood by in case the humans tried to escaped their restraints.

The captain struggled against the hold of the heavy elastic restraints until he saw Donar enter the converted lab. At the sight of the tentacled lizard, the struggling stopped, replaced by a fearful foreboding. "What's this all about? Who are you? Release us now!" he demanded.

Snatak led Donar over to the examination tables and brought his muzzle down to just inches above the startled captain's face. "Patience, Captain. You and your first officer are going to assist me in a great experiment," he said, noting that the captain and his first officer had turned visibly pale. The feeble-looking rat pointed to one of the werewolves standing nearby, then to the trembling first officer on the examination table. "Guard, put that one in the first tube," he instructed.

The guard untied the first officer. Seeing a chance to run, the human made a break for the gymnasium door. Unfortunately for him, though, the two other guards had anticipated his move and quickly intercepted him. The frightened human was knocked to the deck by the blow from an odd-looking energy weapon swung by one of the snarling creatures. Drawing him roughly to his feet, they then dragged him to the tube, holding him by the arms to prevent any additional trouble. As they locked him into the tube, he looked to his captain for help, then resigned himself to his fate as his captain looked away.

The captain looked over at Donar. His fear was quickly replaced with a growing temper of his own. "What are you fiends doing to him?"

Donar looked at Snatak, who was frantically adjusting the controls on an instrument on the other side of the lab. "Yes, Snatak, tell us, what are you going to do to him?"

"I have created a process that allows me to use living genetic matter as a catalyst in the creation of a completely adaptable form of life." He was in constant motion, activating bank after bank of ancient machinery.

"What kind of life?"

"My Lord, you informed me that our agents must be able to move about freely in this universe, did you not?"

"Yes, Snatak. Get on with it."

Snatak pointed again at the werewolf. "Go now. Bring me the test subject from the other room."

The guard bowed to the sorcerer and left the room, then returned seconds later with one of the humanoid servants they'd been using for menial tasks.

"Guard, put the test subject in the larger tube."

The guard shoved the willing servant into the large, clear tube and latched it shut.

Donar watched in puzzled excitement as Snatak went about his business. The scientist moved his hand over blank control surfaces and adjusted connections that fed power from the powerful fusion reactor. He watched more closely as Snatak performed the experiment. He was confused as to what was going to happen, but he was also excited to see it. In the small tube, the human beat his hands ineffectively on the strong, clear material. Donar sensed the terror building in the creature and relished in it.

"My Lord, behold!" Snatak activated the final sequence on his console, and the machines pulsated with an eerie green light. Fire seemed to crackle in and around the small tube. A bright emerald aura surrounded the frantic crewman.

The captain tried to turn his head to see what was happening to his subordinate, but he was too tightly held by the restraints. Snatak again moved his paws over the controls and increased the power to the machine. As the aura surrounding the first officer increased, the human screamed in incredible pain.

"What are you doing to him, you bastards?" the captain cried. "Stop this!"

The man started to dissolve, slowly and horribly, into a

fine mist, his body peeling away in incredible torment, layer by layer: first the skin, revealing the musculature beneath it, and then the bone structure, down to the marrow, bursting into a fine red mist before finally being drawn up into the intake at the top of the tube.

"Very impressive, Snatak...as a casual diversion," Donar said with a grin. "Don't you agree, Captain?"

The captain had closed his eyes and unsuccessfully tried to force out the sounds of his dying friend. He knew his fate wasn't bound to be any better, but he refused to die as a coward. "Drop dead," he spat.

"Captain, I have been a most awful host, haven't I? Guard!" Donar called to one of his werewolves. "Please turn the table so the captain can enjoy the proceedings with the rest of us."

The guard turned the captain's examination table so that he was facing the tubes. The one they had forced his crewman into was now as empty as it had been before he was put there.

Snatak stood before his audience, basking in the attention and his master's pleasure. "My Lord, we are ready for Stage Two."

"Proceed, Snatak."

"The living genetic matter is being altered by the energies within the machine," Snatak explained. He traced the energies from the tube to the machine and finally to the larger tube, where the quivering servant stood. "The living energies are collected in this receptacle," Snatak continued, pointing at a silvery box just above the large tube. "Observe."

When Snatak activated the console for a final time, the collected energies flooded into the transparent chamber. The living crimson mist, now charged with incredible energy, seemed to consume the servant. The humanoid's body, now barely visible, pulsated with power. The form within the tube seemed to grow to at least two meters in height, but that was not what provoked the ship captain's gasp. The body features seemed to be wiped clean, the skin now appearing like moldy clay.

When the morbid procedure finished, Snatak said to the closest werewolf, "Guard, open the latches."

The wolf seemed apprehensive as he stepped to the tube and unlocked it. "Slave, step out of the tube."

The servant, now a humanoid mass of clay, walked out of the tube and stopped in front of Donar.

"How do you feel?" Donar asked the newly formed creature.

"Strange, My Lord," the servant answered. "No pain but strange."

Snatak pushed a small switch on the side of the examination table, lifting the captain into an upright position. Standing by the examination table, he then signaled his creation to join him. "Slave, put your hands on both sides of the human's head."

The creature reached over and did as Snatak ordered. As soon as contact was established, the captain's eyes closed tightly, and his body broke into violent trembles, as if he were caught in some kind of crazed fit. Blood started to slowly drip from his eyes and ears, and Donar looked on in amazement as the crimson rivers began to flow more forcefully out of the man. As the captain's face started thin, literally shriveling, the former servant's face began to fill out and become more defined. The captain shook more violently, and his skin, from head to toe, was soon withered and sunken, till his flesh turned to the consistency of parchment and finally crumbled to dust in the hands of the servant.

Donar stared at his slave. The face that stared back at him was the face of the captain.

Snatak looked over at his lord, his excitement causing him to jump up and down with joy and pride for a job well done.

"Very good, Snatak. You're still full of surprises. Is the transformation...total?"

"Question him, My Lord. See for yourself."

Donar turned to the newly fashioned human standing before him. "What is your name?"

The creature with the face of a man found his answer without any hesitation. "I am Captain William Barton of the Alliance transport ship *Aries*, My Lord."

Donar turned back to his sorcerer, his amazement evident. "How?"

"My process allows any of our warriors to, with a simple touch of just seconds, take the form and memories of anyone you wish to replace," Snatak said, "yet they also retain their old identity and loyalty to you. I call it a 'simulcron.'"

"An appropriate moniker, to be sure. How long does it last?"

"I do not yet know. Perhaps this first one will give us our answer," Snatak said as he gestured to the transformed creature.

Donar wrapped a long, tentacled feeler around the copy of Captain Barton and briefly laughed out loud. "Come with me, Captain. We have a liftoff to prepare and much to talk about."

"Yes, My Lord."

As they walked out of the gymnasium-turned-lab, Donar flashed a smile back at the little sorcerer. "Well done, Snatak, but we will need more raw material for your new toy – much more," he said as the doors shut behind them.

* * *

Two hours later, with the help of the reinvented Captain Barton, *Aries* thundered into the sky and the void beyond. Donar sat in the command chair and watched the stars flash by on the forward viewscreen. They had used Snatak's process twice more since their first successful test. Sitting at the helm and navigation stations were two more of Donar's warriors, recently transformed into transport crewmembers. The captain stood by his side, ready with any information that might be needed.

In the hours prior to liftoff, the simulcron of Barton had filled in all the holes in the information he could not force out of Ank. The Alliance seemed ripe for the taking, but first, they would need another ship. Barton had pointed out that since they'd missed several check-in calls, his ship would be considered missing. A system-wide bulletin would be sent out, and too many questions would have to be answered to explain their failure to respond.

The safest course of action would be to find a habitable planet to use as a base of operations. After that, they would locate another vessel, one that would allow them to travel more freely. Ultimately, more creatures would be needed to feed the transformation machine so the campaign of conquest could begin.

Donar and Barton had spent hours looking at star charts

82

of the systems within range of the transport. A planet was finally chosen, based on its location on the Alliance fringe border and its mainly human colonist population.

They would enter the Nexus system in fourteen hours and would assume orbit around the third planet. Donar already knew they would be welcomed, as Fleet transport ships were rare visitors to those distant colonies, and any assistance and supplies would be appreciated by the local populace.

A short time before, Barton had called ahead to make all of the necessary arrangements with the colony Ruling Council. Besides the fact that Nexus III contained all the living materials he needed, Donar also knew that as a mining colony, other important minerals for his experiments could be obtained there.

Donar looked over at Barton. It had been about twenty-four hours since his rebirth. "How are you feeling?" he asked, recognizing it had been about twenty-four hours since his rebirth.

"Fine, My Lord," the former servant began. "I've been giving a lot of thought to our next move."

"Oh? And what do you think that move should be?" Donar asked, amazed at the quality of the information the copy was able to transfer from the original.

"After we secure the colony, our first goal must be infiltration of the Alliance military structure. Once we have control of Fleet resources, we control the Alliance."

It made perfect sense to Donar, but before they decided on any military action, he first had to consult with Modok. In leaving Lieutenant Ank alive, he had infuriated his war chief. Modok wanted to taste Ank's blood, but Ank was spared as a warning of things to come. *What good is terror if word of it does not spread?* Donar reasoned. He activated the comm unit on his command chair with a flick of a tentacle. "Modok, go to the briefing room. I will meet you there."

"Yes, My Lord," came the reply from the bridge speaker.

As Donar stood from the chair, he motioned to Barton. "Come, Captain. We have a campaign to plan, and I want those plans put into motion before we land."

Barton looked at his master and bowed slightly at the waist. "Yes, My Lord," he said, as they both turned and left the bridge.

CHAPTER 8

*P*ulsar's trip to the Alliance starbase on Juras IV had been uneventful, and Mark Carson was grateful for that. With Melanie keeping a watchful eye on him, Carson saw to it that Sabrina Weltman was handed over to the proper authorities.

With that small favor out of the way, the rescue of the senator's daughter, they were all looking forward to a long period of relaxation on some far-off planetary paradise. Before that, however, they had to call the admiral to report the success of their rescue mission. With any luck, Brooks would approve Carson's request for a slight detour to the resort planet, Argos, where he and Melanie might have an opportunity to see if that pre-mission kiss would lead to anything else.

"Ernie, open a subspace channel to the admiral."

"Aye-aye, Skipper," said the voice of the sentient computer. "I have Admiral Brooks for you on Subspace Channel Two."

Carson looked at the forward viewscreen, where the image of his mentor, Admiral Clayton Brooks appeared. He had known Brooks long enough to realize that he didn't seem to be in a very good mood. "Admiral," he said hesitantly, I'm happy to report that the rescue mission was, indeed, a success. I've already dropped the senator's daughter off on "

"Very good, Carson," Brooks interrupted. "Now, I need

you to make a slight detour to Sector 3676. The coordinates are being fed into Ernie's navigational subsystems as we speak."

Carson peered over at Josh and Melanie, who were wearing expressions of obvious disappointment equal to his own. "Admiral, uh...we were hoping for a little shore leave before our next assignment. This was a bit of a rough one, and – "

"Mark, this will just be a short milk run for you," the admiral implored. "Listen, after you finish this little detour, I'll personally approve any request for leave anywhere in the galaxy." By Carson's silence, Brooks realized it was time to play his trump card. "I'll even pay for it."

Carson contemplated the offer before staring back at the others.

Josh and Melanie both shrugged, then nodded their approval.

"All right Admiral. What's the deal?" Carson asked, curious as to why a so-called "milk run" was worth so much to his penny-pinching boss.

"It seems Alliance Fleet Operations has misplaced a transport," Brooks began. "It was due to make a supply drop to a group of scientists doing archeological research but failed to respond at any communication checks or arrive at its next scheduled destination."

"What about the science team?" Josh asked from his position at the science station.

"Fleet Operations has tried unsuccessfully for the last three days to contact them."

Carson was beginning to get a very bad feeling. "Excuse me for a second, sir. Ernie, do you have those coordinates?"

"Yes, Skipper."

"Give them to me."

When Ernie repeated the coordinates the admiral had transmitted, Carson couldn't believe his ears; those coordinates would place *Pulsar* close to the disputed boundaries separating the Alliance from the Dreedan Empire. "Admiral," he said, "do you, by any chance, realize *where* you're sending us for this, uh...milk run?" Carson asked, hoping the older man had simply screwed up and provided the wrong coordinates

"Mark, with tensions as they are, the Fleet doesn't want to risk sending an armed military cruiser into the area," Brooks replied. "In fact, the request comes personally from Fleet Admiral Olstad."

"You are aware that the Dreedans are not very fond of us, correct?"

"I know, Mark, but it can't be helped," Brooks said. He tried to sound sympathetic, but he knew Carson would never buy it.

"Right. We're on our way," Carson said, resigned to his fate.

"Mark, I believe you might be acquainted with the transport captain."

Carson just stared at him intently, ready for the next bit of good news.

"His name is William Barton."

"Thank you, sir."

"Keep in contact. Brooks out." With that, the image faded from the viewscreen as the communications channel closed.

"Ernie, set a course for the provided coordinates. Give

'er all the speed you've got," Carson said. He didn't even hear Ernie's reply; rather, he just sat quietly in his command chair and stared at the starfield and the planet they were orbiting.

Melanie and Josh moved over to stand by their friend, and Melanie was the first to break the silence. "Mark, what's the matter?" she asked.

At the continuing silence, Josh became a little concerned. "You okay, man? Who is this Captain Barton anyway?"

"Yeah, I'm fine," Carson said, still staring out at the stars as *Pulsar* gracefully pivoted on its aft thrusters before blasting into interstellar space. "William Barton and I went through the Academy together. We shared a room. I guess you could say we hated each other at first, but we still had...a mutual respect," Carson continued in a monotone voice. "Eventually, that respect led to a kind of semi-competitive friendship."

"When did you see him last?" Melanie asked.

"Hmm. It had to be nine or ten years ago. After we left the Academy, we were assigned according to our skills. Bill went into Starship Command, and I moved into Special Forces, then Covert Operations," Carson reflected. "After that, we sort of just lost touch, each of us caught up in our own little world."

"What kind of captain was he?" Josh asked. "I mean, would he miss a scheduled comm check?"

Carson's reply was short. "No. Never."

Melanie looked down at him strangely, feeling that there had to be a little more to their friendship than Carson was telling them. "Ernie, what's our ETA to Sector 3676?"

"At current speed, we should arrive at Planet Solo in five hours, forty-three minutes, fifteen seconds."

Carson stared for several more seconds at the stars blurring by on the forward viewscreen. Finally, he stood and faced his shipmates. "I recommend that we all get as much rest as we can. I don't have a very good feeling about this."

Josh and Melanie nodded their agreement, then turned and walked to the twin doors of the bridge, which swiftly whispered open as they approached.

"Ernie..." Carson said, stopping just before the doors.

"Yes, Skipper?"

"Keep your long-range sensors peeled. We're gonna be traveling through some potentially hostile space, and I don't want anything sneaking up on us."

"Aye-aye, Skipper."

"Also keep an eye out for any wreckage that might have been a military transport," Josh added. "Call us as soon as you power down from hyperspace."

"Affirmative, Josh," Ernie said.

The doors slid quietly shut behind Ernie's three human shipmates. As *Pulsar* cruised through space, the computer reached out in all directions with his sensors. They trusted him, and he was not about to let them down.

Each human member of the team took the opportunity to rest in his or her own way. For Joshua Grant, the time meant freedom to spend a few hours studying his technical journals. In fact, he had so little free time that he assumed that much of what he was reading was already obsolete.

For Melanie Patula, rest was simply that. During her early years, growing up on Helos, she had learned to take sleep whenever and wherever she could. It didn't take more than a few minutes before she dozed off.

Unfortunately, sleep did not come so easily for Carson. His thoughts continued to race, always returning to the mystery ahead of them. *What has Bill Barton gotten himself into now? And why does Brooks find it so crucial for us to investigate? Obviously, he's under a lot of pressure from Fleet Operations, but why? Maybe it's got something to do with the science team Bill's ship was heading for.* One thing was certain: He didn't like their close proximity to Dreedan space.

Brooks had, along with the coordinates of Solo, sent over all the information they had on the science team and what they had discovered so far. Carson noted that they'd already spent a great deal of time searching through the ruins of the enormous city that seemed to span most of the northern hemisphere, but there wasn't any detailed information on their discoveries. The personnel files were extensive, though, especially on the security detachment Fleet Command had provided.

Security was being handled by... What was his name? There it is, a Lieutenant Ank. To Carson's surprise, he found the felinoid's record of achievement to be excellent. It seemed there was little that the security chief couldn't handle.

Looking at his chronometer, Carson realized they were scheduled for system entry in about one hour. With a touch of his hand, Carson deactivated the terminal, turned of the lights, and gently put his head down on his hard pillow. The pillow sensed his movement and conformed to the shape of his head with ease. *With any luck,* Carson thought, *I'll get at least a few minutes of ZZZ's before I'm needed.* He closed his eyes and, as his training allowed, managed to fall into a restless version of sleep.

It seemed to Carson that his eyes had been closed for only a few minutes before he heard the terror-filled scream coming from outside his cabin. Leaping out of bed, he moved quickly through the door.

Seconds later, Joshua Grant met him in the small corridor. "What the hell was that?" he asked, looking at the sleepy Carson in a panic.

Carson stared at Melanie's door, and he and his friend had a similar answer: "Melanie!" they shouted simultaneously as they both headed quickly for her cabin.

When they entered, they found Melanie sitting in a fetal position in the corner of the small cabin, her bed cover gripped tightly in her pale, white hands. She was drenched in sweat, but it was the look in her eyes that most shocked Carson, a look of absolute terror.

Carson moved quickly over to her and knelt by her side. "Melanie, what's wrong?" noticing the obvious fear in her eyes.

Melanie remained unresponsive, not even noticing that she was no longer alone.

Josh ran out of the cabin and returned moments later with a small med-scanner. The sensors in the med-scanner quickly revealed her physical condition.

"How is she?" Carson asked.

"Well, her pulse and respiration are incredibly high. As far as I can tell, she seems to be in shock." Josh removed a small hypo-spray from the med-kit and injected the fluid into Melanie's exposed arm with a low *hiss*.

"What'd you give her?" Carson asked, seeing that

Melanie was starting to relax.

"Just a tranquilizer."

Carson turned back to Melanie. "Mel, can you hear me?"

Melanie finally seemed to hear his voice and looked up into his face. "Mark, is that you?"

"Yes, it's me," Carson said soothingly. "Tell me what happened."

Melanie seemed to concentrate, trying to bring the last few minutes back into focus. "I tried to sleep, but the nightmares..." she said. "They seemed so real, so...horrible. I couldn't get them out of my head."

Josh leaned over to Melanie and gently put her hand in his. "Melanie, do you remember anything specific? What were the nightmares about?"

Tears ran down Melanie's face as she continued her story. "Horrible things, these hairy, terrible beasts. Sharp teeth, dripping blood. They seemed to be everywhere. They were chasing me, but I couldn't run. Mark, I couldn't wake up!"

"But you did. Josh and I heard your scream."

"I don't even remember screaming." She began to tremble again as she looked up a Carson with pleading eyes. "Mark, am I going crazy? I've never had a nightmare like that before. It was so...vivid."

"You're not going crazy," Carson said as he took the crying woman into his arms, hugging her tightly.

Suddenly, they all felt a slight lurch as *Pulsar* moved out of hyperspace. Ernie's voice followed, announcing their entrance into the star system.

"Listen, Melanie. Josh and I have to go to the bridge," Carson said, releasing their hug. "You stay down here and relax. We can take care of things for now."

Melanie gingerly got to her feet. "Not on your life," she said, sounding more like her old self. "You guys aren't gonna leave me alone down here. Just give me a few minutes to change, and I'll meet you on the bridge."

Carson laughed and gave her a small kiss on the cheek. "Melanie Patula, you're quite a woman."

"You bet I am!" Melanie replied, smiling for the first time that evening.

"Ya know," Carson said to Melanie quietly, "that's a bet I just might take you up on."

Josh stood by the door and cleared his throat. "You comin' or what, Carson?"

"Right behind ya, buddy."

The door closed behind them as they left Melanie's cabin and headed for the bridge.

CHAPTER 9

Several minutes later, Melanie arrived on the bridge and found both Josh and Carson immersed in their pre-descent checklist. Planet Solo filled the forward viewscreen, and it certainly wasn't the type of planet one would want to plan a vacation around. There was dense cloud cover but surprisingly few bodies of water.

Carson looked up from the helm.

Noticing the concern on his face, Melanie quietly moved to her station at communications. She really cared about Carson and knew that in his own way, he cared about her. She also knew that for all of them to act as a team, she had to set any stronger personal feelings aside. Their job was often dangerous, and that left little to no room for romance. Still, it was fun to escape that way sometimes, to let those feelings tickle a smile to her lips, and Carson seemed to enjoy the brief respite of basking in their relationship too. *Who knows?* Melanie thought to herself. *Maybe when this is all over, we can make that shore leave a bit of a romantic getaway.*

"How are you feeling?" Carson asked, interrupting her thoughts.

"A lot better. Thanks," Melanie said warmly to both of her friends.

"Good to see you, Melanie," Ernie chimed in from the bridge speaker.

"Thanks, Ernie. You too."

Preparations were complete, and Carson and Josh were strapping themselves in for the landing.

Carson turned to his crewmates and gave Melanie a very suggestive wink. "Okay, people, let's do it. Ernie, begin atmospheric entry."

"Aye-aye, sir," responded the computer.

Pulsar began to angle downward. Force fields activated, enveloping the outer hull in a protective layer of energy as the starship plowed through the dense upper atmosphere of Planet Solo. At the proper time, artificial gravity generators were deactivated, and Ernie took over helm control, guiding them to the site of the massive ruins. With gravity control set for atmospheric flight, the three humans released their safety restraints and began to prep the ship for landing.

"Ernie, give me a tactical scan of the landing area," Josh ordered.

The forward viewscreen lit up, a grid pattern overlaying their intended landing site. The landing area, normally used to receiving supply ships, was empty.

"Ernie, what do sensors show? Any life form readings?" Carson asked.

"None within sensor range."

"Okay. Take the ship in at sixty meters above the city and run a tight high-powered sensor scan," Carson ordered.

They were all amazed at the sheer size of the ruins beneath them, especially since the investigating archeological team had only been able to penetrate about one or two kilometers from their original landing site. That would be the area that they would concentrate on, as anything else would be a waste of time.

"We'll make two sweeps, the second tighter than the

first. If you pick up any life form readings, I want them pinpointed immediately."

"Aye-aye, sir."

"Josh, after that, bring us around and take us to the landing site."

"Right."

Pulsar made its first sweep of the city with no luck, but on the second pass, Ernie came to attention. "I have a life form reading," he reported, as asked.

"Where, Ernie?" Melanie asked.

"Map reference twenty-six by four by nine," the computer responded.

"Ernie, please show our position on the map overlay," Josh requested.

A small white dot lit up on the grid overlay of the city.

"Ernie, can you give me a diagnostic?" Melanie asked.

Usually, Ernie could run a medical diagnostic scan that would provide the condition of the life form on the sensors. "Sorry, Melanie," he said this time. "The composition of the building materials renders a medical scan impossible. It is...impenetrable," answered Ernie, his mechanical voice exhibiting obvious upset that he could not carry out her instructions.

"That's okay, Ernie."

"All right, my friend," Carson said, "take us down."

"Aye-aye, sir."

Pulsar made another lazy sweep before it settled gently on the spot that had, not much more than a day before, been occupied by the transport ship, *Aries*. Inside the small starship, three sets of eyes stared at the large viewscreen on the forward section of the bridge. Ernie was in the process of rotating the outboard scan, giving them a 360-degree view of the landing area.

"Would you look at all that?" Josh said in amazement.

The area was a mess, to say the least. To Josh, it was all quite reminiscent of what the Dreedan raiders had left behind on Arton III, a bizarre combination of things, with wreckage of all sorts littering the ground. At best, it was a junk heap.

"What a mess," added Melanie.

The more Carson saw of the mess outside the ship, the greater his sense of foreboding that something was dangerously wrong. It was time for them to start their investigation, and he hoped they could find that life form they had pinpointed from above the site. "Let's go, folks," he said to his two friends. "But I don't want anybody taking any chances. We all wear sidearms. Josh and I will take the heavy blaster rifles." He then looked over at Melanie. "Mel, take the med-kit and bio-scanner. We'll need you to triangulate Ernie's sensor reading and find whatever we picked up on sensors back there."

"Heavy blaster rifles? That's quite a bit of firepower, Carson. Any particular reason?" Josh asked.

"Just a feeling, Josh."

"I'll get the med-kit and the bio-scanner," Melanie said, then headed off to sickbay to fetch them.

"Ernie…" Carson said to the ship computer.

"Yes, Skipper?"

"I want you to maintain Class A security while we're gone. Allow no one to approach the ship other than us. One of us will contact you every hour. If you don't hear from us, wait an hour after the first missed check-in, then lift off and establish orbit. Then inform Brooks of everything we discover and turn over control of the mission to him." Carson paused for a moment, making sure he hadn't forgotten anything. "Understood?"

"Understood, Skipper," Ernie responded. He was fully aware of what Class A security meant, but he also knew it gave humans a certain amount of personal security to repeat things for their own ears to hear.

"Ernie, the ship's all yours, buddy. Take care of her. Josh," Carson said, gesturing toward the door, "let's get going."

"Right," Josh said.

They walked out, and the bridge doors slid shut quietly behind them.

* * *

Several minutes later, after a brief stop at the armory, Carson and Josh met Melanie at the airlock. All three were outfitted in combat armor. Though light in weight and appearing more like heavy overalls, the armor could absorb the power of a small blaster while allowing the wearer relative ease of motion. The suit wasn't perfect, though, and Carson knew it, but anything that gave them an edge was welcome. At the very least, in a combat situation, the wearer seldom had to worry about small arms fire. Also, because no one was sure of the condition of the power supply, each of them carried a set of light-intensifying goggles.

Noting that they were as prepared as they were ever going to be, Carson adjusted the comm unit on his wrist and activated the airlock hatch.

First the inner and then the outer hatch slid aside. As it did, Melanie felt a shiver rifle down her spine; she was thankful, though, that Carson and Josh didn't seem to notice. She didn't know what they'd find out there, but she agreed with Carson's advice to exercise extreme caution.

As the planetary atmosphere wafted into the ship, it carried a strange, pungent stench, one Carson had smelled all too many times: the stink of death. It was evident then, if it hadn't already been made clear from all the rubble and debris and liter, that a battle had been fought there not too long ago. The smell of charred flesh, as well as other things he was happy he couldn't identify, still loomed heavily in the air. The air was still and humid, with no breeze blowing to dissipate the noxious aroma that assaulted them.

"Let's go," Carson said to the others. "Our first stop will be the security shack."

"What about the life readings?" Melanie asked. "There might be a survivor."

"Yeah, we'll check that out, but first, I wanna see if there's anything on the security cameras that might give us a clue as to what happened here," Carson said as they disembarked from the ship, the hatch quickly closing and sealing behind them.

They walked amidst the carnage of what had been the science station landing area. Sensitive instruments were tossed aside, obviously disregarded by those who had caused the death and destruction. Since the encampment had been constructed right outside the city, their walk was a short one. The security shack had been erected just inside the city perimeter, so it could easily monitor activity inside the massive ruins, as well as any incoming orbital traffic.

When they reached the entrance to the city, Melanie froze in place. Carson and Josh, noticing her sudden halt, both stopped as well.

"Melanie, what's wrong?"

"Nothing, Carson. It's...just a feeling," answered Melanie.

"What kind of feeling?" After what had occurred on *Pulsar*, Carson had a feeling of his own that something close by was behind Melanie's nightmarish visions.

"Like...déjà vu, like I've been here before."

"So have you?" Josh asked curiously.

"I-I don't think so. I'd definitely remember a place like this."

"Well, the security shack's about fifty meters in that direction." Carson pointed a finger northwest, where a large transmission mast jutted out of the top of a prefabricated building.

Moments later, they entered the security shack. The entire room was in shambles. Monitors were smashed, and there was an enormous burn hole in what had been the communications console.

"Josh, take a look at this," Carson said, kneeling by the dark, jagged hole in the panel.

Josh knelt down beside his friend and examined the edges of the blast hole with a portable scanner. "Carson, this console is made of tri-titanium alloy. The power necessary to cause this type of damage would have to be incredible," he said in awe. "It coulda been done by some sort of high-charged plasma bolt." Josh pointed to the edges, then inside the communications unit itself, explaining his theory on how the console was destroyed. "It's really amazing. The plasma energy virtually vaporized the outer casing of the console, then entered where it exploded, destroying the entire unit from the inside."

"Is it compatible to anything we have?"

"Nothing handheld."

"Wonderful," Carson whispered to himself. "Just freaking wonderful." As he got to his feet, he noticed that one of his teammates had disappeared. "Melanie!"

"Right here," she said quietly from behind a collapsed computer panel. "Gimme a hand with this, would ya? The duplicate camera scans should be underneath, in the computer core."

The two men rushed over, and all three began pushing the heavy piece of equipment.

"If it's not too badly burnt out, we should be able to run it through Ernie back at the ship."

"It's coming," Carson said through clenched teeth. "Just a little more."

The panel tipped over to the floor with a loud *crash*. They were not prepared for the sight that greeted them as the bloodied head of Corporal Anderson rolled silently into view. Melanie screamed once before falling hard onto her backside. Carson and Josh just stared at the decapitated head, in utter shock. From the expression permanently etched on the face, the corporal had not died very pleasantly.

"Oh shit," was all Josh could say, words that had to fight their way through a tightening throat.

Carson quickly moved to where Melanie sat, her eyes wide, and lifted her gently to her feet. "Melanie, look at me," he said to her.

She remained silent, staring at the head sitting in front of them.

Carson grabbed her face and turned her so her gaze was

on him and no longer on what was left of Corporal Anderson. "I said look at me!" Carson yelled, finally getting her attention. "Get the backup from the computer core and wait by the door."

Melanie moved quickly to the computer core and pulled the backup cartridge from the computer, then stuck the small disk into her med-kit. Without looking back, she turned and walked out of the security shack and waited by the door.

"Carson," Josh said, "this isn't looking too good."

"No, it's not. Let's find that survivor and get the hell outta here."

As Carson and Josh left the security shack, they found Melanie pacing back and forth outside.

"Melanie, don't worry. If you can't go on, we understand. You can go back to the ship, and Josh and I will look for the survivor."

Melanie straightened up and turned to face her commander. "No! I'm going with you."

"Are you sure?"

"Just try and stop me," she said sternly, pulling out her bio-scanner to start triangulating on the life form signal that had been received by *Pulsar*. "This way."

The power generators the scientists had set up when they landed were still functioning at a reduced power level, so the light-sensitive goggles were not needed. They passed several large chambers as they tracked the signal that led them closer and closer to their objective.

Walking past one chamber, Josh noticed a faint light. "Wait! There's something glowing in there."

"Josh, we don't have time for sightseeing," Melanie said,

staring at the readings from her bio-scanner. "The signals are getting weaker."

Josh noticed that the glow was coming from a large arch at the far end of the chamber. "Just a quick look," he said, then disappeared inside.

Carson and Melanie followed him in. As Melanie walked in, she leaned her hand against the wall and suddenly went stiff, dropping the scanner.

Carson leapt to her side as she emitted a scream that seemed to come straight from Hell, then collapsed to the floor in a heap. "Melanie, what's happening?" Carson asked. "Josh, get over here! Quick!"

Josh rushed over and quickly picked up the bio-scanner. When he passed it over Melanie, he noticed something unusual. "Carson, these are the same readings I got last night, during her nightmare."

Carson slapped Melanie lightly across the face, hoping to jolt her to consciousness. "Melanie, wake up! Mel?"

After a few seconds, her eyes started to open. "Mark, I know why this place is so familiar. It was in my dream last night."

"What happened when you touched the wall?" Carson asked.

"Weird images, blood everywhere. There were these...creatures, made of clay or something, tearing people apart and then *becoming* them somehow. I-I just don't know. The images are really confusing."

Carson could see that Melanie struggling to understand what she had seen. As before, she had presented them with both a clue and a puzzle all at once.

"Take it easy, girl," Josh said, happy to see the bio-scanner readings becoming more steady.

"I'm feeling better," she assured them. "It was just the shock of the vision."

"I thought you had to concentrate to receive anything from a person or an object."

"Josh, the emanations were so strong that they broke through my mental barriers."

So intent were they in their concern for Melanie that neither Josh nor Carson noticed the glow of the arch increasing nor the shape emerging from beyond.

The creature sensed that it had been freed. It had been forgotten by its master and had impatiently waited for his return. When the portal had somehow been activated, it crossed into the arch chamber. Its master was not there, but finely tuned senses informed it that it was not alone. It saw the three humans by the far wall, two leaning over the form of a third, all with their backs turned. Saliva dripped down its jaws. Seeing its chance to surprise them, it leapt from the shadows, claws extended, ready to rip the throats of its prey. Grinning, it could already feel the taste of their blood. In midair, though, the creature saw its mistake too late; one of the small beings on the floor shouted, then pulled the weapon from its holster. The beam of energy from the blaster burned a charred hole through it, hurling it to the ground.

Everything happened so quickly that Carson could hardly grasp it. They were about to help Melanie to her feet when she screamed for them to get down. Instinctively diving to the side and pulling out his weapon, Carson saw Melanie fire her blaster from her hip, striking a dark shape that had tried to jump them from the shadows. The beam hit what looked to be the thing's chest and threw it violently to the ground.

They went over to see what it was that Melanie had shot, and Carson suddenly understood why Melanie was so frightened of her nightmare. The thing, whatever it was, was some sort of haphazard mutation. The body appeared to be of a large wolf. The dark, charred blaster wound was visible along its underside, but it was the head and jaws that disgusted them most. A large shark head was attached to the wolflike body, its jaws distended in death, as if still trying to ensnare its unsuspecting prey.

"Melanie, let's find your survivor and get back to the ship. Josh, call Ernie and let him know what's happening." Carson moved Melanie over to the side as Josh reported to Ernie. "Where did you learn to shoot like that?" he asked.

Melanie looked at him, wearing a smile on her face. "I learned from the best."

Carson laughed quietly as Josh rejoined them.

"Mother wants us to be careful," Josh informed them with a smirk. "I swear, sometimes I think I programmed that computer too well."

"Right. Melanie," Carson said to the young woman, who was now holding the bio-scanner again, "plot the quickest path down to our reading. And Josh..."

"Yes?"

"No detours." Carson gestured to the smoldering creature. "Now that we've had a most unfriendly welcome, I think it'd be wise to keep that blaster rifle ready. If that bio-scanner reading isn't a survivor, we need to be ready."

"Right," replied Josh, cradling the weapon in his arms.

"Melanie, lead the way," Carson said, giving the still-glowing arch one last look as they left the chamber and headed down the dark corridor.

They continued on, the lights flickering around them, powered by generators that seemed to be running low on power. Melanie led the way, her bio-scanner homing on the signal radiated by the life form they were attempting to find. The soft tones of the scanner increased in volume as they got closer. Carson, with his blaster clenched tightly in his hand, and Josh, blaster rifle at the ready, kept a careful watch for any other surprises.

"We must be descending to another level," noticed Josh as the grade of the corridor floor decreased.

The tones from the bio-scanner increased to a fevered pitch, signaling that they were within ten meters of their target. Melanie shut down the scanner and placed it back in the med-kit strapped to her waist. Carson noticed a blaster quickly took its place, and Melanie used it to gesture to the chamber just ahead of them. Quietly, Carson motioned for Melanie to move behind him. When she did, Carson slowly inched his way along, with his back to the wall, till he reached the open entrance. Looking back at Josh, he motioned for him to quickly join him, the rifle armed and ready.

Signaling to Josh that they would move through the door on the count of three, Carson quickly prepared himself. Counting silently, Carson reached three and, in a low crouch, dived through the door, then came up with his blaster ready. Josh crouched by his side, the powerful rifle scanning the area for any sign of trouble.

Carson suddenly and painfully realized that the chamber they had entered had to have been created for one purpose:

pain. There were various devices of torture scattered throughout. Carson slowly started to move through the chamber as Josh gave the okay for Melanie to enter. They investigated further, checking every cell along the way.

Finally, in the last cell, Carson caught a glimpse of the life form they had tracked from the surface. "Melanie, Josh, get over here now!" he shouted as he approached the figure, a felinoid from Cada III, dressed in the tattered uniform of a chief of security. He knew then that it had to be Lieutenant Ank.

The figure was unconscious but on his feet, chained to the cell wall. Seeing the irons that bound both his legs and wrists, Carson quickly removed a small laser-cutting torch from his belt and began to work on the metal restraining bands as he was joined by his two comrades.

"Oh God," Melanie said with a gasp as she retrieved the bio-scanner from her med-kit. So close to her patient, she would be able to run a more detailed scan.

Carson had finished the final restraining iron, and the two men gently lowered the still form of Lieutenant Ank to the cell floor. Melanie prodded the injured Lieutenant gently in the chest and noticed a small gasp of pain when she touched a crack in two ribs. After Melanie finished with her diagnostic check, she reached into her med-kit for a small hypo-injector. After making sure the drug dosage was correct, she placed the small, silvery tube by the base of the unconscious security chief's neck and pressed the small stud on the side, releasing the drug into his system.

"How is he?" Carson asked, noticing that Melanie was working feverishly, trying to stabilize the felinoid's condition.

"Well, the scanner shows a concussion and two broken ribs. He also seems to be suffering from dehydration and a nice little blaster burn on his chest. He'll live, but we have to get him back to the ship and then to better care. We have to get him there fast."

"Is it safe to move him?"

"I gave him a sedative and a painkiller. The wrapping I put around those two cracked ribs should keep them immobile enough until we get back to the ship. I've done all I can do for him here." She hoped Ank wasn't in too much pain as Carson and Josh carried the large felinoid out of the dark chamber.

Holding him under the arms, they slowly retraced their way back to the ship. As they reached the surface, both men seemed to be feeling the strain of carrying the felinoid.

"Shit, this guy is heavy," spat Josh through clenched teeth.

"Put him down and call Ernie," Carson said as they gently lowered Ank to the ground. "Tell him to get sickbay ready and to start the preflight checks."

After the instructions were relayed to the ship, the two men again picked up their heavy burden and continued on their way back to *Pulsar*.

Finally onboard, Ank was brought to the sickbay and strapped down to one of the examination beds. Melanie worked rapidly over the prone figure, attaching the auto-doc to her patient to monitor his condition and adjust medication flow. Noting that she had done all she could, Melanie turned on the automatic monitor and headed for the bridge. If there was any change in condition, Ernie would immediately advise them.

Arriving on the bridge, she noticed that her friends were at work finishing the preflight check Ernie had begun. They had the computer core from the security shack and were trying to get Ernie to scan its contents.

Carson stopped what he was doing as she took a deep breath and settled down in her chair. "How's our guest?"

"I don't know. He seems to be stable, but I think the quicker we get him to actual hospital facilities, the better."

"Ernie, can you scan the visual track on this disk?" Josh asked.

"Of course, Josh. It's only a simple XJ4 computer core," replied Ernie, slightly insulted.

"Is the scan indexed in any way?"

"By date and time prefix, Josh," the computer responded.

Good, Carson thought. "Ernie, cue it up to start two hours before the core burned out and then run it at three times normal speed."

"Right, Skipper," Ernie said.

The small portside monitor illuminated with a replay of the terror that had occurred four days prior. The three humans stood in terrified awe, transfixed by the horror they saw. They watched as both scientists and security were butchered by the things that came from beneath the glowing arch. The death and decapitation of Corporal Anderson played out before their eyes, and then there was a fight between Lieutenant Ank and the large, robed reptile, which eventually burned out the communications panel and the security cameras.

Carson looked over at Melanie and saw that it was all disgustingly familiar to her. He felt like a voyeur, suddenly dropping into the middle of her nightmare uninvited.

The mood was somber and chilling as the images faded from the screen. What they were dealing with was something beyond their understanding. No one said a word; the pictures spoke far more than a thousand words.

Carson pressed a small switch and ejected the disk from Ernie's central processor. "Everybody to their stations," he finally said, quietly settling himself into his command chair. "Ernie, get us the hell outta this freak show, would ya?"

"Course, Skipper?"

"Take us back to the asteroid, back home, and tell the admiral we're on our way."

The dreary silence returned and lingered among them as *Pulsar* leapt into the sky and headed spaceward.

CHAPTER 10

Several light years away, Alliance battlecruiser *Ranger* plowed through the interstellar void. Powerful engines drove her through space at speeds that far exceeded her design limits. On her bridge, Captain Martin Tompkin sat in his command chair, watching the stars blur by on the forward monitor screen. The bridge was a beehive of activity as Tompkin stared out, trying to will more speed out of his cruiser.

They had received the signal from the disaster beacon one hour and fourteen minutes ago, and every crewmember was painfully aware of its significance. More than a distress call, the beacon warned of a space vessel's near-imminent destruction. The signal configuration had confirmed it as the Alliance transport ship *Aries*, and the signal came from somewhere in the Nexus system.

Tompkin stood from his command chair and walked nervously over to his navigator, in spite of his own pile of duties.

The ship navigator and helmsman, seated side by side, both sensed their captain's presence as he stood over them.

"What's our ETA to the disaster beacon?" Tompkin asked.

"Forty-seven minutes, sir," the navigator answered, noting that it was the fourth time the captain had asked him. Considering the fact that the same question came at regular fifteen-minute intervals, he felt Captain Tompkin should have been able to figure it out for himself, but he certainly wasn't going to say so.

"Good," Tompkin said. He then quietly returned to his padded command chair and turned to look at his science officer.

The young lieutenant's eyes were concentrating deeply on the long-range sensor scan in front of him. The interception course would lead *Ranger* along the boundaries of Dreedan space, and although there was an uneasy truce between the two great space powers, Tompkin was never one to take chances.

A tall man in his early forties, Tompkin had captained *Ranger* and her crew of 247 for over 5 years now, and he had seen his share of action. He wasn't sure if the Dreedans had anything to do with the disaster beacon or not, but he hadn't gotten as far as he had without taking precautions. On system entry, the starship defensive shields would be activated, as well her weapons. Until then, there wasn't much any of them could do other than sit and wait.

* * *

Admiral Brooks paced along the spacious Commando, Inc. operations center, Fleet Admiral Olstad a constantly irritating shadow. It was bad enough that he'd had to lie to Carson and the others about the importance of their detour, but for Olstad to big-brother his every footstep was too much. He had received the reports from *Pulsar*, and he only hoped he hadn't gotten his field team in over their heads.

The butchery, for lack of a better term, of the science team had disgusted them all. Unfortunately, Carson had no word on the fate of the *Aries* or her crew. He hoped they could question the science team security chief, when or if he recovered.

From what they were able to put together, they had found something – or rather, something had found them in the ruins of the ancient city they were exploring, and they all paid the price for releasing it with their lives. Hopefully, they wouldn't have much company.

Brooks noted that *Pulsar* would not arrive for at least another two hours. Deciding that there was very little to do until then, he headed back to his office, with Admiral Olstad right on his heels. When Brooks moved behind his large, wooden desk, Olstad settled into the chair opposite him. He harbored a distinct dislike for guests in general, so he'd made sure Olstad would be forced to sit in the most uncomfortable chair that he could. He'd brought it from Earth, and it was actually an antique. The small metal tag on it read, "Property of the Boston Red Sox, 2006." Hoping it proved as painful now as it had in its original position.

He could see that Olstad seemed agitated. "Would you like a drink, Roger?" Brooks asked, already knowing they could both use one.

Olstad nodded slowly; he was agitated and was sure a stiff drink would be quite helpful at alleviating his tensions.

Brooks reached the wall and pressed the palm of his hand against a small plate mounted at eye level. After verifying the admiral's identity, the plate glowed a steady yellow, and a panel slowly slid open to reveal a small bar. Brooks took out two glasses and poured them half-full of rich, amber fluid, then handed one to Olstad.

"Thanks, Clay," Olstad said as he took the glass from Brooks. After downing the drink in two large gulps, he looked up to see his host take his seat back behind his desk, the drink still resting untouched in his hand. "Impressions?" he asked, referring to the replay of the Solo security tape *Pulsar* had transmitted over to them.

"I'm not sure what to make of it right now," Brooks said, finally taking a sip from his glass.

"All that killing," Olstad began, trying to make sense of it, "but where are the bodies? We saw the blood and the bodies on that recording, so why didn't your people find any of it?"

"Most of the ruins went unexplored. Maybe the corpses are deeper in the tunnels. You may have to send in a team to search the city more thoroughly," Brooks said. The things he'd seen on the tape had killed savagely, enjoying the pain and death they caused. That, along with the disappearance of the transport ship, didn't exactly give him a warm, fuzzy feeling, and he knew if those things were loose in the galaxy somewhere, they had to be considered a definite threat. "In any case, we should have our answers shortly."

Before Olstad could say anything else, both men heard a short tone from the comm unit on the desk.

Brooks reached over and pressed a small stud on his desk. "Yes? What is it?"

"Sir," Griffin's voice said, "we've just received another message from *Pulsar*."

Brooks and Olstad suddenly came to attention; any news from his people would go a long way to clearing up some of the holes in an already murky picture. "And what are they saying?"

"Dr. Patula reports that her patient is still unconscious but stable."

At last, some good news, Brooks thought. *Maybe things*

are improving.

"We also have a revised ETA. They've already arrived at the outer perimeter marker. We estimate that they will dock within eighteen minutes."

"Good. Keep me informed," Brooks said to his assistant. "And, Griffin, make sure we have a medical team standing by when they dock."

"Of course, sir."

Brooks felt a slight bit of relief, realizing he might get some answers sooner rather than later. He reached for his drink and gulped it down in one long, fiery swallow.

* * *

Ranger entered the Nexus system on schedule. Captain Tompkin called a shipwide yellow alert and ordered all defensive force fields energized. If nothing else, Tompkin thought of himself as a by-the-book captain. When entering an unknown situation in hostile space, all precautions had to be taken.

Sensors had locked on *Aries's* position, and they would be there in a matter of minutes. The battlecruiser was prepared for a full evacuation, and the chief medical officer had the sickbay set up for casualties. All in all, Captain Tompkin felt his ship was adequately prepared.

"Captain, sensors have picked up *Aries*. She's dead ahead, sir," a *Ranger* science officer reported.

Tompkin stared at the image on the forward viewscreen. "Helm, reduce speed to .25 of light speed."

"Aye, sir," replied the helmsman, his hands moving quickly over his control console, complying with the order and slowing *Ranger* significantly.

"Give me magnification times two on the screen."

"Mag times two? Aye-aye, sir." With another move of the helmsman's hands, the allegedly damaged transport ship leapt into view.

Tompkin analyzed the image on the viewscreen. Surprisingly, for a ship that had just issued a disaster beacon, it seemed to be in very good shape. "Lieutenant, scan the transport. Any sign of damage?"

The young science officer glanced down at his readout, then lifted his head only a few seconds later. "Captain, sensor scan reports no apparent damage."

Tompkin turned his command chair to his communications officer, who was stationed at the rear left of the bridge. "Hail the *Aries*, Ensign."

Turning to her communications board, Ensign Nana White stopped her hand as a small light lit on her console, signaling an incoming hail. "Captain, *Aries* is hailing us."

"Put it on the screen."

The image of *Aries* flickered for a moment before finally being replaced by the image of Captain William Barton. Tompkin wanted answers, for it was a violation of Alliance Fleet law to misuse the disaster beacon when no disaster had actually occurred.

"Hello, Martin," Barton said. "I suppose you're wondering about the disaster beacon."

Tompkin looked at Barton and felt rage boiling up within him. "You bet I am, Barton. You have a lot to explain."

"It's a little complicated, Martin, and I can't explain it to you like this. It's something I have to *show* you."

"All right, Barton, but this had better be good. If I don't like your answer, I'll throw your ass in my brig and haul you off to the nearest starbase! I haven't the time or resources to waste on games."

Barton looked at his fellow captain and smiled. "Okay, Martin. Understood."

"Helm, move us to within 5,000 meters," Tompkin said as he felt his anger begin to ebb.

"Aye-aye, sir."

The engines engaged, and the cruiser moved closer to the mysterious transport.

"Ensign White, inform the hangar bay to prepare a shuttlecraft for immediate departure."

"Yes, sir."

Before this is over, there'll be hell to pay, Tompkin thought. Unfortunately for Captain Tompkin and the crew of *Ranger*, he didn't know how true that thought was and not to his own advantage.

CHAPTER 11

Brooks and Olstad waited on the observation deck that overlooked the massive landing bay. They watched as *Pulsar* came in through the retractable airlock doors and settled onto her berth.

A full medical team stood by as the bay doors silently closed and the area repressurized. Dr. Antar, the chief medical officer, waited impatiently for the environmental display above the inner hatch to inform them that it was safe to enter the area. Seconds later, the display went from a deep red to amber and finally to a steady green, signifying that the bay was pressurized and it was safe to open the hatch. The doctor's hand immediately went to the door release, and the heavy hatch slid open. Wasting very little time, Antar and his team reached *Pulsar* as the starship cargo ramp slid down with an audible *hiss*. He saw Carson and Grant carrying out the felinoid, a clear mask covering the whiskered snout, feeding oxygen to the injured officer.

As the passengers reached the bottom of the ramp, Antar motioned with his hands for the two men to settle the gurney softly on the deck. "We'll take him from here, Carson."

Carson sighed, his relief evident, as he and Josh lowered their unconscious patient to the deck. "Thanks, Doc."

Melanie came down the ramp last and saw the medical team working over her former patient. "Shouldn't we get him to sickbay?"

Antar looked up at her, the expression on his face betraying an obvious distaste for the intrusion. "Miss Patula, we are taking care of the patient, and we will move him to sickbay when I'm ready."

Carson didn't know what to do. He saw Melanie's face reddening, and it was clear that the disdain was mutual between them. Antar was a young, obnoxious snob who just so happened to be one of the most brilliant medical minds in the Alliance, with jurisdiction over any patient brought inside the base. Still, they had rescued Ank from a torture chamber buried under a ruined city half a galaxy away, and he would be damned if he would allow Melanie to be spoken to so disrespectfully by anyone, least of a young punk and a know-it-all. If it wasn't for the fact that they were working over an injured being, Carson was sure Melanie would have already vaporized him on the spot.

"He was my patient long before he was yours," she said, glaring at him with homicidal rage, "and I will see that he is treated properly."

Antar stood and moved his face to within inches of the angered woman. "He will be, if you will just let me do my job," he snapped. "My team works better without unnecessary interference!"

As the tense situation escalated, a loud, authoritative voice could be heard above the screaming.

"Enough already!" Clayton Brooks cried out. "Antar, take your patient to sickbay." He then turned to Melanie, who was trying to regain her composure. "Melanie, go with him."

Antar turned to face the admiral in disbelief, not at all happy with his orders.

The disgruntled look on Antar's face was not lost on Brooks, but the difference between Melanie and him was that he certainly didn't have to take the doctor's attitude. "Do you have a problem with that, Doctor?" Brooks finally asked.

Carson held his tongue and his grin in, secretly hoping Antar would give him the wrong answer.

"No, sir," Antar replied quietly.

An antigravity gurney floated in, and Lieutenant Ank was gently loaded onto it. Antar and the rest of the medical team then turned for the open inner hatch and headed for sickbay.

As soon as she was sure Antar was out of earshot, Melanie approached the admiral, wearing a small smile on her face. "Thanks, sir," she said, then gave the older man a small kiss on the cheek before she turned for the door.

"Melanie?"

Melanie stopped and turned her head. "Yes, Admiral?"

"You're welcome," Brooks said as he suppressed the small smile that almost curled his lips. She was something like a daughter to him. *She's come a long way from Helos,* he thought to himself, beaming proudly. "Now get going. You have a patient to take care of. Let me know when he regains consciousness."

"Right," she said as she left the landing bay.

Brooks noticed Carson and Grant walking behind her, also making their way to the exit. "And where do you two think you're going?" he asked sarcastically.

"Admiral, it's been a long couple days. Josh and I need to get something to eat, then some rest," Carson said, but he could see that the admiral had other ideas – ideas Carson was inevitably not going to like.

"Listen, Carson," Brooks began, "I have a technical team coming now to pull the security tapes and any other related files from *Pulsar*. You," Brooks said, pointing at both of them, "will supervise its removal. Then clean yourselves up and report to Admiral Olstad and me in my office. Is that clear?"

Realizing they were defeated, both men wearily mumbled, "Yes, sir," then headed back up the cargo ramp and into *Pulsar*.

* * *

Donar was pleased with the way his plan was coming along. The subjugation of the colonists of Nexus III had been quick with the help of his Captain Barton and *Aries*. The ship had landed, and Barton had brought the director of the colony onboard to discuss details of the alleged resupply.

From that point, it had been simple to substitute one of Snatak's simulcrons for the real director and send the creature back to its people. Within a day of their arrival, all resistance had been negated, and the human colonists who were not essential to the plan had been killed or imprisoned; the others had either been put to work in the mines or used for raw material for the creation of more simulcrons.

Meanwhile, in space, more and more ships slowly and blindly fell into his trap. The distress call Barton transmitted from *Aries* drew ships from all over into his web. Among them, the prize was the battlecruiser, *Ranger*. With such a powerful vessel under his command, other nearby planets were raided, bringing in new equipment and, more importantly, prisoners for their growing Nexus III base.

The Dreedan Empire was also targeted. From advice

supplied by Barton and Tompkin, Donar decided he would do all in his power to disturb the already fragile, tiny shred of peace that existed between the Alliance and the warlike Dreedans. At the sites of the destructive raids, evidence was left, causing blame to be placed on the other side for the mass killings. Tompkin had assured Donar that he had left nothing behind that could possibly lead anyone to the truth.

Donar's fleet was growing, as was his new army. In an operation so complex, he had a need for experienced soldiers. His creations could kill, but they couldn't pilot starships or handle the advanced concepts of space warfare. To correct this problem, open recruitment was silently established. Barton had told him of a human on Tanda IV, a killer-for-hire who had been easily recruited for other organizations at the right price. Donar had not yet dealt directly with the human, but he knew that as plans progressed, he would be needed to supervise those already sent. In the past few weeks, dozens of the filthy creatures had arrived from throughout the galaxy, but Donar found that he was quite fond of the Luto. Other than their monetary greed, the insects reminded him the most of his own creations.

There were plenty of violent monsters in the galaxy. Other than the mercenaries who would kill their own mothers to stuff their wallets, there were the mentally deranged, those who would gladly kill for the pure enjoyment. There were even those religious zealots who felt betrayed by their own gods and were on the prowl for vengeful retribution. By far, though, the most useful were the raiders. They had the necessary experience, as well as the temperament for Donar's plans, but he would still test and utilize them all. Those who passed would be recruited, but any who failed would become fodder for the transformation machine. In many ways, the self-made monsters exceeded even his creations in their propensity toward violence.

Both Barton and Tompkin, however, had urged the tentacled one to exercise caution in his efforts, so as not to draw too much attention. Even under such careful restraint, the plan was proceeding smoothly. Tompkin and *Ranger* were now being dispatched back to their home base, with a dozen simulcrons onboard to aid them in their first invasion of the Alliance military structure.

Snatak's equipment had, itself, been duplicated and loaded onto *Ranger* for later, when deeper penetration would occur. Tompkin had informed Donar that even at *Ranger*'s top speed, it would still take them three days to reach their command base on Planet Allegre IV. The starbase there had full jurisdiction over that sector of the Alliance and would be important in maintaining their security. It would offer them the opportunity to operate locally with impunity, without the worry of Alliance interference, at least in that sector.

At one time, Donar could have led his warrior hordes from planet to planet, but things had changed. In this new era, guile and cunning were more important than violent savagery. His warriors would also learn to adapt; of that, he had no doubt. After all, sooner or later, blood would be spilled and much of it tasted.

The decision was also made that Barton and the transport would remain where they were. Donar was still leery of his simulcron's life span and wanted him to stay close by for observation. Also, he required much of the information that was still locked inside the creature's thick skull. As jealous as Modok seemed that Donar was spending so much time with Barton, the war chief had also admitted that the information they might obtain from him would prove essential. Donar was aware also that very shortly, he would have to entrust a very important mission to the simulcron. Still, at the first opportunity, Modok would enjoy the chance to crush his new rival, and Donar had to stay on the lookout for any attempt to do so before he was through with him.

Donar contemplated past events for several more seconds as he looked out from behind the plasticine window of his new quarters, formerly the director's, to observe the activity outside. In the distance, he saw *Ranger*, already in final preparations for its return home. Even now, the twelve simulcrons were moving into the battlecruiser cargo bay. Donar laughed quietly to himself; his warriors left a wide berth between themselves and the creatures who were once their brethren. Many more of them could be manufactured. After all, the human rabble seemed to provide the perfect element for the process.

The only problem that lingered in Donar's mind was his wishy-washy faith in Snatak. All had progressed too well for his former assistant, and it was time for the master to return to his work. He had spent long enough depending on others for scientific breakthroughs. *In fact,* Donar thought, *perhaps there is a little something I can whip up for this special occasion.*

He looked out to the hills in the distance. The humans were penned up in the mines, out of sight, in case of the arrival of unwanted visitors. He had duplicated some of the local creatures to use as scenery in case of any uninvited guests. They were also there to act as guards for the work groups they had formed to better transform the mining colony into something more useful. *Yes,* Donar thought to himself, *there is still a great deal to do, but my plans of conquest are well underway.*

CHAPTER 12

Damn. *That was more of an interrogation than a debriefing*, Carson thought to himself as he forced his tired and exhausted body down the darkened corridor. The artificial lights lowered slightly in intensity, giving the illusion of night.

The six-hour endurance test with Josh and the two admirals had lasted into the wee hours of the morning. They had spent the time going over the computer records from the Solo excavation site, as well as the visuals from the security cameras. They had suffered through continuous, computer-enhanced replays of the horrible deaths, hoping it might reveal something they might have missed. Glimpses of creatures, savage and impossible monsters, fluttered in and out of view. While looking at the enhanced playback, Carson realized just what it was that had scared Melanie so much.

The next step was obvious for them all: A return trip to Solo was in order. The glowing arch was only one of the things Carson wanted to examine with the extra time he knew he'd have. The admirals agreed, though Olstad was leery about sending *Pulsar* in alone.

Finally a compromise was reached: An Alliance cruiser would sit in orbit while *Pulsar* and her crew began their investigation of the planet. Providing extra security and support, the cruiser would help protect their position while they explored the old tunnels. With tensions involving the alleged Dreedan raids on the outer settlements increasing, a battlecruiser watching their backs would give them one less thing to worry about. After the meeting, Admiral Olstad departed for the regional starbase in the Solo sector to arrange for *Pulsar*'s escort.

Carson's feet were now moving robotically, by sheer force of will. After thirty-eight sleepless hours, his willpower was also running short. Still, as he continued to his quarters, other, somewhat less important matters weighed on his mind. He'd spent such a long time trying to keep people out of his life since Rigel IV and Dandi that he sometimes found it difficult to figure out how to respond to Melanie, if he could respond at all.

He was certainly attracted to her, and it wasn't hard for anyone to see how she felt about him. He cared deeply for her, but he didn't know if he actually loved her. After all that time, he was surprised he still remembered what the word meant. Before he went to his quarters, he decided to swing past sickbay, where he knew Melanie would still be overseeing her new patient. That way, he could at least tell her goodnight. *That bastard Antar,* Carson reflected, *assigning her to the graveyard shift, just to get revenge for his run-in with Brooks.* Sickbay wasn't too far out of his way, and he thought they could perhaps they could cheer each other up a little.

Sickbay was located twelve decks below the surface, in perhaps the most secure area of the asteroid after the central power core. Carson stepped off the turbo-lift and smiled with the knowledge that his destination was just around the bend in the corridor.

Without warning, his thoughts were interrupted by a loud *crash* from the medical unit ahead.

What now? Carson thought. He ran the remainder of the way and burst quickly into the medical complex. Melanie was lying in the corner of the outer office, and Carson quickly rushed to her side. Kneeling over her, Carson checked her vitals as best he could. He was relieved that besides the large welt on the right side of her head, she seemed to be unharmed.

The small office was a mess, and so was the examination room. Something had torn the room apart, but there was no sign of any intruder. He finally figured out what had done the damage when he saw that the bed that had so recently been occupied by Lieutenant Ank was now empty. Ank was loose in the base, and Carson knew he had to be found before anyone else got hurt. He moved quickly to the comm unit on the wall and pushed the emergency alert button.

As a siren sounded throughout the asteroid, Carson activated the internal comm unit. "Security, this is Carson. Intruder alert! The patient they just brought into sickbay has attacked Dr. Patula and escaped. Warn everyone. We need to keep the corridors clear."

"Yes, sir," came the reply from the speaker.

"Don't kill him," Carson added. "Set all weapons to stun. Got that?"

"Right. Stun, not kill. My men are on the way," the security man responded.

Carson returned to Melanie. She was coming around, but he was sure she was going to have quite a headache.

Melanie put her hands to her head and tried to stand. "Oh! It hurts," she moaned.

"Take it easy, Mel," Carson said as he held her steady. "You've got a nice bump on your head. What happened?"

Melanie leaned against the wall and tried to recall the recent events. "Ank's readings began to improve, but he seemed to be...delirious. When I went over to give him a tranquilizer, he came to and grabbed my arm. He was babbling something about me not being able to fool him again, saying we couldn't hold him. He hit me on the side of the head, then...well, that was it."

Carson helped her over to an examination table, where he started to tend to her injuries.

Minutes later, Josh and Brooks, along with a squad of security men, burst into the room.

"What happened here? Are you all right, Melanie?" Brooks asked.

Carson looked up at them and answered for both of them. "We're fine, sir. It seems our injured friend didn't like the accommodations that we booked for him."

"Well," Josh added, "at least security is looking for him."

"Josh..." Carson asked.

"Yes, Mark?"

"Do me a favor. Check Melanie out. I'm gonna find that lunatic before he hurts somebody else," Carson said, getting up to head for the door. He stopped by a burly security man who was standing by the door. "McCann, give me your weapon."

Without a word of question or complaint, the security man handed the needler to Carson.

"Thanks." Carson opened the chamber to verify that the load consisted of tranquilizer darts and nothing more lethal.

"Mark, are really up to this? I mean, you've been up for quite a while, and – "

"I'm fine, Admiral. I won't be able to sleep with Ank

loose anyway." With that, Carson turned and winked at Melanie, then turned to leave. *Funny,* he thought on his way out of the medical complex. *Every time I get a chance to be alone with her, something always comes up. Is that some kind of sign or what?*

* * *

The search for the felinoid had been ongoing for several hours, to no avail. Security was tightened around key areas of the asteroid, such as the power core and operations center.

Carson was quickly developing a certain respect for the cat. Even in such an injured condition, Ank had a cunning that surprised even him; he was certainly not acting like a wounded animal. Whatever was going through Ank's mind, Carson was sure he knew that the landing bay would be too well guarded. Suddenly, as he pondered it a bit further, Carson had his answer. Unfortunately, he would have to handle it himself, as more security might spook Ank off or push him into doing something far more hazardous.

Carson rushed to the nearest turbo-lift and ascended almost to surface level. Of course the main landing bay was heavily guarded, but there was a small maintenance bay that was accessible without the need to go through the larger bay.

Minutes later, he reached the bay and found one lone technician lying on the deck, unconscious. A small shuttle was prepping for liftoff. Test flights were scheduled from that bay all the time, so a departing shuttle would not typically cause any alarm.

Carson moved quickly. He closed the pressure hatch behind him and scurried to gain access to the shuttle before the small maintenance hangar doors opened and the vacuum of space killed him. He saw a revolving red light, signaling that the inner seals of the hanger doors were releasing, and he heard the alarm warning of the imminent depressurization of the bay. The shuttle was moving into position as Carson reached the airlock door. The air began to thin, and he hurriedly input the emergency release code into the lock. It was becoming more and more difficult for him to concentrate as the hangar pumps began to equalize the pressure inside with the vacuum outside. On the verge of unconsciousness, Carson input the final sequence, and the airlock doors silently slid open.

Carson abruptly fell inside the small chamber and quickly closed the hatch behind him. The airlock cycled shut, and oxygen began to fill his starving lungs. After taking several deep, replenishing breaths, he removed the commandeered needler and advanced to the flight deck of the shuttle. As the doors opened, he moved cautiously, holding the weapon out in front of him.

They had cleared the asteroid, but the pilot's chair was unsettlingly empty. *Where is he? Here, kitty-kitty,* Carson thought and almost said aloud but thought better of it.

As he moved to the pilot's station, a large, hairy paw came from out of nowhere, hitting his hand and knocking his needler to the deck. Ank stood there, looking none too happy and none too sane. "I won't let you take me back, Donar," the cat said with a growl. "I'll kill you first." He had picked up the weapon and had it pointed at the human.

Carson was confused. *Donar? What the hell is he talking about?* "Listen to me, Lieutenant," he appealed. "My name is Carson, not Donar. Please put the gun down."

Ank seemed to waiver, pulling the gun down slightly

before raising it again. "No! Before, you looked like me. Now you look like this. You killed Anderson, and now you die!" Ank screamed, then fired.

Carson, however, had already started to move before the felinoid fired, so the darts harmlessly hit the inner hull. Diving to the deck, he hid behind the pilot's chair; two more darts made impact on the back of the chair. He spotted a power wrench sitting by the engineering station only two meters away. Unfortunately, out of the corner of his eye, he also saw Ank coming closer. He knew if he lost his cover, he was finished.

Making a quick decision, Carson dived for the wrench just as Ank pulled the chair aside. Carson picked up the titanium alloy bar, about half a meter in length. He hurled it at the startled Ank with all his might.

Ank stuck out his paw to ward off the projectile, but the needler was again knocked to the deck. Off balance from the attack, Ank could not stop Carson from picking up the weapon. Still, the sight of the gun in Carson's hands did not stop Ank from slowly advancing on the human.

"Stop where you are, Ank. Stop, or I'll shoot." When Carson saw that Ank was obviously not going to heed his warning, he fired one dart into the center of the big felinoid's hairy chest.

Ank staggered as he pulled out the dart and angrily hurled it on the deck. After three more darts were fired into him, he finally lurched to the deck, unconscious.

Checking the needler, Carson noticed that the gun was now empty, so he set it down on the pilot's chair and made quick work of tying up his captive. After finishing, Carson looked out the forward viewport and saw that the shuttle was on a collision course with one of the smaller asteroids in the belt. Quickly leaping to the control console, Carson fired the starboard maneuvering rockets on full thrust as the shuttle hurled closer to the large hunk of space rock. He was finally able to breathe a sigh of relief as the shuttle turned and narrowly avoided the collision. Collapsing into the pilot's station, he moved his hands over the helm controls and set a course to head back to the hangar bay.

Next, he activated the short-range transmitter and informed the admiral that all was okay and that a security and medical team should be ready at the main landing bay.

Carson then set the shuttle on autopilot and went back to check on the unconscious lieutenant. To his surprise, Ank was already regaining consciousness; he had pumped enough drugs into the large felinoid to put twenty men to sleep for forty-eight hours. Cautiously, he retrieved the power wrench and stood about two meters away from the groggy lieutenant. "How ya feelin', big fella?" Carson asked, trying to keep a respectable distance between the two of them.

"Sleepy," Ank slurred, his muzzle feeling about as numb as the rest of his body. "I'm sorry for all this. I don't know what happened to me. I thought I was back on Solo and that everyone was trying to kill me. It was a nightmare."

Carson was sure Ank was sincere, and his explanation was eerily similar to Melanie's back on *Pulsar*. "Turn around," Carson said to him.

As he turned, Ank felt Carson cutting the sealing tape from his arms, releasing them from behind his back. "Did I hurt anybody?" Ank asked nervously.

"Just a few bumps and bruises, nothing too serious,"

Carson answered as he helped the weak Ank to his feet and into the copilot's seat.

"I remember a young woman. Did I hurt her?"

"Just a big, ugly bruise and a bit of a headache."

Ank lowered his chin onto his chest in regret.

"Really, she'll be all right," Carson assured the big cat. "We should be landing in a few minutes. You can apologize to her yourself," Carson said.

Soon, the large, shell-like hangar doors of the main landing bay opened in front of them. With skill and precision wrought from hundreds of similar landings, Carson brought the shuttle to a perfect touchdown on the berth that had recently been occupied by *Pulsar*. As he powered down the shuttle systems, he noticed a large security force waiting by the pressure hatch.

Ank was wearing a nervous expression. After all, as recently as an hour ago he had tried to kill several of them, and he wasn't quite sure how he would be treated.

Carson saw how apprehensive Ank was and reached out his hand to grab Ank's large paw. "Listen to me. When the hatch opens, I'll go out first. You'll be fine. They'll will wanna talk to you though. I'm sure they'll ask you about what happened on Solo. Can you handle that?"

Ank looked at him and nodded slowly, his two paws closing on the human's hand. Their eyes met, and Ank silently swore an oath to the human, a debt he had every intention of repaying.

They both stood, and Carson walked ahead of him down the lowered ramp as the security men rushed in. Carson spoke with the men for a second, then motioned for him to step down from the shuttle. The security personnel were understandably tense, their hands never straying far from their weapons as Ank joined Carson on the hangar deck. Behind them, the shuttle was lowered back down to the maintenance deck.

Carson turned to his new friend. "Ank, the admiral wants to see us in his quarters. These men are here to escort us. Don't worry, my friend. You will not go alone. I've got nothing better to do."

As his mind started to clear, Ank could see he was inside some sort of asteroid. As they walked, questions began to spark up in his mind. "Where am I, Carson?"

"You're in the asteroid base of Commando, Inc."

"I've heard of you. You have quite a reputation, even among my people."

Carson nodded, silently accepting the compliment.

To Ank, the human seemed different from the puny creatures he had served with. He gave some thought to the man he was being taken to. "Shall we see Admiral Clayton Brooks, by any chance?" Ank asked curiously.

"Yeah, that's him," Carson replied slowly as the door to the admiral's office slid open in front of them.

As they entered, Brooks stood from his chair and stared at the felinoid. He had been cleaned up, fed, and given a Commando, Inc. uniform, and the large size suited him quite well. "Please sit, Lieutenant," Brooks said, motioning to a chair in front of his desk. "You too, Mark." As both took a seat, Brooks noticed that the five-man security escort team seemed a bit confused as to what to do next. "You men can leave now," Brooks barked.

"Yes, sir!" they sang in unison, then turned and left the room.

Brooks sat down and looked at the two figures seated in front of him. He shook his head; both of them looked like shit. After almost two days without sleep, exhaustion was taking its toll on the younger man. Ank also appeared to be dead on his feet, hardly the crazed creature who had thrown his base into so much confusion and chaos only hours before. Nevertheless, as tired as they were, the meeting could not be postponed or avoided, for he needed Carson to be there for Ank's debriefing. A move of some kind had to be made quickly, and the cat was, quite possibly, the keeper of the key pieces of information that they needed to proceed.

"Lieutenant, are you feeling well enough for a few questions?" Brooks asked.

"I'll be fine, Admiral," Ank responded. All in all, except for needing to sleep for several years, he felt no lasting effects. "My sincerest apologies, though, for what I've put you and your people through."

"No damage done," the admiral said, with a dismissive wave of the hand. "Now, I want you to tell me everything you know about what happened on Solo," Brooks said as he activated the compact vid-recorder on his desk.

Ank began with the discovery of Chamber 102 and the strange, glowing portal within. As he continued the story, both Carson and Brooks were transfixed, hanging on his every word. They listened closely, interrupting only for clarification of certain points. They listened as the horror of what had been released from the portal was made as real as the chairs that they were sitting in. Ank told them of the horrifying creatures and of their leader, Donar, who could supposedly change his form and become anyone at anytime.

At the end of his detailed disclosure, a silence hung in

the room as all three thought about what had just been said. While they didn't have all the answers, one thing was certain: It was now critical for a mission to leave for Solo as soon as possible.

Brooks turned to Carson, who seemed to have aged an additional ten years in the last two hours. "Get a few hours of sleep. You look like you're ready to drop. Then get *Pulsar* and the others ready. You're going to Solo," he said, glancing down at his chronometer. "Departure will be in eight hours."

"Right," Carson said, standing.

"Admiral, I'd like to go along," Ank said more than asked as he also stood, his whiskers twitching in anticipation.

Brooks looked at him closely before he answered, "I was hoping you'd say that, Ank." He then offered his hand to the newest team member.

Ank reached over to shake the man's hand, wearing a smile on his muzzle for the first time in a long time.

"Welcome aboard, friend."

"Thank you, sir," Ank said. He then turned and followed Carson out of the admiral's office.

After they left, Brooks looked at the printout of Ank's service record. He had already discussed the lieutenant with Olstad. He was a perfect complement for Carson's team. In fact, he had wanted to recruit Ank for quite some time, but he had never been able to pry him loose from Olstad until now. After what happened on Solo, Ank seemed to have much to prove, seemingly more to himself than to anyone else. If he proved in the field that he was valuable and it in, with Carson's approval, the admiral would make him a permanent addition. After all that time, Brooks hoped he'd found the final member of his field team. He also hoped it would not be their first and last mission together.

Brooks activated his comm unit link to his operations section. "Griffin, open a channel to Admiral Olstad's ship." Brooks thought it was about time that he clued Olstad in on his conversation with Ank. With the *Pulsar* launch less than eight hours out, Olstad would need time to secure a ship.

"Yes, sir."

"And get me an update on the Dreedan border raids."

As he waited for the connection of the secure channel, Brooks realized his old friend was going to have a lot to do once he reached Allegre IV.

CHAPTER 13

Admiral Olstad thought he had chosen wisely. The small light cruiser starship had been built more for speed than for combat, and his conversation with Brooks had confirmed that speed was a necessity. He was also happy to hear that Lieutenant Ank had recovered and would accompany the expedition to Solo. Olstad had approved the security man's discharge from the service because Brooks wanted him; God only knew how many favors he owed the retired admiral. He had called ahead to his command base and informed them of the situation.

Fortunately, they had some good news. Thirty-six hours earlier, an Alliance battlecruiser had entered orbit for resupply and crew replacements. *At least we won't have to try to dig up a ship on such short notice*, Olstad thought.

As the cruiser reduced speed to sub-light, Olstad could see Allegre IV coming into view on the forward viewscreen. Taking his seat to the right of the captain, he noted that the crew was preparing the ship for landing, and he didn't want to get in their way. On a ship so small, planetary landings required everyone's full attention.

"Admiral, it looks like we're gonna have some company," Captain Evers said, pointing at the viewscreen.

The battlecruiser was coming into view, and their atmospheric entry course would bring them even closer. As they passed, both men were able to make out the ship name and registry number on the side of the shiny hull.

"It's *Ranger*. Captain, please raise Captain Tompkin on visual."

It was almost too perfect. Olstad needed a battlecruiser, and now the pride of the Alliance fleet, with one of the service's finest commanding officers, was in sight.

A moment later, the view of the powerful starship dissolved, replaced with the tall figure of its captain. "Admiral, to what do I owe this unforeseen pleasure?" Captain Martin Tompkin asked from his command chair.

Olstad noticed a great deal of activity on the battlecruiser bridge, but that wasn't at all surprising for a ship in orbit around a starbase. "I'm sorry to invade on your shore leave, Captain, but I'm gonna need you and your ship for a very important mission, almost immediately."

"I'll re-call my command crew, Admiral. We should be able to leave within the hour. But what, may I ask, is the mission, sir?"

"I'm afraid I can't disclose that over an open channel. Meet me in my office in forty-five minutes for a briefing."

Tompkin's image started to break up as the cruiser began its atmospheric entry. "I'll be there," the *Ranger* captain said as the cruiser plunged through the atmosphere and the transmission ended.

For a moment, Olstad thought the blunt disconnection a bit strange, and he could have sworn he had seen an untimely grin on the face of Captain Tompkin. A smile itself would not have been so alarming from anyone else, but in all the years he had known Martin Tompkin, he had never seen one curl the man's lips.

If Admiral Roger Olstad had been on the *Ranger* bridge, he would have witnessed the miracle firsthand. Not only was

Captain Tompkin smiling, but so was the entire bridge crew. *This is too simple,* Tompkin thought. His master figured that, sooner or later, some kind of expeditionary force would be sent to their home world, and he couldn't have been more right.

He thought of his upcoming meeting with Admiral Olstad and congratulated himself for saving one simulcron from the dozen that they had brought. The other eleven had been used to secure key positions on the starbase below, controlling operations, security, and medical. *Shortly,* Tompkin thought, with some amount of pride, *I'll add a Fleet admiral!* But first, he had several transmissions to make.

"Ensign White!" he bellowed; they had decided to use their new identities, even when alone, to help them to adapt more to their new form. "Send a tight-beamed, scrambled transmission to Nexus III. I need to talk to Lord Donar immediately!"

"Yes, Captain," the duplicate ensign said as she sent out the powerful transmission.

The transmission would be almost impossible to detect from planetside. Even if they did detect it, though, the communications chief on the planet below was one of them.

"I have Lord Donar on the screen," the faux ensign said.

Tompkin turned to see his master's reptilian face on the forward viewscreen.

"Speak, Tompkin. What have you to report?"

"My Lord, while in orbit around Allegre IV, we were hailed by Fleet Admiral Olstad. It seems he'd like to send my ship on a mission."

"And what mission is that, Captain?"

"Unknown as of yet, My Lord. I am to report for a briefing in thirty minutes."

Donar remained quiet for several seconds, as if contemplating his next move. "Are there any simulcrons remaining?"

"I saved one...for just such a special occasion, sir." Tompkin was delighted to see that he had said the proper thing; his master was clearly pleased with his foresight.

"Excellent. Arrange to take one of the creatures down with you, and use it to take control of the admiral," Donar said, then paused a moment for effect. "Do I make myself clear?"

"Yes, My Lord. And what of the mission?" Tompkin asked.

"Lead it as planned. If your destination is the home world, go. If anything of importance is found, bring it to me."

"And if they resist?"

"Then kill them all, save one. You know which one I speak of, and you will bring him to me. If there are others who are aware of our existence, we must know who they are before we destroy them. If necessary, I will use a simulcron to extract the information, but that takes so much fun out of interrogations, doesn't it?" Donar said, his mouth open in a demonic grin, revealing his sharp teeth.

"And if they find nothing?"

"Then arrange...an accident."

Tompkin knew what his master wanted, and he wouldn't disappoint him. "Yes, My Lord," he said. As the connection severed from the other end, he remembered what it was like to rip the creatures apart. *And the blood!* Oh, how he missed the salty-sweet, crimson, warm delicacy dripping off his fangs and down his throat.

A look of disappointment crossed his face as he realized that in his current puny form, he had no fangs or powerful jaws with which to feast. "Ensign," he said again to White, "raise starbase communications."

Moments later, the connection established, and Lieutenant Malone appeared on the viewscreen. "Yes, *Ranger*?" Malone was one of the first of the base personnel replacements, as control of communications had been a priority.

"I will be shuttling down shortly for a meeting with Admiral Olstad. I have a package for him. Please see to it that it remains a surprise until I'm able to present it."

"I will see that security clears the area for your arrival," Malone said. As soon as the frequency was closed, Malone quickly opened up a secure internal channel to security. "This is Lieutenant Malone. I'd like to speak to Security Chief Thurmond."

In less than thirty seconds, Chief Thurmond's voice came over the comm unit. "This is Thurmond."

"Are you alone? Can anyone hear us?"

"No," came the reply.

"Tompkin will be arriving with a package for Olstad. The old man is to be next."

"Right," was all that was said before the conversation ended with an audible *click*.

Malone knew there would be no problem smuggling the simulcron down to the base. However, Thurmond would, as he had done several times before, keep the corridors cleared between the landing bay and the admiral's office.

A second later, the announcement about the radiation leak drill appeared on his status board. It would keep all personnel in their current location, until the alleged emergency was over. It was the tenth and last time he would have to make these arrangements for the arrival of a simulcron. The fact that nobody reacted to ten situations in less than four days did not really surprise him. The bureaucracy with which the base was run was the same one that had granted him the authority to organize the distractions. The corridors had to be kept clear; even hidden under the bulkiest uniform, they were noticeable. Though there were 11 of them in key positions there, it was still out of a complement of over 300 support personnel. Now, adding the knowledge of Admiral Olstad to their cause would contribute greatly to the success of his master's plan.

The shuttle with Tompkin and the simulcron were on final approach, and the takeover of Starbase Allegre was almost complete.

* * *

Olstad sat behind his desk, happy to be back in familiar surroundings after his stay at the asteroid. He had tried, just a few moments before, to complete a message to Brooks about his sending of *Ranger*, but the communications chief had informed him of the malfunction in some of the gear. He did promise, however, to send the message out as soon as repairs were completed. Now, all that was left was to brief Tompkin on his mission to support Carson and his people when they reached Solo.

Before Tompkin's arrival, Olstad moved to his liquor cabinet and removed a vintage bottle of scotch whiskey. He'd been waiting for an excuse to open it, and he was sure

Tompkin would need a nip or two once he heard the details of his mission.

As he poured the two small glasses, Olstad heard a short tone at his door, signaling that the *Ranger* captain had arrived. "Come," he said, sitting back behind his desk with his two drinks.

The door slid aside, and Captain Tompkin walked in.

"Have a seat, Captain."

"Thank you, sir," Tompkin said, but he continued to stand above the seat. "Admiral, before we begin, there's someone outside I'd like you to meet. I think he will be very beneficial to my mission, whatever it is."

"What are you talking about, Tompkin?" Olstad asked, unnerved and curious at Tompkin's strange behavior.

"Sir, I think it might be better if I show you. It will only take a moment. He's waiting in your outer office," Tompkin said. "You won't regret it, Admiral."

Olstad sat there for a moment, trying to fathom what Tompkin could possibly be talking about. Releasing a frustrated sigh, he got up and moved toward the door. As he passed his desk, he picked up both glasses and handed one to Tompkin. "Here. Take this. And whoever it is, this had better be good. We don't have much time."

"Oh, it's good, Admiral. It's very good."

As they walked out, Olstad saw a large figure standing by the wall, his back to the two of them. *I need to speak to the quartermaster,* Olstad thought. *This man needs a bigger uniform. My God, he's bursting at the seams!*

"Admiral Olstad, I'd like you to meet...Admiral Olstad!" Tompkin said as the visitor turned around.

Olstad didn't understand what was going on until the

figure turned to face them – or at least it would have if it had a face.

"He might not look like you now, but he soon will."

A shock went prickled up and down Olstad's spine, and his glass of precious scotch fell from his hand, drenching the carpeted floor with dark liquid and peppering it with shards of glass as the thing started to approach him. It was humanoid in shape, but it had no features of any kind. It was like a walking mass of clay.

Olstad moved back as the thing advanced. "Tompkin, what's going on? What the hell is this thing?" He turned to retreat into his office, but Tompkin stood in the way. Instantly, the panicked and confused Olstad ran to the comm panel on the wall and frantically stabbed the activation stud with his index finger. "Security to the admiral's office STAT! Emergency! Security, answer me!"

"No answer, Admiral?" Tompkin said, now standing next to the creature, moving ever closer to the admiral. "Don't worry. You'll understand it all in a few minutes. Everything will become blatantly clear."

Helpless, Admiral Olstad backed up to the wall.

Tompkin relished the look of terror on the human's face as the creature reached out its large, misshapen hands and placed them on both sides of the older man's head.

Olstad screamed as the terrible pain hit him, making him feel as though his head was imploding from within. His body went slack and would have fallen to the floor if not for the two gargantuan hands holding him by his head. Uncontrollable spasms hit as every orifice of his head hemorrhaged simultaneously. Blood flowed freely, and the admiral felt his mind being quickly ripped away.

Tompkin watched the simulcron and the human as the transformation procedure progressed. The two shook uncontrollably, as if engaged in some powerful, orgasmic dance. It had always fascinated him. The gushing blood seemed to feed the simulcron, nourishing it until it totally devoured the essence of the human. Tompkin realized that he, too, was once a simulcron, a mass of clay, but now he was considered one of the chosen. He licked his lips as reminisced about what the creature was feeling, the power of knowledge feeding it, giving it purpose. It was their destiny. In his prior form, he had lusted after the blood of his victims, but now, as he watched the body of Admiral Olstad grow thinner and thinner, finally crumbling to dust within the now empty uniform, he tasted a more intense victory. They consumed the pathetic creatures entirely, and that brought a smile to his face.

The creature dropped the remnants of Admiral Roger Olstad to the floor and turned to face Tompkin.

Tompkin was very pleased as he looked into the face of the new Admiral Olstad. "Welcome, Admiral. First, let's get rid of this mess," he said, pointing to the mass of crumbling flesh that had been his commanding officer. "Then we'll find you a uniform that fits properly. After that, I believe we have a briefing to get to, do we not?"

The newly transformed simulcron looked at him and smiled. "Yes, Captain. We have much to discuss...and I could use another drink."

CHAPTER 14

Carson sat in his command chair and went through the standard preflight checks. Liftoff would be in twenty-three minutes, and he and Ernie would see that everything would go smoothly. Using the forward viewscreen, he scanned the large hangar bay, where he found Melanie and Josh stowing the equipment needed for their trip.

Ank was close by, supervising the loading of some specialized weaponry he had insisted they carry. Carson didn't know what to make of the large cat-man, but if a fight broke out, he would certainly be glad to have him on their side. Ank had apologized long and hard to Melanie, and Melanie had quickly accepted, but Ank so regretted what had happened that he now followed her wherever she went.

"Skipper, there is a call coming in from Admiral Brooks," Ernie said calmly.

The computer-generated voice jolted Carson back to the present. "Thanks, Ernie." He pressed a small button on the side of his command chair, opening a communication channel. "Yes, Admiral?"

"I just spoke to Olstad," Brooks said, his voice a bit anxious. "He informed me that Captain Tompkin and *Ranger* will meet you at Solo."

Carson knew Tompkin, and though he felt the man was a little stuffy, he and *Ranger* were the ideal choice to keep watch over them. He was sure there had to be some other explanation for the admiral's uneasiness. "Is something wrong, sir?"

"I-I don't know, Mark. Just a feeling, I guess."

The line went silent for a moment.

Finally, Brooks continued, "Listen, it's probably nothing." Then he paused again, as if to weigh his words carefully. "Just do an old man a big favor."

"Anything, sir."

"Be careful, son."

"I will. But, Admiral..."

"Yes, Mark?"

"Just hold down the fort here. I have a feeling there are ten miles of suffering on the way."

"No problem there. Good luck," Brooks said, and the channel closed.

Carson leaned back into his cushioned command chair. The admiral had never been so apprehensive about a mission before, and he wondered what was really on the old man's mind. *Was it something Olstad said?* From the very beginning, the whole thing had been a mystery. As soon as he thought they had one part all figured out, another equally bizarre question jumped up to take its place.

The bridge door behind him opened with a low sigh, and his three comrades entered and took their stations.

Melanie walked over to Carson and placed her slender hand on his shoulder. "You look...deep in thought. What's up?"

"Nothing," Carson said, staring blankly ahead. "The admiral just called to wish us luck."

"What's so strange about that?" Ank asked from his station at the tactical console.

"Well, big guy," Josh said, turning in his seat to face

him, "it just so happens to be the first time our leader has expressed this particular wish."

"All right, boys and girl, to your stations. We have a rendezvous to make," Carson said.

Melanie took her seat by the communications board.

"Skipper, Operations requests our status," Ernie said from the bridge speaker.

"Ernie, you can report that we're all set."

The ship shuddered as *Pulsar* rose on its pad to her launch position in the landing bay. When the lift came to a rest, external umbilical cables, which had, until that moment, supplied *Pulsar* with power, released and drew back into modular power outlets on the aft section of the pad. Ernie automatically switched to internal power as he brought the powerful fusion reactors online. *Pulsar* gently rose and spun on her axis as the massive hanger doors silently slid open. The vacuum of space quickly filled the bay, and the starship became fully operational.

"Take 'er out, Ernie," Carson said.

Pulsar started to move forward, toward the opening hangar doors.

"As soon as we're clear of the belt, kick in the hyperdrive."

"Right, Skipper."

Pulsar moved out into space on the power of her retro thrusters. As soon as they cleared the base perimeter, the powerful fusion engine activated, propelling them through the belt. They were surrounded by thousands of floating, mineral-laden boulders of all sizes, so Carson allowed Ernie the task of navigation. It helped that their progress was being monitored by sensors installed in various asteroids scattered throughout the belt. As soon as they were clear, security would reactivate the powerful pulse weapons system. That would ensure that base security was maintained, an important condition considering current events.

"Ernie, activate the forward viewscreen, please," Carson ordered.

The screen came to life before them, and they all watched as they cleared the belt, leaving the last of the asteroids behind.

"All clear, Carson," Josh said.

"Ernie, engage hyperdrive. Set course for Solo."

"Right, Skipper," Ernie said.

As *Pulsar* thundered into hyperspace, Admiral Brooks stood in the operations center and watched, till the ship disappeared from their sensors. Mark Carson knew him very well. He hadn't intended his concern to eke through his voice, but he should have known he could never fool the boy. Among his many other talents, Carson was a trained intelligence operative and could easily read a change in voice inflection, especially in one he knew so well.

Something was troubling Brooks though, ever since his last communication with Olstad. Upon Olstad's departure, he'd been greatly concerned about the problem on Solo spreading to other inhabited worlds, but now he seemed willing to dismiss it as nothing more than an isolated incident. *Why is he suddenly treating this problem so lightly?* Olstad had seen the horrendous tape of the massacre, and the effect off it on the fleet admiral had been quite evident.

Well, I won't figure any of this out standing here

worrying about it, Brooks finally told himself. Deciding that he had to find the answer himself, Brooks returned to his office and immediately called his executive assistant.

Seconds later, Griffin entered and stood before his superior. "Yes, sir?" Griffin asked.

Brooks could see that he looked out of breath, and he could only assume he hadn't been at his desk in the outer office when he called. "Ready my shuttle, and I'll need a pilot."

Griffin was caught by surprise by Brooks's order. He couldn't believe the Admiral was making travel plans at that particular juncture, and his face in fact reflected his confusion. "Sir, you're leaving the base?" Griffin asked, only realizing how ridiculous his question was after it left his mouth.

"No, Griffin," Brooks answered sarcastically. "Just get the ship ready and put a pilot in it so I can cruise the landing bay."

"Yes, sir. I mean...no, sir," Griffin stammered out.

"Griffin, relax and listen closely," Brooks said quietly. "You will prep my ship for launch and get me a pilot to fly it. Do you understand?"

"Yes, sir. May I ask your destination?"

"I need to get to Allegre IV. Something's...not quite right."

Griffin hesitated a moment, thinking closely about what to say next. "Do you want me to come with you?"

Brooks looked at his executive assistant and was actually touched at the offer. Unfortunately, he needed Griffin to stay behind and run the show till he got back. "No. You'll be needed here. Someone has to coordinate that data on the border raids."

"Admiral, I must insist, then, that you take someone from security with you," Griffin said, privately relieved that Brooks had not taken him up on his offer.

Brooks thought for a moment and realized Griffin was right. *I'd be a fool to walk into anything suspicious without help. If Olstad asks about the extra security, I'll just fib and say the guard's a consultant, there to evaluate Allegre IV's own security force.*

"All right, Griffin, you win," Brooks said, switching on his comm unit. "Security, this is Admiral Brooks. Have Security Chief Noga report to me on the hangar bay in thirty minutes."

"Yes, sir," came the reply from the small communications speaker.

"I'll take Noga with me, if that's all right with you?" Brooks asked his assistant, seeing that Griffin was enjoying his moment.

"The perfect choice, sir," Griffin said as he stood and headed for the door. "I'll see you to your ship."

Brooks waved his hand at Griffin.

The assistant, not looking to push his unusually good fortune, turned and left. He understood why everyone disliked the smug bastard, but he was the best at what he did, and that was why he was there.

Brooks had to pack a few things for the trip, but he stopped on the way out to pour himself a drink. After downing it in one quick swallow, he walked out of his office and into his quarters which, for the sake of expedience, were situated right next to his office. As he entered, he went for the bed and removed a small traveling case from beneath it.

He contemplated the case as he placed it on the bed and sat beside it. He always kept a full case ready, in case he was needed elsewhere at the spur of the moment. Brooks looked around his quarters, wondering if it was the last time he would lay eyes on it. Very few people had ever been invited there. It was his inner sanctuary, and except for his small circle of friends, no one had ever seen it.

Pictures of family and friends, some long gone, adorned the walls. Pictures of himself with Mark, Melanie, and Josh hung by the bed, something of a family portrait. In fact, he took great pleasure in telling people that the key moments of his life could be found there. As he opened the case and inserted the small, lethal blaster that he usually kept under his pillow, he hoped he'd see them again.

When he reached the hangar bay, a team of technicians were busy prepping his ship for launch. Standing by the shuttle, he noticed Noga doing what security people seemed to do best: looking threatening. Of course, Noga didn't have to do much to accomplish that. At a shade under seven feet tall and vaguely primate in appearance, he was as fearsome a sight as Ank. Brooks only found one small fault in his head of security: He lacked any sense of humor. Originally from Planet Elba II, Noga was the spawn of a warrior clan who felt the ultimate act of honor would be to die in combat, as long as he took his opponent with him.

Elba II was situated in disputed space, between the Alliance and the Dreedan Empire. It was, therefore, constantly under attack by Dreedan raiders. It wasn't long before the Alliance offered the people of Elba II status as a member planet. The Elbans, though, were a prideful people, and after a series of negotiations, a treaty was born: The

Alliance Fleet provided protection, while Elba II provided an outpost to monitor Dreedan border activity, an alliance built on fulfilling mutual needs.

As Brooks approached the shuttle, Noga snapped to attention.

The admiral merely looked at him as he passed and shook his head. "C'mon, Noga. Let's board. We have a lot to discuss."

Without a word, Noga fell in behind the admiral and followed him into the shuttle. The door slid shut behind them, and the hangar elevator lifted the small shuttle to the landing bay. Both Brooks and Noga took their seats as the shuttle reached launch position.

Brooks cringed at the sight of the pilot as the ship rose and accelerated for the opening hangar doors. Glick was the total opposite of Noga; once he got going, he was impossible to shut up. *I've got a feeling this is going to be a long trip,* Brooks thought with much dismay.

* * *

Traveling at full speed, *Ranger* arrived a full day before *Pulsar*. Tompkin had planned the early arrival in order to give them time to set up an ambush on the planet below. His memories of Carson were strong in that form, and there lingered a definite dislike of the Commando, Inc. field leader, accompanied by a distinct respect for his abilities. Carson was bound to discover something, and if he did, he would take him back to Donar or kill them all. He was too much of a threat to be allowed to live with any new information, and they couldn't replace Carson with a simulcron either. His orders from Donar were to bring back a live captive for interrogation. *But,* Tompkin thought,

Donar isn't here, is he? If he deemed it necessary, he was quite prepared to kill them all – every last one.

Ten of his crew would accompany Carson and his people to the planet surface. Tompkin wished he could send more, but of the 247 humans who had made up the crew, only 75 simulcrons had been created to replace them.

He had told his men that Lord Donar needed at least one of the creatures alive for interrogation, and they all knew it was not healthy to cross Donar. Tompkin sat on the bridge and thought about that. If the decision were his, things would be different. The first thing he would do would be to obliterate the ruins on the planet below. Where there was no evidence, there would be no crime. Next, he would kill Carson as soon as he entered orbit by blasting *Pulsar* out of space. It was that other simulcron that kept Donar from taking action; Barton made him rely more on caution than destruction. Modok, he knew, would gladly destroy them all and watch as their blood soaked the ground. Tompkin's ship was the pride of the Alliance Fleet, he didn't see the need for caution, and he assumed that was simply a side effect of his former werewolf thought patterns.

"Captain, a message from *Pulsar*," Ensign White said from her communications station, interrupting Tompkin's thoughts. "She just entered the system. Her ETA to our position is twenty-three minutes."

Ranger was one of the most powerful Alliance battlecruisers, and just one blast from her photon cannons would reduce *Pulsar* to dust. Unfortunately, in Tompkin's opinion, that wasn't Donar's plan. "Very good, Ensign. Open a channel, and let's welcome our friends," Tompkin said gleefully, licking his lips in anticipation of things to come.

CHAPTER 15

After system entry, Carson assumed helm control and guided *Pulsar* toward Solo. Long-range sensors had established that *Ranger* was waiting for them in orbit, her large hull clearly visible on the bridge viewscreen.

Josh was the first to comment on the size of the battlecruiser, whistling out loud. "Whew! Look at the size of that baby!"

Ranger easily dwarfed them. In fact, her hangar deck was large enough to admit *Pulsar* with room to spare. Powerful photon cannon emplacements were also evident along her outer hull. Drawing its destructive energy directly from her powerful engines, *Ranger* had the power to devastate an entire planet. That particular class of starship could hold its own in almost any fight.

"Carson, we're being hailed by *Ranger*," Melanie said as the communication console registered the incoming message.

"Put it on the screen."

They watched as the image of *Ranger* dissolved into the face of Captain Martin Tompkin, not a change for the better, in Carson's opinion.

"Hello, Carson. Good to see you again," the *Ranger* captain said, somewhat sarcastically.

Carson could hear Ank growling behind him, and he grinned and looked back to the screen. "Same here, Tompkin. Nice to have you along for support."

"Well, Admiral Olstad briefed me on the mission. It seems you're in overall command on this one," Tompkin retorted. "I'm only here to provide perimeter security. I have a team standing by to join you on the planet surface."

"Thank you, Captain. We appreciate your help."

"Carson, would you and your people care to come aboard? Perhaps a drink before we begin?"

"Maybe later. We should really get underway ASAP," Carson answered, finding it hard to believe that Tompkin had been accurately apprised of the situation.

"You are correct, of course," Tompkin replied. "My security team will leave immediately for the surface and will rendezvous with you at the primary landing site by the city entrance."

"That will be fine. *Pulsar* out." Carson stood from his chair and paced the bridge.

"Carson, that didn't sound like the Martin Tompkin I remember," Ank said, his whiskers twitching slightly. He had told them during the long trip that he'd served briefly with Tompkin, and it hadn't been an experience to remember. "He was much too...friendly."

"This whole thing is starting to sound a little strange," Melanie added.

"Well, anyway, what's next on the agenda?" Josh asked.

Carson thought for a second before he sat back down. "We land and do our job. I want you all to be very careful though. Ernie..."

"Yes, Skipper?"

"Set the landing vectors and take us down to the same coordinates as before. Everybody get in landing position." Since he didn't have to concentrate on the landing, Carson could focus more on their next move.

The bridge was bathed in red light as the small starship angled downward and began its decent to the planet surface.

Tompkin watched as *Pulsar* entered the planetary atmosphere in preparation for landing. He was upset that Carson and the others had refused to board *Ranger*, as that would have made things easier for everyone. The shuttle carrying his security team was also on the way down. His orders had been explicit: He was not to interfere with them unless they discovered something significant, at which point they should report back.

The cat was there, too, the one they had tortured after the glorious moment of their release. If they found nothing, they would all be killed on the way back to their ship. He would then destroy all evidence of their existence and conjure up a convincing story. It would be easy enough to blame Dreedan raiders for everything, and with Admiral Olstad on his side, whatever tale he told would not be challenged. As he looked down toward the cloud-shrouded planet, Tompkin couldn't help but think of what War Chief Modok's reaction would be when he told him he'd destroyed the cat.

* * *

Pulsar settled gently on the pad it had occupied only several days before.

Carson, the first out of his seat, walked over to Josh at his science station. "Anything going on out there?"

Josh ran his hands across his console, transferring the sensor readings to a display just above them. Information on their immediate surroundings flashed across the screen. "Well," Josh said, perusing the accumulated data, "temperature's down a little. The atmosphere is still breathable, as long as you don't inhale too deeply. And, last but not least, there are no life form readings within sensor range."

Carson looked at the display as new information came from their sensor sweep. "Well, it looks like we've got company," he said noting the arrival of the *Ranger* personnel.

The small Alliance shuttle set down fifty meters port of their position, and the security team was already approaching.

"Ernie..."

"Yes, Skipper?"

"You know the routine. Maintain Class A security until we get back. Under no circumstances is anyone but us to have access to this ship. Is that understood?"

"Aye-aye, sir," the computer responded.

"Let's move, people. Our escort awaits," Carson said, and they each exited through the bridge doors.

Before they left the ship, though, Ank detoured them to the weapons storage area he had set up prior to their departure from the asteroid. It was usually utilized to hold supplies and often remained empty. However, now, it was evident that Ank had been working quite hard to fill it. Practically from floor to ceiling, the room was chockfull of weapons, ammo, and artillery, an impressive armory if there ever was one.

"Wow," Josh said as he gazed around at the arsenal Ank had stockpiled. "Don't tell me you're expecting trouble," he said sarcastically as they shrugged into their protective body armor.

Ank stared at Josh, and a low growl filled the chamber before he turned back to Carson. "It is best to be prepared. Since we number only four, I have included more powerful weapons. When I checked the armory, I found it...lacking. Now our little quartet will be sufficiently armed."

Ank certainly knew his weapons. Blasters of different sizes hung from the wall, and to one side of the chamber sat a portable photon cannon that Carson thought might seem more at home sitting on the hull of *Ranger*.

Each of them selected a hand blaster and affixed it to their belt. With the security force on hand, three of them didn't find it necessary to carry anything more powerful. Ank, on the other hand, insisted on taking the photon cannon. Cradled in the crook of his powerful arms, the weapon seemed like somewhat of a trinket, but it certainly wouldn't fire like one.

Melanie looked at him in disbelief. "Are you sure you wanna carry that bulky thing, Ank?"

Ank looked at her, then at the cannon slung over his broad shoulders. "Yes," he said, as if the topic was not open to discussion. After all, he recalled the powerful weapons used by Donar's followers. "Last time, I was caught unprepared. That will not happen again."

Carson gathered up his own equipment, including the two small daggers secured to his wrists, then joined the others by the corridor. Melanie was carrying a med-kit with her sidearm. Josh had a blaster pistol in his holster, but he also had a portable sensor-recorder, clipped to his belt. Carson turned to Ank, who seemed impatient to leave. The only specialized equipment the big cat held was the photon cannon. They all checked their comm units, making certain the small devices were securely strapped to their wrists, then exited the ship from the cargo bay airlock.

Stepping out last, Carson closed the airlock, and the door closed with a soft *hiss*. He joined the others as the security force from *Ranger* arrived. As they approached, Carson tried to size up the situation, wondering if they could be trusted. He cast a cursory glance over at the cat-man and saw the felinoid stiffen slightly, bringing the photon cannon up just a little more than before.

Carson stepped forward as one of them came closer. "My name's Carson. I'm – "

"Yes, I know who you are," a particularly ugly specimen of humankind interrupted. "I'm Security Chief Dowd. We're here under orders from Captain Tompkin."

Carson hesitated briefly before starting over, overcome by the same bad feeling he'd sensed while talking with Tompkin. "Dowd, assign four of your men to monitor the perimeter and guard the ships. Four others will stay at the security shack to serve as a communications relay and backup, and you and another of your men will accompany us to the city."

After Carson finished, Dowd stood motionless for a moment, just staring at him, an insubordinate, rebellious look Carson knew and did not appreciate. Carson started to dress him down, but Dowd turned and went back to his men. Not sure what else to do, Carson returned to his own small group to a collection of confused stares.

Melanie was the first to inquire. "What was all that about?" she asked.

"I don't know, but something very weird is going on here," he said.

Dowd suddenly returned, with another burly security man in tow. "It's taken care of, Carson," he said. "Are you ready?"

"Ank, take the point. Chief, take the rear position," Carson said, his voice beginning to give away his anger.

Carson joined Ank at the lead as they entered the dark, subterranean tunnels. "The next move is up to you, big guy," he said to the felinoid. "Where to?"

"The trouble started in Chamber 102. That is where we begin."

They moved silently down the dark corridors, weapons drawn and ready. When they reached the chamber, the yellow glow was still illuminating the outer corridor.

Ank led the way in, his photon weapon up, scanning the chamber for any sign of danger or ambush. The others cautiously entered behind him, but Dowd and his security man stopped at the chamber entrance.

Melanie looked around, this time careful to avoid contact with the walls. "This is the same chamber we were in when that creature attacked us."

Josh stared at the arch, glowing, as if it was alive with power. He removed his scanner and started to take readings. "Carson, I don't know where this thing is getting power from," he said, pointing at the arch, "but the readings are off the scale."

"Do you remember what happened before the arch opened? What were Clarkson and the others doing?" Carson asked, placing a comforting hand on Ank's shoulder.

"The doctor was standing at that console over there," Ank said, staring at the large, glowing enigma.

Josh stepped over to the console and saw that its face

was blank. He could find no trace of a control surface, not a button or a switch. Without thinking, he leaned a hand against the smooth surface, and the machine came to life. Josh stepped back involuntarily, startled by the sudden activity.

The arch glowed brighter in response, as more power fed into the strange construct. As the glow intensified, a translucent mist could be seen forming below the arch. They watched closely as the mist began to reveal something behind it, something other than the wall.

So engrossed they were by what was forming under the arch that they didn't notice the two *Ranger* security men slipping away into the corridor.

Carson moved closer to the arch, trying to get a better look at what was forming. Ank was right behind him, and a shiver ran up and down his furry spine as he recalled the last time the arch had been activated. The image became sharper, revealing a strange planetary surface with a threatening red sky above it.

"Dowd, call the others...and inform Tompkin. I think we've found something," Carson called out without turning.

"I already have," came the humorless reply from the chamber entrance.

When Carson turned to look at him and scold him for his tone, he saw Dowd standing with one arm wrapped around Melanie's neck, the other holding a blaster at her head. "What the hell, Dowd? What's going on here?" Carson demanded, angry at himself for being caught off guard.

"Drop your weapons now!" Dowd ordered as the remainder of his force stood behind him.

Carson saw Ank nervously pawing his weapon, clearly

angry by the threat on Melanie's life. "Do as he says, Ank. Josh, you too," Carson said placing his own blaster pistol on the floor.

"Very smart, Carson. You might just live a little longer," the security chief said as he loosened his hold on Melanie's throat and passed her back to his men behind him. "Take her back to the ship," he ordered.

Ank growled at her mistreatment.

Dowd turned to the cat and smiled. "What's the matter, kitty? You don't like the way I treat the lady. You weren't that frisky when we had you here last."

At that moment, it all came together for Carson, the telling feelings he'd experienced before. The things they had seen on the tape made sense, and his stomach churned at the thought. "Take it easy, Ank," he said to his large friend.

"Yes, pussycat, take it easy. Do you know how happy Modok will be to see you again?" Dowd pointed his blaster at Ank, his finger tightening on the trigger. "I'm sure he'd understand if I brought you back a little...damaged."

While Dowd was speaking, Carson quietly released a small dagger into his right hand. He knew if he didn't act fast, Ank would be fried. Dowd was too busy enjoying the moment to notice him quickly snap the small knife through the air. The enemy did notice, though, with great satisfaction, the pain as the blade hit him in his gun hand, forcing him to drop the weapon to the floor.

Ank moved fast and dived for the floor where his blaster pistol rested. In one smooth, choreographed blur, he moved to his feet and fired, hitting a guard in the chest and blasting him to the wall.

Josh and Carson had also recovered their weapons and

were shooting away. Unfortunately, the remaining security men had taken cover and were returning their fire.

Carson crawled over to Ank as a barrage of blaster fire sprayed just above their heads. He noticed one of Dowd's men vying for better position and quickly picked him off with a shot, almost ripping the simulcron's head from its body.

"Pull back to the shuttle," Dowd shouted to the remainder of his team.

Josh stood from his cover to get a clear shot at Dowd, but the security man turned and fired first. The blast hit Josh and spun him over the console behind him.

"Josh!" Carson screamed. He rolled to the side and fired wildly; he struck another guard but missed Dowd. "Ank, can you see Josh?" he asked, unable to verify his friend's condition.

"No, Carson," the cat answered, ducking his tall frame another barrage of fire.

"Carson!" came Dowd's voice from the corridor. "You're both going to die now, you and that wretched cat!" Then, cradling his injured hand, Dowd tossed a small object into the chamber.

Carson and Ank saw the object rolling toward them from the entrance, and they didn't have to get a close look at it to realize what it was.

"Grenade!" Ank screamed.

He then picked up Carson and tried to dive out of the way as the grenade exploded. The blast caught them and tossed the two through the air like ragdolls in a hurricane. Unable to stop their flight, they tumbled through the arch and disappeared.

CHAPTER 16

The sleek shuttle landed without incident on Allegre IV. Brooks and Noga were met by Starbase Security Chief Thurmond as they stepped off the small starship. Brooks had ordered Glick to remain with the shuttle and to expect hourly check-in calls. "If a scheduled check-in is missed for any reason," he'd said, "head back to base and inform Griffin of trouble. Otherwise, be ready for us here, in case we need to make a hasty retreat."

As Thurmond approached, both Brooks and Noga appraised the muscular human. Dressed in a red jumpsuit embroidered with the nova star patch of a security chief, Thurmond looked young for a man in such an esteemed position. He also seemed to possess the humorless demeanor common to all those in his profession. Brooks glanced over at Noga and saw that his head of security was also sizing up the human as a possible opponent.

"Admiral Brooks, welcome to Starbase Allegre. Admiral Olstad is waiting. Please come with me," Thurmond said to them.

Brooks nodded his thanks to the security chief, and the three walked the short distance to the terminal building.

Thurmond was silent as he led them to Admiral Olstad's outer reception area. "Please wait here," he said quietly, then turned and entered Olstad's office.

"Might as well have a seat, Noga," Brooks said, patting the couch by the wall.

Noga plopped his large bulk uncomfortably down in a chair obviously meant for more human-sized hindquarters.

Several moments later, the door opened, and Thurmond reappeared. He signaled for them to rise and motioned to the office. "The admiral will see you know."

When they entered, they found Olstad sitting behind his large, oak desk, a piece of furniture he'd had transferred to Allegre IV all the way from Earth. Chairs or desks, rank did have its privileges.

Olstad didn't seem to pay them much notice as they entered; his eyes were glued to a monitor on his desk. "Gentlemen, please sit down," he said without bothering to look away from his readout. Only when he finished reading did he reach over and shut down his display. As the monitor went dark, he turned to his guests sitting before him. "Now, what can I do for you, Clayton?"

"I thought it might be prudent to discuss internal security, Admiral, both yours and mine. With situations as uncertain as they are, I thought it was important enough to stop by with my head of security," Brooks said, hoping Olstad wouldn't see through his ploy.

"Clayton, my security is in good hands," Olstad said. "If that's the only reason you're here, you're wasting your time and mine."

Brooks glanced back at the door and noticed that Thurmond was standing next to it. *We're friends,* he thought, *glancing back at Olstad, so what's with the armed guard?* "Actually, I've been a bit worried about...*you,* Roger."

Olstad looked him in the face and smiled, moving his hands to his lap under his desk. "Why should you be worried about me? I'm fine. If you should be worried about anyone's health, it should be your own, Clayton."

"Huh? I'm afraid I don't understand," Brooks said, trying to keep the nervousness out of his voice.

"Come now. We both know why you're really here."

Brooks glanced back at the door and saw that Thurmond now had his blaster out, pointed at their heads. He turned back to Olstad and saw a needler also pointed at them.

"Chief Noga, please drop your weapon on the floor."

Noga reluctantly did as he was told, but he was clearly anxious to make some kind of move. When Thurmond, still holding his blaster on them, bent down to retrieve Noga's gun, Noga lashed out, sending a booted foot harshly into Thurmond's midsection. The blow seemed to knock the breath out of the presumably human security guard as Noga pounced on him.

Before he could deliver a blow with his large fists, Brooks heard the soft popping of Olstad's needler as he fired three times into Noga's broad back. Quickly, the darts pumped their cargo of tranquilizer into his body. Noga collapsed like a demolished building, weakened by the drug, his weight falling on top of Thurmond.

With a scream Brooks didn't think any human could produce, Thurmond kicked Noga off him and bared his teeth before giving the unconscious security officer a violent kick to the ribs.

"Easy, Thurmond. You don't want Admiral Brooks to think we are poor hosts," Olstad said, now pointing his needler squarely at Brooks.

Brooks looked back at the strange being who used to be his very good friend. "You look and sound like Roger Olstad, but you're not him. You're some kind of...imposter. Now where is he!?" His temper was on the rise, and he no longer cared that escape was practically hopeless.

"Technically, I suppose I could say I killed him."

Brooks wanted to tear the murderous thing apart, rip him into pieces, gun or no gun.

Olstad realized the man's hostility and lifted the needler and pointed the weapon at his head. "I wouldn't try anything if I were you, Clayton. Olstad's memories of you are, for the most part, good ones. I would hate to ask Thurmond to kill you."

Not swayed at all by the threat, Brooks contemplated his next move, if he even had a chance to make one. He knew his time was almost up; the hour was ticking away, and without the check-in call, Glick would flee for help. He had to keep the thing busy until that help arrived. "What do you want from me?" he asked calmly, trying to buy time.

Before Olstad could answer, the comm unit on the desk beeped, and the red light flashed.

"Excuse me, Admiral," Olstad said to Brooks before turning his attention to the speaker. "Yes? What is it?"

"Admiral, an unauthorized ship has just lifted from the spaceport," Malone said. "I've issued orders to the perimeter ships that it be treated as hostile and destroyed."

"Thank you, Malone. Don't let them escape." Olstad then switched off the intercom and smiled at Brooks. "It appears that someone has stolen your shuttle. I'm afraid it will now have to be destroyed, in the interest of base security."

"You conniving bastard!" Brooks said, slumping down in his chair. It looked like the cavalry wasn't going to come charging over the hill after all.

"Oh, by the way, I forgot to tell you that we received a mission update from *Ranger* before you landed. Captain Tompkin says they found nothing, but there was an unfortunate accident."

Brooks's stomach twisted into knots as he awaited the news he dreaded to hear.

"An underground explosion, so I'm told," Olstad continued. "Your team is dead, buried under solid rock, except for Dr. Patula, who is now our guest."

Mark dead? Brooks couldn't believe it. *Josh and Ank buried with him in an explosion? No! It can't be!* "You sick son-of-a-bitch," Brooks said. He quickly made up his mind to take whatever vengeance he could and, faster than he thought possible, Brooks leapt across the desk. Midway to his prey, he felt the sting of a needler dart as it connected with his upper arm. His last thought was of Melanie, the sole survivor, and the fact that she was still not the lucky one.

Olstad stood and callously shoved Brooks's body off his desk. "Don't worry, Clayton. You and Dr. Patula will see each other very shortly." He turned to Thurmond, who holstered his blaster, and pulled Brooks's limp body over to where Noga was lying. "Call Tompkin. Tell him to change course and get his ship back here. We have a gift for Lord Donar."

* * *

Glick glanced at the shuttle chronometer and saw that the admiral's call was, indeed, late. He had waited an extra ten minutes, but the old man had been specific in his orders. Glick powered up the shuttle and keyed his transmitter onto the starbase flight frequency.

"Operations, this is *Shuttle CI-1,* requesting clearance for immediate departure." Glick had completed his preflight check during the previous hour and now just needed proper clearance before he could leave.

"*Shuttle CI-1*, this is Operations. You do *not* have clearance. Please deactivate your engines immediately," the voice said.

Glick looked out his forward viewport. A squad of security men were rushing out, weapons drawn. *This must have been what the admiral suspected,* he thought as he punched his flight controls and sent the shuttle barreling into the night sky.

Energy washed across his rear deflector screen as ineffective ground fire from the men below lanced up at his vessel. With or without clearance, Admiral Brooks had ordered him to rush back to the base if any check-ins were missed. Orders or not, though, Glick hated to abandon the admiral.

He laughed to himself as he realized that it was exactly why Griffin had assigned him to the chauffeur's job. "That bastard *expected* trouble!" he muttered, and trouble was definitely what he had, because the shuttle sensors picked up four high-speed targets leaving the planet and closing in quick, right on his tail.

Bringing the engines up to full power, Glick tried evasive maneuvers, hoping to lose his pursuers. This shuttle was nothing like the high-tech attack fighter he was used to, but it had a few surprises. The admiral had had the foresight to have the shuttle systems completely refit. A strong, alloyed armor had been used to reinforce the hull, and the engine could rival that of many space fighters. It was definitely not standard equipment. Unfortunately, the only offensive weapon the shuttle possessed was a photon cannon beneath the bow. To use it, Glick would have to face the fighters head on, and he knew that would be a suicide mission.

His power levels had gone into the red zone, and the enemies were still closing. *Well, outrunning them is out,* he thought. His computer readout told him that at his present speed, they'd be within firing range in less than one minute.

Left with very few options, Glick began to turn the small shuttle back on his attackers. As he started his turn, a different plan came to mind. He remembered that Allegre IV had a pair of moons. *It's better than nothing,* he decided as he corrected his course and headed for the orbiting planetoids, the fighters still in hot pursuit.

"Shit," Glick said out loud as a photon blast rocked his ship. The cabin lights dimmed but powered back up after a brief moment. "That was too close."

He knew the only reason he had lasted so long was because they had underestimated the capabilities of his shuttle and held back. Now they were firing for range, getting too damn close for his own good. He dived the shuttle over the bleak lunar landscape, his engines already whining in protest as a photon blast obliterated the cratered ridge he had just flown over. He knew if he didn't do something soon, his engines would overheat and blow, or else he'd be shot out of the sky. Neither choice thrilled him.

Glick checked his topographic scan as a photon blast connected with the rear of the shuttle. Alarms sounded, and the internal lights flickered again. If not for the new armor, the first direct hit would have been the last. His power dropped down to 45 percent, and Glick knew his time was quickly running out. The blast had burned out the engine cooling system, and an explosion was imminent if he didn't put her down soon.

He looked at the sensor scan and saw a nearby mountain range. *Hmm. If I can make it there in one piece,* he thought, *I might be able to hide and make repairs.* Another near miss from a fighter convinced him that it wasn't going to be that easy.

Using every last bit of energy he could squeeze out of his crippled engines, Glick reached the mountains ahead of his pursuit. Ducking under an arch of rock, he pulled his shuttle into a tight turn and waited for the fighters to arrive.

He didn't have to wait long before two of the fighters burst through the arch. Seeing him too late, they fired wide, the energy blast missing his ship by thirty meters. Glick targeted both ships and quickly fired off a shot for each of them. His excellent marksmanship was rewarded as his two targets exploded silently and crashed violently to the surface.

While the attack had been successful, it had also depleted Glick's emergency reserves. He couldn't be bothered looking for the other two fighters; instead, he had to scout out a secluded place to set down. When he spotted an opening in the side of the mountain, he used all available power and maneuvered the ship toward it. With the skill of a surgeon, Glick threaded his battered vessel into the dark abyss. He shut down the engines, and the tired, bruised shuttle settled down hard on the rocky surface beneath it. Glick quickly shut off the cabin lights as the fighters crisscrossed outside.

Realizing that he was safe for the moment, he turned to his computer and called up the self-diagnostic program. As the machine automatically checked vital shuttle systems,

Glick could tell from the smoke that the prognosis would not be good. He looked at the damage readout on the display and saw that he had a lot of work ahead of him before he could lift off.

He unbuckled the safety harness and retrieved the emergency toolkit from the supply cabinet. He wasn't really a mechanic, and he knew it, but he was confident that with a little work and a whole lot of luck, he could get the shuttle back into space. As he worked on the burnt-out, melted circuitry, Glick activated his receiver, figuring he might as well monitor the happenings outside while he was busy making repairs.

* * *

Olstad was insane with rage as he listened to Malone's report. "What do you mean, he escaped?"

"The fighters chased the shuttle to the surface of the outer moon. Somehow, it destroyed two of the craft and disappeared," Malone said, not at all happy that he was taking such abuse from Olstad. They were both from the same stock, but the human he had become made it difficult for him to stand up to Olstad in any way.

"Well, find him. Lord Donar will not appreciate it if word gets out, endangering his holy crusade. You will find the shuttle and destroy it, or I will destroy you."

Malone shuddered at the threat. "His ship took a lot of damage in the skirmish. The two remaining fighters have verified it."

"Then his ship should be easy enough to find. Put more fighters into space and destroy it now!" Olstad screamed, then slammed his hand down and ended the conversation.

Malone sat in Operations and tried to think of an excuse

that would coerce more of the humans to risk their lives for him. They were very gullible, and he only had to find the right cause to inspire the fools. *They aren't that different after all,* he thought, with a smile on his face.

* * *

Tompkin sat on the bridge of *Ranger* as it left orbit around Allegre IV. The audacity of Olstad, forcing me to join the search for the shuttle. *The mindless dope has let his new body and memories get the best of him.* If he didn't need the presence of Admiral Olstad to cover for him, he would have killed the fool already.

He had important cargo for Lord Donar – not only the girl but her leader as well. He was certain his master would be quite pleased, and he leaned back in his seat feeling accomplished, knowing that things were going well.

As he relaxed, his intercom flashed on the arm of his chair. "Yes? What is it?" Tompkin snapped grumpily into the comm unit.

"This is sickbay. Could you come down here, Captain?"

"For what reason?" Tompkin asked, not even clear as to why the human sickbay had been reactivated; it was certainly not equipped for anyone of his kind.

"I fell it would be easier to show you, sir," the voice said, fear oozing from it.

"This had better be important, Doctor. I'm on the way," Tompkin said. He then closed the internal channel and left the bridge.

When he reached sickbay, he saw Dowd lying, unconscious, on the examination couch, his body covered to his neck with a blanket.

Tompkin approached the table where the ship doctor

182

was bending over Dowd. "What's wrong with him?" he asked impatiently.

"See for yourself," the doctor said, pulling the blanket away from Dowd's body.

Tompkin, startled, took several steps backward. The body seemed to be slowly decaying, turning back into the claylike mass it had been before and then breaking down. "But what... How did this happen?" Tompkin demanded, revolted by the sight of the decaying mass.

"Dowd came back with a knife wound on the back of his hand," the doctor said, looking helplessly down at his seemingly doomed patient. "I bandaged the wound and put him back on duty. Two hours later, his whole arm had changed. Whatever it is, it's moving quickly through his entire body."

"Can the decay be reversed?" Tompkin asked, hoping for some good news, as Dowd's chances for long-term survival did not look good for any of them.

"No." The doctor then pulled the blanket up over Dowd's head.

Tompkin was none too happy that he now had bad news to report to his master. Not only that, but he realized he had to be very careful himself, if he was going to avoid suffering the same grim fate as Dowd. Donar's army of simulcrons had one major fault: They were extremely fragile and could be destroyed by even the smallest battle wound.

As Tompkin headed back to the bridge, one thought lingered in his mind: *I certainly wouldn't want to be Snatak, once Donar finds out the bitter truth about the little rat's amazing invention.*

CHAPTER 17

Ank opened his eyes and stared up into the bleak red sky. He remembered the grenade explosion, he and Carson hurtling through the air toward the arch. He had tried to throw the human out of the way of the blast, but they were both caught in the tumult. Turning and wincing as a sharp pain lanced through his side, he saw Carson lying a meter away. He was sure he'd re-cracked a rib or two while trying to shield the frail human from the brunt of the explosion, but he didn't regret it.

Ank moved to his unconscious friend and felt his neck for a pulse. When he felt a steady beat beneath his paw, he removed a small med-scanner from the emergency kit on his belt and ran it above the fallen Carson. Except for a slight concussion, the human seemed to be fine. With a groan, the big cat sat back down on the desolate ground, giving the pain in his aching ribs a chance to subside.

He was relieved that Carson would live, for he respected the human almost as an equal. He had heard of Mark Carson and Commando, Inc. before; their exploits were legendary throughout the galaxy. The fact that Admiral Brooks wanted him even after his failure on Solo was a source of pride for Ank. He had enjoyed serving in the Alliance military, but until now, he had never felt as if he'd had a family, at least beyond the surface of Cada III.

Ank shook the emotional thoughts from his mind, as he knew they had more pressing matters to tend to. *This must be the world those creatures came from,* he thought to himself. *No wonder they wanted to leave.* Ank looked at the bleak landscape and wondered if he would ever see home again. The red sky flashed above them, arcs of lightning illuminating the sky, but no rain fell. In fact, he had a feeling that not a drop had touched the thirsty surface in quite some time.

Whatever they did, he knew they couldn't remain there any longer. If they were going to survive, they would have to find food and water. He was sure there had to be some solution, because Donar and his beasts had somehow survived here during their lengthy stay, and they couldn't have used up all the resources. Ank wondered what direction he should go; while Carson would be unconscious for several more hours, he couldn't wait that long to start his trek.

He decided it would be smart to first take an inventory of all the equipment they had at their disposal. They had one blaster pistol, which Carson had been holding during the explosion; Ank picked up the weapon and stuck it in his belt holster. He laid everything else in front of him, though there wasn't much to sort out. There was one canteen, half-full, and he would have to stretch the water as long as he could. The most important piece of equipment they had was Carson's small bio-scanner still clipped to his belt.

Ank activated the scanner and was relieved to see that the instrument still worked. He turned it slowly, searching for signs of life within its five-kilometer range. Just when he was beginning to think his search would prove futile, when the scanner indicated a faint bioreading just inside its range limit. Unfortunately, from that distance, the scanner could not be more specific about the type of life form or the concentration in the area.

Seeing no alternative, Ank collected the rest of his working equipment and, as gently as possible, heaved Carson over his left shoulder. He then started out, planning to head to the location about four and a half kilometers northeast. He was sure that if he could maintain a decent pace, he would reach the life forms within two hours.

* * *

Ank trudged along, the burden on his shoulder becoming heavier and his damaged ribs throbbing more painfully with each step. He would not stop until he found help for Carson, despite the strain. Ank willed his legs to keep moving, knowing that if he faltered, they were both finished.

Ahead of them was a ridge of blackened rock. The bio-scanner quietly insisted that the life form readings were coming from just beyond the other side. He put Carson down and ran the med-scanner over his friend again; he was happy to see that Carson's system seemed to be stabilizing. Ank decided to leave him there, and he ran the rest of the way alone to scout out what was beyond the ridge.

When he reached the ridge and looked beyond, the sight that greeted him was one of nightmarish fascination. Surrounded by great stone walls on every side, a castle stood in the distance, its two tall towers penetrating the red sky. The structure looked ancient, but the bio-scanner sensed that the only living things in the area were concentrated there. As he returned to Carson, he realized there were few alternatives.

Upon reaching Carson, Ank prepared himself for the final part of their journey. He didn't know what awaited them at the castle, but it was the only shelter in the area. Ank turned quickly at the sound of movement coming from behind him. He was elated to see that Carson had regained consciousness and was attempting to rise to his feet.

"Ank, wh-what's going on?" Carson stuttered. "Where are we?" he asked weakly as he unsteadily straightened, then collapsed down to his knees.

Ank rushed over to his friend and gently eased him to the ground. "Take it easy, my friend. You have a concussion."

Carson glanced up at his feline comrade. "Oh? So that's why my head feels like it's been kicked by a gondak. What the hell happened?"

Ank smiled at the image of his friend being kicked by a muscular, one-legged beast. "We were caught in the blast at the cave, and the force threw us through the arch. I am not sure where we are, but it is where we ended up."

"How long have I been out?"

"About three hours," Ank said, then filled Carson in on what he had discovered over the ridge.

"I guess we haven't much choice than to storm the castle then. Are we armed?"

"We have only this blaster," Ank replied, holding up the weapon.

"Then it will have to do." Carson stood but didn't move; something was clearly bothering his team leader.

"Thinking of the others?" Ank asked, something that had been on his own mind during most of their trek.

"Yes. We've gotta get back. Those bastards took Melanie, and I won't believe Josh is dead till I see his body for myself."

"Then in that case, we should get moving. If that's Donar's lair, we might find something there to help us get back."

Carson couldn't argue with his friend's logic. He collected himself and followed the felinoid up the ridge, then down to the castle, even though they weren't armed for trouble. The blaster was only charged at 40 percent, and he had one dagger remaining on his left wrist.

As they approached the castle, Carson couldn't help but remember the old horror stories he had loved while growing up. *Evil mad scientists and vampires often reside in similar structures,* Carson thought.

It took only a few moments for the mismatched pair to reach the stone barrier that separated them from the structure within. The weather, or lack thereof, seemed to grow more violent by the minute. Fire, seemingly generated from Hell itself, flashed across the deep red sky, but the temperature dropped as the wind picked up in intensity.

"We've gotta find a way inside. We won't last much longer out here," Carson said, observing their need for shelter from the harsh elements.

Ank wrapped his large arms around his body; he had a great dislike for the cold. Cada III was a relatively warm world, and its people were rarely subjected to extremes in temperature. "You are right, Carson. We must scout for an entrance," he said with a shiver.

"Right. We'll circle around the barrier together. Let's go," Carson said as he gathered their few supplies.

As they walked the outside of the stone perimeter, stopping occasionally to examine certain weak-looking sections of the ancient walls, Ank suddenly froze in place.

Carson looked over at his friend and realized the felinoid's body had stopped moving, but his eyes were scanning the terrain. "What's the matter?" he asked.

With his back to the wall, Ank announced, "We are being watched." The blaster had quickly made its way to his large paw. "There, about twenty-five meters out," he said, pointing. "Do you see them?"

Carson peered out into the darkness. While he couldn't see anything, he trusted Ank's eyes, which were far more sensitive than his own, especially in the dark. When fire again flashed across the sky, illuminating the area Ank had pointed to, Carson could barely make out several lumbering shapes, and they were coming closer. "I saw something," he said. "I'm not sure what it is though." His left wrist turned to release his remaining dagger into his hand. As his eyes readjusted to the darkness following the atmospheric flash, Carson made out pairs of glowing orbs moving ever closer. "Whoever they are, they're coming this way."

"They are stalking us, trying to surround us," Ank said, the fur on his back standing on end as he tracked their unseen enemy with the blaster.

Carson and Ank froze as a loud, piercing howl filled the darkness.

Ank began to fire his weapon when the creatures attacked, felling them as quickly as he could. As one fell, though, another quickly moved in to take its place.

Out of the corner of his right eye, Carson saw one of the creatures lunge at him, baring its large, sharp teeth. With a flick of his wrist, he buried his remaining dagger in the creature's throat, dropping it to the ground. Whatever it was, it was quite similar to the distorted thing that had attacked them in the arch chamber several days prior. "How many of these things are there?" Carson said as he tried to keep track of the creatures out in the darkness.

They were becoming more wary in their attacks, for at least a dozen of them littered the ground. For a moment, the onslaught stopped, as if they were regrouping for their next attack run. For the moment, the blaster had given them a slight edge.

"There are more out there, and my blaster is almost depleted," Ank announced.

When the power pack in the grip of the blaster approached a 10 percent charge, the indicator blinked amber, indicating the need for replacement. When it was red, the weapon would be powerless, allowing their enemies to tear them apart.

"Ank, to the left!" Carson cried when he saw another creature charging.

Ank fired, and the blast tore the creature in half. After that shot, the indicator glowed a steady red, signaling that their time was almost up. He held the weapon up so Carson could see the scarlet glow.

"Don't tell me the blaster's drained already," Carson said, hoping the sky was to blame for the red hue.

"Sorry, but it is." To prove his point, Ank squeezed the trigger, producing only a sharp *click*.

"I asked you not to tell me that," Carson said as they backed closer to the wall.

The creatures seemed to sense a change in the situation and grew bolder. They came at them slowly and methodically as they realized their prey was now helpless. When they got within two meters, though, they stopped.

A brave one started to move forward on its own. It was huge, a furry body supporting a large, bulbous head. Its jaws were open, and saliva dripped to the ground from sharp teeth. It seemed to be the pack leader, as it was easily twice the size of the others, and it seemed to be granted the honor of shedding their blood first. After the first kill, the others would join in.

Frantically, Carson and Ank looked around for a rock or club, anything they could employ as a weapon. It seemed hopeless, though, as nothing feasible could be found. They would have to fight hand to hand, or rather, hand to jaws. Unfortunately, against those freakish jaws, even Ank had no chance.

The other creatures howled with impatience, ready to feast.

The huge, nightmarish creature crouched low and sprung, its jaws open and its claws extended.

Ank and Carson stood, each awaiting his fate in his own way. Ank growled loudly, but Carson stood silently as the end hungrily approached.

* * *

Melanie opened her eyes and stared blankly at the ceiling above her. Her body felt numb as the drug they had given her on Solo began to wear off. She leaned up on her elbows and took in her new surroundings. She was obviously not onboard a ship, as the night sky was visible through a plasticine window at the far end of the room.

It was not the average detention cell either, because the bed beneath her was quite comfortable, and a small dressing table and mirror stood to the left of the window, with a plain wooden chair sitting in front of it.

Melanie slowly stood. The room spun around her, so she grabbed the side of the bed to steady herself. She moved carefully to the wall and felt it in several places, until she found a small switch. When she flicked it, the room was bathed in light. As her eyes adjusted to the brilliant onslaught, she was finally able to see more clearly, and she gave the room a closer inspection. She found that besides the bed, the chair, and the table, the room was barren.

Melanie did notice two doors though. One led to a lavatory, which she would need very shortly, but the other was locked; where that door led, she didn't know. She walked over to the door and examined the locking mechanism. Had she not been stripped of her tools, she could have opened it in no time.

Raising her fists, she pounded hard on the door. "Let me out of here!" she screamed, hoping someone would come.

Frustrated, she sat back on the bed. She had no idea what had happened to Mark and the others, for Dowd had thrown her back to his men before the explosion. The blast had brought the ceiling crashing down, effectively sealing off the chamber.

Before she'd even had time to contemplate her capture, Dowd had come back smiling. Holding his injured hand, he'd told her that her friends were dead. At that point, she had lashed out at him. Breaking free of the others, she'd delivered a hard kick to Dowd's head, sending him to the ground. Before they could restrain her, she had dived on top of the startled security chief, wrapping her hands tightly around his thick throat. The others had to pull her off, but not before an amazing vision had come to her. As she had squeezed his neck, she'd seen a strange world, cloaked in a blood-red sky. As she was pulled free, Melanie could have sworn she saw Mark and Ank there as well.

Dowd had not been very happy with her, and he had promptly backhanded her; she would have sagged to the floor if the others had not held her up. Dowd had then grabbed at her long hair, and she had spat in his face. Enraged, he'd bared his teeth, snarled, and kicked her in the stomach, then finally stuck a hypo roughly into her arm, drugging her unconscious.

How much time had passed, she did not know, nor did she know where she was. She lay back on the bed, hoping Mark and the others were all right and that her vision of him under that fantastic crimson sky was true. If that was the case, he was still alive, and she held on to that small shred of hope as she closed her eyes and fell quickly asleep.

* * *

Some time later, light streamed into her room, and Melanie opened her eyes. Feeling a bit more refreshed than the night before, she got out of bed and moved to the window. Beyond the clear, alloyed windows, she saw people loading a transport ship with supplies. Her vantage point was only a few meters above the surface, so she couldn't make out very much detail.

As she tried to get a better view, something threw itself against the outside of her window. Startled by the projectile, Melanie stumbled back and fell on her posterior. She screamed when she saw that it was similar to the wolflike thing that had chased her in her nightmare. She dropped back and hid behind the bed as the thing tried to get at her, powerfully slamming its body against the window in a frenzy.

"No!" she screamed into her hands when she heard the window crack.

Finally, unable to take the strain of the pounding, the creature jumped into the room, the window exploding into thousands of sharp pieces.

Melanie looked up as the creature approached. She saw the bloodlust in its glowing eyes. It growled at her as it approached, its mouth open and its fangs dripping saliva. She crouched behind the bed and threw a pillow at it. The werewolf raised a sharp-clawed paw and shredded the soft object, sending it to the floor.

"Get away!" Melanie cried as it reached out and threw the bed to the side.

It stood over her and howled, the horrifying sound filling the small room. As the creature bent down, its sharp teeth ready to tear into her soft flesh, Melanie lashed out with her booted feet, kicking the face of the startled creature and causing it to stagger. Enraged and in pain, the creature charged her, and all Melanie could do was sit against the wall, awaiting her cruel fate.

Just as she closed her eyes, though, she heard the unmistakable sound of a blaster, and the nightmarish teeth-gnasher was flung back and crashed into the desk by the window.

She quickly stood and looked at the source of the blast. She was surprised to see Mark Carson standing by the door, the barrel of the blaster pistol cooling in his hand.

"Are you all right?" Carson asked.

She stared at him, not believing her own eyes. "Mark, is that you? How did you find me?"

"Of course it's me," he said matter-of-factly. "Who did

you expect?"

"I don't know, but I'm happy to see you," Melanie finally stammered. "Where are the others?"

"They're dead, Melanie. They were both crushed by debris when the explosion brought the ceiling down. I barely made it out alive myself."

Melanie dropped down to the bed. She just stared ahead, her face a blank page. Josh had been more than a close friend; he was more like an older brother. As for Ank, even though she had not known him long, he'd quickly become part of her extended family. She struggled to make sense of everything that had happened, and her grief felt like an open wound. *No. Grief is a normal human feeling, and I should not have such luxuries*, she thought as she stood and walked over to the dead creature on the floor.

Melanie stuck out her foot and kick the creature in the side of the head. She had hoped the gesture would ease her sorrow, but it didn't. "That thing tried to kill me." She looked at the werewolf Carson had shot and the large, dark hole burnt into its chest. Even in death, the thing seemed to be reaching out for her, trying to devour her from some unknown afterlife.

Feeling a sense of revulsion for the thing that had just tried to kill her and desperately needing some comforting, she turned and ran over to Carson.

Strangely, Carson held his hand out, stopping her before she reached him.

"Mark, what's the matter?"

He looked at her, then glanced down the corridor. "We have to get out of here. There are a whole lot more of those things lurking about," he said as he motioned for her to follow him. He then led her out of the room and through the building, as if he'd been there a thousand times.

"Mark, where are we going?" she asked when she realized they were winding downward; that was quite odd, since they had started out at ground level.

"We have to free one of the other prisoners before we head back to the ship," he said as he opened the door before them, then led her down to the subbasement level.

A long, dark corridor welcomed them, lined with barred cages on each side. They walked slowly to a cell at the far end of the block, then stopped. Melanie saw a ragged figure huddled on the floor at the rear of the cell. When the pile of rags shifted, a face became visible.

She let out a startled cry as she realized that it was the face of Admiral Clayton Brooks. "Admiral, is that you?" she asked, moving closer to the ancient, rusty bars.

The battered face looked up at her. "Melanie?" the voice said weakly.

"Mark, we have to get him out," she cried out to Carson.

"I don't think so," Carson said. He then gripped her shoulder and pulled her into a tight hug.

With the contact, visions rushed through Melanie's mind, all disjointed and horrible. She tried to pull away but was locked into the tight embrace. "Let me go!" she screamed hysterically.

"Why? Isn't this where you've always wanted to end up, in my arms?"

The visions became a form of physical punishment as the Carson evil twin held her tightly to him. It took every ounce of her concentration to ward off the horrible images. Deep in her mind, Melanie felt herself running; something was chasing her, its sharp teeth flashing in the darkness. A deep panic grew within her. The images were somehow force-fed into her, and she was ill equipped to block them. She knew if she couldn't stop them soon, insanity would soon follow.

In her mind, she saw Mark and ran to him. He smiled at her, and her fear eased. Suddenly she froze in terror as his smile revealed sharp fangs, blood dripping from them. "No!" she screamed as the rape of her mind continued.

Reeling from the horrible mental attack, Melanie was unprepared for the next shock. The figure that was holding her quivered and changed, its shape altering. Her nightmare suddenly entered waking reality as Melanie looked up and saw a long, reptilian head full of sharp teeth and staring menacingly down at her. The arms that were wrapped around her had transformed into tentacled feelers.

Melanie did the only thing anyone could do in a situation like hers: She fainted.

Donar glanced down at the woman he was holding in his grasp and laughed quietly to himself. "Was it something I said, my dear?" he joked to himself as he lifted her up and carried her to the admiral's cell. *It would be so easy to snap the poor little creature's neck,* Donar thought. *No, there will be time for that later, after I have no further use for her.*

Brooks stirred as Donar opened the cell door and carried Melanie inside.

"Look, Admiral. I've brought you a present," he said as he dropped her on the hard floor.

Brooks pulled his battered body over to Melanie and cradled her head in his lap. Tears came to his eyes as he held the unconscious woman who was like a daughter to him. He looked up at Donar, staring into his black, emotionless eyes, and rage filled him. "I'll kill you," he murmured from between cracked lips.

Donar stopped as he closed the cell door behind him. "Admiral Brooks, believe me when I tell you that in a very short time, you will not want to kill me. In fact, I will become the most important thing in your life. Unfortunately, you will not be around to enjoy it."

Donar then turned and left the chamber, his laughter chilling Brooks to his very soul. They had cruelly tortured his mind and body, and now that they had Melanie, he felt completely downtrodden and defeated. He had seen what they had done to Olstad and the others, and he was sure they had the same fate in mind for him and for the young woman he so adored.

"Don't worry, Melanie," he whispered, petting her hair. "I won't let them hurt you," he promised, though he knew he was quite powerless to stop them.

CHAPTER 18

Carson and Ank lunged quickly in opposite directions as the creature cleaved the air between them. Growing angrier that its slices fell short, the creature glared at them on either side of it and snarled. Carson tumbled over and hopped to his feet as it turned toward him to make another attempt at a kill. Seeing that their prey was now divided, the pack began to close in on the human as well. The large creature, though, still wanted the first kill and growled at its inferiors, causing them to retreat a few steps.

Since all of its attention was now on Carson, Ank made his move. Silently moving behind the stalking creature, Ank grabbed it by its muscular tail. With all his strength, he tossed the beast several meters through the air. With a yelp of pain, it landed amongst the pack with a dull *thud*. Ank moved quickly to Carson and helped him up even before it landed.

"Thanks," Carson said as he slowly got to his feet.

Ank nodded as they both backed to the wall.

The creature was now enraged. Taking no chances, it advanced again, this time backed up by the pack.

Carson was shocked by an unexpected vibration behind him as the wall began to shake, then slid back. Two small, black-cloaked figures ran out, clutching silvery tubes in their hands. Stepping in front of the startled pair, they pointed the tubes at the advancing beasts. Concentrated streams of energy lashed out, their power lighting the darkness, and wherever they touched, they left death in their wake. In no time, the pack was decimated as the bright yellow beam slashed through their ranks.

Carson and Ank watched in amazement as the few remaining creatures turned and ran off into the darkness.

"Thank you," Carson finally said. "My name is – "

Before he could finish his introduction, the two figures turned and pointed the deadly weapons at them.

Ank tensed, as if he planned to make a move of his own.

Carson put a hand on his friend's muscular shoulder. "Relax, Ank."

The strangers pointed their weapons into the darkness of the corridor they had just stepped out of, gesturing for them to enter.

Ank seemed hesitant till Carson nodded his approval and started in first.

As they entered the corridor, they saw lit torches hanging in wall sconces, illuminating the passage in a ghostly greenish-yellow, flickering glow. Carson glanced back and saw that their two tiny rescuers were still behind them, but the powerful weapons were still pointed at their backs. The wall slid into place, sealing them in.

Silently, they walked down the corridor until they reached a featureless wall. One of the figures handed his weapon to the other and moved to the rocky surface. The small one placed a hand on the wall and asserted pressure on three points, then stood back. With a loud, rumbling vibration, the wall slid aside. Once both cloaked figures had a weapon in hand again, they motioned for Carson and Ank to move forward.

"You guys aren't real talkative, are ya?" Carson said to

the two armed but silent figures as the inner wall slid shut behind them.

As they entered the large inner courtyard, Ank gazed up at the massive towers. "Well, we're inside. Now what?"

"I don't know. Let's take it one step at a time."

Ank nodded as they were marched up a narrow path, toward the entrance of the castle. The size of the structure was impressive, but that wasn't the cause for the shiver that peppered Carson's spine. He couldn't explain it, but if evil had a physical manifestation, that was it.

As they passed through the front courtyard, they saw others gathering to gawk at them, strange and curious creatures who wanted to get a better look at the giant newcomers. Carson slowed to look back at them, but the muzzle of one of the shiny silvery weapons pushed into his back. He took the hint, and after glaring back at his diminutive captor, increased his pace.

The doors seemed to open on their own as they entered the ancient edifice. The interior was in the same condition as the outside; age and deterioration had taken its toll. As they walked through the enormous foyer, Carson had a feeling that the structure had been dying for a long time and had just recently entered its terminal phase.

They entered another room, where a fireplace glowed with warmth at the far end. By the front of the fireplace sat a chair. One of their small captures moved to the door and slowly shut it, preventing the warmth from escaping the small room.

A form began to stir in the large chair.

Carson motioned for Ank to be on his guard.

"Put your weapons down, my children, and get our

guests something to drink," a voice quietly said from the chair.

The two small figures disappeared.

The source of the voice slowly stood and turned to meet them. "Gentlemen, please have a seat." An ancient human stood before them, adorned in a simple cloth robe. He pointed a gnarled finger at two chairs that were sitting near the fire.

"Thank you," Carson said, and he and Ank both sat down. "My name is – "

Again, his introduction was interrupted, for the two black-cloaked figures returned, each with a mug containing a steaming-hot, thick, red liquid.

"Carson," the old one said. "Yes, I know your names, but for now, please drink. I do hope you like it. The broth is made of local herbs and a few of my own spices," the old man said to them.

Carson and Ank looked at each other as they took the mugs.

"There are easier ways to kill you than poison, of course," the withered man explained.

"Of course," Carson said. He slowly moved the steaming liquid up to his lips and took a small, tentative sip. "Mmm. Not bad. Try some, Ank."

Ank sniffed the concoction carefully before bringing the mug to his muzzle. With his first taste satisfactory, Ank quickly finished the rest. "It is very good. Thank you. You know our names, yet we do not know yours."

"You may call me Atlo," the elderly man said.

The two mysterious figures returned and stood beside him, one on each side.

"I am pleased that you like it, for it will help you regain your strength quickly. Now, if you could be so kind, perhaps you could tell me what you are doing here."

Carson took one more sip from his mug before he began his story. Filling in as much as he could with Ank's help, he slowly, and with as much detail as possible, told Atlo of what had transpired during the past week.

When they finished their terrible tale, the old man sat back in his chair, his face drained of color.

The two figures that flanked him seemed restless, and one leaned over and whispered to the seated man.

"Atlo, are you all right?" Carson asked, sensing the grief on the man's face.

Atlo turned back to his guests. "I will be fine. Donar escaped from here. I am sorry I could not stop him."

Carson sighed and leaned back into his chair. "Can you explain?"

Both he and Ank could see the pained expression on Atlo's face as he began his own tale of terror. "Where should I begin?" he said, as much to himself as for the others.

"The beginning is usually sufficient," Ank said, placing the empty mug down on a small table by the side of his chair.

"Well, my story begins uncounted centuries ago," Atlo commenced quietly. "Believe it or not, this wrinkled one before you is a brilliant geneticist, and my research was everything to me. I looked for ways to improve the human condition, for the world was so encumbered by needless suffering. Disease was destroying people before their time, making them suffer. The air and water were grossly polluted, making life more difficult every day. I tried to create an...ultimate survivor, one who could thrive in the darkest of futures. I combined the genetic material of several of the hardier species, from several planets, with human DNA."

"And were you successful?" Ank asked.

"At first, I was. I created a whole new form of life – human but with all the best traits the universe could offer. It was equipped with superior intelligence and physical strength far beyond the normal ranges. I raised it and taught my protégée everything I knew about genetics, but something went horribly wrong."

When a solitary tear rolled down the old man's weathered cheek, two robed figures each grabbed an arm in a comforting hold.

"What went wrong?" Carson coaxed. He had already pieced most of it together himself, but he wanted Atlo to finish the story.

Atlo took a deep breath and continued, "Arrogance, greed, ambition...and quite a bit more, I'm sure you can imagine, my boy. Sometimes, even the best things of others cannot peacefully coexist. The more my creation learned, the more superior he felt over everyone and everything else."

"You're talking about Donar, aren't you?" Carson said quietly.

Atlo stiffened at the sound of his name. "Yes, though the name I gave him was 'Patac,'" he said, a glimmer of pride sparkling in his eye. "In the language of my people, it means 'peace.' He took that foul name when he rejected all I tried to teach him about life. He perverted my experiments, turned them into horrors." The concealed rage Carson had noticed lurking behind the surface of the old one's countenance suddenly rushed out into the open. "Life was no longer sacred to him, and he made a mockery of it, carelessly genetically combining completely unknown creatures into bloodthirsty mutants. He even experimented on his own cell structure."

"His transformations?" Ank said in a growl.

Atlo slowly nodded. "Yes. He can alter his own molecular structure to whatever form he chooses."

"What happened next?" Carson asked.

"Donar saw the possibilities in his mutant army. He wanted to spread his form of genetic perfection throughout the universe. First, he subjugated his own people, and then he and his creatures took their unholy crusade to the stars."

Carson looked at the tired old man thoughtfully. "Those ruins on the other side of the portal? That was your city," he said more than asked.

"Yes," Atlo said sadly. "My people revolted, and Donar had them destroyed, all but me. He needed me, or so he said. Donar used his home world as a base to strike out at neighboring sectors of space."

Carson could see the old man tiring from his story, as if it needed an extreme force of will to continue. "Go on," he prodded.

"He forced me to go along with his vile plans, forced me to help him make monsters." Atlo looked down at his feet, unable to make eye contact with either of his guests.

Carson felt pity for the man sitting before him, a man who'd harbored such a huge burden of guilt for countless centuries. "Wasn't there any resistance by the other worlds?"

Atlo looked up at Carson and sighed. "Donar approached each in a different form. Sometimes he was a messiah he'd uncovered from their religious past or as a trader bringing needed goods. There were many other disguises he wore to exploit them, depending on the planet. Once he garnered their trust, he turned on them, releasing his hordes of monsters to rip them to shreds. Some of them even joined him and helped to destroy their own people."

"He experimented on the inhabitants of each planet?"

"Yes, Ank, and he used his captives for a variety of reasons. Those he did not use for experiments, he killed or put to work as slaves. If they turned out correctly, they joined his army. If not, they were destroyed or cast out. You have already met two examples," Atlo said.

Carson and Ank both looked at him curiously.

The old human's face finally broke into a smile.

Carson, seeing the grin on Alto's face, decided to take a guess. "The first are obviously those things outside. Were they too dangerous even for Donar?"

"Dangerous indeed. The first he created attacked and almost killed him. The second are my two friends here," he said, placing his arms around the waists of the two cloaked figures. "All right, my children. It is time to show your manners."

The two small figures each pulled down their hoods, revealing their faces to the two amazed visitors.

"Incredible," Carson said quietly.

The two figures before him had the faces of children, both identical but different in some way. Their soft, round faces were topped with curly, blond hair. The only thing that differentiated them from human children were the pointy ears on the sides of their heads.

"Introduce yourselves," Atlo prompted them.

They both stepped forward, extending their small hands.

Carson took the offered hand and shook it, noticing how soft and smooth it was, like a babe's.

"Hello, Carson. My name is Dute," the childlike voice said. Though soft, the voice had a definite masculine quality to it.

"My pleasure, Dute," Carson said with a smile.

After their hands disengaged, Dute moved over to Ank and repeated the introduction.

The other elflike figure walked over and extended a hand to Carson. "Hello, Carson. My name is Lota."

Carson noted that the voice, though as soft as Dute's, was otherwise feminine. Lota was not as quick as her companion to release his hand, and her bright, blue-green eyes seemed to melt into his soul. "Hello, Lota. It's nice to meet you," he said as he flashed the brightest smile he could offer her.

She still stared at him as she repeated the greeting to Ank, albeit not with the same excitement.

Dute walked over and shook his companion by her small shoulders, finally pulling her gaze off him and her body back to Atlo's chair.

As the elfish creatures took their places again by Atlo's side, the old man continued, "First, Donar created those horrible killing machines outside. They were too violent to control, even for him. Then," he said, looking at Dute and Lota, "he created them, creatures incapable of violence."

"They seemed quite capable outside," Ank said sarcastically.

Lota stepped forward, wearing a stern look appearing on her face. "We didn't want to hurt them, but we had to save you," she said, her eyes still on Carson.

Ank took the reprimand in stride. "My apologies, little one...and also my thanks."

That seemed to pacify Lota, who smiled again and took her place by Atlo.

"He used them as servants, then gave them to his troops for training," Atlo said with distaste.

Carson nodded, understanding what Atlo didn't care to put into words: The peaceful creatures were given to Donar's troops and torn apart for pleasure. "How was he stopped?"

"I finally convinced the authorities of the threat. They began to fight back, eventually forcing him back to our decaying city. By that time, the galactic forces had decimated much of Donar's army. They had us trapped, but even after all he had done, I couldn't bear to see him destroyed," Atlo said, his eyes pleading.

"So you used the arch?" Carson said, finishing the old man's thought.

"Yes. I told them I would help, for a price. I asked that his life be spared."

Ank stared at the old man, his anger difficult to hide. "Why?"

"He was my creation...my son, in many ways," he said, almost choking on the words.

"Who built the arch?" Carson asked.

"I was involved with the project in its early construction. Donar thought he could use it for escape. It was originally designed to transport matter anywhere in the galaxy, but I reprogrammed it and sent him here," Atlo said defiantly. "The arch was too unstable, deemed too hazardous for use. It had been deactivated by the Science Council, the chamber sealed off."

"If it was unstable, why did Donar risk using it?"

Atlo shrugged his shoulders in response to Carson's question. "He was desperate. His soldiers were decimated, and for all intents and purposes, he had lost. He really did not have much of a choice. I went ahead to set the machine, but he sent his lackey, Modok, along with me."

Carson could see Ank stiffen momentarily but turned his attention back to Atlo. "He didn't trust you?"

"No. Donar trusts no one," Atlo said, shaking his head. "He would only go if I went first. I managed to program my DNA pattern into the console so that only a true human could reopen the portal, not one of his mutant army. I hoped that after an extended time away from other beings, he might understand where he'd gone wrong and change."

Carson stood from his chair and looked around. "Atlo, what is this place? Where are we, exactly?"

"The arch allowed me to open a doorway to a parallel dimension. I searched for a place of beauty, someplace where Donar's thoughts might turn from the terrible course he had locked his life on."

Carson had a hard time imagining the decrepit, dried-up planet as a paradise. "It obviously didn't work," he said.

"No, it did not. He resumed his research, experimenting with the local life forms. I had locked the planet inside a force field to keep the occupants of this dimension from discovering Donar and the remnants of his dangerous creations. Unbeknownst to me, though, it also kept the effects of time out as well," Atlo said with regret. "He had plenty of time for his experiments."

"And he discovered that you had helped to trap him?" Ank asked.

"Yes."

"Why didn't he just kill you? He doesn't seem to be the very forgiving type."

"I am not sure why, exactly, but he instead transformed himself into that hideous reptile thing as a reminder to me of the horror he would visit on the outside if he ever broke free. When your science expedition to my planet opened the arch, it gave Donar his opportunity."

"Why didn't he take you with him?" Ank asked.

"He wants me to remain a prisoner here, along with his other disappointments until he needs me again."

"Is there any way back?" Carson asked.

Atlo shook his head. "I'm sorry, but I do not know of any. The arch can only be activated from the console in the arch chamber, but you said your friend was shot down and the chamber was sealed off."

"So we're trapped?" Ank said, scratching his head with an extended claw from his paw.

"I am afraid so, my friends. You are welcome to join us," Atlo offered.

Carson sat down and considered his options. "We saw some of the others out front. How many are here?"

Atlo thought to himself for a moment. "In the compound? About forty."

"Are they all like Dute and Lota?" Carson inquired.

"No. Donar left a number of different mutations here. Why do you ask?" Atlo asked, trying to figure out Carson's line of reasoning.

"If we're going to survive here for very long, we have to start reclaiming the planet. For all of Dute's and Lota's wonderful qualities, I'm sure they are not typically used to killing those things outside," Carson responded. He would be damned if he was just going to exist forever on that barren rock.

Dute and Lota seemed confused by his words.

"Why would we want to go outside the walls, Carson?" the small female asked.

"We have everything we want here – food, water, friends, shelter, and everything to sustain us. Why should we risk hardship and death outside?" her male counterpart added.

Before Carson could say anything in response, Atlo answered, "I understand what Carson is saying, my children. To sustain oneself is not enough. Life is meant to be lived, not merely survived." He turned to Carson and nodded. "I agree. To simply exist is not enough. We will help, won't we, little ones?"

Dute and Lota seemed to consider it briefly, then nodded almost simultaneously.

Carson turned to Ank, who seemed to be lost in thought. "What about you, my friend?"

Ank stood and walked over to his human friend. He stopped in front of him and put both of his paws on Carson's shoulders. "As I told you before, I will be there when you need me. Besides, we have no other choice. Still, I will not give up on the idea of getting home."

"Agreed," Carson said to his large, furry friend.

"Atlo, can I ask you for a favor?" Ank asked, turning to face the old man.

"Ask, and if it is in my power, it is yours."

"Do you have any more of that broth? I'm quite hungry," the felinoid said, rubbing his rumbling stomach with a furry paw.

Carson laughed hard and fell back into his chair. His laughter was contagious, and Atlo and the two elves soon joined him in a chorus of chuckles.

"Of course. Lota," Atlo said, and the female elf scurried off to fetch more of the tasty broth. "Gentleman, please sit with me before the fire. We have much to discuss."

Carson pulled up his chair and sat down next to the miniature inferno. He was concerned about getting home, but for the time being, they were in the best place they could possibly be. For now, he could only hope everything in their universe was working out for the best.

CHAPTER 19

Donar sat in the back of the heavily armored land skimmer as the small craft carried him to the operations center. The inspection had gone well, and he approved of the work that had been done to turn the small mining colony into an armed camp. *There is no further reason to hide our existence,* he thought as he passed row after row of assorted space vessels.

They had been on Nexus III for nearly a month, during which his base had been built into a fortress stronghold. Barracks had been constructed to house his own creations, as well as his growing hordes of hired mercenaries, who worked cheaply and without question.

The landing field contained a great variety of spacecraft, many of which were still being adapted to his needs by mercenary technicians. His selection of acquired and donated vessels was vast; he had everything from a battlecruiser to small, single-seat fighters, all fueled and ready for his command to launch. He was especially proud of the ten Dreedan starcruisers Tompkin had appropriated during a raid on a Dreedan military depot just within their Imperial boundaries. Even now, he had plans for the delta-winged starships, as well as for all the others sitting on the field.

The raids into both Dreedan and Alliance territory had gone well. Accusations and counteraccusations between the two galactic powers had stretched tensions almost to the breaking point. Vast fleets of battlecraft were gathering in the stars above at opposite sides of the frontier boundary. War was a certainty. With one final push, the killing would begin.

The Olstad simulcron had counseled him about the changing times. Space was too vast for either galactic power to properly safeguard all their outer colonies. Thus, those colonies were ripe for the taking, but attacking the heart of the Alliance was another story entirely. As they were, they were no match for the Alliance Fleet. Eventually, Donar would be stopped, and all their efforts would prove futile.

It was certainly not how he preferred to operate. Too many uncontrollable variables remained, but he was patient, if nothing else. After waiting centuries for vengeance, a few more days or even weeks would not matter. The mighty star fleets of both of his enemies would destroy each other, leaving their throats open for his strike to follow. In the chaos of destruction, he would lead his followers to their rightful place in creation.

While they were occupied in space with their meaningless combat, he would rip out the belly of the Alliance, and he would not wait for the end of the war to start. All of his agents, human and simulcron alike, had been summoned for a conference of war. The time for waiting was over. Both he and his followers needed the universe to bleed again. At that very moment, the werewolf guard was growing impatient, hungry for blood, and there had already been incidents between his creatures and the human rabble he had hired. Some of the vermin had died, but that was to be expected; sooner or later, they would all meet their end.

The skimmer stopped by the entrance of the operations

center. Once used to house the administrative government of Nexus III, the multilevel structure was the only one large enough to suit his purposes. Two werewolf guards stood at attention as their master stepped down from the vehicle and walked past them and into the building.

As he entered, he saw Modok lumbering toward him. The war chief fell in by his master's side as they continued down the corridor.

"Is all in order?" Donar asked.

"Yes, My Lord. They are all waiting for you in the briefing area."

"Good. We will begin immediately."

They continued down the long corridor until they reached a pair of heavy wooden doors. A werewolf stood guard, clutching its energy weapon tightly in sharp-clawed paws. Moving past the guard, Modok swung the doors open and allowed his master to enter ahead of him.

Donar took his place at the head of the large, rectangular table. Modok sat to his right, opposite Barton, who sat to his master's left. The other simulcrons gravitated together. Joining Barton on Donar's left were Tompkin, Olstad, Thurmond, and the recently transformed Noga. To Modok's right sat Snatak and three of the mercenaries, two humans and a Luto.

Barton stood and gestured to the three figures at the far end of the table. "My Lord, allow me to introduce our mercenary recruiter, Regar Weent."

Donar turned to the human and immediately sized him up as someone who was not to be trusted.

After the introduction, Weent stood to introduce his two companions. "I decided to bring my second-in-command,

Jackson, to the meeting. This is D'ucto," Weent said, pointing to the Luto. Weent's distaste for the alien was quite apparent in the manner in which he introduced the tall insect. "He represents the interests of the members of his race who will be working with us."

"Sit down, Weent." The human disgusted Donar, but for the moment, he needed him.

At the sound of Donar's voice, Weent quickly took his seat.

Once he had everyone's attention, Donar stood and faced his seated War Council. "Good. Now I will dispense with any formalities and begin with the reason you have all been summoned. It is time for our conquest to begin."

"With all due respect, My Lord, it is about time!"

"Silence, Modok," Donar snapped.

"My Lord, is it advisable to move this quickly?"

At the sound of the ridiculous question, Donar turned to face Barton. "The time for stealth is over, simulcron. We own this system and control the others that border us. Our people are growing restless, with good reason. It is time for the crusade to begin."

Tompkin nodded his agreement and faced his master. "Master, what is your plan?"

"First, we will remove the two obstacles. Admiral Olstad..." Donar motioned to the older simulcron.

"Yes, Lord?"

"What is the alert status of the Alliance base on Allegre IV?"

"We're still looking for the wreckage of Brooks's shuttle. All of the base pilots and attackcraft are occupied in the search."

"Good. You will return there with Thurmond and prepare for my eventual arrival. It will serve as my command base in this sector."

"What of the remaining humans?"

"They will be eliminated. I will send a large enough force of captured Dreedan attack craft with you to destroy any resistance. The appearance of a Dreedan attack on an Alliance installation will also cause panic. The creatures in the military will call for rapid retaliation, and war will further escalate. Do I make myself clear?"

"Yes, My Lord," Olstad responded quickly. "I will personally see to it that a distress call is sent at the proper time, identifying our attackers. But what of our need for continued secrecy of operations?"

"When events begin to unfold, there will be no further need for these games." Donar sat back down in his seat and continued his briefing. "Noga..."

"Yes, My Lord?" the large simulcron called out as he leapt to his feet.

"There is a small light-speed cruiser waiting at the landing field. Take Weent and two others and return to your Commando, Inc. asteroid headquarters."

"What if they question the location of Admiral Brooks?" Noga asked.

"You will simply tell them that he decided to remain on Allegre IV with Admiral Olstad to discuss...battle tactics," Donar said with a brief hesitation.

"Perhaps it would be better if I went alone, My Lord."

"No! Your lie will not hold up under deep scrutiny. The operation must be accomplished with haste. Even without Brooks or Carson, they are still a threat and must be destroyed."

"Yes, My Lord," Noga said, nodding.

"Once they have allowed you to land, you must use your advantage of surprise."

"The security force is well trained. The creature would accept no less. If we are going to use force, how do we penetrate security? It will be especially difficult around the fusion reactor."

Donar reached into one of the deep pockets of his long robe and pulled out a small capsule. Holding it out to the others, with a whip-like snap of his tentacle, he quickly threw the small object into the far corner of the room. As it impacted with the floor, the capsule burst open. Billows of dense smoke drifted up to the ceiling of the large room.

The members of the War Council quickly panicked as the smoke began to drift toward them.

Donar put both large tentacles out in front of them and blocked their escape. "Everyone stay where you are," he said. "It is a simple smoke capsule, and it's already clearing."

Everyone saw, to their relief, that his words rang true. The smoke was dense, but it did not seem harmful in any way.

"This, Noga, is how you will accomplish your task. When filled to capacity with my micro-condensed gas, there will be more than enough to incapacitate the entire complement. It will be colorless and odorless, and they will have no time to react, for they will fall unconscious immediately after exposure." Donar then removed another capsule and placed it on the desk in front of Noga.

The simulcron looked at it, then glanced questioningly back up at his master.

"You do know what to do with it, don't you?" Donar asked.

Noga slowly nodded his head, his grin growing wider and wider. "There is an emergency life support station outside the landing bay. All I have to do is release the contents of the capsule, then leave it to the base ventilation system to carry the gas along."

"Good. You will then make your way to the fusion reactor and destroy any who have not been affected by the gas. Am I correct that an overload of the core will result in an explosion that will vaporize the entire asteroid?"

"Yes, My Lord. The memories of this creature are very specific on the subject. He also has extensive knowledge of the correct process for manual override of the fail-safe system."

Weent quietly raised his left arm in the air.

"Yes, Weent?" Donar asked impatiently.

"Why should we destroy the base? They've got secrets and things there that we could use," he slurred out in his usual elegant way.

"They will be destroyed because I will take no chances. Do you understand?"

"Yeah, I got it," the mercenary said wearily.

"Donar..." rasped the voice of the Luto.

"Yes?"

"My people will want more money."

Enraged, Weent jumped to his feet. "You lousy insect! We all agreed on a price."

The Luto just sat in his seat, its two antenna quivering. "That was before the command for combat," D'ucto voice rasped from between two sharp mandibles.

Donar stared at the creature before him for several seconds. "We will not offer you more for your services."

"Then I am sorry, but I must withdraw my people from your service."

"Very well," Donar said, placing his tentacled arms on the tabletop. "I will not hold you to your contract. You are free to go."

D'ucto stood and bowed to his former employer. "Thank you. I hope we can work with each other in the future." At Donar's nod, D'ucto walked out the door.

Donar glanced at Modok, then toward the double-doors. "Destroy it quickly, before it leaves the building. As I said, I will take no chances."

Modok stood and bowed his large, simian head. "Yes, My Lord," he said as he, too, turned and exited the room.

As the doors closed behind his war chief, Donar turned to the two human mercenaries. "Weent, I hope you will be able to control the remaining Luto."

Weent removed his blaster from his holster and gently placed it on the table. "The Luto are a reasonable race. I'll just make 'em an offer they can't refuse," the human said with a smile. He noted, though, that he was the only one who understood the humor of the ancient Earth movie line.

Barton looked up at his master, a puzzled expression etched across his face. "My Lord, what of me?"

"You, Barton, have an important task to perform. You will find a captured Dreedan cruiser that is being prepared on the landing field. You will use it to return to our home world. There, you will locate and retrieve the antimatter power core."

"Why, My Lord?"

Donar reached a tentacled arm over to the viewscreen on the wall behind his chair and activated the monitor. The image sharpened to reveal the open cargo bay of the Dreedan light cruiser. A large, cylindrical, metallic container was being loaded onto it.

"Do you all see the metallic device being loaded onto the cruiser?" Donar glanced at the others as they nodded their assent. "The casing is designed to hold the core, and once it is activated it will – "

"Explode!" Weent interrupted, jumping to his feet. "You're putting together an antimatter bomb, aren't ya?"

"Correct, human. Now allow me to finish. I do not appreciate interruptions."

Weent nodded and returned to his seat.

Donar again turned to Barton and continued, "You will then transport the device to its final destination."

"Which is?" Olstad asked.

"Why, the seat of the Alliance, of course." Donar activated the viewscreen, and the image of blue and white world appeared.

"Earth?" Weent said with a shudder.

"Yes. Do you have any objections, Weent?"

Weent slowly shook his head and leaned back in his chair, realizing he'd obviously bitten off a little more than he had originally bargained for.

"Good," Donar said with a snarl that ended further conversation.

Raiding's one thing, Weent thought, *but destroying my own home world is a little much.* He didn't know what he could do about it, though, because the lizard had taken care of any contingency. He had beaten the foulest things the universe had thrown at him, but Donar was something different. Weent didn't trust the ugly creature for a minute, but he'd also seen with his own eyes what would happen to anyone who came under the slightest suspicion of betrayal, and he didn't want to have it happen to him as well. Weent was no genius, but it wasn't hard for even him to see that his employer was truly insane.

Donar stared at each of the other members of the Council. The room was totally silent for several minutes before Donar calmly continued, "The installation of the core into the bomb casing is quite simple. You will be informed on the proper procedure before you depart. When you reach the wretched planet, all you need to do is enter orbit and release the device. It will enter the atmosphere and detonate. The resulting firestorm will wipe all life off the face of Earth. Of course the Dreedan Empire will be blamed for this wanton act of destruction, removing the final stumbling block to war."

"What if we run into any Alliance warships?" Barton asked. "The closer we get to Earth, the more we will be challenged."

"The bulk of the Alliance battle strength is patrolling elsewhere, in preparation for hostilities. There will be very little to challenge you, but I would not allow even the smallest chance of you being stopped. When you have retrieved the antimatter core, you will proceed to Allegre IV. After the starbase is taken, you will take command of the Fleet, and they will escort you the remainder of the way to your objective. On the way there, you will destroy any ship you come into contact with. Word of your advance must not spread, at least not until it is too late."

"Yes, My Lord."

"Are there any other questions?"

Olstad slowly raised his right hand in the air.

"Yes?"

"My Lord, the Dreedan Empire will deny any responsibility for the planet's destruction."

"It will not matter, for they will have their own problems to deal with. I have my own special plans for the so-called mighty Dreedan Empire." Seeing that he had everyone's attention, Donar continued, "The final part of my plan involves a small experiment. While the initial stages of our plan were set in motion, I returned to the laboratory. I have created a serum that...well, perhaps it would be enlightening to show you. Modok," he said to his clawed war chief, "activate the wall monitor."

Modok activated a small control on the table with a slight touch of his claw. The viewscreen instantly came to life behind Donar, showing Snatak's laboratory and a human figure strapped helplessly to an examination table. When the image zoomed in on the figure on the table, they all recognized the subject.

"As you can see, Admiral Brooks has reluctantly agreed to be our test subject."

Brooks struggled without hope against the straps that bound him to the hard metal surface. Surgical tape had been placed across his mouth in an effort to keep him silent.

Snatak bolted up in his chair, his pointed nose twitching nervously. "My Lord, why wasn't I informed of this?"

"Because you had no need to know." Donar seemed angered by the question from Snatak but quickly regained his composure seconds later.

One of Snatak's assistants stood by the side of the table, a pneumatic hypo clutched in its paw. It seemed to be waiting for a command from Donar to begin the experiment.

"I'm sorry to keep you waiting so long, Admiral. You may begin," Donar said to the werewolf in the white laboratory smock.

The werewolf pressed the tip of the injector to the base of the human's neck and depressed the activation stud. A slight hissing sound followed as the contents were injected. For several seconds, nothing happened.

"Well, what's goin' on?" Weent asked.

Just as he finished his question, he decided he really didn't want an answer, as he saw Brooks snap his head back in what must have been incredible pain. Brooks was changing. Hair began to quickly grow over the surface of his body as he jerked spastically under the restraints. A chill went through Weent as he saw what the Commando, Inc. chief was transforming into.

In a matter of seconds, a once-prominent nose elongated to a canine-like muzzle. It ripped the tape from its face, and large fangs filled its hellish mouth. When the transformation was finally complete, very little remained of Admiral Clayton Brooks. The resulting creature, more animal than human, strained against its restraints.

Donar looked at it proudly; it made his werewolves look like tranquil puppies in comparison. He could also see his laboratory assistants frantically trying to tighten the restraints before they worked loose, and that brought him glee as well.

"My Lord, what should we do?" the smocked werewolf inquired in panic.

"Tranquilize him and place the admiral in an adjoining cell to Dr. Patula."

"Yes, My Lord," the lab assistant said.

Donar severed the connection and grinned proudly at the shocked onlookers.

"My Lord," Snatak asked, "what is the effect on the creature's mind?"

"His mind is quite intact, except for an overpowering bloodlust, which, if unsatiated, will sooner or later drive him mad." Donar turned to face the Council once again. "Tompkin..."

"Yes, My Lord?"

"Do you know the location of the home world of the Dreedan Empire?"

"Yes, My Lord," Tompkin answered.

"You will bring the Dreedan people a gift from me. Your ship missile batteries are now being adapted to carry a special payload, which you will deliver upon your arrival."

"Why, My Lord?" Modok asked curiously.

"Not that I owe you any explanation, but with the governments of both the Alliance and the Dreedan Empire in chaos, one of two things will inevitably happen. Either I will have the war I so desire, or they will simply collapse with their leadership gone, allowing me to easily defeat them both. Whichever the case, I will win."

"The Dreedan battlecruisers may detect me on the way in or coming out."

"That is the point."

"But I may be destroyed."

"Then so be it, but you will survive long enough to accomplish your mission. Beyond that...well, such is the price of success."

"Understood," Tompkin said reluctantly, though he silently vowed that he would not be sacrificed so easily for Donar's lofty ambitions. *After I return, he'll find out what the real price is!* he thought.

"Barton, you will gather whatever you need and leave within the hour."

"Yes, My Lord," the simulcron said as he stood and quickly left the room.

As soon as the door was closed again, Donar continued, "All modifications will be completed on *Ranger* within three hours. Unfortunately, it will take another twelve or thirteen to mass-produce enough serum to poison the entire atmosphere of the planet. Your departure will take place immediately after all is completed. If there are no further questions, you may go."

The others all rose slowly and headed for the door.

"Snatak, stay," Donar said to the small sorcerer before he could scurry out of the room. "I would like a word with you."

As the door closed, leaving the two mismatched creatures in the briefing room, Snatak turned to face his master. "Yes, My Lord?"

"You will never question me again, Snatak. If you have a problem with that, I will be happy to feed you to one of your own unimpressive machines. Do you understand?"

The small scientist said nothing and nodded his head.

Donar walked to the window. "What of this problem with the simulcrons? Have you found an answer yet?"

"Not yet, My Lord. It seems the problem is in the stability of their basic genetic material."

"Fool! If a simple wound can cause their cell structure to break down, what good are they to me in a battle?"

Snatak seemed at a loss for words. "Perhaps if I experiment with the prisoners, I might find an answer," he mumbled, terrified.

Donar turned in rage.

Snatak, at the sight of his master, began to fear for his life.

"Experiment on anyone you wish, but do not touch the girl. I will not risk her until you have perfected your pathetically fallible process! Crawl back to your laboratory and correct your mistakes! I do not want to see your misshapen form until you have an answer. Now go!"

Snatak bent his head low as he hurried out the door, leaving Donar alone with his thoughts.

Donar felt the bloodlust coming over him, and in anger, he slammed a tentacled arm down hard on the table, splitting it in half. As he concentrated, his reptilian form wavered. When he finally solidified, he had reassumed his human guise.

He walked over to a mirror hanging on a far wall and looked into the face of Patac. He laughed out loud, with no fear that his voice would carry beyond the heavy wooden doors; he could not allow his creations to know of his true form, for in that puny body, he would have no hope of maintaining his hold over the others. He needed the terror-inspiring form of Donar to keep them in line.

"Atlo, you fool," he said to the face in the mirror. "You made me the perfect human, but in doing so, you provided me with all the qualities I need to succeed with my plans. It is only fair, as the superior species, that I should be the one to conquer and rule the galaxy as I see fit. Maybe when the time comes, I will bring you back to me. I will show you what your brainchild has become. Then, when your dread no longer amuses me, I will rip out your heart and throw your dead carcass to your grandchildren!"

Donar's reflection shimmered again, and he once again stared into his familiar reptilian face. With a fearsome swing of a tentacled arm, the mirror shattered into several hundred jagged shards, as sharp as his teeth. In his heart, he felt that a glorious time had arrived; very shortly, his operation would begin, and the galaxy would again tremble at the sound of his name. With the sound of hideous laughter filling the briefing room, Donar threw open the wooden double-doors and stepped into the corridor on the way to his destiny.

CHAPTER 20

Josh Grant opened his eyes and wondered if he would be greeted by a choir of angels or something much worse. He tried to sit up, but a flash of pain lanced through his shoulder, causing him to collapse back onto the dust-covered floor. He had taken a laser blast in the left shoulder during the shootout with Dowd's security people, and the force of the impact had sent him spiraling over the control console. *It's a good thing Ank made me wear this heavy combat armor though,* he thought. *I owe that guy. Hey, speaking of him, where is he? And where the hell is Carson?*

He tried to sit up again and, ignoring the pain, finally struggled to his feet. "Shit," he said as he ran his hand over his injured left shoulder. He looked around the chamber for signs of his missing friends, but he only saw an empty Alliance security uniform containing a white, clay-like substance.

"What the hell is this?" Josh leaned over the uniform and removed his bio-scanner. A quick reading of the strange substance gave him puzzling, inconclusive results. Using a specimen slide from his medical kit, he placed a sample of the decaying matter into a small sample container and returned it to the med-kit on his belt. Then, stiffly, he made his way to the chamber entrance.

"Well, we're not gonna get out this way," he muttered quietly to himself after observing the blocked exit.

Something had obviously happened to the others, and

he couldn't remain sealed in there for too long; the oxygen would eventually run out. *There has to be a way out, but how? Maybe they made it out before the ceiling came down, he thought.* Either way, he had to find out.

Josh felt along his right wrist for his comm unit. He activated the device and brought the transmitter up to his lips. "This is Josh. Can anybody hear me? Please respond."

Only the steady *hiss* of static replied.

He repeated his plea twice before he noticed a signal trying to punch its way through the barrier of electronic noise: "Josh, this is Ernie. Can you hear me?" came the voice of the *Pulsar* sentient computer. It was faint but discernible as Josh tried to ignore the background hiss.

"Ernie! Am I glad to hear your voice," he said with relief. "Do you know where the others are?"

"Melanie was taken to *Ranger* by the security men, and I assumed the skipper and Ank were with you."

Josh was stunned into silence. They took Melanie but not Ank or Carson? Then where the hell could they have disappeared to? His wondering ceased when he saw the still-glowing arch. It seemed alive, beckoning him with its hypnotic light. "Ernie, fill me in on what's been going on. How long have I been out?" Josh asked as he tried his hand at the control console.

"It's been 16.7 hours since Melanie was taken out of the city perimeter," Ernie stated matter-of-factly.

"What happened after they took her?" Josh said, keeping the conversation going as he struggled to figure out the complexities of the console.

"After they took Melanie up in the shuttle, Dowd tried to gain access to me. I kept all security shields active and prevented him from doing so. Forty-seven minutes after their shuttle lifted, my sensors registered a photon bolt fired from *Ranger,* targeted for my position. I was able to maneuver out of the way before impact."

"Why didn't you warn headquarters?" Josh asked, his hands still busy trying to activate the arch.

"There is an eighteen-hour delay built into my program to ascertain crew status before I am allowed to carry out such an order."

"Don't bullshit me, Ernie. I'm responsible for most of your programming. I know nothing like that exists in you."

"I couldn't just leave you here."

"Well, thanks for staying." Josh stopped fumbling with the console as something dawned on him. "Ernie, I think I know where they are!"

"Where, Josh?"

"Can you link up to my comm unit for a scan?"

"Yes...but why?"

"I want you to scan a control console that is right in front of me."

"All right."

Josh removed the communications unit from his wrist and placed it on the featureless console before taking two small steps backward.

"I am scanning the console, Josh. It seems to be preprogrammed to operate the arch. I will attempt to instruct you on its operation."

Josh stood over the console and held his hands above the control surface. "I'm right next to the console, Ernie. Now what?"

"Place your left hand thirty-three degrees off the center

position and your right fourteen degrees to the right," Ernie instructed.

Josh did as he was told and watched as the arch began to glow. "It's working, Ernie!"

The portal beneath the arch began to shimmer, revealing an alien landscape on the other side.

"I'm going through the arch to look for Carson and Ank."

"Josh, when you go through the portal, the console will automatically deactivate. You'll be trapped."

Josh stopped to consider Ernie's words. "What choice do I have, Ernie? I can't just leave them there. I'll leave the circuit open. While I'm gone, find some kind of override," he said as he picked up his blaster and returned it to his belt holster.

"I cannot guarantee that I can accomplish that," Ernie said quietly.

"Well, buddy, give it your best shot." Josh looked at his chronometer on his wrist and thought for a moment. "Ernie, if you can, activate the arch six hours from now. If you can't, then you are to return to headquarters to fill everybody in. Understood?"

Ernie hesitated at first, accessing his central processor to try to find a loophole in his programming that would allow him to disobey a direct order. Finding none, he responded sadly, "Understood."

Before he walked through the arch, Josh made certain that all his equipment was secured. He noticed a glint of metal on the chamber floor by the arch and bent down to find Ank's heavy photon cannon. He strapped it over his uninjured shoulder. Once he was finally prepared, he stopped and turned. "Ernie?"

"Yes, Josh?"

"If I don't see you again...well, take care, man," Josh said as he stepped through the gateway and disappeared.

As Ernie predicted, the portal began to power down after transport was completed. With all the skill and power Ernie could muster, the computer kept a single spark of power flowing through the console. He hoped that meager effort would keep the arch from completely shutting down and allow enough time for an override to be discovered.

Even if he had to burn out his entire computational matrix to accomplish his task, he would find a way to reactivate the arch in the six hours Josh was going to give him. They were his friends, his family, and he could not fail them. *I am the most sophisticated computer in the universe,* Ernie thought to himself. *It is time I earn my pay.*

* * *

In a flash, Josh stepped into a world totally unlike any he'd ever seen before. There was no sign of the portal. In fact, all he could see for kilometers in any direction was bleak desolation. "Well, Toto," he said quietly to himself, "this sure isn't Kansas."

Still, Josh was somewhat relieved that he wasn't trapped in the arch chamber anymore. He only hoped he had made the right decision in stepping through it. A lot depended on Ernie; if he couldn't find a way to reopen the portal, it really wouldn't matter if he found the others or not.

One way or another, he would have to find his way back to that exact spot within six hours. From a small compartment on his belt, he removed a homing tracker and carefully placed it in the sand where he judged the portal to be.

235

Josh looked up at the threatening red sky and decided to abandon his combat armor. Not only would the bulky equipment slow him down, but it would also cook him in his own juices. In such unforgiving heat, he could take no such chances.

With the six-hour countdown well underway, Josh removed the bio-scanner from his belt and swept the area. The small device began to register a small assortment of life forms in the area. Shaking his head, Josh realized they were not worth investigation. He could afford no mistakes; if he didn't choose the right direction the first time, he would have no hope of returning in time. His best guess was to move in the direction of the highest life form concentration and hope for the best.

Happy that the pain in his left shoulder had subsided to a dull throb, Josh adjusted the photon cannon across his back and checked his chronometer before finally starting off in what he hoped was the right direction.

CHAPTER 21

Carson covered the small electronic motion sensor and moved to the next placement position around the castle perimeter Ank had insisted that before anything else was done, they had to find some way of ensuring an outer security perimeter, at least temporarily.. Constructed of bits and pieces of his and Ank's remaining equipment and attuned to their one remaining comm unit, Carson hoped the three units would provide enough perimeter coverage to offer sufficient early warning if the mutants returned. *Well,* Carson thought as he patted the silvery tubed weapon at his side, *I'll be ready for them if they do show their ugly faces around here again.*

Though there was really not much of a difference between night and day on that planet, the sky seemed to be darkening just a bit. With a yawn, Carson was reminded that he hadn't had a wink of sleep since their arrival. After the last sensor was placed, it would be time to head back to the castle to see how Ank was progressing. The big feline was inspecting the castle supplies for any signs of shortage or contamination. Whatever he found had to last them for quite a while; reclaiming the barren soil would not be easy.

When the final sensor was in place, Carson rose and stretched his tired muscles. *This is one fine mess I've gotten us into,* he thought. Carson still felt that he was to blame for what had happened on Solo. There was something he could've done to prevent things from turning out the way they had. He had suspected trouble, but he had reacted too slowly. For all he knew, Josh was dead, Melanie captured by Dowd, and he and Ank were definitely stranded. *Not a very advantageous position*, he thought as he started his journey back to the ancient structure.

Night fell by the time Carson finally arrived back at the castle. Due to the peculiar rotation of the planet, periods of night and day were always different. The one constant was the presence of firestorms, flaming across the sky regardless of the hour.

Walking wearily into the great structure, Carson removed the silvery energy weapon from his shoulder and placed it in a wooden rack that held the only three others like it on the planet. Breathing a sigh of exhaustion, he found the closest chair and settled himself into it. It was hard to believe they had accomplished so much in the eighteen or so hours since they had arrived at the castle. Carson and Ank had begun by teaching Donar's assorted misfits the fundamentals of security and had quickly set up a squad to keep watch at the top of the castle walls.

Carson shut his eyes only for a moment before Ank walked in, with Dute and Lota in tow. He liked the two elves but thought Lota's infatuation for him was beginning to get out of hand.

Lota ran to Carson and placed her two small hands on his tired right arm. "Carson, you're back! I've missed you."

Carson looked up at Ank, hoping the big feline would somehow help him out of the unnerving situation.

Ank met his friend's gaze, offering him little sympathy.

"How goes the inventory, Ank?" Carson asked, trying to ignore the pressure of the two small arms clinging to him.

"Quite well, more than enough till we're able to revitalize the dead soil." Ank looked over at the small elf as she gazed lovingly at Carson. He was amused by the situation the human now found himself in, but he also realized his friend was very uncomfortable. "Lota, we still have much to do. Please take Dute and to the food storage room. I will meet you there shortly."

Lota pouted as she released Carson's arm. "Oh, all right. Dute, let's go." As she walked away with her companion, she stopped suddenly and smiled at Carson. "I'll see you later, Carson."

"Right," Carson replied wearily as Lota and Dute left the room. After they were gone, he slowly turned his head to Ank. "Where's Atlo?"

"The old man does not seem to be feeling very well...and you don't look very well yourself."

Carson turned a weary eye as he struggled to get comfortable in the big chair. "Don't worry about me. I'm just tired." Straining slightly, Carson slid his comm unit from his wrist and held it out for Ank. "At least this should warn us in advance if anything approaches."

As Ank took the small, square device, a red light began to blink on it. "Carson, it seems something has triggered your early warning system."

Carson shook his head and tiredly stood. "I'll check it out."

Ank stuck a furry paw on his friend's tired shoulder. "Are you sure you're up to it?"

"I'm fine," Carson said, gently pulling away.

"Let me go with you."

"Suit yourself." Carson went again to the wooden

weapons rack and removed two silvery tubes. He threw one to Ank, then opened the door and went out into the night.

* * *

Josh moved quickly across the deserted wasteland. He knew time was running out; within an hour, Ernie would have the portal open. How long he could keep it open was anyone's guess. Josh's bio-scanner led him to the largest concentration of life forms within its limited range. If Carson and Ank weren't there, he would have to head back to the portal, for he had no time to check elsewhere.

The sight of the castle both amazed and repulsed him. It was the type of structure nightmares were made of. He re-shouldered the heavy blaster cannon and continued on his trek.

Sliding down the ridge, he quickly made his way down to the castle, its immense structure seemingly growing in size with each step toward it. Josh began to feel jumpy as fire danced across the sky, illuminating everything in a shadowy, ghostly glow. The large blaster came quickly down into his hands as the atmospheric fire lit up two advancing forms ahead of him.

So far, he had seen no signs of life, but he knew it would only be a matter of time until he encountered something or someone. He crouched low as he heard movement off to his left and right. Whatever it was, it was trying to outflank him. He looked down at the weapon at his side. *Whatever it is, it's in for a surprise.*

When the large shape rose from the rocks ahead, Josh fired a quick burst from the cannon. The intense stream of energy shattered the rock into thousands of small pebbles. As he turned to search for his other target, he saw, albeit too late, a form leap on him from the rocks above. He watched helplessly as his weapon rolled away in his struggle with the thing on top of him.

The figure then picked up a large rock, ostensibly to crush his head, but a suddenly flash of fire from the sky illuminated his adversary.

"Mark, no!" he shouted as he saw who was about to kill him.

Carson hesitated as he quickly recognized the voice. "Josh? Is that you?"

"Yeah, man. Now get off of me, would ya? It's hard enough to breathe here as is."

Carson dropped the rock to his side and quickly scrambled to his feet.

With the pressure from his chest removed, Josh stood by his friend's side.

"Josh," Carson said in amazement. "I-I thought you were dead."

"Almost was, but the body armor took some of the edge off that blast. I've got Ank to thank for that. Is he here?"

"Right behind you, Doctor," the felinoid said from the shadows.

"You don't know how happy I am to see you guys," Josh said as the three tightly embraced in a brotherly hug.

As they broke apart, Carson looked again at Josh, as if he was a desert mirage that would soon disappear. He handed Ank his blaster cannon. The felinoid seemed very happy to have the weapon back, but he was no happier than Josh, who'd been toting the heavy thing for much longer than his protesting shoulder could bear.

"How did you get here?" Carson asked.

"We don't have much time for gabbing and reminiscing, Carson," Josh said, glancing at his wrist chronometer. "We've gotta be back at the portal entry point in forty-five minutes, or else y'all can start to plan the construction of your retirement condo by the castle."

"There are others there. We can't just leave them behind."

"All right, but let's move."

On the way to the castle, Josh quickly recounted the events of the past day, trying to be as concise as possible, bearing in mind the short time they had remaining.

They entered the vast lower foyer of the castle and quickly looked for any sign of Atlo. They found the old man sitting by his fireplace, with the two elves by his side, as always.

"Atlo, we must go now. Our friend here," Ank said, pointing a furry paw toward Josh, "has opened a way back for us, but we have to move."

Atlo simply sat and stared at the flames before him. Finally, he turned slowly in his chair to face the three visitors. "I'm sorry, Ank, but I must remain here."

Carson stepped forward and knelt before the chair. "Why? What've you to gain by staying?"

"I cannot abandon the others. There may be more on this planet who will eventually find their way here. You must hurry, though, Carson. Donar must be stopped, at any and all costs."

Carson glanced over at the elves. Dute and Lota both nodded at him, indicating that they would not leave their dear friend behind.

Lota walked slowly over to Carson, with her head bowed.

When she reached him, she leaned down and placed a small farewell kiss on his cheek before looking back up at him. "Have a safe trip, Carson," the little elf said as she returned to the old man's side.

Josh stepped forward and put a hand on his friend's shoulder. "Carson, we really don't have much time. We gotta go."

"Right." As Carson stood, he extended his right hand out to Atlo. "Goodbye, Atlo," he said.

The old man grasped it firmly in both of his and smiled up at Carson. "Goodbye, Carson. Remember what I told you."

Ank stepped forward and extended a paw that Atlo also took between his two gnarled hands. "Be well, old man." Ank then stared strongly at the two elves. "You two behave and be well, or I will hear of it."

The two elves nodded their agreement.

And with that, Carson led his two friends out of the castle and into the darkness.

CHAPTER 22

Melanie sat, cross-legged, on the floor of her cell, trying to make sense of the events that had brought her there. Admiral Brooks had shared her cell until only a few hours earlier, when Donar's foul werewolves had come to haul him away. *At least the sensory bombardment has let up,* she thought, trying to find some bright spot in a very dark place. Given time to sort things out, her mental shields would only grow stronger.

Donar had caught her by surprise the first time. Thinking he was Carson, she had let her defenses down. That contact with the alien mind had flooded her with a series of images she was just now beginning to sort out. The more she saw of her captures, the less her nightmares scared her; knowing what she had to defend against made all the difference. One thing she knew for certain was that Donar was pure evil. She also knew she had to do something to stop whatever he was planning to do or get word out to someone who could. She'd been told that the others were dead, but she still felt a strong link to Carson. *Either that scaly bastard lied to Brooks and me, or he really thinks Carson and the others are gone. The thing is, he doesn't know Carson like I do. No one does.*

Melanie looked over at her neighbor in the adjoining cell. It was difficult to keep track of time, but she estimated they must have brought the unconscious thing in not more than twenty-five or thirty minutes ago. The others were horrible to look at, but the one she gazed upon now must have been the great-granddaddy of them all. Whatever the thing was, the other werewolves simply threw it in the cell and quickly locked the door behind them, and the nondescript beast had remained quiet since.

She knew she had to find some way to escape. *But how?* They had searched her thoroughly and removed the special lock picks she carried. Melanie turned her predicament over and over in her mind, trying to find an answer.

Suddenly, the sound of the cellblock door opening brought her to standing attention. The sight of Donar made her think she might just have run out of time.

This time, the fiend was not alone; rather, he was accompanied by a hideous creature that looked like a gorilla with lobster claws. Any other time, in any other circumstances, Melanie would have been horrified, but now she found some comical amusement in their mutated zoo exhibits, each more grotesque than the last. As they stood in front of her cell, Melanie began to laugh, long and hard.

Donar looked at her curiously. "My dear, what do you find so amusing?"

For a moment, the question did nothing more than push her to a new plateau of laughter. "It's just your friend here, Donar. I've never seen surf-and-turf in living form before." Melanie felt the hysterical laughter looking for a way out and did nothing to stop it from surfacing. "I was just wondering, is it best to serve him with melted butter or steak sauce?" she asked, collapsing to the floor in uncontrollable, delirious laughter, her hand clasped to her stomach as she struggled to catch her breath from the side-splitting hilarity.

"I will kill you for that, human bitch," Modok said,

thrusting a large claw through the bars toward Melanie.

"Modok, leave her alone!" Donar said as Melanie quickly pushed herself back to the far wall, well out of reach of Modok's powerful claw.

"My Lord, we cannot overlook or forgive such insults. She must pay!" Modok cried out.

Melanie could see that the creature was losing control as its claw lashed out, snapping a mere foot from her throat.

Donar wrapped a long tentacle around Modok's neck and, with a tug, threw his maddened war chief to the ground. "You will obey me, or *you* will be the one who pays! I will not tolerate insubordination!"

Modok sat against the stone wall and massaged his throat gently with the side of his claw. He looked up at his master, then meekly lowered his head. "Yes, My Lord."

Donar turned again to face Melanie. She was sitting again, crossing her legs over each other. The humor seemed to finally have gone out of her in the face of her near decapitation. Still, there was a hardness etched in her expression; even after what had almost happened to her, she wasn't afraid. Donar clearly observed that the look on her face was more defiance then terror.

"Donar, I think you should consider getting a leash for your pet. Also, if you have him fixed, he'll be less likely to wander. I'd be more than happy to do it for you, though I may need a magnifying glass." Melanie stood and moved to the cell door, wanting to prove how brave she was, even though she could see that Donar barely had the large creature restrained.

"Dr. Patula, it will do you no good to antagonize Modok. If you do not please me, I will give you over to him and his tender caresses."

Melanie stood quietly. It was one thing to be courageous, but considering the consequences, she did not want to overstep those narrow boundaries. "What do you want?" she finally snapped.

"Merely to see how you and the admiral are feeling."

"Your hairy friends took him a while ago. Don't you have any idea what's going on around here?"

Donar's lizard-like muzzle split to reveal great rows of dagger-sharp teeth. "Do you mean to tell me no one has informed you about our other guest? Modok, please wake him up."

Modok pulled out a hypo-injector and, handling the instrument clumsily in his large, clawed hands, stuck it through the cell bars and pressed the end into the hairy side of the unconscious creature. The injector hissed as the drug found its way into the thing's system. The stimulant worked quickly, jolting the hideous creature back to life. With its senses finally restored, the creature threw itself at the bars in an attempt to reach Donar.

Melanie was quite confused by the situation as she watched the creature's murderous attempts to get out. "What's going on?"

At the sound of Melanie's voice, the creature suddenly stopped its assault on the bars. It turned to the girl and slowly walked over to the bars that separated the two cells.

Melanie took a step back, putting as much distance as she could between herself and the hairy beast.

It looked at her, its rage all but gone. Its face softened a little, and it didn't seem so terrible anymore. It reached a hairy, muscular arm slowly into the cell.

Melanie sat back and shook her head at the poor creature.

"Don't you recognize our friend, Melanie?" Donar said, interrupting her thoughts.

Melanie stared at the creature closely. She slowly stood to her feet again and walked over. Staying out of arms' reach, she noticed tears flowing from the creature's blue eyes, which seemed eerily familiar. It was trying to move its mouth, as if talking was some unfamiliar act.

"Melanie..." the thing said in a soft, harsh whisper.

She turned to Donar, shaking her head.

"Oh, I see you finally understand. He may not look like himself, but the admiral has been here all the time."

With tears streaming down her face, Melanie reached over and grabbed the hairy paw in her own hands. Dropping her mental shields, she concentrated deeply. After only a few seconds, she realized that Donar was right: She was looking at Admiral Clayton Brooks. "What have you done to him, you son-of-a-bitch?" Melanie screamed out, her tears now flowing freely.

Donar seemed amused by the situation. "Nothing much, just a species readjustment."

Modok stepped to his master's side. "Nothing to laugh about anymore, bitch, is there?" he said smugly.

Melanie didn't answer. She merely collapsed to the floor, holding her head in her hands as she cried. Now, the laughter was coming from the other side of her imprisonment.

"Come, Modok. Let us leave our friends to get reacquainted." Donar knelt by the bars and looked at Melanie. "You will be mine," he said matter-of-factly. "I need you and your abilities, and one way or another, I will have them. It has been a long time since I have pleasured myself on human flesh, especially female." He then stood and pulled his robe away from his body. "See what pleasures I will give you...with this."

Melanie watched with horrific fascination as Donar closed his reptilian eyes and concentrated. From between his scaly legs, an appendage grew. Phallic in appearance, it approached her through the bars, stopping several inches from her face. Suddenly, the end began to transform. It shimmered like a desert mirage, and when it solidified, she was looking at the face of Mark Carson.

"Mark?" she asked quietly through her tears.

"Melanie, I love you. Come closer," the face said.

Melanie moved a bit closer and reached a hand out to the familiar face. As her hand reached out, the features altered again, quickly shaping into a serpentine form, its great mouth open wide to reveal sharp fangs and a flickering, forked tongue. Without warning, the snake struck at Melanie. Screaming, she quickly pulled her hand away as the horrible appendage closed down on air.

The scaly appendage then quickly retracted back into Donar's body as he closed his robe. "My dear, think it over. The next time you see me, we will have a wonderful time – just you, me, and my friend here," he said, pointing between his legs.

Donar turned, and he and Modok walked away.

Before they reached the cellblock door, Melanie stood and moved quickly to the front of her cell. "Donar, I'm going to kill you!" she screamed as the door slammed shut, cutting off her tormentor's laughter. She turned from the door and looked at Brooks, at what he'd become. When his eyes met hers, she could feel her mentor's emotions, even from where she was: almost an equal mixture of terror, sadness, and embarrassment. There was another feeling, though, one so strong that it viciously beat back all the others: a hate so strong that she wasn't sure if anyone would be safe.

Melanie felt her own intense hatred as she sat back down, facing Brooks. She thought of what the future held and knew being raped by Donar with that foul growth would not be part of it. Her knowledge that Donar was going to die, even at the cost of her own life, consumed her mind. All she had to do was figure out how.

* * *

Several light years away, Glick worked feverishly on his crippled shuttle. The damage he had taken in the battle with the Alliance fighters had left much of the circuitry a molten mess of metal and plastic. He had spent the better part of the last thirty-five or so hours jury-rigging much of what was still operational. The main problem, though, was life support. There wasn't much time remaining before the system would cut out completely, so getting the flight systems operational was a priority.

The other problem revolved around the transmissions he'd intercepted from Allegre IV to someone in the Nexus star system. Since the communications gear in the shuttle was a step above anything else available in the Alliance, he was able to listen in on a great deal of the tight-beamed signals, though reception depended on the orbital track of the moon where he was stranded. Admiral Brooks had been right in his suspicions that there was trouble brewing. Now, Glick had to get out of here to warn Griffin of what was happening.

He plopped down in the pilot's chair and pulled on a water bulb from the emergency rations as he contemplated the electronic clipboard in his lap. Going down the checklist, Glick discovered good news and bad news. "Let see," the pilot said to himself. "The good news is that the flight systems should survive the trip back home. Unfortunately, about halfway there, life support will conk out on us. Game over."

The rest of his discoveries were a mixture of good and bad. The weapons system was a burnt-out piece of junk, the comm system would only receive, and his defensive shields couldn't take more than a token pounding before dropping entirely.

On the good side, his engines and flight controls were still in pretty decent shape, and his long- and short-range sensors were still operating. He was happy that the sensors were still feeding him useful information. After a futile search for him, the fighters had been recalled to the starbase. With any luck, they had considered him dead; that would give him the slight edge he needed to escape the system.

Replacing the clipboard under the chair, Glick began the procedure of powering up his onboard systems. He had to do everything manually, with the computer-monitored autopilot hardware that was wired into his life support. "Well, here goes nothing."

With a low rumble, the power levels rose sufficiently for a flight attempt. Glick reached out a tentative hand to activate the maneuvering thrusters, but the alarm he had wired to the sensors filled the flight deck with a wailing siren.

"Shit! What now?" he said as he pulled the sensor display up on his forward display.

In amazement, he stared at the reading on the long-range sensor scan. Entering the system at a high speed was a fleet of twelve ships. Moving quickly, Glick patched the library computer into the sensor display and did an identification scan on the approaching ships.

"Dreedans," he said, slamming his left hand down hard on the armrest. It was certainly not a glee-worthy development. Sneaking out of the system was not going to be easy anyway, and the Dreedan ships were a problem that would not disappear quickly.

Obviously, Allegre IV was their destination; it was the Alliance's only outpost in that sector. *But how did they get past the Alliance?* It was pretty common knowledge that the two fleets had faced off against each other on either side of the frontier boundary, but undetected penetration that deep into Alliance territory by that many enemy ships seemed impossible; if it wasn't for the fact that he was seeing it with his own eyes, he wouldn't have believed it.

Glick activated the comm system. If I can just figure out what's going on, I might have a chance.

The speaker came alive with a voice he had heard before. "Malone, this is Olstad," the voice said through the static. "It is time for us to take control."

"Admiral, the fighters scrambled as soon as your ships entered the system. I couldn't stop them," Malone replied.

"No worries. My ships will take care of them."

"What about the remaining humans here?"

"Donar wants them all eliminated."

Glick couldn't believe what he was hearing, a fleet admiral ordering the murder of his entire complement.

"Lower the shields so my ships can land."

"It will be done immediately," Malone voice said.

Glick had to take the chance, had to make everyone aware of Admiral Brooks's suspicions. He had thought it was pure fantasy, that he was just following the orders of a crazy old man, but now? The truth was, he couldn't think about what was going on now.

He activated the thrusters, and the shuttle slowly moved out of its dark sanctuary. Working only the small maneuvering jets, Glick drove the damaged shuttle just a few meters above the surface. While everyone was busy with Allegre IV, he would sneak along the surface to the far side of the small moon. There, with a little luck, the bulk of that orb would cover his escape.

* * *

All went well for Olstad and his armada of Dreedan warships, as the small squadron of fighters was easily outgunned and blasted out of space. Malone opened a hole in the starbase shields, allowing one of the warships to penetrate and eliminate the planetary defensive emplacements.

Quickly securing the landing field, the first ship was quickly joined by the remainder, as a combined force of over 900 mercenaries, along with Donar's werewolves, savagely went on the attack. Again, the human forces of Allegre IV were no match for the sheer numbers that overwhelmed them. The security force fought bravely, but for every werewolf they shot down, two took its place. Held back from their bloodlust for so long, the werewolves abandoned their energy weapons and began to rip the humans apart.

In their wild savagery, not even their mercenary accomplices were safe. Of those mercenaries who went out on the attack, half of their casualties came as a result of being in the way of their comrades. For this reason, Olstad and most of the other humanoids remained onboard their ships until the brief battle was over.

Olstad surveyed the death and destruction. Part of him was sorry for the carnage he had caused. Sometimes it took a great amount of will to keep that which was Admiral Olstad submerged. Taking on the identity of humans was dangerous, as more than their memories seemed to transfer. He felt things he had never felt before. Nevertheless, Donar said it was to be done, and Donar was his master. Unfortunately, the Olstad in him kept telling him that was no way for a soldier to die.

Olstad found Malone in Operations. The simulcron had hidden himself from the attack after making it possible for the ships to land. Now, it was time to clean up the mess and prepare for Donar's arrival. Malone was coming over to him, and he clearly wasn't happy.

"Admiral, we have a problem," he said. Malone looked frightened half to death, which was no surprise after how fragile he'd been after the transformation.

"What problem?"

"The werewolves, sir. They refuse to listen to me. Some have taken dead human bodies with them to the sub-maintenance levels. Gralik is in charge of them."

Olstad had wondered how long it would take. Now, without Donar's supervision, they were losing control. "Did you tell them they are to obey Lord Donar's orders?"

"Yes, and they simply told me to leave or they would see if simulcron blood is as tasty as a human's."

A wellspring of rage rose up within Olstad. They had all been of the same stock before the transformation had forever changed him. His own bloodlust, as well as that of his fellow simulcrons, had been diluted with the absorption of the humans. That had given them more of a sense of duty to the cause. "Thurmond!" he called out to his humongous security chief. "Go with Malone. Some of the guards are blatantly refusing to obey the word of the master. Show them what happens when they stray."

Without saying a word, Thurmond simply nodded and went with Malone to the lower maintenance level. They found Gralik sitting in the corner of a maintenance bay with two other blood-drenched werewolves, each munching on a different limb from the corpse of a security guard in front of them. Shreds of red security cloth still covered the remains.

Gralik saw them as they entered, and a snarl came from deep within his throat. "Ah, Malone. You've brought me some meat. Leave me, Thurmond, or join this one on my plate."

Thurmond looked down at the corpse sadly. He remembered the young security ensign from his squad. Like Olstad, memories and feelings had become part of his makeup, and the dead human had been a friend. "Gralik, come with me."

Gralik and the two other werewolves howled with laughter at the command.

Thurmond removed his blaster from his belt and adjusted the weapon to the highest setting.

The three werewolves stopped their feast for a moment

and looked fearfully at the long barrel of the deadly weapon.

"I will not ask again," Thurmond said quietly.

Gralik grabbed hold of a yet-untouched leg of the human body and ripped it free at the joint. "Thurmond," the werewolf said menacingly, "I will see you dead first."

Thurmond merely pointed the weapon squarely at the beast's chest and fired, sending a beam carving through Gralik's hairy body.

For a moment, Gralik stood and looked down at the charred hole where his chest used to be. He looked back up at Thurmond before collapsing in a bloody heap atop the dead ensign. His final thought was how tasty the smell of his burnt flesh and fur smelled.

"Do I have to make an example of you too?" Thurmond asked the two remaining werewolves.

They had obviously seen enough, as they both fought each other to be first out.

With his job done for the moment, Thurmond turned and started for the door.

Malone caught up and followed him the rest of the way out.

* * *

Glick had carefully followed the contours of the moon till he felt safe enough to engage his main engines. With a lurching hesitation, the shuttle shot away, into space. He'd managed to place the moon between his intended course and Allegre IV.

Looking at his communications equipment, Glick knew it would be useless at that point. Any transmission would be picked up and, in all probability, jammed. With his ship in such a failing, helpless condition, finding him would have posed no problem.

He unbuckled his safety harness and went to check the condition of his fragile ship. He thought he had done a fair job on the repairs, but he was certainly not a mechanic. So far, things seemed to be holding together, all except for life support. The computer had calculated that at his current acceleration, he would arrive home about four hours after his air ran out. His only option was to go on minimum life support and try to keep his ship pointed in the right direction. He had an emergency air supply, but that would only give him about twenty extra minutes of life.

Glick removed the emergency air and another bulb of water, exhausting the supply cabinet, then sat down back at his pilot station. After taking a long drink from the last water bulb in the emergency rations, he reached under the padded seat and pulled out the electronic clipboard to compose what would be his final message, in case his ship arrived too late. He was definitely not a fatalist; in fact, he considered himself quite optimistic as compared to many beings he knew. He was also a bit of a realist, though, so as he looked at the board and tried to think of what to say, he knew the odds were not exactly with him.

CHAPTER 23

Jagged bolts of energy flashed across the darkening red sky as Josh led his two friends to the portal position he had marked. The signal given off by the tracker led them quickly to the exact spot. "Well, this is the place," he said as he dug under the sand and came out with the small transmitter. He handed the device to Carson, then sat his exhausted body down on what was once the trunk of an enormous tree, now dead and blackened by the years and the planetary decay.

"How much time do we have left?" Carson asked.

Josh looked at his chronometer, and relief was apparent on his face as he announced, "We made it with about three minutes to spare."

"Great. Now let's hope Ernie has done as well on his side," Carson said, plopping down beside Josh with a groan and a sigh.

After the hectic pace of the past few days, they were all showing signs of exhaustion. Even Ank seemed to strain a bit as he paced in front of them.

The time went quickly, and Josh glanced down for a time check. Before he was able to give them an update, they all heard a loud whine, and the portal shimmered back into existence.

"Let's go!" Ank said restlessly.

Both men looked at their feline friend and nodded their agreement.

"All right. Follow me through," Carson said. He turned

to the shimmering air and looked closely, making out the portal chamber behind it. With a running start, he leapt through the swirling mist and found himself back in the massive chamber. As he ambled to his feet, Ank and Josh came through together.

Josh recovered his comm unit from the control console.

Meanwhile, Ank looked around the chamber and noted the sealed entrance. "We have to break out soon. The air is getting too thin."

Carson looked at the blaster cannon on Ank's shoulder, likely their only hope. "I guess were gonna have to blast our way out," he said reluctantly.

Ank brought the heavy weapon down from his shoulder as Carson and Josh took cover. As soon as he saw that the others were safe, Ank squeezed the trigger and sent an intense stream of energy into the rubble that blocked their escape. The force of the impact scattered rock over the chamber as more and more of it was blasted away.

In a matter of moments, Ank had blasted a hole in the debris, barely large enough for the three to fit through. As they moved through the tight squeeze, they were greeted by the smell of fresh air filling the chamber.

Ank handed Carson his weapon and fit himself through the hole.

Carson put the gun down and turned to Josh. "Josh, let me have your comm unit."

"Right," Josh said, handing the transmitter over.

"Ernie, this is Carson. Do you read?"

"Yes, Skipper! So good to hear your voice again," the computer responded happily.

"Same here, Ernie. We're on our way out to you. Prepare

the ship for launch. I want to be in space two minutes after we get back."

"Aye-aye, sir. No problem."

"Good. Carson out." After handing the device back to Josh, he gestured for his friend to go out next. When he was on the other side of the rubble, Carson handed the blaster cannon through the opening, then crawled out himself.

Together again, they quickly made their way to the surface and finally to *Pulsar,* still resting by the entrance to the city.

Carson glanced over at the crater in the landing area where Ernie had avoided the shot from *Ranger.* He was so happy to be leaving the planet, even though they were short one member of their team. All in all, things could have been much worse.

When they reached the starship, the airlock doors opened, allowing them entry. Ank took all the weapons and equipment back to the armory and storage lockers, while Carson and Josh headed for the bridge.

As they took their positions, the bridge doors opened, and Ank entered and took his station.

Carson glanced at his two crewmates and began the preflight check. "Ernie, what's the ship status?"

"All systems are fully operational, Skipper. Are we going after Melanie now?"

Ernie's question took Carson by surprise, leaving him speechless. Josh and Ank looked first at each other, then at Carson, each wondering what their leader would say; they were curious themselves as to their next move.

"Ernie, as soon as we figure out where she is, we'll get her," Carson said in all sincerity. "For now, initiate lift-off procedure."

"Aye-aye, skipper."

All power systems were operating at their peak as *Pulsar* rose into the sky, turned, and accelerated free of the planet's gravity well.

The bridge was silent. Between the exhaustion brought on by the events on Solo and Melanie missing, the mood was somber.

"Ernie, set course for home, full speed."

"Aye-aye, Skipper." Ernie took navigation and helm control from his tired human companions.

There was hardly any notice of the minor course correction as the starship blasted into hyperspace and out of the system. Unfortunately for Carson and the others, if Ernie had delayed their entry into hyperspace for another few seconds, *Pulsar's* powerful sensor array might have been able to detect the Dreedan cruiser that had entered the Solo orbit.

Carson pivoted in his command chair and stared out at the stars on the forward viewscreen. There were so many things he'd wanted to say to Melanie. He knew he'd made a real mess of things on Solo, and he very well could have gotten all four of them killed. *From now on,* Carson swore to himself, *I'll take no chances with anyone's life but my own.*

"Josh, why don't you and Ank go below and get some sleep? I'll watch things up here."

"What about you?" Josh asked. "You gotta be tired."

"I'll be down in a few minutes. I just want to check in with Admiral Brooks."

"Right. All right, time for a little shut-eye," Josh said as he stood and walked over to Ank.

"I will go, but Carson, please call if you need us," Ank said as they reluctantly left the bridge.

When he was alone, Carson went over to Melanie's communications console and sat down. "Ernie ... "

"Yes, Skipper?" the voice of *Pulsar* responded.

"Raise the base for me please."

"No problem, Skipper." There was a momentary pause while Ernie established the subspace link with their asteroid headquarters. "The admiral is unavailable, but I have Griffin for you."

"Thank you, Ernie. Transfer him to the main viewscreen."

The picture on the main viewscreen shifted. The stars blurring by the ship faded out, replaced by the face of Griffin.

"Where have you been, Carson?" the chubby second-in-command of Commando, Inc. asked. "You don't look so hot."

"We had a problem on Solo. *Ranger* turned on us. They took Melanie, and I'm assuming Tompkins thinks we're all dead. Where's the admiral?"

"He should be at the starbase on Allegre IV. He had suspicions that Admiral Olstad is involved in something, so —"

"What!? Why did you let him go, Griffin?" Carson snapped.

"Carson, I tried my best, but you know the admiral. I sent Noga to keep him out of trouble and Glick to fly his shuttle," Griffin said.

Carson knew Griffin would have had no chance of stopping Brooks. The man was stubborn enough to willingly stick his head in a lion's mouth and let no one talk him out of it.

"But," Griffin continued, "I haven't been able to reach either the base or Glick's shuttle in almost two days."

"Listen, Griffin. I'm setting a course for Allegre IV. If you hear anything from the admiral, call me. You got that? Anything!"

"Got it," Griffin answered meekly. "Carson, there's been one other major event you should be aware of."

"What's that?" Carson asked, rubbing his tired eyes.

"Tensions between the Alliance and the Dreedan Empire have almost reached the breaking point. Both sides are accusing one another of committing atrocities against the outer colonies of the others. Fleets from both sides are facing off on the frontier boundary, trying to instigate the other into making the first move."

"Well, we both know who's behind this, don't we?"

"You mean the admiral's suspicions are true?"

Carson looked at the surprised expression on the man's face. He hadn't really believed Brooks, but at the very least, he had sent Noga and Glick to babysit the admiral. "Yes, and I have a feeling that the admiral is in way over his head. I'm changing course, Griffin. Stay in touch. Out." Carson then severed the connection and contemplated the events occurring around him. He had no choice but to head for Allegre IV. He just hoped that he wasn't too late.

"Skipper, should I readjust our course?" Ernie inquired.

"Yes, Ernie. Take us to Allegre IV. What's our ETA, at maximum speed?"

"Three hours and fifteen minutes," Ernie responded almost instantaneously.

"Good. I'm going below before I drop. Keep your sensors peeled, buddy. If you run across anything unusual, let me know. If not...well, handle it the best you can." Carson stood slowly from the communications station and made his way for the door.

"When should I wake you, Skipper?"

"If nothing happens, just before system entry."

"Yes, sir," Ernie said as the doors closed behind Carson.

In his quarters, Carson collapsed immediately onto his bed. Unlike his previous attempt, he was asleep before his head hit the pillow.

* * *

Glick sat in his pilot's chair and wondered what god he'd offended to land himself in his current precarious situation. There had been one bit of damage he knew nothing about. During the strain he had put on the shuttle in the battle over the moon, the coolant system for the powerful main engine had been severely weakened. Repeating that similar strain on his high-speed escape had weakened it even further, eventually causing the system to malfunction and shut down.

Red lights and emergency alarms had alerted him to the problem, but it was too late to stop the engines from burning out. All he had left at his disposal were the small exterior thruster motors. They would push him along, but now, with the main engines down, he figured it would take him about seventy or eighty years to make it back to the asteroid belt. *Somehow*, Glick thought, *I don't think that will be in time.*

He had finished dictating his story into the electronic clipboard, for whatever good it would serve. With power levels dropping and his life support just about depleted,

Glick felt he had nothing to lose, so he activated the shuttle disaster beacon. Under full power, the beacon could broadcast its signal for many light years in every direction, but now the faint pulse he was sending out could only be picked up by a ship in his near vicinity.

Glick put the clipboard on the flight controls in front of him and leaned back in his chair. Reaching a hand up to a wall-mounted console, he deactivated every system not needed to prolong his own life or aid in his detection from another ship, so their power could be transferred to the beacon.

Suddenly, his efforts were interrupted by yet another alarm. Quickly punching up a diagnostic of his ship systems, he saw the words he'd dreaded seeing: "Life Support Malfunction," blinking brightly on his terminal display.

The air's getting pretty thin up here, Glick thought to himself as he brought the tank of emergency oxygen onto his lap. He put the facemask on and turned the small nozzle on top of the cylinder to release the life-giving gas into his lungs. A regulation emergency bottle of oxygen could last anywhere from twenty to thirty minutes, depending on how wisely it was used. He would see that he got as much of that thirty minutes as he could.

Glick sat and stared at the stars. Ever since he was a boy growing up in the atmospheric domes of the Martian colonies, space always had a strong attraction for him. His father had wanted him to work in the merchant service; after all, that was his father's life and his father's before him. Glick, though, craved excitement, and he knew he would not find that in piloting a ferry or a merchant ship in the local star systems. Thus, he had disobeyed his father's orders and enrolled at the Alliance Military Academy. There, he became adept at a variety of fighter craft, and he could fly just about anything. After his term of duty was up, he was quickly snatched up by Admiral Brooks for his Commando, Inc. project.

Glick stopped reminiscing when he began to feel dizzy. He brought the tank up for a look at the pressure gauge; it was just about at zero.

He wondered what it would be like to die quietly in space, drifting off as his oxygen-starved brain shut down. Somehow, it was not the end he had pictured for himself. He'd been certain he would meet his death during a pitched battle in space, that some enemy would sneak up behind him, firing a blast of energy, blowing him and his ship up.

He felt his eyes closing, and it was getting harder and harder to stay awake. He laughed out loud; for some reason, he found it funny that he simply couldn't breathe anymore. For that matter, everything was funny.

Out of the corner of his eye, Glick saw or at least thought he saw something coming at his ship. *Pretty blinking lights? Is it death? Is God coming for me?* He didn't really care anymore as he closed his eyes and surrendered to the blackness.

CHAPTER 24

Ernie had done as Carson had instructed. With his long-range sensors scanning at maximum capability, he would be able to discover potential problems before they endangered the ship or its crew.

Carson had authorized him to use his own judgment, unless a situation necessitated his presence. Using internal sensors and tied to medical monitors in sickbay, Ernie had determined that the others needed to get as much sleep as possible, and he was determined to see that they got it.

Only a small percentage of Ernie's powerful computer memory was needed for the task he'd been assigned to. The rest of the time, he spent in a kind of computational introspection. He had much time to ponder most mysteries, especially those related to why, as a machine, the matrix that held what was essentially his brain referred to his existence as "he."

Ernie knew he was not human, a creature of flesh and blood, but he shared many of the same feelings as those of his human crew. They were his friends, and when they were in danger, he experienced worry. He felt it now for Melanie. Josh had constructed him, and Mark Carson commanded him, but she had been the first to befriend him. She had always treated him as more than the machine many of the others thought he was. Without her there, Ernie felt as if part of him was missing. He knew the others, especially Carson, shared his feelings.

Concluding his self-analysis for the time being, Ernie scanned his assorted systems for the source of the interruption. Long-range sensors had discovered a metallic object floating slowly on a track, Ernie computed, that would carry it out of the Allegre system. Using the judgment Carson seemed to be so confident in, Ernie changed course to intercept the foreign and indeterminable object.

An analysis of the readings confirmed its identity as a modified Class 1 shuttle. Maneuvering closer, Ernie was able to enhance the transmission of the weak but operating disaster beacon. The recorded transmission washed uncomfortably over Ernie's memory banks.

"This is *Commando, Inc. Shuttle One*. We have an emergency and require immediate assistance. This is *Commando, Inc. Shuttle One*. We have..." the message repeated over and over.

Ernie decided then that it was time to wake the others, and he signaled them to hurry to the bridge. He knew their human bodies required more sleep than what they had gotten, but human decision-making was now required.

At the summons from Ernie, Carson bolted upright in bed. He quickly checked the chronometer on the wall and realized he had been allowed the luxury of about two hours of uninterrupted sleep, more than he'd had in the last four days. He knew the computer sometimes acted as a nursemaid to them, so it was unlikely that Ernie would have woken them unless they were facing something beyond the scope of Ernie's authority or capability.

He reached the bridge just before Ank or Josh, though they were right behind him. "What's going on, Ernie?" he asked as he took his central command chair.

"Sensors indicated a metallic object intersecting our course. Upon changing course and investigating, I discovered it to be the admiral's missing shuttle," Ernie reported.

"Ernie, check for life signs," Josh ordered.

"My sensors indicate one life form aboard. Readings indicate that environmental systems are now nonoperational. Life signs are beginning to fail."

"Shit!" Carson shouted. "Ernie, activate a tractor beam and pull the shuttle into docking position."

"Skipper, the docking port on the shuttle has been compromised," Ernie reported. "System damage will not allow the port on the shuttle to engage."

"Great," Carson thought aloud. "Ank, let's get to the airlock. I need to get into a suit and get over there." He then ran to the door with Ank trailing behind him. "Josh, get sickbay operational," he yelled before the doors closed behind him.

Down below, Carson struggled quickly into his white, formfitting spacesuit. Ank, wanting to assist, climbed into a similar but larger version of the one Carson had sealed himself into, then double-checked the seals on Carson's suit.

The inner hatch opened, and the two commandos walked into the pressurized chamber, Ank carrying a med-kit in case additional care was needed. Carson pressed a control stud on the inside wall, and the green safe light glowed red, signaling that the atmospheric pressure in the chamber had dropped below the capacity necessary for humans. Slowly, with the airlock chamber now void of air, the outer door slid open.

The spacesuits were equipped with a special thruster

pack on the back, for manned maneuvering. With only ten meters separating the two space vessels, both suits fired off a small burst from their thrusters and floated over to the airlock entrance of the shuttle. On the way over, Carson looked at the damage the shuttle had sustained. Large sections of the craft had been charred black by laser fire. Blast damage had also exposed circuitry, power still arcing between the open circuits.

Ank reached the side of the shuttle first and tried to activate the door release by the airlock hatch. Nothing happened, even when he punched the button over and over again. "The airlock controls are not responding," he announced grimly over his suit transmitter.

"Look!" Carson pointed his finger at the scorched, black, ionized metal crossing over the seam of the outer hatch. "It's fused."

Ank removed his laser torch from his belt and placed it against the fused section. "We'll have to cut it open."

"Well, you'd better do something fast. Life signs are taking a dip way down," Josh said through the helmet speakers of both suits.

Carson stood and thought for a moment as he watched Ank cut through the heavily fused section of metal. He wished there was a faster way; if they didn't move quickly, there wouldn't be anyone alive inside to rescue. "Ank, stop cutting. I have an idea," Carson finally said.

Ank did as he was told and holstered the torch.

"This shuttle has a double-hatch, just like the one in *Pulsar*. All we have to do is blast this door in, then use the inner one as a substitute. Once we're inside, we'll just seal the inner door before we open the hatch to the flight deck."

"How do we blow the outer hatch?" Ank asked.

"Ernie, are you following all this?"

"Yes, Skipper. What do you want me to do?"

"Fire a quick pulse from the forward cannon. Aim it dead center on the airlock door. Use only enough power to destroy the outer door, without harming anything else. Can you do it?"

"No problem, Skipper. I just need you and Ank to clear the area."

Carson and Ank both moved toward the stern of the shuttle and took cover behind the bulk of the main engine. They watched as *Pulsar* pulled away from the shuttle. Within seconds, the ship executed a 180-degree turn and angled back toward them. Stopping within seventy-five meters of the shuttle, Carson could see a bright pulse of light from the forward weapons pod and felt the impact as the measured bolt of energy struck the crippled vessel.

Again, the thrusters hurled them to the airlock. The blast had punched a jagged hole in the door. Carson squeezed through and turned to see Ank trying to force his wide shoulders past the blasted metal. Pulling away from the hatch, Ank released the cutting torch and its power pack from his back and tried again. Carson tugged on his arms from the inside and finally managed to get Ank into the cramped space of the inner lock. Once they were inside, Carson triggered the interior hatch, which slid silently upward.

"Let's shut this door," Carson said to Ank as they both entered.

Once the inner hatch was down and secured, they proceeded through the chamber and out past another door, into the passenger section. Finding no one, they moved to the flight deck, where Glick was still seated in his pilot's chair, the empty emergency air still strapped to his face.

"Ank, it's Glick. Give me that oxygen from the med-kit."

Ank quickly handed the small unit to Carson, who quickly used it to replace the depleted one. Ank then removed a hypo from the kit and pressed it quickly to the base of Glick's neck, releasing the drug into his body. "This tri-oxy solution should enrich the O_2 supply to his brain, if we aren't too late."

Carson ran the diagnostic scanner over Glick and was relieved to see that they'd made it just in time. *Another few seconds and... No, I don't want to think about it.*

"His vitals aren't very stable. We'd better get him back to the ship."

Without a spare suit for Glick, Carson removed a small sphere about the size of a grapefruit from his belt. With a quick turn of a ring that circled the round object, the sphere began to grow. They watched as it expanded large enough for them to insert Glick. The sphere contained its own environmental system and would protect Glick from the space atmosphere for up to three hours. It was useful in situations when it was necessary to make an emergency escape without a spacesuit.

After Glick was sealed inside, Ank picked up the rigid sphere and carried it to the airlock.

Carson stayed behind to look for anything they could salvage, but all he found that he thought might prove useful was the electronic clipboard Glick had left on the console in front of his seat. After retrieving the data board, Carson turned back to the flight deck one last time before heading aft to meet Ank.

Ank stopped and stared at the outer hatch. The hole *Pulsar* had made for them to enter was still too small for the life support sphere to fit. "What now?" Ank asked as Carson joined him.

"We'll have to blow it from the inside. Take Glick out of the compartment."

Ank carried the sphere out of the compartment and waited for Carson, fully aware that the human planned to activate the six explosive bolts that held the hatch in place.

"Ank, get ready," Carson said through his helmet speaker. "When I activate the explosive bolts, it'll blow in five seconds."

"Acknowledged."

"Five...four...three..." Carson counted as he threw himself out of the small compartment. "Two...one... Now!"

Even though the noise of the six small explosions was swallowed by the vacuum of space, they both felt the rumbling of the shaking ship. Then, to their surprise, the shuttle began to move away from *Pulsar*.

Inside *Pulsar*, Josh and Ernie witnessed the explosion and watched as the craft began to float away.

"Ernie, activate thrusters and throw another tractor beam on the shuttle before it gets too far out of reach," Josh ordered.

"Right, Josh." *Pulsar* quickly moved in pursuit of the tumbling ship. Once Ernie had them back in range, he reactivated the tractor beam and pulled the shuttle back to within ten meters.

Together, Ank and Carson pushed the sphere out of the shuttle and steered the life capsule with its living occupant toward *Pulsar*. As they reached the ship, the hatch opened for them. Pushing the sphere ahead, they entered the small chamber and locked the hatch behind them, where Ank, nearest to the airlock controls, began re-pressurization procedures. This time, the light went from red to green, and they saw Josh on the other side with an antigravity stretcher at the ready. As the inner door opened, Josh rushed forward and settled the sphere down gently on the deck.

Carson and Ank quickly shed their suits and helped Josh put Glick on the stretcher. Josh replaced the small oxygen mask on Glick's face with another and pushed the stretcher through the doors, which closed behind him with a pneumatic *hiss.*

Floating on a cushion of magnetic force, Josh pushed the stretcher down the short corridor, into the sickbay. Ank helped move the unconscious body onto the diagnostic bed the felinoid had occupied only days before.

As soon as Glick was secured in bed, Josh activated the auto-doc to monitor his systems. He eventually turned the auto-doc over to Ernie and waited for the computer to complete its diagnosis. Even though they were all qualified to render medical aid in such a situation, Josh felt more comfortable letting Ernie do the initial examination. His medical database had been programmed by Melanie and contained assorted treatments for almost any ailment or injury. It wasn't long before Ernie had completed his examination of Glick and deactivated the auto-doc with an audible tone.

"Well, Ernie, how's Glick?" Josh asked.

"My examination," Ernie began, speaking to Josh, Carson, and Ank, "reveals that the subject, though stable, is suffering from severe exposure and oxygen deprivation."

"What's your recommendation, Ernie?" Carson asked, looking down at Glick. He still looked like the same kid he and Brooks had recruited more than two years ago.

"A minimum of 4.7 hours in a decompression chamber is required, but emergency treatment was started soon enough to avoid permanent damage. I suggest that we maintain the flow of oxygen into his body until we can get him to the medical center at the base."

"Ernie..."

"Yes, Skipper?"

"Set our course for home, full speed."

"Aye-aye, sir."

"Josh, you stay here and keep an eye on Glick. If he comes to, I wanna know about it. Ank and I will be on the bridge."

As the two exited, Josh turned back to his patient. He was a little uncomfortable playing doctor; that was Melanie's bag, not his, as he was far more at home around machines than people. He looked down at Glick, who was sleeping peacefully on the bed, the mask on his face feeding life-giving oxygen into his body. He was happy that they had gotten to him in time. Though he never saw much of Glick, Josh knew he was one of the best pilots they had. He also had one of the sickest senses of humor, and Josh himself had, more than once, been the brunt of his practical jokes, though none were ever too cruel. Still, he was a lot of fun to be around.

Time passed slowly as the *Pulsar* engines accelerated, carrying the ship through hyperspace faster than any ship before. Still, no matter how fast they seemed to travel, it always seemed too slow.

Carson sat on the bridge in his command chair and stared at the stars as they whizzed by. *I'm so tired of this,* he quietly complained. From the very beginning, it had seemed they were always one step behind current events. He looked over at Ank, who seemed to be growing more and more familiar with the ship and its controls. *At least,* Carson realized, *he's getting more time to familiarize himself with all the equipment while Josh and I get to know him.*

Carson had already checked with Ernie twice, and they were still more than an hour from home, even at top speed. He felt a feeling he despised: uselessness. So far, his timing had been terrible, and now he was paying for it by having to play catch-up. He wanted answers, and he wanted them immediately. He had a feeling that something terrible was about to happen and that it would happen soon. He wasn't psychic, though Melanie had claimed she could sense something in him that she couldn't quite explain. *Maybe I do have some sort of sixth sense,* Carson considered, *like a built-in early warning system.*

He quickly stood from his chair and walked over to Ank. "Hey, keep watch up here, I'm going below to sickbay." Without waiting for a reply, Carson made his exit.

When Carson entered sickbay, he found Glick still lying on the diagnostic bed.

Josh was sitting at the small desk, entering his report in the terminal. "What's up, Carson?" he asked, turning to look at his friend.

"How's our patient?" Carson asked, motioning over to Glick.

"Not bad. Why?"

Carson stood over his unconscious friend and looked down into his boyish face. "I want you to bring him around...now."

Josh stood and faced Carson. "Glick's been through hell, Carson. He needs his rest."

"Give him a stimulant, Josh. We need information. I can't keep flying blindly through this."

With a sigh, Josh picked up a hypo-injector from the medical supply cabinet and snapped in a cartridge containing a strong stimulant. "And you're gonna take full responsibility for this, right?"

"Don't I always? Just give him the shot, Josh."

Josh shrugged his shoulders and pressed the end of the injector to the base of Glick's neck. With a touch of the activation stud, the injector released the stimulant.

Carson watched as Glick began to stir. A low moan escaped the injured man's lips as his eyes slowly fluttered open.

"Glick, can you hear me? It's Carson."

Glick looked up at Carson, his eyes still somewhat glazed from his recent experience. "Carson?" he asked weakly. "God, my head is killing me. Talk about a hangover. You got any aspirin?"

"Later, Glick. What happened? Where's Admiral Brooks?"

Glick almost bolted upright at the sound of the admiral's name. "Brooks! We gotta go back for him. They've got him!"

"Who? Who's got him?" Carson said slowly.

Glick pushed his head back into the pillow and shook it from side to side. "He suspected Olstad, said he had to get there. He ordered me to wait for a check-in call, but it never came, and...uh..."

Glick paused, but he was becoming a little more coherent. Something had lured the admiral to Allegre IV and captured him, causing Glick to attempt a high-speed getaway.

"And what, Glick?"

Glick sat back and tried to concentrate.

"Enough for now, Carson," Josh said, placing his arm on Carson's. "Let the man rest. This is all too much, and – "

"No, there's more," Glick said from the bed. "After they chased me to the Allegre IV moon, I intercepted transmissions to the starbase from deep space."

"Where did they come from?" Carson asked as he pulled from Josh's grasp.

"The shuttle was damaged, but I think it came from one of the outer systems, somewhere in the Nexus system, I think. That's probably where they took Noga and the admiral. You gotta change course and go there now." Glick struggled to get off the bed, but Carson and Josh held him down.

"Easy, man," Josh said quietly. "Take it easy."

Glick took a deep breath and settled down a little. When the men released their grip, he stopped struggling and continued, "Before I left the moon, the starbase was attacked by a squadron of Dreedan battlecruisers."

Carson leaned over Glick, absorbing every word with great interest. "Olstad led that attack. That coldblooded bastard actually ordered the murder of his own people."

"Josh," Carson said, leading his friend to the far side of the small sickbay, "remember Dowd and Tompkin?"

"Right, Mark. This is beginning to sound familiar."

"Yeah, right," Carson said as he activated the wall intercom. "Ank, are we within range of the belt yet?"

"We are just within scanning range," came the reply.

"Raise Griffin. I need to speak to him."

Several seconds later, the voice over the speaker changed to that of Griffin. "Carson, what the hell is going on?"

"I just found the admiral's shuttle, dead and floating in space. The only one aboard was Glick, barely alive. The admiral and Noga are missing."

There was a short pause before Griffin stuttered out, "What do you mean, missing? Noga's landing his ship in the bay now. He said Admiral Brooks is still on Allegre IV, discussing battle tactics."

Glick rolled out of bed and hit the floor with a *thud*. "No! Carson, it can't be Noga," he said, grabbing his ribcage and wincing in pain.

"Carson, is that Glick? What's he babbling about?" Griffin asked.

Carson thought for a second, then said, "Griffin, get a security team to the landing bay. That's not Noga."

"Carson, are you crazy? Do you expect me to..." Griffin hesitated for a moment while someone spoke to him in the background. "Carson, there's a problem in the hangar bay."

"What kind of problem? Answer me, Griffin!" Carson yelled into the intercom.

Suddenly, they heard coughing coming from the operations center through the speaker.

"Wh-what's going on? I-I can't breathe... Gas... Carson, I..."

Then the transmission abruptly broke, and contact was

lost.

"Griffin, can you hear me? Griffin, come in! Ank, are you following all this?"

"Yes, Carson. We're at the edge of the belt now."

"Good. I'm on my way. Josh, I'm gonna need you. Let's go. Glick stay here."

Glick stood to his feet and used the bed to brace himself. "Not on your life, Carson. I'm coming with you."

"Fine, but let's get moving." Even as he said it, Carson hoped he had made the right decision and that Glick wouldn't drop on them when they reached the bridge.

Pulsar cruised up and stopped at the edge of the belt. The three men arrived at the bridge and found Ank at his tactical console, arguing with Ernie.

"Ernie," Ank screamed at the computer, "take us in."

"I'm sorry, Ank, but the security field is in full operation. We cannot proceed."

Carson stepped over to his chair and sat down. "Ank, what's the problem?"

"Ernie refuses to allow *Pulsar* to enter the belt."

"Ernie..."

"Yes, Skipper?"

"Why can't we proceed? We can override security from here, can't we?" Carson asked.

"I'm sorry, Skipper, but the main computer refuses to acknowledge my signal. We cannot shut down asteroid defensive systems."

"Josh, see what you can do."

"Right, Carson," Josh said as he sat at his science station. "Well," he said a moment later, "Ernie's right. We're locked out."

"There has to be a way in."

"There is one way," Josh proposed to the captain. "Ernie, bring up a schematic of the defensive field, and put it on the main viewscreen."

The image of the asteroids in the distance vanished and was replaced by a map of laser battery emplacements and the asteroids they were located on.

"As you can see," Josh began, "the laser batteries are placed in such a way as to negate almost any type of entrance, save one."

Ank looked at Josh in amazement. "You don't mean..."

"Yep. A fly-through, at high speed. It'll be a quick-draw contest to see who gets blasted first, us or each asteroid we fly past."

"Ernie," Carson asked, "can you plot a course through the field and blast the asteroids out?"

"I can set the course for you, but I cannot control either flight controls or weapons systems on entry."

"Why?"

"An energy-dampening field is being utilized. I will lose all control of my higher functions as soon as we enter the field. I am sorry."

Glick stumbled over to the manual helm station and collapsed heavily into the padded chair. "I'll handle the ship, if someone else will take weapons control."

"Glick," Josh said with a shake of his head, "you're insane. You can hardly stand."

Glick considered Josh's comment for a second before turning to face the engineer. "Well, Josh, if I remember correctly, this tin box can be flown from the seated position. How about you, Ank? Think you can handle weapons control?"

"No problem at all, but it is Carson's decision."

All eyes turned to Mark Carson, who really wished he was anyplace else. "Ernie, plot the course. Let's do it."

The bridge was tense as Ernie ran through the necessary calculations for the high-speed trip through the asteroid minefield.

"Skipper, I have fed the course into the navigation console," Ernie announced.

"Well, Glick, can it be done?" Carson asked.

He scanned the readouts on the monitor and seemed satisfied with the results. "It won't be easy, but I think I can do it."

Carson sighed as he sat back in his chair, decidedly resigned to whatever the near future held. "Ank, stand by on weapons. Josh, activate defensive shields and feed target data to Ank. Okay, Glick, engage those engines and take us in."

Without answering, Glick activated the engines, and *Pulsar* surged ahead into the field.

CHAPTER 25

Everything had progressed according to plan, Weent thought, as he watched Noga reactivate all defensive systems. They had been allowed to land in the bay without incident. The excuse that Noga had given to Commando, Inc. second-in-command had proved enough as they had been granted immediate clearance. Passing through the belt had been a tense experience for Weent and the two other mercenaries. They had been briefed on the potential destructive power of the weapons built into many of the asteroids and it had been a source of great concern.

Noga brought the small cruiser through unharmed and into the open hangar bay. Except for the simulcron, the others watched the approach through the cockpit viewscreen. The sheer size of the asteroid headquarters amazed them.

The ship had settled down and then taxied to a secondary hangar out of the flow of traffic. As soon as Noga had the shuttle powered down, Weent handed blaster rifles out and stood by the hatch until Noga joined them.

The hangar crew never had a chance as they were all gunned down as the hatch opened. They were vicious and thorough – no one was allowed to leave the hangar alive. After they had secured the hangar and maintenance bays, Noga and Weent, both in Commando, Inc. uniforms had exited the hangar bay and quickly entered another room only a few meters down the corridor. On the door Weent could see that it simply said, AUXILIARY LIFE SUPPORT – NO ADMITTANCE. Noga had just grinned at him before inputting his security code into the lock. The door had then, in acknowledgement of the correct code, opened to admit them.

After that it was an easy matter to find the ventilation access controls and introduce the sleep gas provided by Donar. After taking less than three minutes, both Noga and Weent, their faces covered by oxygen respirators, left the small room and headed back for the hangar bay.

There they were reunited with the two other mercenaries – similar respirators covering their faces. The second time they left the bay, they could see that the drug had done its job; everyone laid on the deck unconscious.

The first stop that Noga had led them to was the operations center. He had warned them that they had to reestablish the defensive zone so that no one could enter, and only they could leave.

Weent removed the respirator from his face as Noga gave him and the two human mercenaries the clear sign. He had taken the two humans with them for two reasons: the first being that if they were discovered, they could pass more easily for part of the normal complement, and secondly, he couldn't trust or control any of Donar's creatures.

Noga finished his work at the security console and turned to face the three humans. "Come now. I've already removed all fail-safe controls and manual overrides that control the core from here."

"Can't we destroy it from here?" the human mercenary called Jones asked.

Noga shook his head. "No. We have to go to the fusion

reactor core itself to start the overload."

Weent looked around the control room and felt it was a shame that he couldn't take anything with him. They had been given a certain length of time to accomplish their mission and then to return to Nexus III.

"Weent, are you coming?" Noga asked as he noticed the human still standing by the operations console.

"Yeah, I'm coming," he said as he followed them out into the corridor.

In space, unknown to the four terrorists, *Pulsar* was engaged in a life or death game with the already targeting laser mounted asteroids. Glick had played the helm console like a concert pianist as *Pulsar* swerved from side to side in an intense effort to avoid being hit by the intense energy pulses released by the gun emplacements.

Carson felt useless again as he knew that it all depended on the flying skills of Glick and the marksmanship of Ank with equipment that he was still not quite comfortable with. Suddenly, the ship took a hit on her shields and the lights dimmed for a very long second.

"Josh, damage control!" Carson yelled over as he gripped the armrests of his chair tightly.

Josh accessed the areas of the central computer that were not affected by the jamming and called up a quick diagnostic. "A hit on the port shield – she's still holding!"

Carson gave a small sigh of relief. They had progressed about one-quarter of the way through and had taken only two ineffective hits. He knew he had Glick to thank for that. He had never seen anyone with half the instinctive skills that this man at the controls of his ship seemed to possess.

Pulsar barrel rolled, between two asteroids as a beam of

energy lashed out, vaporizing a small chunk of asteroid just behind them. Ank reacted quickly and fired as they passed as the asteroid exploded in a shower of rock and metal fragments.

Glick looked intensely at the course plotted by Ernie. He knew the laser weapons were self-correcting and it would get more difficult the closer he got. He didn't know if he or the others would make it through this alive, but he was having the time of his life piloting *Pulsar*. This vessel was like no other in space, and showed it.

Ank fired off burst after burst from *Pulsar*'s blaster cannon. With a firing radius of 360 degrees around the ship, there wasn't much that Ank couldn't hit. Taking the sensor feed that Josh Grant kept feeding him, he could take out multiple targets simultaneously.

As Ank fired, the ship was jarred by another burst from behind. Had this been a ship with a less powerful deflector shield, *Pulsar* would now be in more pieces then anyone would care to count. The lights flickered again, this time replaced by red emergency lights.

"Josh, activate emergency power." Carson didn't want to take any chances that the main core would go down from all the punishment that the ship was taking. The lights stabilized as emergency power fed from solar panels in the stern of the ship.

Finally, they passed the last asteroid housed laser and slowly approached the base.

"Everybody all right?" Carson asked as he settled about three inches down into his seat.

"Fine, though barely," Josh said as he rubbed the sweat from his head.

"All right," said Ank from the weapons console.

"How about you, Glick?" Josh asked smiling.

Glick swiveled his chair to face the others who could see that he was soaked through from the intense concentration. "What a ride, man. Now what?"

Carson stood and walked over to the viewscreen – the visual showing the asteroid headquarters floating silently in the distance. "Well, it all depends on whether or not we have Ernie back."

"I'm fine now, skipper," came Ernie's voice from the bridge speaker.

"Great," Carson said. "Run a diagnostic on all systems, Ernie."

A few seconds later Carson got the answer that he was looking for. "Minor damage to the deflector generator, and the power core is down 33 percent. I have already started automated repairs."

"Nice going, Ernie," Josh added with a smile.

"Ernie, we're going to have to find a way in. Can you open the doors on the main landing bay?" Carson asked.

There was a momentary pause as Ernie sent out a signal that would activate the large hangar doors. When nothing happened, Ernie informed them of his failure. "Hangar doors access is restricted. All codes have been changed, skipper."

Carson paced back and forth across the bridge. Suddenly, he stopped and looked at Ank. "Ank, remember when you thought Donar was still holding you, and you stole the shuttle?"

"Yes," Ank answered.

"Do you remember where you took it from?" Carson

looked at him, the answer was so obvious.

It was even obvious to Ank as he realized what Carson was talking about. "The maintenance bay."

"Right, the maintenance bay. Glick take us there. Ernie, try the activation access code. It should be at a security level too low for Noga to be concerned about."

Pulsar maneuvered to the smaller repair and test bay where Ernie again sent out a signal. This time, the single, armored door began to slide open.

"Skipper, I have a positive response on the access code," Ernie reported.

"Good. Glick, take us in."

"Right," Glick said as he slowly guided *Pulsar* onto the repair birth within the small hangar. When the ship was secured, Ernie sent out another signal closing the hangar door and repressurizing the bay.

Within seconds, Ernie announced that the atmosphere on the outside of the ship was equalized with inside, signaling that it was safe to leave. Before leaving though, Carson handed everyone a blaster pistol, while he added a small needler to a clip attached to the rear of his belt.

Ernie monitored them as they headed for the operations center. All around them lay motionless bodies. Josh stopped occasionally to verify that they were only sleeping and not dead. Eventually, they made it to the central control room where they found Griffin, also unconscious, slumped over the communications console.

Josh checked Griffin and found that he was in the same condition. "Well, they're all unconscious. Whatever it was that they used, it worked quickly. Nobody was able to make a move for the emergency support equipment."

Carson sat by the master computer and ran an internal sensor check. Ank walked over and stood over him. "What are you doing, Carson?"

"Considering the fact that everyone is out cold. I'm running a motion-sensor scan to see if I can find our intruders," Carson said as his hands played over the controls. They all looked up at the main viewscreen that dominated the forward section of the operations center as Carson transferred data from the sensors to the larger display. Starting with a holographic view of the asteroid, Carson scanned each level one at a time. After several tense seconds he had success. "Got them. They're heading for level twenty-two."

"Carson, it has to be the fusion reactor," Josh said tensely. "The fail-safe's been disabled." They all knew the implications of that statement. With the fail-safe control disabled here, the only way of handling a potential emergency of the fusion core was from the reactor control room itself.

"Ank, you come with me. Josh, you and Glick stay here. See if you can repair the fail-safe." Carson motioned for Ank to follow him and the two ran out leaving Glick and Josh behind.

Once they were gone, Josh removed the panel and stared at the damage that Noga had done to the system. "All right, Glick. Lets see if you can fix things as well as you can fly."

Glick looked at him and shook his head. "We're really in trouble then," he said with a smile as they went to work.

Weent watched as Noga worked the controls of the massive fusion reactor. It was an awesome experience,

Weent thought; the power core stretched downward, seemingly to the very core of the asteroid. He walked over and watched Noga build the awesome power into a destructive force that would probably create a small sun from the unstable materials that would be vaporized in the explosion.

Weent began to think about the fate that awaited his home planet. Why, he thought, did it bother him so much that in a matter of a few hours, Earth would cease to exist? Did he care one way or the other what happened? There seemed to be no easy answer. Earth had given him his chosen "profession" and very little else. Maybe he was becoming to old for all this, he thought.

A high-pitched whining broke the spell of his thoughts and brought him back to the matter at hand. He could see the instruments going wild as the reactor began to generate more and more power while channeling its massive energies absolutely nowhere. The resulting overload and explosion would destroy everything in the belt and dead-zone this area of space for centuries.

"Weent, it is done," Noga said as he moved past Weent. "Where are the men?"

"Watching the corridor. How much time do we have?"

"No more than twenty minutes."

As the door closed behind them, Weent looked down the corridor before looking curiously at Noga.

"What is the matter?" Noga asked, impatient to leave.

"The men. I left them here. Now they're gone."

Noga saw from a glance at his chronometer that there wasn't much time to give the human beasts a second thought. "Perhaps they're back at the ship. We must not waste anymore time."

Carson looked down at the two mercenaries at his feet. He had taken each one out with a well-placed needler shot – the tranquilizer in the darts quickly knocking the two human intruders unconscious. Looking over at Ank, Carson could see the big felinoid pointing down the corridor. Both Weent and Noga were walking right toward them.

He had about enough of Weent, Carson thought. This time he wasn't going to give the mercenary a second chance. He adjusted the earphone from his comm unit as Josh's voice came through the small receiver.

"Carson, listen closely. The core is in overload. I figure about eighteen minutes till detonation." Not being able to respond verbally, Carson sent an electronic confirmation of what Josh had told him.

He couldn't depend on Josh fixing the fail-safe controls. Signaling Ank, Carson tumbled into the corridor and came up with his needler in his hand.

"Stop – both of you! Drop the weapons." Carson ordered as Weent and Noga froze into place.

"Carson, you're supposed to be dead." Weent said, confused by the events. "I might have known that Donar's people would screw that up too."

"Shut up, Weent," Noga growled.

"Listen, Weent, drop the blaster – now!"

"Hey, Carson, no problem," he said as the gun clattered to the floor.

"You too, Noga, or whatever you are. Drop it."

"Of course, Carson." Noga pulled his blaster out of the large holster in his belt and threw it down to the floor. As Carson stood up from his crouch, Noga pulled a small object from his belt and threw it down the corridor.

"Grenade," Ank shouted as he rushed from his place of concealment and again knock Carson out of the way. The grenade landed just in front of Weent, the explosion blasting him against the corridor wall.

When the smoke had cleared, Ank helped Carson to his feet before dusting off his own uniform. "Are you all right?"

"Thanks again, Ank. But next time please, just a warning. One of these days I think these rescues are going to kill me."

Ank smiled at the attempt at humor on Carson's part. He knew that if a similar situation occurred again, he would take the same action, and probably suffer through the same joke.

Carson could see as the smoke dissipated, Weent lying by the side of the wall where the grenade had exploded. As Carson knelt by the injured man he was surprised to see that he was still alive.

"Ank, give me the first aid kit."

Ank handed him the small med-kit as he looked down at the broken body of his old friend.

Weent moved his head from side to side in obvious pain. The reading that Carson had from the medical diagnostic scanner was not very good. He was bleeding internally, and beyond the medical care that he could give him.

He prepared a hypo, but was stopped by Weent. "No, Carson. It's too late," he said from between clenched teeth.

"Let me give you something for the pain."

"The reactor. It's set to blow. Stop it." It seemed as though it was an effort for Weent to talk and his head settled back to the floor.

Ank leaned over to Carson, and put a paw on the man's shoulder. "Carson, Noga is back in the reactor chamber."

"How much time is left?" Carson asked as he kept his eyes on Weent. Even after all that had happened, he still remembered the friendship that they had once had.

"Twelve minutes."

As he stood, Weent pulled him back down. "Carson," Weent said through the pain, "they're crazy. Ship was sent with anti-matter bomb...destroy Earth. You have to stop them."

"What about Melanie?"

"The doc? She's with Brooks. Donar's holding them."

"Carson, time is running out," Ank interrupted.

Carson looked up at Ank and then back at Weent. "Where are they, Regar?"

"If I tell you, will you kill Donar for me?"

"Tell me!"

"Promise me," Weent cried.

"I promise," Carson said softly.

"Nexus III, Carson. I'm sorry. We were friends once, weren't we?" Weent asked as his grip tightened on Carson's arm.

"Once."

"Good. Now get Noga before I kick your ass into space. Right into..." Weent closed his eyes, his hand dropping from the tight grip he had on Carson's arm.

Carson activated the intercom on the wall and signaled the operations center. "Josh, what's your status?"

"If you don't have that core under control in eight minutes, you won't need a ship to fly through space," came Josh's tense voice.

"I'll take care of it," he said as he closed the channel.

"He's locked the door – now what?" Ank asked.

"That thing seems to know everything that Noga knew. He'll know every possible way into that room, and have them all covered. The only way I can see is to quickly overwhelm him."

Carson outlined his plan. A two pronged assault: he would head through the ventilation system while Ank would blow open the door and try a more frontal assault.

Handing Ank his blaster, Carson outlined how to overload the weapon's power pack. The resulting explosion should be enough to open the heavy door. With Noga's attention diverted, Carson thought that he might have a chance of reaching the control board and shutting down the runaway core.

With five minutes remaining, Carson ran to an air ventilation junction grid and opened the access hatch. He crawled through the maze of tunnels heading to what he hoped was the reactor room.

With only two minutes remaining, Carson looked down on Noga as the simulcron paced back and forth across the dimly lit chamber. Sending a silent electronic signal to Ank, Carson braced for the explosion. Several seconds later the door blew inward, stunning Noga for a brief time. Carson leapt to the floor and made a mad dash for the reactor control. Noga turned and fired at Carson, the blast grazing him and sending him flying to the floor.

Noga stood over the fallen Carson and brought the blaster down for a final killing shot. Just before he could pull the trigger, a heavy paw smashed against the back of his neck, sending him sprawling. Ank pulled his blaster from its holster as Noga quickly stood and charged, headfirst.

Carson opened his eyes to see Ank and Noga in a brutal fight. Noga hit Ank with a heavy fist, sending the felinoid down to the floor. Spotting his blaster, Noga dived to the floor, quickly coming up with the weapon.

Remembering that he still had the needler, Carson saw where Ank still laid. "Ank, catch," Carson yelled as he hurled the needler to his friend. Ank caught the weapon and before Noga could react fired a dart. The small dart struck the simulcron in the eye. Yellow colored fluid spurted out as the pain sent him backward into the main power grid.

The energy of a small sun momentarily lit Noga up in a glowing haze, until his atoms lost their adhesion and the alien disintegrated into a milky white mist. The whining had intensified as Carson made a quick dive for the control panel. He quickly got control of the core as the whine slowed to a low hum.

Carson pulled himself to his feet and slowly slid back down to the floor as the adrenal rush faded. The pain of the blaster burn on his upper shoulder was intense but tolerable. Ank helped Carson back to his feet as Josh and Glick entered with their weapons drawn.

Ank looked at them both as he pulled Carson up. "It's done. Help me get Carson to sickbay."

As they helped Carson into the corridor, signs of life were quickly returning to the base as the effects of the gas began to wear off. By the time they reached the medical center, Dr. Antar was standing by to assist.

Carson sat on the examination table as Dr. Antar cut away the top of his uniform to reveal the section of his shoulder burned and blistered by the blaster graze.

"This isn't too bad, is it?" Antar joked as he sprayed the wound with an antiseptic. The look that Carson had given him convinced Antar to keep any further jokes to himself.

As the treatment continued Carson filled in Ank and Griffin on the conversation that he had with Weent before the mercenary had died.

After he was finished, Griffin stepped forward with the first question. "Can you trust him?"

Carson thought for a moment while Antar bandaged the wound. "I do. Weent knew he was dying. What would he have to gain by lying at this stage?"

"If that's true, than the Earth, along with the Alliance Council is in great danger," Ank said.

"I guess we'd better act on it," Griffin said as he scratched the top of his balding head.

"Based on what Glick told me," Carson said as he hopped off the table, "there was a hell of a large force assembling out by Allegre IV. What's the status of the Alliance fleet?"

"They're out at the frontier facing off against the Dreedan fleet, each blaming the other for the raids on their frontier colonies. Unfortunately, the fleet is too far out to possibly catch up."

"But we're not," Carson added as he pulled on a fresh uniform. "Griffin, have Glick put together the fastest ships he can and have them ready to move out in one hour. Also, put in a call to Admiral Stack, he should be in command of the fleet strike force. We'd better advise him on current events."

"What about Admiral Brooks and Dr. Patula?"

"Let's head for Operations and I'll tell you on the way."

By the time they had reached the busy operations center, Griffin tried to digest what Carson had told him. Communications meanwhile had opened a channel to Admiral Stack who sat on the bridge of his flagship waiting for Carson's arrival.

"Admiral, good to see you again sir," Carson said to the figure on the large monitor.

Stack's face brightened at the sight of Carson. Stack had been his commanding officer in the war and they shared a mutual respect for each other's abilities. "Carson, what's going on here? I've got a fleet of Dreedan Imperial warships close enough to spit at. I don't have time for casual chit chat."

"Admiral, please listen closely to what I have to say, and for both of our sakes please believe me." For the next several minutes Carson told Stack, as quickly as possible, what had transpired in the past several weeks. He had to give the admiral credit; he was taking the story quite seriously and didn't interrupt once. When he was finished, Stack let out a long breath and stared at him from the other side of the screen.

"You believe this story is true and that Earth is in danger?"

"I do, sir," Carson responded quickly.

"Well, they certainly caught us with our pants down, son. There's no way I can get enough ships back there in time to stop them."

"I know, admiral. I'm setting up a strike force here that should be ready to leave in about twenty-three minutes."

"What about Brooks and the girl. If I can arrange some

kind of truce with the Dreedans, I can lead my fleet over there and dig them out."

"I don't advise that. They could be in danger if they detect your fleet heading toward them."

"Then what do you suggest."

"I'm allowing *Pulsar* to intercept the enemy ships without me," Ank stood abruptly at this part of Carson's plan. "I'll take Weent's cruiser and return with it to Nexus III; we can't take a chance that Donar would hear about the failure of any of this – he'd probably kill them both. After the enemy fleet has been destroyed, the ships will rendezvous to offer support at Nexus III."

Stack nodded his head at what Carson was saying, seemingly at total, though reluctant agreement. "We'll go with your plan, but I'm going to have a couple of battlecruisers standing by just off system. We can't let this Donar escape. When you need me, I'll be there."

"Thank you, sir."

"Don't thank me yet, Carson. I still have to convince the Dreedans that Donar has made idiots out of all of us and then try to convince the rest of my fleet of your crazy story. Good luck. Stack out," the fleet admiral said as he closed the communications channel.

As Carson turned to the others he was made aware immediately of the criticism of his plan.

"Carson, you can't go in alone," Ank said angrily.

"Sure I can. Someone has to be there when news of your saving Earth comes in. I don't think that Donar takes failure very well."

Griffin walked over with a communiqué and handed it to Carson. As Carson read the message, Griffin paraphrased it for the others. "It seems that any ship that fleet of yours comes across is being blown out of space." Seven ships, including a passenger transport with 840 people onboard, were already known victims of Donar's strike fleet.

"They're certainly leaving a trail," Carson said as he crumbled the communiqué into a ball and tossed it to Josh.

"Can you estimate, based on this, where the fleet is?" Ank asked.

"About six hours from Earth. What little that can intercept them has already been destroyed," Glick said depressingly.

Carson did some quick mental calculations in his head before facing the others. "Well, as close as I can figure it, if the ships leave on schedule, you should be able to intercept them just outside the orbit of Mars."

"To close," Griffin said after a deep breath.

Ank turned from the group and stared down at his black uniform boots. Carson walked over and put a comforting hand on his friend's shoulder. "What's the matter, Ank?"

"I don't feel right about seeing you face Donar alone. You don't know the extent of his power like I do."

"Ank, I have one major advantage; He thinks we're dead."

Ank found it hard to argue with his friend's logic. "You won't take any unnecessary chances?"

Carson looked his friend in the eye and smiled. "I've done this kind of thing before. If I have a problem, I'll keep them busy until you guys show up."

Ank shook his head. "You didn't answer my question."

Carson shrugged. "I can't promise anything, but I'll try."

Ank nodded, even though he still looked at Carson with

a wary eye. "That I will accept."

"Good," Carson said. "We have ten minutes before liftoff, so let's move."

A few minutes later they found Josh and Glick waiting for them in the hangar bay. Spread out over the massive hangar, Carson could see technicians equipping the small fleet of nine cruisers with extra armament.

"It's about time you two showed up," Josh said to them as they entered the hangar.

Carson ignored Josh and turned to Glick. "What's the fleet's status?"

"Well, the "fleet" as you called it consists of nine ships," Glick said sarcastically, "but they're all combat ready."

"Good. What about Weent's cruiser?" Carson asked as he pointed at the small ship still sitting where it was left.

"No problem, as far as I can see."

"Great," Carson said as he began to cross the hanger in the direction of the small cruiser.

"Will someone explain to me what is going on?" Glick called to Carson.

"See Ank, he's already explaining it to Josh," Carson called back as he continued on to the cruiser.

When he reached the main hatch he turned to look back at his friends. He smiled as he could see that Josh wasn't reacting very well to his plans. He could swear that he heard Josh calling his name as he shut the hatch behind him.

Moving to the small flight deck, Carson sat down and began to familiarize himself with the helm and navigational systems. It had been a long time since he had to manually pilot a ship of this kind by himself; Ernie had really spoiled him.

Punching up an external display, he saw Josh give up his argument with Ank, throw up his arms, and head through the hatch into *Pulsar* resigned to accept the plan as it was. He had purposely avoided saying goodbye to any of them. Both of their missions could wind up costing any or all of them their lives, but he somehow thought that he'd be seeing them again.

Powering up the cruiser's systems, Carson reported to Griffin that he was ready. Within another thirty seconds, *Pulsar* and the nine other cruisers each reported the similar status. With *Pulsar* leading the pack, and with Glick at the helm, he had few doubts that they'd fail.

One by one, Carson watched as the fleet of ten ships was lifted to the landing bay in their preparation for launch. Before the lift could take him up to the landing bay, Carson turned at the sound of the flight deck's inner hatch sliding open.

"Ank!" Carson said at the sight of the felinoid. "What the hell are you doing here? You're supposed to be in command of those ships out there."

Ank approached and took a seat by the communications/science station. "Glick is capable enough to lead the strike force. It's a violation of my code of honor to allow you to go alone."

"Interesting code..." Carson saw that he hadn't the time to argue as the small cruiser was lifted to it's launch position just in time to see *Pulsar*, followed by the other ships, head off into space.

"OK, strap in."

"Yes, sir," Ank said as he flashed Carson a pathetic salute.

"Good luck to us all," Carson said quietly to himself as he activated his main thrusters and launched into space.

CHAPTER 26

Eleven delta-winged Dreedan warships exited silently out of hyperspace. In a triangular formation they plowed through space past the planet Pluto. Powerful sensors, orbiting eighty-7,000 kilometers beyond Pluto's orbit transmitted data on the size and location of the enemy fleet to a receiving station on the small planet's surface. Knowledge of the detection was quickly forwarded to Fleet Command Headquarters on Earth with predictable results – the entire system went to red alert.

On orders from Earth, Colonel Samuel Majors ordered his small squadron of fighters to intercept the intruders but were easily swept aside – no match for the firepower of the small fleet. Two Dreedan Destroyers broke formation just long enough to each fire four missiles off at the Plutonian threat. The eight missiles streaked through space on the power of small ion thrusters. Each warhead was targeted for the pressure dome which covered the outpost.

"Eight contacts. All incoming, sir," the young ensign on sensors reported.

Majors looked at the readout and knew there was very little that he could do. "Activate counter-measures, and lock on point-missile defense system!"

Electronic countermeasures were activated in an attempt to scramble the tracking mechanisms of the incoming weapons. Anti-missile missiles fired off in multiple salvos from small hidden launchers to intercept any that got through.

Three missiles were intercepted high above Pluto's surface – their explosions lighting up the pitch black sky. Two of the missiles flew wide of the dome and impacted on the desolate surface seventy-five kilometers away. The impact rumbled through the outpost as cracks began to show along the dome.

Majors grabbed tightly onto a console in front of him as circuits shorted out all through the control room. "Damage control report! Damage control..."

"Colonel, three missiles are locked onto us!" the ensign interrupted. "Impact in five, four..."

"Oh, my god," Majors murmured to himself.

"...two, one."

The three remaining missiles struck the outpost simultaneously on its titanium atmospheric pressure dome. The resultant explosion vaporized not only the outpost, but one-eighth of the planet's surface. In the space of less than a second, the Pluto outpost and 147 men and women ceased to exist.

Barton, in the lead ship, was well aware of the dangers this close to the seat of Alliance power. He regretted the need to destroy the small outpost, but there was very little choice. He was not like the others. True, he was a simulcron, but his original stock was elfin, not werewolf. Those limitations though would not hinder him from completing his mission.

The flight to the Terran star system, otherwise, had been uneventful, Barton thought as he sat on the bridge of what had been the Dreedan battlecruiser Dreadnought. They had been challenged by several ships which had attempted to stop his fleet. His superior force had destroyed them all. With the best of the Alliance fleet dancing with their Dreedan counterparts at the frontier border, nothing remained powerful enough to stop them.

Since the battle of an hour ago, his ships were now crossing past the ringed planet that he knew from his stolen memories was called Saturn. It would only be a matter of not more than another hour now before they reached their destination: Earth. For some unknown reason, there was a certain sadness in what he would soon be doing. The memories of this planet were strong; as this was the birthplace of the human who was part of him.

He would not disappoint his master though. As soon as orbit was established, he would launch the completed anti-matter device from one of the adapted missile batteries and sever the head of the Alliance government from its galactic body. He would do as he was commanded to, in spite of the doubts caused by his alien memories.

Meanwhile, at the edge of the solar system, *Pulsar* exited hyperspace and continued in pursuit, her engines pushed to their limits. With her superior speed, she had arrived well in advance of her own small fleet. Glick, sitting in the command chair, hoped that they could delay them long enough for the other ships of his strike force to arrive. He turned in his chair and faced Josh who now sat at the tactical console. After Ank had left him in command to go off with Carson, it had just left the three of them – just Josh, Ernie, and himself. It was just as well; Ernie could handle many of the complex ship's functions, leaving the two humans to handle the combat chores.

"Glick, long range sensors have located eleven warships

of Dreedan design ahead of us, currently crossing the orbit of Jupiter," Ernie reported from the data received from his long range sensors.

"Ernie, what's our ETA to intercept?" Glick asked calmly.

"We will intercept the enemy ships in twelve minutes if we maintain our current speed."

"What about the rest of the strike force?"

Again the response came immediately. "At current speed they will arrive five minutes ten seconds after we engage."

It looked like they had their work cut out for them. "Let's do it. Shields to full power," Glick called out.

"Shields are up, and all weapons charged to full power," Josh reported.

"We're being scanned," Ernie reported as his sensitive receivers picked up the scan of enemy sensors.

"Josh, activate sensor jamming – blind 'em!"

Josh ran his hand over the tactical activating the proper controls that would confuse any sensor readings to the Dreedan ships, causing them to be unreliable. Long-range communications would also be impossible, giving Ank and Carson more time to accomplish their part of the mission at Nexus III.

Glick quickly jumped to the helm station and took full helm control. He thought he'd be of very little use to any of them tied to the command chair.

"I have them on tactical sensors," Josh said from the rear of the bridge. "I'm transferring to the main viewscreen." The forward screen dissolved into the sensor-generated view of the triangular formation of warships before them.

"OK, gang," Glick said as he concentrated on

maneuvering *Pulsar* in for a rear assault. "Let's rock and roll."

Barton reacted as he was told of the ship now closing on the rear quarter of his force. "Dispatch Predator and Eliminator to intercept. Keep the rest of the force on course."

In space, the two outer points of the triangle peeled away and turned to face *Pulsar*. The captains of both ships had done this same maneuver many times before and had instantly destroyed all that had come, including the human's outpost on Pluto. Needless to say they were both over confident as their ships closed on the lone prey.

On *Pulsar*, both Glick and Josh saw the two ships peel away from the body of the fleet and head leisurely back toward them.

"Two Dreedan cruisers at 6,000 kilometers and closing," Josh reported. "Their shields are up and sensors indicate weapons are at full power."

"We can't waste time with them," Glick called out. "I'm going to take the ship between them. Fire as we pass."

"Right," Josh said as he targeted the attacking ships.

They knew that it was a risky maneuver, but they had to reach the lead ship and delay it until the others showed up.

An alarm sounded as sensors picked up incoming fire. "They're firing," Josh screamed. Photon fire washed over *Pulsar*'s shields. Ninety percent was fully absorbed, but the other 10 percent leaked through to rock them in their seats.

"Hold your fire, we have to make the shots count," Glick called out.

Again the shields absorbed the fire from the two Dreedan cruisers. The bridge lights dimmed as Ernie channeled more power to the defensive systems. "That was a close one. Damage report, Ernie."

"Damage to port and starboard shields. I have rerouted power to compensate."

"Ernie, call off range to target," Glick called out.

"Four thousand kilometers...3,000...2,000..." Ernie called out.

"Fire!" Glick screamed.

Josh pushed down on the firing stud and two intense beams of energy lanced out at the enemy ships at point-blank range. The beams struck the two ships at close range, and despite their shields, punched through the hulls of each cruiser. As they passed the damaged ships, a second salvo was fired. At the impact, both cruisers momentarily flared and then disappeared, each exploding in incandescent brilliance. *Pulsar* continued on as debris from the destroyed ships bounced harmlessly off her still glowing shields.

"Yeah!" Glick screamed.

In the Dreadnought, Barton viewed the events with fear. This one craft had destroyed both of his picket ships and was still coming. He would not be stopped this close to his objective.

Turning to his communications station he made a decision. "Order the rest of the fleet to turn and attack the intruder. Warn them not to be as careless as their two destroyed brothers, but to destroy that ship at all costs."

Barton sat back in his command chair as the Dreadnought crossed the orbit Mars. What ship did the Alliance have that could destroy two of his ships that easily. "Fool!" he called to the science station. "Run an identification scan of the intruder."

Moments later the science officer turned his face white, as he thought of how he'd give his report.

"What do you report?" Barton growled.

"The configuration of the ship is not in the Dreedan computer banks," the science officer said before turning back to his sensors.

"Give me a visual of the configuration on the main viewscreen," Barton ordered. The viewscreen now displayed the configuration of a ship that Barton, with terror growing, recognized. "That's *Pulsar*...they must be alive. Communications raise Nexus III. I must talk to Lord Donar."

The communications officer turned to his console and activated his subspace transmitter. As he attempted to send the signal, a high-pitched squeal came through his earphone almost deafening him.

"Someone is jamming our signal," the officer moaned as he brought a hand up to a numb ear.

That someone, Barton realized, had to be *Pulsar*. It was a powerful ship, but it couldn't be a match for eight fully prepared Dreedan warships – could it?

The computerized scan showed all the remaining ships turning back toward them – only the point ship continued on.

"Shit," Josh said quietly. Eight on one are not the best of odds.

"Ernie, where's the rest of our ships?" Glick frantically called out.

"Two minutes behind."

"Send them a signal to burnout their engines if they have to, we need help."

"Right, Glick," Ernie sent the message as they saw the Dreedan ships close.

"What's their range?" Glick said as he pointed to the enemy ships.

"Five thousand kilometers, and closing," Josh reported from tactical before Ernie.

"Ernie, what's ships status?" Glick asked.

"Shield capacity is down 23 percent; all other systems are fully functional."

"They're all firing!" Josh called out.

Long-range fire came in from all eight ships. Not accurate, but spread for effect, seven of the eight initial bursts passed harmlessly, the eighth though impacted – the blast causing the lights to flicker again.

Glick took *Pulsar* through evasive maneuvers as he tried to find a way past the ships without taking too much punishment. Josh activated the powerful weapons again, and space lit up with high-energy death. *Pulsar* took two other hits as the lights went out and red emergency lights came up to take its place.

"Shields are down to 15 percent. Starboard shields have dropped. Structural damage to the sensor grid. Automated repairs beginning," Ernie reported, his computer created voice reflecting the pain of each blast.

Josh fired his weapons until an override shut them down due to overheating. They had disabled two of the ships and had damaged three others, but they were still in pursuit. A photon blast ripped into her shields above the bridge causing the lights to go out. Caught in a surge of energy the tactical station exploded in electric fire.

"Glick, fire on the bridge," Josh called out as the intense

heat forced him back from the hot panel. "Ernie, activate emergency extinguishers...Ernie!"

Hearing no answer, Josh grabbed the small extinguisher bottle from beneath his seat and quickly sprayed the flames. Glick, meanwhile tried in vain to keep *Pulsar* out of range of the attacking ships. Glick sadly felt resigned to the fact that if something didn't happen soon, *Pulsar* was a goner, and not much later, the Earth.

A Dreedan warship came up in front of them, weapons primed. Without Ernie, Josh check the tactical status board and saw that the shields would not stop another hit.

"Josh, I'm sorry. This is..."

Before Glick could finish, the Dreedan cruiser erupted in a cloud of expanding gas. Over the comm system they heard a message coming through.

"You guys okay," came a familiar voice.

Glick could see the rest of the strike force as it struck from behind, taking the remaining enemy ships by complete surprise. Glick brought up auxiliary power, as Josh made his way to the communications console.

"Were fine, thanks," Josh said as the nine Commando, Inc. light cruisers overwhelmed the enemy battlecruisers. They had used their surprise to destroy the more powerful warships.

Glick didn't pause, as he channeled all remaining power into the engines and *Pulsar* accelerated into action. "Josh, tell those ships to follow us when they get control, and then get your arse back to tactical. What's damage control like?"

"Well, Ernie is out. Sensors are at minimum power, and I have even better news," Josh said glumly.

"What's that?"

"Weapons banks are exhausted. The emitters are all but burnt out."

"Are they totally inoperative?" Glick asked without turning.

"Not totally, we've only got one or two shots before we lose the emitters."

"What about the photon launchers?"

"We lost them early on."

It was frustrating. Even if they caught the last ship, they didn't have enough left to penetrate their shields before it was too late.

"Give me what you can," Glick said as he pushed the damaged *Pulsar* even harder. "Where is he?"

"Just passing lunar orbit. We won't reach him in time," Josh added dejectedly.

Glick pounded his hand against the helm console. This was too much, he'd been shot at, stranded in space, and survived a battle against ten Dreedan battlecruisers. He'd be damned if he'd be stopped now.

"Josh!" Glick called out. "Get to communications. Get me that bastard."

"Why?"

"Don't ask. Just do it!"

Josh tried to establish contact with the Dreedan cruiser. Sensors reported that it was within minutes of entering Earth orbit – time was running out. Seconds later the tactical view on the forward screen faded and was replaced by a face that Glick found familiar.

"Bill Barton?" Glick said more in amazement more to himself than to the figure on the screen.

"Hello, Glick. You don't look very well."

"You've got to stop your ship. You can't do this," Glick pleaded.

"I understand what you mean, Glick. Unfortunately, Barton is not in control of this situation," the simulcron added.

"You must be one of those creatures," Glick said impolitely to the image on the screen.

"No, I am a higher form of life, you are the creature," Barton sneered from where he sat.

"Glick," Josh said quietly, "he's in orbit."

Glick turned back to the screen, he had to buy a little more time.

"Barton," Glick said, not knowing what else to call the creature, "there must be part of you left in there. Fight it. Don't let the thing win; it's your home planet too."

There seemed to be a slight conflict within Barton as he looked from side to side. "Remember your family...your mother and sister – they're on Earth. You can't kill them, can you?"

Barton seemed confused now, as he stood from his chair and stumbled to his feet. "My mother and sister...memories of them are strong. I loved them...but what is love." Perhaps that was the feeling he had felt before, Barton thought.

Josh could see the indecision that Glick had caused in the simulcron. The memories of its previous owner seemed to threaten to tear their way out.

Eventually, Barton straightened out and faced Glick. He could see the saddened look on what had once been his friend's face. "I'm sorry, Glick. I have no control." Suddenly the connection was cut and there was only darkness.

"We're within range," Josh said. "But his shields are up."

Glick leapt from his position and joined Josh at the tactical station. "Where would he release that bomb from?"

"Possibly the forward missile launching bay. Why?" Josh looked at him and then shook his head. "You can't mean what I think you mean."

"You got it. We have to hit that anti-matter bomb as soon as it's launched." Glick intensified all remaining sensor power and tightened it into a tight short-range display. "Transfer weapons to manual tracking control and route as much power as we can into the shields." With Ernie non-responsive, he had no choice but try to line up the shot himself.

Josh completed the connection and they waited. The wait wasn't long as the anti-matter device, gleaming in the sunlight, ejected from the bow of the enemy vessel. Glick lined the cross-hair from the manual fire control system on the large metallic canister. With a quiet prayer he pressed a thumb down onto the firing stud. Silently, an intense beam of energy shot out from *Pulsar* and impacted with the anti-matter bomb. The power of the explosion lashed out in all directions. Josh hoped the atmosphere would offer protection to the Earth, but for them there was none; with the shields at only 25 percent of full power he hoped that whatever happened to them was quick.

They waited as the expanding ball of white light approached them. Glick saw the ball of highly charged energy consume Barton's ship and then approach *Pulsar*. With a silent prayer he braced himself for impact. When the shock wave struck, Glick fell back, his head hitting the hard armrest of the command chair. His final thought as darkness closed around him concerned the possible existence of god, and if a Supreme Being did in fact exist, what had he done to deserve all this?

CHAPTER 27

Several dozen light-years away, a small Vixen class light cruiser decelerated out of hyperspace just beyond the outer fringes of the Nexus star system. Switching immediately to its fusion drive engines, Carson set a parabolic course that would bring them to Nexus III for a landing well into nightfall. He and Ank had hoped that the darkness would provide enough cover to enter the enemy camp; the search for Melanie and the admiral had to progress as silently as possible.

Ank's sensor scan of the system had come up clean, signaling no potential problems in their way. Satisfied that there wouldn't be any serious problems for at least several minutes, Carson went to the rear storage area to check on the supplies that he had loaded. Ank joined him there as the ship's navigational computer guided the small cruiser to its destination.

"You seem worried," Ank said as he saw Carson going through his inventory checklist. "I am." Carson turned back to the supplies as Ank came closer to help uncrate the supplies.

"We will not know for certain whether *Pulsar* has succeeded until this operation is finished, but we must stay focused on our own task," the felinoid said as he removed the compact photon cannon from its storage case.

"I realize that, Ank." Carson was aware that they had to proceed at total communications blackout; it was after all his plan. Out of one crate Carson pulled out two black jumpsuits and threw the larger one to Ank. Ank caught the one-piece garment and looked at the human – a mixture of surprise and astonishment on his face.

"You had this loaded all the time. How did you know that I'd be coming along?"

As Carson shrugged into his own night black jumpsuit he regarded Ank with a smile. "Just a guess."

He began to strap his assorted accessories to his combat belt when Ank turned to face him – the photon cannon strapped to his side.

"What's our first step after we land? You do have more experience at this sort of thing than I do."

"Well, the first thing we do is create a diversion to keep everybody busy while we're on our way out." Carson removed four small square metallic devices and laid them carefully on the deck.

"What are those?" Ank asked as he knelt down to examine one of them. To him they seemed nothing more than a perfect cube: three inches across on each black side. There was also a small display on one side with a red button just beneath it.

"A little something I cooked up in my spare time," Carson said as he picked one of them up. "High explosives, with a built in timer. We just place a few of them in areas where they'll cause the most trouble, and in up to an hour later – boom. The perfect diversion. But remember, once you push that button, there's no way to shut it down.

"Very good. Then we split up and look for the others."

"Right – and remember Ank no straying. I know you'd love to get your claws into Donar, but we have to get the others out first – that's our priority. Understand me?"

"Understood," Ank replied as he turned and walked out of the supply area and back to the flight deck.

Carson finished readying his weapons pack with an emphasis on silence and stealth. If he was right, the horrors that Nexus III concealed where best left to a larger, more prepared force. His thoughts drifted back to Ank. He had known that he would include himself at the last minute, but he'd hoped that the felinoid's motive consisted only of helping him rescue the others and not one of vengeance. He had enough on his mind about the operation without having to worry about watching his back.

Making sure that all the supplies were secured, he headed to the flight deck to join Ank. He could see the planet in the distance as Ank strapped himself into the co-pilot seat.

Carson sat down in the pilot's seat and began his final system checks. He looked over at Ank and noticed that he seemed absorbed in the planetary data the sensors were reading. He had hoped that he hadn't offended his friend with his little speech on priorities. "Ank?" he asked.

"Yes?" Ank responded without facing him.

"I want you to know that I didn't mean any offense back there. I just want this mission to succeed," Carson explained.

"I am not offended, my friend. I will be there when you need me – I've told you that before."

Carson nodded. "I know. Thanks for coming."

"Thanks is unnecessary, Carson. We both know that you could have done this without my help," Ank pointed out. Suddenly, they were interrupted by a blinking light from the comm system. "A signal coming in."

"It's show-time, Ank. Put it on audio." Ank swiveled in his chair to reach the controls for the cruisers communications system.

"The channel is open," Ank said as he turned back.

"Cruiser approaching Nexus III identify yourself," came the low rumbling voice.

"This is Weent, the mission was a success. I request permission to land," he said in his best imitation of the dead mercenary.

There was a hesitation before the voice came back on. "Weent, that doesn't sound very much like you." Both Carson and Ank could hear a snarl at the end of the statement. They both knew what was on the other end.

"I got a whiff of that gas...it affected my throat," Carson choked out. He did have one last card to play though. "I got important information for Donar. You wanna take responsibility if he doesn't get it in time?"

"All right," came the quick reply. "Follow the homing beacon to the landing area. We will have a security squad meet you when you land." The connection was cut off from planet side as Carson cleared his throat.

"Carson, I know how Weent sounds. That didn't sound anything like him," Ank said.

"Maybe we all sound alike to them," Carson said sarcastically as he picked up the homing beacon and altered course to follow it down.

As Carson guided the ship down toward the surface, he reflected on the conversation. He didn't like the idea that there would be a reception for them. One or two guards would be easy enough to handle, but more than that would make things almost impossible. A crazy plan came to mind, possibly just crazy enough to work.

"Ank, listen to me closely. Go to the back and get the supplies ready fast."

"Why?"

"We can't risk being discovered at the landing field. So I'm going to crash us outside the compound."

"You're what?!" Ank growled.

"Get the supplies and two antigravity parachutes. We'll do one low level fly by, get a picture of the compound, and then jump." The antigravity parachute generated just enough power for one slow atmospheric descent.

"This is crazy," Ank said as he unbuckled and went for the supplies.

"Not as crazy as fighting all those things down there at once. You don't want that to happen? What's the matter, Ank – afraid of heights?" Carson asked jokingly as he brought the ship into a tight dive that would take them over Donar's compound before they bailed out.

Ank came back to the flight deck with two packs of supplies and two of the electronic parachutes. The antigravity unit consisted of a harness with a small boxlike device attached that worked against the magnetic field of a planet.

"Look down there," Carson said as he took the ship over the landing field. They could see hundreds of space vessels just sitting, waiting, as if for a command to rise.

"Carson, there are enough raider vessels down there to..."

"I know," Carson interrupted, "to handle anything we would have left, if we lost the fleet in a war."

The small cruiser flew out of the perimeter of the

compound below as Ank took notice of the terrain below. Closer in, right after the landing field, it reminded him greatly of the wasteland on the planet that Donar had been imprisoned on – further out it was lush with growing vegetation.

The cruiser gained altitude as Carson knew the belts had a minimum altitude to work. "All right, Ank," he said as he took the antigravity belt and one of the packs. "Let's get to the escape hatch – quick!"

After setting the auto-distress system, he programmed the ship into a tight turn, which would be followed by a steep dive into the hills thirty kilometers away. By the time they discovered who'd been aboard, it would be too late.

They reached the emergency escape hatch as Carson felt the ship turn to the hills and execute its pre-programmed orders to dive. He saw Ank flip open the protective tab that covered the activation controls that would blow the hatch. Pushing the small button with a touch of his paw, the sound of the explosive bolt blasting the hatch into the night sky was quiet compared to the sound of the air as it rushed by.

"Jump!" Carson called out. Ank threw himself out of the diving cruiser. As he tumbled through the sky, he saw Carson follow him out. Quickly adjusting the controls on his antigravity belt he was able to gain control of his plunge. Carson too had gained control of his fall and they both began to fall gently to the ground. They could hear the whining sound of the cruiser's out of control engines as it plummeted toward the hills northwest of them. After several seconds they had to cover their eyes as the explosion lit up the night for kilometers.

The belts had simple attitude controls and they were

able to maneuver a bit closer to their objective. Carson gave Ank a thumbs up signal as the ground came up to meet them. They came down not more than 100 yards from the point where the dead ground met the living soil.

Quickly dispensing with their antigravity belts, they removed their field packs to get at their supplies. Each was now outfitted in form fitting black outfits; Carson with his needler and blaster holstered by his side along with his two throwing daggers clipped in their special spring releases on his wrists. Except for the daggers, Ank carried the same, along with the extra power of his photon cannon. Both also carried small, but powerful grenades attached to a web belt that crossed their chests. The only things that remained in their packs were the small explosive devices with their one-hour timers.

After making the 100 yards to the tree line, Carson knew that their diversionary crash must had generated incredible chaos. He just hoped that it kept them all busy until they were finished.

Through his binoculars he could tell that lights had gone on all over the armed compound and there seemed to be a great deal of activity. Heavily armed guards, both alien and human alike were boarding large land skimmers in preparation Carson hoped was for a long trip into the hills to investigate the crash site.

There was still plenty of trouble waiting for them in the compound though. He could still see guards patrolling; human, alien, and some other things that he wasn't quite sure of. The humans were raiders - he was sure of that. The others seemed to be a collection of mercs brought together from all over the galaxy. It figured, Carson thought. The only one who could get this kind of assortment together was Regar Weent. There had to be a hole in the defenses – but the question was where?

Ank tapped him on the shoulder to get his attention and pointed to the landing field where the fleet of ships stood. Carson immediately got his meaning. Even though it was about 200 yards through open ground, it wasn't heavily guarded, though it did offer enough cover for them. Once they made it to the perimeter of the field it would be easy enough to make it the rest of the way to the main buildings of the compound.

Carson nodded, and then signaled that he'd be the first to make the trip. Assuming a runners three-point stance, he wanted to get across as quickly as possible. He only hoped that there weren't any security devices planted around the perimeter. Knowing as much about Donar as he already did, he doubted that his ego would allow him to believe anybody could get this far.

Moving quickly, Carson made it to the edge of the landing field. Pulling his needler from its holster, he signaled for Ank to join him. Within seconds the felinoid was by his side. Carson removed the sensor photo that he had taken on the fly-by from the inside of his jumpsuit and spread it out on the ground before them.

"Look," Carson whispered quietly, "most of the buildings on the other side of the compound are from the original colony, the others are prefab."

"Then that's where we start."

Carson nodded his agreement. "But first a little mischief."

Ank smiled and withdrew one of the small explosive

charges from the pack. "How long do we set the timer for?"

"Set them for one hour." Carson patted him on the back and they began to place the charges throughout the field of space vessels.

Carson returned first and waited for Ank to finish setting the charges that he had taken. He took one last look at the photo when he noticed a large shape standing over him.

"Ank, sit down," Carson said without looking up.

He only looked up when he heard the growl. There wasn't much in this galaxy that could scare him, Carson thought, but if he made a top-ten list, this would certainly be on top.

"I am not, Ank. But you are mine!" the werewolf said as he opened his jaw to reveal row after row of sharp yellowed teeth. It reached down to him and grasped him tightly around the throat. Carson felt the blood beginning to well up in his head as the thing began to choke the life out of him. Unfortunately, he didn't think that he'd die from suffocation as he was slowly being lifted to that jaw full of dagger shaped teeth.

Suddenly the pressure disappeared and he collapsed to the ground. Looking up he saw Ank with the werewolf's head in his large paws. With a twist, Carson could hear bones break in the creature's neck as Ank lower it to the ground.

"Thanks," Carson choked out through his bruised windpipe.

"You're welcome," Ank said as he helped Carson to his feet. "By the way, now you sound like Weent."

"Right. Let's go," Carson said as they began to slowly make their way to the end of the field.

Stopping at the edge of the field, they spotted another guard – this one of the human variety. Carson took out his needler and fired once – the dart hitting the man in the side of the neck. Ank caught the man before he hit the ground and pulled him over to where Carson crouched.

"Give me a hand with this," he said to Ank as he stripped the uniform off of the unconscious mercenary.

Several moments later, Carson stood in front of Ank in the somewhat large uniform. At least, Carson thought, he'd be able to wear his jumpsuit and the rest of his equipment underneath.

Ank just shook his head. "You must have a wonderful tailor."

"Wait here. If I find them I'll get you." Carson stood and walked slowly toward the administration building. He passed several guards along the way and tried to remain as inconspicuous as possible as he entered the building.

Carson made his way down the dark corridor. With every step his eyes became more accustomed to the darkness. Suddenly, lights came on, blinding him for an instant.

"Mark Carson, I presume," the voice said in front of him. When he finally saw what it was that had addressed him, Carson decided that the werewolf wasn't so bad after all.

"Let me introduce myself," the nightmarish thing said as it brought its huge crustacean-like claws to its hairy chest. "My name is Modok, and I have been sent here to welcome you." With the huge claws held out before him, Modok moved toward the stunned human.

CHAPTER 28

The thing that had spoken to him was huge. Its ape-like body stood at almost seven feet, but that wasn't what bothered him the most. The long, hairy arms ended in huge, pincer-tipped claws, like those of a lobster. Covered in a hard red shell, the deadly limbs reached out to him.

With his back to the wall, Carson pulled his blaster from its holster inside the burly merc uniform he wore. Modok, though, reacted quickly. Thrusting out his claw, he plucked the weapon from Carson's hand while he battered the human to the floor with the other. As he lay on the floor, Carson watched as Modok applied pressure, snapping the weapon into two pieces that clattered to the floor.

"Now, Carson, it is your turn."

Modok's strength was unbelievable, and he knew if he didn't make a move soon, he would certainly end up in the same condition as the blaster. He stood as the huge mutant made its move. Modok swung his claw at the left side of Carson's head. Agilely avoiding the attack, he ducked the heavy blow, causing the claw to miss and smash violently into the wall behind him; if Carson had been hit, he probably wouldn't have fared any better than the wall that now had a deep gouge cut into it. For a counterattack, he kicked sharply against Modok's inner thigh, drawing a cry of pain before throwing another kick to the creature's simian face.

Modok staggered backward only a few steps before he grinned, showing his teeth. "Very good, human," Modok said, running his long tongue over the blood from his wounded lip.

Carson swallowed hard as he saw how much Modok enjoyed the taste of his own blood. However, it was not any part of his plan to allow the monster any taste of his. "Not good enough, because you're still breathing," he said.

Carson rushed in, attempting to bowl Modok onto the floor. He was stopped in his attempt as Modok caught him around the waist with an open claw. The creature laughed as Carson felt the air exploding from his lungs, the pressure from the jointed claw threatening to snap his spine like a twig. Feeling his vertebrae straining to their breaking point, he tried the only move he had left. He spread his arms apart and, with all the strength he could muster, brought his hands together and smashed them against Modok's pointed ears.

Modok howled in pain as he released Carson. Grabbing his back and tumbling to the floor, Carson knew he was physically outmatched. Matters only grew worse for Carson when Modok reached between his back and pulled out a heavy battleaxe from the back of his belt.

"How sweet your blood will taste when I am finished carving you up, Carson," Modok said gleefully. "You have given me a small challenge, and I will reward you with a slow and painful death."

Carson felt the pain in his back dull to a throbbing ache as he wondered what he could possibly do. Against that axe, his daggers were useless, and he doubted that his needler could penetrate the evil one's thick hide. He had only one option left, and he quickly found the small, round object connected to a belt under his stolen uniform. He pulled the object out and showed it to Modok. "Do you know what this is?" he said.

Modok hesitated for a moment, trying to remember. His advance came to an abrupt halt as he finally recalled its purpose. "If you use it, we both die," Modok said with a snarl.

"Well," Carson said, finally finding reason to smile, "the way I see it, if I don't use it, I'm going to be the only one dying around here, and I really don't think that's fair. So you see my problem, right?"

Modok could see that the human had a point: He didn't have much to lose. "What if I let you live?"

Carson's smile vanished as abruptly as it had come. He ignored the question and pressed forward with his own. "Where are they? Where are Brooks and the girl?"

Modok was enraged at the situation that the human beast had put him in. He decided he would give the foolish human the information he was demanding, but as soon as he was caught off guard, his head would fly from his shoulders. "They are in the basement cellblock, down those steps," he said, pointing to a door on the far end of the corridor.

"Good. Now drop the axe and back away," Carson ordered.

Modok dropped the battleaxe but refused to move out of Carson's path. "You will not get past me, Carson. Use your toy if you must. I will survive, but I doubt you will. It will likely offer you a far kinder demise than I will!"

With his bluff called, Carson had very little choice but to follow through on his threat and take his chances. With a little luck, he thought he might survive, though he doubted it. He primed the grenade with a twist of the pin, then prepared to throw it at the nightmarish obstacle that blocked his path. When he brought his arm back, something seemed to catch it, preventing it from coming forward.

"Carson, there is no need for that," said a voice behind him with a growl.

Carson turned around and saw Ank standing behind him, holding his hand in his strong feline paw.

Modok saw him and smiled. "Pussycat! How nice of you to return. I can't tell you how much I've missed you."

Ank took off his photon cannon and handed it to Carson. "Get the others. I will deal with this scum."

"You sure?" Carson asked as he took the weapon. He knew it would be a simple matter for Ank to blast Modok, but if that was all Ank intended for the beast, he would have already done it. Modok was one of the reasons Ank had insisted on coming along, and now he'd found the perfect excuse to exact his vengeance.

"Yes, now go," Ank said as he turned to face Modok.

Modok regarded them carefully. "What makes you think I will allow either of you to pass?"

Carson leveled the weapon at the creature's chest and raised his eyes upward.

Modok looked down the barrel of the large weapon and saw that Carson was more than prepared to use it.

"I offer you a chance for honor, Modok. If you refuse, I have no time to waste on you," Ank said, nodding to Carson and the large weapon.

Modok let out a loud chattering laugh. "All right, pussycat. You will die first." He turned to Carson and snapped his two-clawed arms together. "Don't worry, Carson. You will be next."

Carson watched Modok carefully as he moved quickly. The weapon sights never left the mutant, not for a second. Once he was past him, he bolted for the door and the stairs that would take him down to the cells.

After Carson was out of sight, Modok turned to face Ank. "Have I ever told you how your pathetic Corporal Anderson begged for his life before I killed him? The fear made his blood so much sweeter."

Ank realized, with his rage growing, that Modok was trying to force him into attacking recklessly. "I am sure your blood will be just as sweet, mutant."

Modok retrieved the battleaxe and grasped it tightly.

With his adversary now armed, Ank stood in a defensive crouch, his hands held out in front of him.

"Then let us begin!" Modok screamed as he charged, holding the menacing axe high above his head.

Ank stood his ground and blocked the long arm that was holding the down-swinging weapon as it cleaved past his head, knocking Modok off balance. Taking advantage of his opportunity, Ank attacked. As the war chief fell past him, Ank delivered a stunning open hand to the back of Modok's neck, causing the creature to fall to the floor. He knew he had to remove the axe from the fight, as there was little chance that he could defeat his adversary while he was so heavily armed. While Modok was dazed, Ank kicked at the claw that held the axe, sending the weapon hurtling down the corridor.

Ank glared down angrily. "Get up, mutant," he growled. "Let's see if you have the courage for a fair fight."

Until that moment, Modok had never faced Ank without a weapon close at hand, and the prospect terrified him.

Flexing his claw where Ank's booted foot had struck him, Modok stood. *Fight fair?* he thought. *This has gone too far.* "Guards!" he screamed.

Ank took his defense stance again and waited for the werewolves to enter. When no one responded to the call, Ank was not the only one who was mystified. "Problem?" he asked.

"Guards! Miserable dog-spawn," he screamed, seemingly to the emptiness. After all, Donar had promised him backup. Finally, the reality of the situation sank in: Donar had abandoned him. *Curse his tentacled body!* Modok thought, glaring at Ank. *Now I have to fight this cat myself.*

"Seems they've deserted you," Ank said with a soft sigh.

Modok, with his large, jointed claws raised in front of him, charged madly at Ank. "Now you die!"

"I don't think so," was all Ank had time to say as he met the charge with one of his own, his sharp claws flashing out to rake across Modok's chest.

Now, since neither of them holding an advantage, the battle was on.

* * *

Carson slowly descended the darkened staircase. He wished he could've stayed behind and helped Ank, but time was too precious, and he was sure that Ank wouldn't have allowed him to anyway. Finally, at the bottom of the staircase, he found a heavy, locked door. He placed the photon cannon down by the stairs, then began removing the confining enemy uniform, giving him easier access to the supplies he carried.

Carefully, he unclipped a small explosive charge from

his belt and set the timer for ten seconds. He placed it on the door above the lock, activated the device, and sought cover several stairs above the landing. The force of the explosion blew the lock out and threw open the door.

Moving cautiously, Carson entered the outer corridor of the cellblock. Without warning, a werewolf guard rose from behind a desk and charged him. Carson brought the heavy weapon up to his hip and fired. The powerful pulse of energy struck the creature and flung it back down the corridor. As he passed the prone body, he saw that the beam had drilled right through the werewolf. The wound had already cauterized, letting little blood, but the result was still just as fatal.

On the other side of the small corridor, another door blocked his path. This one was constructed of heavy lumber, like most of the other doors, with a plasticine window at about his eye level.

Carson went back to the dead guard and knelt by his side. Turning the body over, he found what he was looking for: a set of keys dangling from a metal ring on the dead creature's belt. The smell of roasted wolf flesh choked him as he turned back to the door. One by one, Carson inserted the keys. He was rewarded on the third try, when the key turned and the lock snapped open.

Standing back a step, Carson kicked his right foot out, forcing the door to fly open with brute force. In true commando style, Carson bolted into the next corridor with his gun held high. This corridor was deserted, but there was a row of jail cells starting on his right. He saw that the line of cells stretched for more than fifty meters, but none seemed to be occupied.

Slowly, he walked past each cell, examining them carefully. Carson stopped suddenly when he spotted one that held a familiar prisoner, a figure sitting on a bunk, holding his head in his hands. "Admiral, is that you?" Carson asked.

"Mark! Am I glad to see you," the haggard face said, looking up at him. Brooks rushed to the bars that held him prisoner and reached out for the younger man.

Carson grabbed his arm tightly before releasing it and stepping back. "I've gotta get you out of there, sir." Carson raised his photon cannon and pointed it at the lock. "Admiral, stand back."

Brooks stood at the rear of the cell as Carson fired. The energy bolt cut through the lock like a hot knife through butter, and the door slammed backward on its rusty hinges.

Brooks rushed out and hugged Carson tightly. "Son, you don't know what they've been putting me through all this time. Are the others here?"

"No, sir, just Ank and myself. Where's Melanie?" he asked as he scanned the row of cells.

Brooks released him and began to walk down the corridor. "Follow me, Mark. I think I heard her down here."

Carson followed as Brooks led him deeper into the corridor. The older man stopped before a cell and gestured with his hand to the occupant inside. Carson moved closer and saw Melanie, all trussed up, with a heavy piece of tape across her mouth. She looked up at him with pure panic in her eyes. Carson again fired, and the lock melted into slag. He threw the gun down, dropped to his knees, and began to take the restraints off of Melanie's arms. Once he was finished freeing her limbs from their cold, cruel bonds, he pulled the tape from her mouth as carefully as he could.

She took a deep breath and pointed at Brooks.

Carson turned his head to look at what she was pointing at. "Melanie, what's the matter?"

Melanie started to breathe heavily, almost hyper-ventilating. "Him," she said, still pointing.

"Melanie, what's wrong? It's the admiral."

"No it isn't!" she screamed hoarsely.

Carson looked again at Brooks and realized he'd been tricked. A scaly tentacle had wrapped itself around his photon cannon and pulled it out of the cell. "Donar, I presume?" Carson said as he helped Melanie to her feet.

Donar bowed his head as his tentacled arms fondled the unfamiliar weapon the way a pervert might grope an unfortunate young woman. "It is a pleasure to finally meet you in person."

Carson regarded the robed creature with disgust. "Believe me, the pleasure is all yours."

Donar let out what Carson thought was laughter from his long muzzle. "Very good, Carson. I like you."

"Believe me, Patac, the feelings aren't mutual." Carson saw Donar visibly stiffen at the mention of the ancient name. "Sorry. I failed to mention before that I had a nice, long chat with an old friend of yours."

"Atlo," Donar said, as if the name would curse him to hell.

Carson saw that he had him. "He said you haven't been a very good son lately." *If he were human,* Carson thought, *Donar would be a deep red.* The anger was quite apparent to Carson as Donar tightened his grip on the large weapon.

"Guards!" Donar seemed to scream insanely into thin air.

Before the echo of his scream died down, doors on either side of the corridor erupted, and armored werewolves poured in, clutching their silvery-tubed weapons tightly in their sharp-clawed paws.

Carson pushed Melanie behind him, fearing that the situation might turn ugly. "Where's Brooks?" he asked, noting that the odds had suddenly taken a sudden turn for the worst; he counted at least ten of the vicious creatures.

Melanie tapped him on the shoulder, then pointed to an adjoining cell where a solitary werewolf lay.

Carson looked closely at the black-furred creature and then at Donar.

The reptile's muzzle pulled back into an evil grin. "Yes, Carson," he said gleefully, "that ugly, hairy thing is Admiral Brooks. You," he said to one of his guards, "wake the beast."

The werewolf walked over to the cell and prodded the sleeping beast with the muzzle of his weapon.

Stirring, he let out a sorrowful moan as it realized what was going on. When he caught sight of Carson with Melanie, he let out a feral growl and lunged against the bars of his cell, straight at Donar.

The same guard who had prodded the transformed Brooks awake swung the butt of his weapon against the bars. The impact forced Brooks to fall back to the bunk on the far side of the cramped cell, where he growled at Donar.

"You bastard," Carson said. He had never wanted to kill anyone so badly. Furious, he moved to the side of the cell and stared deeply at the tortured creature. "Admiral, is that you?" he asked quietly.

The werewolf sat there for a moment, until its lips moved to form one word. "Mark," Brooks said quietly, in more of a low growl than an actual pronunciation.

Finally convinced, Carson slumped down to the floor cell. He looked back at Donar as he unsteadily got back to his feet. "You won't win," he said with a sneer.

"Carson, based on your appearance here in Weent's ship, I can only assume your asteroid headquarters is unharmed, and I have heard nothing from my armada sent to destroy your Alliance capital, but I will not lose. My fleet of warships will – "

Before he could complete his statement, a series of explosions was heard by all in the basement cellblock. Everyone, with the exception of Carson, looked around in shock as the walls shook at the power of the explosions.

"What is happening?" Donar called to his guards.

Carson looked at his wrist chronometer, then up at Donar, shaking his head. "Well, Donar, I wouldn't depend too much on those ships of yours now."

Donar raged, and for a moment, Carson feared that the lizard would shoot them all down right then and there. "Fool! What have you done?"

"Nothing much. Just...ended this nightmare."

"Mark," Melanie said from behind him, "before you landed, *Ranger* was sent out on a suicide mission into Dreedan space. They're gonna use that werewolf serum on the Dreedan Imperial home planet. He's using *Ranger* to start the - "

"War, Carson," Donar interrupted. "The Dreedan Empire, for as much as you've told them, will only believe their eyes when they see an Alliance battlecruiser heading to their home world. Regretfully, *Ranger* will probably be destroyed, but the war will start, and the Alliance will die.

Then I will regroup and take control during the chaos. Unfortunately, there is no room for any of you in my plans," Donar said, pointing the gun at Carson and Melanie.

Carson and Melanie tensed as they saw a tentacle tightening on the trigger of the cannon. At that range, one blast would be sufficient to reduce them into their molecular components. As they backed to the wall, Carson dropped a small dagger into his right hand from the spring release on his wrist.

Before either could react, though, a powerful explosion rocked the cellblock to its foundation. *What the...? That was no explosive charge,* Carson thought.

"What have you done now, Carson?" Donar raged. The reptile held the photon cannon as if he intended to beat him with it rather than shoot him.

"It sounds like you have a problem. Unfortunately, I can't take credit for it," Carson said sarcastically.

"I have no more time to waste on the likes of you," Donar said as he again pointed the weapon at Carson.

With one quick snap of his wrist, Carson fired the dagger at Donar.

The tall reptilian figure moved almost as quickly as the dagger buried itself into the gun-clutching tentacle. With a scream of pain, Donar dropped the gun and grabbed his injured arm. Suddenly, Donar started to lose control of his form, switching from his human form of Patac and back again to his reptilian form. "Kill them all!" he screamed to the werewolf guards.

They stood where they were as their small brains tried to understand what was happening to their master.

"Kill them, I said. Kill them now!" Donar screamed, both

in anger and in agony as he moved for the exit.

Finally spurred by their master's commands, the werewolves advanced. They held their weapons out in front of them, but Carson could clearly see they weren't going to use them to kill.

"Stand behind me," he said to Melanie as he flicked the remaining dagger into his hand.

"No way," Melanie responded as she stood side to side with Carson.

As the first creature reached the entrance to the cell, the building was rocked by another blast.

"That was no explosive, Mark," Melanie said, taking a defensive stance.

"I know. It sounded like an orbital bombardment," Carson said as he chose the first and only target for his dagger. He was just about to let the other dagger fly when the building rocked again.

"Look out!" Melanie screamed as the ceiling came down on them all.

Carson slowly opened his eyes. *If I survive this, I'm taking one hell of a vacation,* he thought to himself. However, the first thing he saw didn't quite stack the odds in his favor. A werewolf was standing over him, its jaws wide. The dagger was still clutched in his hand, and he thrust it upward, ramming it to the hilt into the beast's throat.

Grabbing at the weapon in vain, the werewolf gave a final growl before toppling to the floor.

Rolling to his feet, Carson picked up one of the shiny silver weapons he had used in the other-dimensional world and turned to face the other guards, but only then did he realize they were alone. All the monsters had been buried under a section of the retaining wall that had supported the ceiling over the central corridor. There were a few moans coming from the corridor but too few for him to worry about.

Carson turned back to where Melanie lay. She had pushed him to the floor when the ceiling started to collapse and was now buried for it. He rushed to where she was and quickly pulled her out from under the debris. Without a bio-scanner, he had to depend on his more limited human skills as he pressed the edge of his fingertips against her neck in search for a pulse. "Thank God," he said to himself as he found a strong beat. He heard a low moan come from her lips, and her eyes fluttered open. "Melanie, can you hear me?" Carson asked.

"Mark?" she asked as her eyes caressed his face.

"Yep. It's me. You okay?"

"Except for a headache, I-I think so. Help me up."

Carson offered his hand and pulled her to her feet. She stumbled slightly, but Carson held her with a steady hand. "Are you sure you're all right?"

Melanie nodded before looking past Carson into the other cell. "Where's Admiral Brooks?" Her voice seemed to be on the edge of panic.

Carson had all but forgotten about the transformed man. "There he is!" Carson said as he pointed to the furry hand sticking out from under parts of the collapsed ceiling. Hurrying over to the other cell, Carson picked up the alien weapon he had retrieved earlier and used it to melt the lock on the cage. He hurried into the cell and began to throw off the rock and plasticine that had buried Brooks.

"Mark, be careful. We don't know how he'll react when

he comes to."

Carson took that as good advice. *After all, how much of Admiral Brooks is in this creature? Will he still attack those he cares for?* Carson didn't want to take any chances, but he didn't really have a choice. "Melanie, give me a hand with this."

Melanie walked over and helped Carson heave a final heavy piece of plasticine from Brooks's body. When he was finally out of the debris, Melanie tried her best to ascertain his condition.

"Well?" Carson asked.

"I think he may have a concussion, but his transformed body is stronger than his old one, and that probably saved his life."

"We've got to get him out of here. Find Ank, if he's still alive, then get a ship. We've got to alert the fleet about – " Carson heard a sound by the door and dived out of the cell. Coming up on one knee, he sighted the silvery energy weapon at the source of the sound and prepared to fire.

"Wait, Carson!" Melanie called.

Carson froze and saw Ank staggering through the doorway, holding a blaster pistol in his hand. His friend was wounded in several places, and red blood was dripping to the floor. "You look like shit," Carson said with a smile.

"Yeah, well, you should see the other guy," said a voice from behind him.

Ank merely nodded and leaned up against the wall.

"Josh, is that you?"

"In the flesh," Josh Grant said as he walked out from behind Ank.

Carson dropped the weapon and pulled his friend into a

tight hug.

"Melanie, are you all right?" Josh asked after Carson released his hold.

"I'm fine, but the admiral is ... hurt."

Josh looked around, not quite understanding the situation. "Where, exactly, is the admiral?"

Melanie stood and pointed down at the beast she was trying to treat.

"You're kidding, right? This has gotta be some kind of joke." When no one answered, Josh shook his head. "Shit! How did this happen? Donar?"

"Right," Carson answered, "but we have worse problems. Where's the ship?"

"We had some fight out there. Ernie took a hit. Glick's trying to get him operational."

"What about those explosions?"

"When we arrived in the system, we found four Alliance Titan-class battlecruisers waiting in orbit. When your explosives began to blow, they took it as a signal and began to bombard the entire compound. Glick and I brought the ship in, and I found Ank with his arms wrapped around this thing's throat," Josh added.

"I take it your honor has been settled?" Carson asked.

Ank nodded as he settled his tired body down on the floor.

"Good. Then get up and help us with the admiral."

"Where is Donar?" Ank growled as he stood.

"I don't know. I stabbed him with a dagger, but then the ceiling came down." Carson shook his head slowly. "Sorry, Ank. He's gone."

Ank reluctantly moved to the cell, and the three of them

lifted the admiral out into the corridor.

"What's so important anyway?" Josh asked.

"I'll explain on the way to the ship," Carson said as they carried Brooks up the stairs.

When they had exited the building, Josh put a call through to Glick, who was powering *Pulsar* in for a quick pickup. Carson saw that the area was bedlam as an attack transport from one of the Titan-class ships had landed with a division of marines. They had come down prepared for the werewolves, with armor and heavy weapons. The wolves flashed their sharp teeth, but they were quickly mowed down by advanced Alliance weapons.

Melanie pointed up as *Pulsar* came in for a quick touchdown.

"Let's move!" Carson yelled as they carried Brooks into the ship.

As they shut the hatch, Melanie and Josh took the unconscious Brooks down the corridor. "Melanie!" Carson called out, stopping her and Josh. "Keep him sedated. We don't need him prowling the corridors."

"Right," she said as they entered the sickbay and attached security restraints.

Carson and Ank reached the bridge to find Glick busy under the helm control panel, wires in each hand.

"Glick, what are you doing?" Carson asked.

"Trying to complete the repairs," he said as he stuck his head back under the panel.

"We need to lift off now!"

"Wait just one minute. There! Got it!" As Glick finished the final connection, power levels throughout the ship approached normal. "Ernie, can you hear me?"

"Yes, Glick," answered the voice of the ship computer.

"Good," Glick said. He then turned back to Carson. "She's as ready as she'll ever be." He stiffened and saluted Carson. "The ship's all yours...sir!"

Carson shook his head. "Take us up. Ernie..."

"Yes, Skipper?"

"We're gonna need all the speed you can give us."

"I've heard that command before, Skipper," Ernie answered.

"Where to, Carson?" Glick asked as he brought the fusion engines back online.

"The Dreedan home planet," Carson said from his command chair.

"What!?" Glick screamed in amazement as *Pulsar* accelerated off the planet and into space.

* * *

The bombardment from space had softened up any resistance from the mercenary squad, many of whom found very little to fight about once their employers had been destroyed. The werewolves, on the other hand, found chaos to their liking. They attacked and savaged anything that moved, friend or foe.

Lieutenant Simmons had seen plenty of action on his tour of duty on the outer frontier, but nothing could have prepared him or his men for what they now encountered. In front of him, two werewolves were sitting by the body of one of his men. They sensed his presence by scent alone, and they turned to face the young lieutenant.

Simmons was shocked to see the blood of his corporal dripping from their muzzles. The corporal had been gruesomely ripped open, and now his internal organs were floating in a sea of red. The beasts growled at Simmons as they protected their prize. With shaky hands, he carefully unholstered his blaster and blew a large hole through the chest of each of them.

"Very good, Lieutenant."

Simmons saw the figure in bloody combat fatigues coming to him with his hand out. Seeing the captain's emblem on his uniform, Simmons stuck his hand in return. "Thank you, sir," he said as the captain shook his hand.

Unfortunately, he did not notice the scaly face beneath the combat helmet. A long tongue came from between the sharp teeth and wrapped itself around his throat. Simmons tried, with his remaining hand, to remove the tongue as it tightened, cutting off the air supply to his brain. His face turned purple as he felt a sharp pain in his chest. He tried to find the source of his problem with his free hand, but death found him first.

"You're welcome," Donar said as his tongue returned to his mouth. Sitting down by the body, he removed the dagger Carson had dared to throw at him and placed it in a pocket of his uniform. Quickly, he grabbed the body by its legs and pulled it into a darkened corner. As he turned around, he was startled to see a marine in a uniform, with a blaster aimed at him.

"Simmons, we're bugging out. Let's go," the marine said.

"Right," Simmons said.

As the lieutenant passed him, the marine squad leader stopped and shook his head. The flickering lights must have been playing tricks on him, because he could have sworn he had seen Simmons's eyes glowing red in the darkness. Thinking it was a trick of the lights and not wanting to spend unnecessary time in sickbay for a psych check, the squad leader, with Simmons by his side, gathered the rest of the squad and boarded their armored personnel skimmer for their short ride outside the compound, where their attack shuttle had been readied for liftoff. Moments later, the squad had secured their supplies for the trip back to the ship.

Hovering momentarily, the shuttle pivoted and accelerated into space. One pair of eyes, though, remained focused on the surface as it shrank to nothing in the distance. Ancient hate clouded those eyes that were somewhat out of place on the face of such a young man, reflecting thoughts of brutal vengeance.

Ruined, Donar thought. He had planned every detail, down to the smallest eventuality, yet his plans were still thwarted by Carson and his people. Everything that had taken a millennium to build was now destroyed. Still, he had Tompkin and *Ranger. Perhaps there is still a chance for success,* he thought, *but first I have a ship to steal and accounts to settle.*

For the first time, Donar, in his new human form, put his head back and relaxed as best as his nature would allow him and planned his vengeance.

* * *

Pulsar drove through hyperspace, her engines strained to the limit as she attempted to catch up with *Ranger.* On the bridge, Glick and Ank completed, as best they could, temporary repairs on their combat systems, while Carson attempted to reach Admiral Stack and the Alliance Fleet.

As Carson sent the message for the fourth time, the comm system came to life. "Mark, I hear you. Where are you?"

"Admiral, I'm heading into Dreedan space, on *Ranger*'s tale," Carson told him over the audio frequency.

"For God's sake, why?"

Carson spent the next thirty seconds filling Admiral Stack in on what *Ranger* planned to do when it reached the Dreedan home planet.

The channel went quiet as Stack considered the implications. Finally, he said, "We're too far away. *Ranger* is one of the most powerful ships in the fleet. Can you take him with a damaged ship?"

"I have to try, sir."

"Is there anything I can do to help?"

"Actually, there *is* something you can do, Admiral."

"Just name it."

"Let them know that I'm coming and the reason for it. My reputation isn't exactly stellar in this part of space."

"Good luck, son. Stack out." After the channel went quiet, Carson turned to Ank and Glick.

"He doesn't seem to think much of our chances," Ank observed from under the tactical console.

"Well, we're admittedly not in the best condition, and *Ranger* has us outgunned even under ideal conditions," Glick added.

Carson stood and walked over to the bridge doors, then stopped. "Well, the admiral will advise the Dreedans. They might be able to get us some support. Ernie?" Carson said.

"Yes, Skipper?" the computer replied.

"How are those long-range sensors coming?"

"They are at 95 percent of operational strength, Skipper."

"Good. Keep them on full and let me know when they pick up *Ranger*." Carson didn't hear Ernie's reply as the doors closed behind him. After what they had put the ship through to reach Earth in time, she had little left to give. *When this is over, if we survive, she's gonna need a complete overhaul,* he thought. As it was, there was only a 50/50 chance that they could even catch up to *Ranger* with the battlecruiser's head start.

Carson had other things on his mind as he turned the corridor on his way to sickbay. Entering, he found Melanie and Josh working over the werewolf body of Admiral Clayton Brooks.

"How is he?" Carson asked.

"He's sedated right now," Melanie said.

Josh activated the bio-scanner, then looked over at Carson. "Carson, take a look at this," he said as he led him to the medical analysis monitor.

The screen came on with what Carson knew was a representation of a DNA pattern, the strangest pattern he had ever seen.

"Weird, huh?" Josh asked.

Carson nodded. "That isn't a normal pattern, is it?"

"Nope. Somehow, this new DNA string has been fused onto the admiral's," Josh said, pointing at the monitor.

"Is it possible to remove it?" Carson asked.

Melanie walked over and joined the two men at the monitor. "Not according to our science," she said before Josh could answer.

"Are you telling me there's no hope?" Carson said as he stared into her eyes.

Melanie grabbed him by the arm and led him out into

the corridor. When the doors closed behind them, she stared angrily back at him. "Don't you think I've tried? Alliance medical science just is not that advanced. I can't just wave some magic wand and turn him into a human again."

He put his hand on her arm and tried to pull her closer, but she pulled away and turned her back on him. "Melanie, we can't give up," he said softly.

When she turned back to him, tears were streaming down her face. "Mark, unless you know something I don't ... well, we can't really count on that. Excuse me," she said as her control began to slip, "but I've got a patient to take care of."

As she went inside, Carson realized he might know someone who could help. Since he was doing no good there, he began to walk back to the bridge.

Before he took more than a few steps, Melanie ran out, calling his name.

"What's wrong?" Carson asked.

"He's conscious," Melanie began, "and he wants to speak to you."

Carson walked back into sickbay with Melanie and over to the diagnostic bed, where Brooks was buckled down. "Admiral Brooks," he said as he leaned over the furry form.

The dark eyes opened, and for a second, there was no recognition in them. Brooks growled at them, his sharp teeth flashing.

"Mark, if he keeps this up I'm gonna have to knock him out again," Melanie said as she prepared the hypo.

"Admiral, it's me, Mark. Can you understand me?"

Brooks stopped struggling as his eyes locked on Carson's. "Marrrk..." His name seemed to fight its way out of the wild brain.

"Yes, sir. It's me."

"Wherrre amm I?" The words slurred as Brooks struggled to retain the human side of his mind.

"You're aboard *Pulsar*."

Brooks moved his furry paw over to Carson's hand. "Kill me," he forced out, tears rolling down his furry cheeks. "Pleeease," Brooks begged.

Carson pulled away as his attention was drawn to the intercom and Ank's voice. "Carson, you'd better get up here."

"What's the problem?" Carson asked quietly into the intercom.

"It's *Ranger*. She's dead ahead."

"That's impossible, Ank. We couldn't have caught up that fast."

"*Ranger* has just stopped. What, Glick?" Carson heard Ank say to the human. "*Ranger* just hailed us. Tompkin wants to speak to you."

"I'll be right there. Carson out," he said, then closed the internal channel. "Melanie, take care of him. Josh, you'd better come with me."

"Right," Josh said as he shut down the monitor. "Melanie, call if you need us."

She gave him a weak smile and a slight nod before turning back to Brooks.

After Carson and Josh were gone, she put her hands on Brooks's furry arm and concentrated. What she saw puzzled her but seemed to give her hope for the future. *Maybe that's what Mark has in mind*, she thought silently as she gave Brooks another sedative injection.

CHAPTER 29

Carson stepped onto the bridge and saw that Tompkin was already waiting on the main viewscreen.

"Carson, good of you to speak to me," the *Ranger* captain said. "Why have you been following me?"

Sitting in his command chair, Carson tried to figure out what kind of game Tompkin-or whatever it was -had decided to play with them. "It's over, Tompkin. The base on Nexus III has been destroyed."

"It is far from over, Carson. First, I will destroy you and your ship, and then I'm going to carry out my mission."

"Why? Donar can't win. He's gone, and there is no sense in carrying out his insane plan"

"This isn't for Donar. If he's out of the way, that's all the better. I have his werewolf serum. After the war is over, I'll use it to create my own army."

"You won't get away with it, Tompkin."

"Don't be so cliché, Carson. I will get away with it and more. Now, if you'll excuse me, I'll just take a moment to destroy you, then be on my way," Tompkin said before he abruptly closed the channel.

"Red alert!" Carson screamed. "Shields up."

Defensive screens activated, surrounding *Pulsar* in their protective glow.

"Glick, get us outta here."

Glick's hands flew over the helm control panel, and *Pulsar* accelerated into a hard-banking turn.

"*Ranger* has fired," Ank said calmly.

The photon charge glanced off the *Pulsar* forward shields. Had they been where they were only seconds before, the blast probably would have bored through their weakened shields and, at the very least, disabled them.

"Shield power down 23 percent," Josh reported from the engineering station.

"Scan for him," Carson ordered. "Where is he?"

"He's at bearing 424 by 621 and coming fast," Ank reported.

"Lay down a spread of missile and photon fire. Let him know it won't be that easy."

"Aye-aye," Ank said as he triggered off a full salvo at the fully shielded battlecruiser.

"Glick, gimme some distance," Carson said, envisioning the battlecruiser running right into his weapons salvo.

"Direct hit on his forward shields by the photon charge," Ank reported. "The missiles are closing. Impact in five ... four ... three ..." Ank could not finish his countdown before the missile salvo exploded. "They were intercepted."

"Any damage from the photon blast?" Carson asked.

"Slight damage to forward shields but nothing more," Ank informed them.

"Wonderful," Glick said as he swerved the ship in time to avoid another photon barrage. "Carson, *Ranger*'s closing."

"Full power acceleration! Let's keep our distance, people."

Pulsar began to pull away. Carson only hoped Tompkin was obsessed enough to keep following them, at least until the Dreedan ships showed up. Thoughts of escape vanished, though, as a loud alarm signaled from Josh's engineering console.

"Engine burnout!" Josh called out as he tried to force more coolant into the assemblies to keep them from blowing. "Shutting down main drive."

"Transfer all shield power to the aft sections," Carson called to Ank.

Without the main engines, all they could do was maneuver pitifully slowly on their thrusters before the fully operational warship. *Pulsar* slowed down and began to feel the brunt of the firepower from *Ranger*. Shields began to glow an incandescent red before they, too, began to overload and flicker off as systems supplying their power went offline.

"Ernie," Carson said quietly as smoke filled the bridge from circuit burnouts, "what do we have left?"

Ernie quickly ran a diagnostic of ship systems and came back with depressing news. "Main drive is out. Shields are out. Internal power systems are at 45 percent. Weapons are operational at three-quarter power. Missile systems are operational from Launcher Two."

"*Ranger* is closing in," Glick reported nervously.

"Ank, target everything we have left at the *Ranger* main sensor array. With a bit of luck, maybe we can blind 'em for a time."

"All weapons locked on," Ank said quietly.

"Get ready to fi – "

"Carson, we're being hailed by *Ranger*," Ank said quickly.

Carson looked around at all of them before turning to stare at the main viewscreen. "Put him on, Ank."

The screen again filled with the image of Martin

Tompkin. "Carson, it appears that it is finally over, at least for you. Believe me when I tell you I've been looking forward to this moment for a long time. Even this human form I inhabit finds something rather satisfying about your impending death. Still, I'm not totally heartless. I'm prepared to hear any last words you have to say." Tompkin sat back in his command chair and smiled.

You wanna hear my last words? How about these, you bastard? Carson thought. "Ank, fire!"

Pulsar lashed out with twin bursts of concentrated energy, as well as the power of its sole remaining missile launcher. Caught by surprise and at close range, the *Pulsar* assault penetrated the *Ranger* shielding and heavy armor and found its target, her main sensor array.

Carson smiled as he saw Tompkin's frantic reaction to his surprise last words.

"Carson, I'm going to kill you!" Tompkin screamed.

"Watch that temper, Tompkin. You have to find me first." Carson turned to Ank and ran his finger across his throat, signaling for him to close communications. When Tompkin was gone from the screen, Carson sat down. "Glick, evasive maneuvers. Give it everything we've got."

"Right," Glick said, and *Pulsar* began to slowly move away.

"They're firing blindly," Ank said from tactical.

Carson knew what game they were playing now: the blind man's bluff. In this case, though, if the blind man found them, they were dead in the sky. Their shields were down, and any impact would be fatal.

"Skipper..." Ernie said, his modulated voice breaking the silence.

"Yes, Ernie?"

"My long-range sensors are picking up three warships of the Dreedan Dreadnought class, quickly approaching."

"Glick, can you gimme any more speed," Carson pleaded.

"Sorry. She's already at full impulse thrust."

"Ernie, activate the forward monitor, full magnification."

The forward screen revealed *Ranger,* still firing off in the distance. By chance, one of her shots struck the lead Dreedan cruiser. The two other cruisers broke from their formation and closed with the Alliance battlecruiser. Suddenly, the Dreedan cruisers opened up with full weapons and fired, point blank, at *Ranger.* The impact of the intense energy struck *Ranger* at her aft engineering deck.

"Carson, there's a call coming from *Ranger.*"

"Put it on audio, Ank."

"Carson, what are you doing? How can you do this to me?"

They could hear the panic in his voice as his ship began to breakup all around him.

"Carson!"

More energy from the weapons fire from the two Dreedan cruisers struck the damaged battlecruiser. Carson and the others watched as the huge warship began to glow, and then *Ranger* simply ceased to exist. The explosion was so intense that not even the automatic filters Ernie dropped electronically in place over the image on the viewscreen could totally eliminate the blinding light of the exploding starship.

"Go to Hell, Tompkin," Carson said softly to the screen

as the blinding light was finally swallowed by the darkness of space.

"Yeah!" Glick yelled, pounding the console triumphantly.

"It's not over yet," Josh said above the cheering.

The bridge fell silent as they all saw the two Dreedan cruisers attaching tractor beams to their damaged comrade.

"Sensors report three Dreedan ships closing in on our position."

Even without Ernie's sensor report, it was clear that the ships were quickly approaching.

Suddenly, the bridge doors opened, and Melanie stepped over to Carson. "I watched from down in sickbay," she said, placing a hand on Carson's shoulder.

Carson looked up at her and patted her hand with his. "What's their range, Ernie?"

"Five thousand kilometers and closing. Correction. They have stopped their engines and are holding at 5,000."

"Carson," Ank said from behind him, "the Dreedan ship is hailing us."

"Put it on visual." Carson straightened in his chair as the view of the three ships vanished and was replaced by what Carson knew was the bridge of one of the Dreedan cruisers – more specifically, a chair facing away from the screen.

When the ship commander swiveled the chair around, Carson had to admire their wonderful taste, for she was a beautiful woman. Long red locks cascaded over her tight-fitting uniform. Her blue skin contrasted brilliantly with her crimson hair, reminding Carson of someone else.

"My sensors show you to be *Pulsar*," she said. "Mark Carson, I believe?"

"Yes, thank you, Captain…"

"Actually, it's Admiral Banat, and Captain Carson, I must thank you, from all my people."

"It was a pleasure. I'm just happy you got to *Ranger* before they got to us."

"Your Admiral Stack called and advised us of your predicament. I have to admit that very few of us believed him."

"Then why did you come?" Carson asked, knowing that the Dreedans were usually a very suspicious people. He didn't understand why they had shown up at all, particularly that fast.

"Perhaps it would be best to show you," Banat said.

Carson waited several seconds before Banat showed him the reason, smiling back at him from the other side of the screen. Carson couldn't believe his eyes. *An Alliance Fleet admiral on the bridge of a Dreedan warship? God, I've seen everything now.* "Admiral Stack?"

"Yes, Mark. Are your people all right?"

"Barely, sir. We've sustained quite a bit of damage, but you guys got here just in time."

"And they say the cavalry never arrives in the nick of time anymore."

Stack had turned from the screen and was talking to Admiral Banat. "Mark," Admiral Stack said, turning back to face Carson, "Admiral Banat has offered you the complete assistance of her people in getting *Pulsar* repaired. She has also informed me that, we will, and I quote, get ourselves and your ship out of her space." Stack had a wide grin on his face when he finished.

"Believe me when I say I can't wait to oblige her. Thank the admiral for her help."

"You're welcome, Carson," Banat said from Stack's side. "Stand by while we tractor you into our landing bay."

"Thank you. *Pulsar* standing by."

Banat nodded as the channel closed and her image faded back to reveal her three ships, one of which was approaching closer.

Carson looked up at Melanie, who was wearing one of her infamous looks. "What's the matter with you?" he asked, even though he already knew.

Melanie stared down at him. "You didn't have to thank her *that* much, you know."

Before Carson could say another word, Melanie pivoted quickly on her heels and left the bridge. Any words Carson had for her died a quick death before they even reached his lips.

They felt the ship lurch slightly and move forward toward the Dreedan ship as the warship turned completely around.

"They've got a tractor beam on us," Glick said, watching the landing bay doors open to swallow them. "It's huge," Glick said of the cavernous interior as they were gently set down.

"The bay is pressurized," Josh added, relaying on the exterior readings of his sensor.

Carson stood and gestured toward the door. "Well, gentlemen, let's go and greet our Dreedan saviors," he said with a sigh. As they all filtered out, Carson was thankful that the problem of repairs for the ship was now in the hands of others. He just wanted to sleep for about 1,000 years, and that was exactly what he intended to do, after he met that pretty admiral.

CHAPTER 30

Inside the hangar of the warship, they were extended every courtesy except one: They were not allowed to leave the cavernous chamber for any reason. All necessary materials or technicians were provided by Admiral Banat. Even though they were heroes in every sense of the word, trust was something the Dreedans still would not give easily.

It was a double-edged sword though. Admiral Stack refused to let any of the Dreedan engineers anywhere near *Pulsar,* fearing that they'd steal her secrets. That delayed completion of repairs longer than any of them wanted. As soon as Josh and Glick pronounced the ship space worthy, Carson ordered them to prepare for launch.

With all preflight checks completed, Carson looked around his bridge. Ank was still at tactical, Josh at his science station, and Glick at the helm. Admiral Stack had chosen to remain below with Melanie to keep watch on Admiral Brooks.

Glick, though, was another story. He had proven himself an asset to the team, but there was no use for a helmsman once Ernie was fully operational. Carson had to smile, thinking they were just the types of technical problems he preferred to suffer from. In any case, it was time to go home.

"Admiral Banat, this is *Pulsar.* We're set for launch."

The main viewscreen activated, and Admiral Banat appeared, looking as calm as she had when they'd first seen her. "You have clearance to leave, Carson. Remember what I said though. Do not return to Dreedan space for any reason. Oh, and have a safe trip. Banat out," the redhead said with a seductive smile before the channel closed.

Carson shook his head as the twin doors of the hangar bay opened. He couldn't wait to put it all behind him.

Glick activated the main engines, and *Pulsar* emerged into space.

"Set course for Allegre IV," Carson said to Glick.

"Right. Allegre IV it is."

After the crisis had passed, Stark had ordered his task force to Allegre IV to retake the Alliance base there. From the reports, the operation had gone smoothly, and the marine force was now mopping up. Stack would supervise the remainder of the reactivation. The werewolves had all been eliminated, but there was no sign of the simulcron copy of Olstad – just a decaying clay-like substance found in his office. It would only be a quick stop, for they still had to deal with Admiral Brooks.

Twenty hours later, with Admiral Stack safely on Allegre IV, *Pulsar* entered orbit around Planet Solo. It was fitting, Carson thought as he viewed the planet from high in orbit, that things would hopefully end where they had begun.

Ernie, already loaded with coordinates from two previous landings, took the ship down. The computer seemed to look forward to returning to the base; Ernie had grown very tired of Glick.

Pulsar slowed through the atmosphere and settled in almost the same spot it had occupied before. Carson decided that Glick should remain with the ship, despite complaints from Ernie, while the others took Brooks through the arch. Carson hoped that perhaps Atlo could somehow reverse what his protégé had done; the old man seemed to be their only hope.

When they arrived, Melanie was already preparing Brooks for his journey. She had him sedated and restrained, with heavy titanium cuffs around his wrists. He seemed to be more in control of his violent actions, but at certain moments, he seemed prepared to lose all control of himself. None of them would be safe if that happened.

"Are we ready?" Carson asked.

"I think so," Melanie answered. "How are you feeling, Admiral?"

Brooks nodded weakly. He obviously considered it all a waste of time and seemed to be humoring them.

Josh stood with Melanie behind Brooks as Carson led them to the airlock. Ank was there to meet them and handed them each a blaster pistol and a holster. Carson and Josh looked at Ank, then at each other, then laughed out loud. Even Admiral Brooks found something humorous and laughed as best as his transformed body would allow.

"What's so funny?" Ank asked, confused.

"You tell him," Josh said to Carson, his laughter beginning to subside.

"No, Josh, you tell him. I know you really want to."

"Will you three move?" Melanie interrupted. "We have important things to do."

"No," Ank said adamantly, "not till they tell me."

Melanie looked angrily at Josh. "Will you just spill it so we can get on with this?"

"Josh, go on."

"All right, Carson," Josh said as he walked over to Ank. "Now, Ank, don't get me wrong, but aren't you a little too…overarmed?"

Ank was carrying his photon cannon, along with three blaster pistols and a variety of grenades, all attached to various parts of his body.

"It is always best to be prepared," the cat-man defensively snapped.

"Well, whatever makes you comfortable. Let's go," Carson said as he opened the inner and outer airlock doors. "Glick?" he said into the intercom by the inner door.

"Yes, Boss?" Glick answered.

"We're on our way. Take care of things while we're gone."

"I will," Ernie answered for both of them.

* * *

They entered the city through the same tunnel they had used previously. For some reason, the natural light that the corridors had radiated out, and electric torches now lit the darkness. When they reached the portal room, they were almost blinded by the intensity of the light. The arch was being fed power from some indeterminable source.

Josh extinguished his light and examined the power readings on the console. "Carson…"

"Yes, Josh? What is it?"

"Look." He pointed. "The arch is functioning on a backup generator."

"Hmm. Is it possible that the generator kicked in when the mains went out?" Carson asked.

"I don't know."

"Well, it doesn't matter. Let's do it."

Josh pulled out his comm unit and activated the ship frequency. "Ernie, do you read me?"

"Loud and clear, Josh. Go ahead," came Ernie's reply.

"We're all set. Remember to activate the arch every twelve hours. If you don't hear from us, you are to take Glick back with you to headquarters. Got that, Glick?"

"Got it," came the reluctant answer.

"Okay, Ernie. It's all yours." Josh put the comm unit back on his belt and looked at the portal as Ernie once again took control.

The arch glowed, and an image again began to form. When it had taken its full form, Carson led them silently through it, into chaos.

Strong, swirling winds lashed at them as the sky seemed about to explode in fury. The weather had been bad before, but that had been nothing like it was now. Suddenly, without any warning, the winds ceased, and all was quiet. Somehow, the silence was more ominous than storm that had preceded it.

"Nice weather," Melanie commented.

"Yeah, right. C'mon. Let's move before it starts again," Carson said as they headed in the direction of Atlo's castle.

The sky again flashed with fire as Ank took point. Streaks of energy lit the angry red sky, and the wind again began its assault.

"Admiral, no!" Carson heard Melanie scream.

Brooks was trying to break free from Josh and Melanie, who were trying to holding him still and avoid his sharp teeth at the same time. Suddenly, before Carson could help them, Brooks broke loose and began to run.

"Ank!" Carson shouted above the increasing sound of the wind and atmospheric explosions. "Brooks got away!"

Ank dropped his cannon and made a dive for Brooks's

furry legs. He managed to trip him up, and they both fell to the ground. Josh and Carson dropped on top of Brooks, and Melanie dropped to her knees, hypo in hand.

"Quick!" Josh screamed. "Give him the shot."

Melanie applied the injector to Brooks's neck, and the struggle was over within seconds.

"Give me a hand with him, Josh," Carson said as they lifted the heavy body between them.

Less than an hour later, they were within sight of the dark castle.

"Why does the weather seem to worsen the closer we get?" Melanie asked to no one in particular.

"I don't know," Josh replied, "but look at those clouds."

They all looked up at the strange pattern forming over the castle and spiraled outward. Dense red clouds seemed full of a blood-red rain they knew would never come.

"We're not far. Let's go. Maybe Atlo can explain it," Carson said as Ank this time helped him carry Brooks.

The sedative was beginning to wear off already, and before long, they would have to give him another shot or take their chances.

As they final found their way to the hidden entrance, Carson heard a murmuring growl from Brooks. He placed him down onto the ground and bent over to listen to what he was trying to say. "I can't hear you, Admiral."

"I'm sorry. I'm all right now." The lips formed the words as well as they could as Carson helped the werewolf to his feet.

Ank had gone to the side of the wall and was looking for the release that would open it for them. Finally, the wall slid slowly to the side.

They walked into the pitch-black corridor, and Ank and Josh pulled out their electric torches and lit the darkness.

Melanie moved closer to Carson and stopped him.

"What is it, Mel?"

"Something's wrong. I'm not sure what it is though. Wait here for a second," she said as she moved to the side and felt along the rock wall. Closing her eyes, Melanie concentrated.

The rest watched intently, knowing that the psychic emanations had to be strong if she could sense something without making physical contact.

"Death is here," she said, her voice shaky.

Carson and Ank looked at each other, then back to Melanie.

"Castle ... darkness ... small and furry ... I don't know what..."

Carson made a mental note of everything she said. When the images were disjointed like that, it usually meant they were invading Melanie's mind faster than she could process them.

"Werewolves, small ones ... sharp teeth ... a laughing old man..." she said. Then she slowly pulled away and almost collapsed.

Carson caught her before she hit the ground and brought her back though unsteadily to her feet. "Are you okay?" he asked.

She nodded as she felt her strength return. "Incredible evil. It was almost like a blanket being thrown over my head."

"Could it have been leftover feelings from when Donar was here?" Ank asked.

"I-I'm not sure."

Carson shined his light further up the corridor, toward the inner door that led to the castle yard. "We'll figure it out as we go. Bring the admiral, and let's get to Atlo."

They all nodded their agreement and followed him to the door. With a press of his hand against the preselected spots on the wall, the inner door slid open. They were all shocked to see that the wind and storms that had increased in intensity with their every step were not present there.

"Let's get inside," Josh suggested.

They quickly crossed the empty courtyard. Ank pushed the large door open, and they stepped inside the large front foyer.

"Atlo!" Carson called. *There should be someone here,* he thought, but even Dute or Lota were not to be seen.

Ank scouted the nearby rooms but found no sign of the old man or either of the elves. "Now what?" he asked Carson.

"Let's go to the living room and wait."

They went into the now-frigid room. Someone had put out the fire, and there was an icy presence where the warmth had once been.

Carson paced the room as the others found places to sit. "Ank, come with me. They can't all be gone." Carson recalled Atlo telling him that besides himself and the two elves, there were perhaps thirty or forty others there.

Ank stood and followed Carson to the door, which opened by itself without them having to push on it. Carson put his hand out to stop Ank, and they both watched as the door swung open the remainder of the way to reveal a figure standing in the doorway.

"Atlo?" Ank asked.

"Carson, what are you doing back here?" the old man said as he walked past him. "I see you've brought others." As he looked at the others, his eyes seemed to bore right into Melanie.

She looked back at him, and a visible shiver went through her body.

"Good to see you, too, Atlo," Carson said.

"I'm sorry, Carson," he said, turning to him. "What is it you want?"

Carson pointed over to Brooks, who was sitting on the couch.

"Is that your pet?"

Brooks looked up and growled. His jaws opened to reveal his sharp fangs, and both Melanie and Josh had to hold him down.

"Admiral, no!" Melanie said, pulling the hypo out again. This time, she didn't wait for Carson's order before she pressed it against the furry neck and injected the sedative.

Carson turned back to the old man, his anger growing. "What was that for, Atlo? He was transformed into that by Donar."

Atlo smiled. "Donar, you say? Well, then my student is certainly improving. But be that as it may, I assume you want me to change him back."

"Yes. Can you?" Melanie pleaded.

Atlo put a hand up to his white, wiry beard and rubbed his chin. "Come with me to my laboratory, and bring the thing with you," he said, pointing to Admiral Brooks.

Josh and Melanie carried Brooks between them.

Carson reached out his hand to stop Ank.

"You sense it too?" Ank asked quietly.

Carson nodded. "Something isn't right here. Where are Dute and Lota? The last time we were here, they wouldn't leave the old man's side. So where are they now?"

Ank shrugged as they followed the others down to the basement. He clutched his heavy weapon tightly, and Carson's hand never strayed far from his blaster.

Atlo opened the door to his laboratory and pushed a switch on the wall, activating argon gas lights that had been placed around the chamber. "Place your friend on the table, and put the restraints on him," Atlo said, pointing a bony finger at the bare examination table.

Josh removed the security cuffs and, together with Melanie, placed Brooks on the table and strapped him down.

"Good," Atlo said as he walked to a table containing beakers of unknown chemical agents.

Carson became more and more suspicious of the old man and his actions. After he had Ank's attention, he signaled his friend to move to the other side of the room while he approached Atlo. "Atlo, these lights," he said, waving his arms around, "Where did they come from? I thought you didn't have electric power, just candles and torches?"

"Um, Donar left a generator here," he explained as he began to mix chemicals.

"You're lying! In fact, you're Donar!"

"Mark, what are you saying?" Melanie asked in shock.

Atlo put down his beaker of liquid and faced Carson. "Carson, why do you make such a hurtful accusation?" he asked, smiling.

Carson pulled his blaster from its holster and pointed it at Atlo. "Where are Dute and Lota?"

"Carson, put that away," Melanie said, walking over to the old one. "Are you insane?"

"I'm sorry, Carson," Atlo said, a bit too charmingly. "My children, come to me."

From the darkness, two small but horribly transformed creatures stepped out of the shadows. Their eyes were blazing red, their jaws oversized and misshapen.

Melanie screamed in disgust before Atlo stuck out a surprisingly powerful arm and wrapped it around her neck.

"Do you mean these creatures, Carson?" Atlo said, laughing out loud.

Carson examined them carefully and found a tear welling up in his eye. "Dute? Lota? Is that you?"

They stopped for a moment, then moved closer to Atlo.

Carson looked at them more closely. They were miniature versions of what Brooks had become, with one exception: Their teeth had been replaced with a powerful, insect-like mandibles, surely strong enough to cut any of them in half. Carson then looked back at Atlo, who was still holding Melanie tightly by the throat. "Why don't we drop the charade?"

"As you wish." Atlo shimmered and dissolved, finally reforming into the reptilian body of Donar.

"What have you done with Atlo?" Ank growled.

"Do not worry about him. I still need the old fool."

Carson saw Melanie struggling in Donar's grasp. "Let her go," he demanded angrily.

"No can do, Carson. My plans are ruined. You and your friends have gotten in my way for the last time. I knew you would come to see Atlo, for the old fool is the only one who would possibly have the knowledge or the pathetic desire to save your friend."

"That explains why the backup power was operational," Josh said.

"Brilliant, human. It truly is amazing what your tiny brains can fathom. I came here just four days ago, and look how many wonders I've accomplished in such a short time!"

"What about the storms?" Carson asked.

"My experiments to create another gateway to your universe had a few ... unforeseen byproducts," Donar explained. "Put your weapons down."

Carson nodded to the others, and they all placed their weapons on the floor before them. As soon as they were down, Donar signaled for Dute and Lota to collect them and bring them to him.

"Before I kill you, Carson, look to your left."

Carson turned his head and noticed that the far end of the chamber as lighting up. In the corner, suspended by wrist chains, was poor Atlo. The old man seemed to recognize them but gave no indications that he was all right.

Donar moved another switch, and a stone wall slid back to reveal a swirling spectrum of lights and shapes. "Behold my new arch, Carson. It is still a bit unstable, but it will soon transport me instantly to anywhere I wish to go."

"Not if I can help it," Carson said as he advanced on Donar.

Donar quickly reached into his large robe and pulled out a sharp object that he held to Melanie's neck. "Do you recognize this dagger, Carson?"

He nodded slowly; it was the very dagger he had thrown at Donar on Nexus III. "Yes," he said quietly.

"Don't worry. I will not kill her, unless she displeases

me. Melanie and I have much to discuss, don't we, my dear?"

Ank growled as he moved closer to them.

"Stay back, pussycat."

Ank stopped when saw the blade press into her neck and the drop of blood it drew.

"No, Patac. Don't do this. It is wrong," Atlo weakly begged.

"Shut up, old man! I have grown weary of these games, tired of my uninvited guests. Kill them, children."

Josh backed up to where Carson and Ank stood as the two transformed elves approached them, a milky-white secretion dripping from their mouths.

Carson got down on one knee and looked at them. "Lota," he said gently, "it's me, Carson. Don't you recognize me?"

"They are mine, Carson, and they haven't fed for days," Donar said with a grin.

Ignoring him, Carson tried again. "Lota, remember us? When we were together? Remember how we held hands? You're my friend."

Lota stopped for a moment, her mandible moving from side to side as she tried to say something.

"Kill them, I said!" Donar screamed insanely.

The other, the sick version of Dute, began to advance again. Lota stuck out a powerful paw to her mate and pulled him to a halt. She looked at him and growled. Dute must have understood, because he, too, held his ground.

"You will obey me!"

"They won't kill for you, Donar," Carson said, smiling at the elves.

"Then I will kill for myself!" Donar cried, tightening his grip on Melanie.

"Oh no you won't," Melanie said, shifting her weight. She threw an elbow into Donar's chest and managed to break his hold. He still had the dagger and tried to use it on her, but she was too quick. Using the unarmed combat skills Carson had taught her, along with the skills she'd learned evading gang rape on Helos, she pivoted and grabbed the tentacled feeler that held the dagger. With all her strength, she spun the dagger around and thrust it high into the scaly, reptilian chest.

Carson flew in high and dropkicked the surprised Donar to the floor as Melanie threw herself out of the way. Donar was having trouble maintaining his reptilian form as he shifted back and forth between it and his human form.

Finally, unable to hold his transformation, he remained as Patac, and his hands were busy trying to remove the dagger from his chest. The blood flowed freely over his hand as he pulled the weapon free and picked the blaster up from the floor.

Carson took note of the curly blond hair and smooth features; Patac was little more than a boy.

Patac staggered over to one of the control panels as blood dripped to the floor.

"Stop him!" Atlo cried. "That console controls the gate."

"No, it's too late for that," he said, coughing up blood through his smile.

"Donar!" Ank growled as he leapt.

Patac brought the weapon up and fired, striking Ank squarely in the chest and knocking him to the floor.

It was all the time Carson needed. From behind his

back, he pulled the small needler and fired two shots, both of which struck Patac in the throat. The drug staggered him as he tried again to reach for the console controls, a failed attempt since Melanie rose up and stood in his way. She threw a hard left fist to his face and sent Patac crashing down by Atlo's feet.

His efforts to fight back were feeble; the wound to his chest and the drug had taken their toll. Melanie hit him again, sending him again to the floor.

Josh rushed over and held her back. "Stop! It's over," he said to her.

Carson, meanwhile, was leaning over the fallen cat, running a bio-scanner over his wounds.

Patac stared at Melanie from his humbled position on the floor. He tried to will his body into another transformation but didn't have the strength. "Do you want to kill me?" He smiled, and that seemed to enrage Melanie even more. "Your people do not have the strength to kill. Humans are so weak."

With strength born of rage, Melanie twisted and threw Josh over her hip. He landed with a *thud* but seemed all right. She reached down for the blaster that lay at her feet and grabbed a handful of Patac's curly blond hair in one hand, pressing the barrel of the blaster against his head with the other. "Remember what I said to you from the cell about killing you?" she said with a sneer.

Donar, now truly Patac, cringed against her pull.

"You've killed my friends and done even worse to others. Now you're going to pay."

"Don't do it, Melanie," Josh pleaded, steadying himself against the examination table.

Melanie stared into Patac's eyes and took a deep breath, then finally let go of his hair and turned away.

"A coward, like the rest of your species," Patac spat at her.

Without any warning, Melanie swung her leg around and delivered a powerful kick to his face. As he wiped the blood away, she glared down at him. "There are worse things than death, pig." Melanie grabbed him by the robe and ran him right into the chaos of the faulty arch. They all heard the horrible scream of terror as he disappeared.

Josh glared at her. "Melanie!"

"Well," she said innocently, "I didn't kill him, did I?" She saw Carson leaning silently over Ank and rushed over to them. "Is he all right?"

Carson shook his head and, for the first time, she began to cry.

Ank opened his eyes and lifted a paw to brush Melanie's long blonde hair out of her face. "Don't, Melanie. I owed you and Carson my life. Consider the debt paid," he said as he stiffened in pain. His eyes closed slowly, and his paw dropped down to his side.

Melanie buried her head in the crook of Carson's arm and wept for the friend she hadn't even had time to get to know.

CHAPTER 31

Josh released Atlo from his chains before going to comfort his friends. The elves seemed confused by the situation, but at least Carson saw them as less of a threat.

Carson wished he had something to cover the body with. He wanted to give some dignity and honor to Ank's final moments.

Atlo paused for a moment to massage the circulation back into his wrists. He then sent his wolfish elves scurrying away; he would make time for them later. "Carson, let me help your friend," he said, gesturing to Ank.

"It's too late. He's dead."

"Listen to me. Do you know the real reason Patac kept me alive?"

Carson half-heard him as he sat with the others around Ank. "No. Why?"

"Put him on the examination table, and I will show you."

Josh looked up at Atlo and shook his head. "What the hell are you talking about?"

Melanie stood up and faced the old man. "Are you saying you can bring him back from death?"

"Yes, but only if we hurry," he said.

"Josh give me a hand with him. We've got nothing to lose," Carson said. Josh picked Ank up by the legs as Carson grabbed his arms.

"Do you believe this guy?" Josh said quietly as they laid the still figure on the table opposite Brooks.

"My Patac was a brilliant scientist," Atlo began. "He had all my secrets for genetic engineering and quite a few of his own, but there was one I wouldn't give him." Atlo poured together a strange mixture of chemicals from the lab table and carried it over to Ank's body. "See, the brain remains active well after the death of the body. Perhaps in your own culture, you've heard stories of ... out-of-body experiences."

Atlo poured the glowing solution into the black, open wound. On contact with the burnt flesh, the chemical began to foam. As soon as the beaker was empty, Atlo returned it to the shelf and stood over the table. As the three humans watched, Atlo placed his hands on the seeping wound. They all stepped back from the table as the wound and Atlo's hands began to glow a fiery yellow.

"Look!" Melanie said in amazement.

The glow spread until Ank's entire body was encased in a blinding aura. They all had to cover their eyes as the intensity increased, but then there was nothing. When Carson turned back to the table, Atlo had vanished.

"Where did he go?" Josh wondered out loud.

"I don't know, but look!" Carson shouted as Ank began to sit up on the table.

They all gathered around Ank silently, none of them aware of what words should be said to a cat stealing back one of his proverbial nine lives.

Ank looked back at them, very confused himself. "Why are you all staring at me with those stupid smiles on your faces?"

Josh looked amused. "You don't remember, big guy?"

"Remember what?"

"Donar killed you. He hit you in the chest with a blaster

beam," Carson told him.

"I certified you dead myself, Ank," Melanie said, "but look at your chest now! The beam cut through your body armor and left you a bloody mess. Now, though, your fur isn't even burnt."

"How? I mean, I don't know. If I died, why am I...alive?" Ank asked them.

"Atlo," Carson said, "the old man somehow brought you back, but I have no idea where he went."

"He is fixing Dute, Mark Carson." They all turned to the entrance to see the little elf Lota, back in her normal form, standing by the entrance. "Atlo sent me to tell you all that he will be back soon to help your other friend."

Carson stepped over to the elf and knelt down before her on one knee. "Lota, I must thank you again, sweet friend," he said as he took one of her small hands with his. "It must have taken a great deal of strength to resist Donar."

"You helped, Carson." Lota beamed at all the attention as the others also knelt down around her. "I am happy to see you, too, Ank," she said as she rubbed his furry head.

Carson stood and walked over to where Admiral Brooks lay. He looked down into the sad eyes and wondered just how much he had really understood. "Admiral, you'll be back to normal soon enough. Just try to relax, old friend."

Less than an hour later, Atlo returned. Ank was the first one by his side and thanked him for returning his life.

"Please, Ank, it is you I owe. Without the help of you and your friends, Donar would be using us to create his next evil."

"Do you know where the gate took him?" Josh asked.

"I can't really say. To another world or even another

dimension, but I am not sure. Perhaps he is even destined to wander in limbo, between realities."

"Atlo, can I have a word with you?"

"Yes, Carson."

After the two moved to the entrance, away from the others, Carson asked, "Who are you really, Atlo? The truth now."

Atlo stood silently for a moment, as if weighing his answer. "Carson, you are a unique man, so I will tell you my unique secret. I have gone by many names in the past."

"Such as?"

"Moses, Hippocrates, Prometheus, Merlin, and perhaps several others you may or may not be aware of. Two thousand of your years ago, my ship was damaged by meteorite bombardment in orbit around Earth. I crashed onto your lush green and blue world. It was a land of violence and death, with a culture so primitive that it took me almost 1,000 years to finish my repairs and leave. My travels wearied me, but I wanted to do my research, and for a while, the people of Solo allowed me to work undisturbed."

"I don't understand. Why the hoax?"

"Privacy, Carson. How much of it do you think I would have had if anyone had known the truth?" When Carson didn't answer, he continued, "I saw what Patac did with my science of alchemy, how he perverted it, turned it into evil. I cannot allow my secrets to ever again be used in such a way. Promise me that you will do something for me when you leave."

Carson met Atlo's eyes with his own. "I owe you that and more. Just name it."

Moments later, Atlo and Carson stepped back into the

laboratory.

"You guys through with your little secrets?" Josh asked sarcastically.

Carson ignored him and walked over to where Brooks lay. "No worries, Admiral. Atlo is gonna take care of everything. We'll meet you outside." Carson put his arms around Josh and Melanie and led them to the door. "You, too, Ank. Atlo needs his room to work. Lota and Dute have already set up food for us upstairs."

Ank immediately came to attention. "Food, you say? I don't think I've eaten yet in this lifetime."

Carson and Melanie laughed as they saw him fly past them and up the stairs.

As they started up the stairs, Melanie hugged Carson tightly around the waist. "Mark, what did you and Atlo discuss?"

"Maybe I'll tell you one day," he said as they closed the basement door behind them.

CHAPTER 32

They sat in the large living room, full from the generous meal prepared by Dute and Lota, waiting for Atlo to undo Donar's curse on Admiral Brooks.

Lota, as before, stayed close to Carson, until Melanie politely shooed the elf away and encouraged her to take a very long walk.

The conversation was light among the four of them, though there was an underlying tension. Despite what Atlo had done for Ank, he still had to prove it again with Brooks.

"I wish he'd finish already," Josh said impatiently. "I'm not good at this waiting thing."

"Carson, do you think the admiral will be...well, himself?" Melanie asked.

"Why don't you see for yourself?" came the voice from the door.

They turned to see Admiral Clayton Brooks standing there, wearing one of Atlo's long robes.

"Admiral! Are we glad to see you," Carson said for all of them. "How do you feel, sir?"

"A little weak, a little ... strange," Brooks said, shaking his head, "And I have the weirdest taste in my mouth."

Atlo followed him in several seconds later and stood by the door with Lota and Dute.

"Thank you for your help, Atlo ... and for the fabulous attire," Brooks said as he tightened the belt of his borrowed robe.

Atlo simply nodded and smiled somewhat sheepishly. "I can't help feeling somewhat responsible for what has occurred."

"Don't blame yourself, Atlo," Melanie said to him, trying to sound consoling.

"Thank you, my dear."

Carson stepped forward and offered his hand to the old man. "We have to be going now. I again thank you and Dute and Lota for all your help."

One by one, they said their goodbyes as they left the castle for the trek to the portal.

"Remember your promise!" Atlo yelled out once more as Carson walked away.

* * *

As they journeyed to the arch, Josh couldn't help but notice something that was obvious to them all. "Look," he said. "The weather's cleared."

The sky seemed to actually be brightening, possibly for the first time in 1,000 years, Carson thought.

The wait for the arch was a mere forty-five minutes as Ernie had activated the portal on schedule. Thirty-five minutes later, they were back onboard *Pulsar,* heading into space.

Once orbit was established, Carson activated the main viewscreen. "Ernie," he said, "put a nuke online. Set it for surface detonation."

Brooks stepped down to Carson's command chair. "What are you up to?"

Carson just stared at the screen. "Just keeping a promise to a friend."

"Skipper, I have loaded and armed a fifty-kiloton

Quasar-class missile into Launcher Two," Ernie reported.

"Ank, lock it to coordinates 120 meters west of our landing zone," Carson ordered.

"The arch?" Brooks asked.

"Atlo made me promise to remove any access to him forever," Carson finally explained.

"Mark, think about what we can learn from the science that created the arch." Brooks tried his best, but he was outvoted by all the eyes staring harshly at such a suggestion. "Fine, Carson. Blow it then," he finally conceded.

"Coordinates locked," Ank said.

"Goodbye, Atlo," Carson said quietly. "Fire!"

The missile pulled away from its portside launcher and accelerated toward the planet surface.

Ank read the telemetry as the missile approached its target: "Five seconds to impact ... three ... two ... one ... Impact!"

They all looked on as the explosion of energy sent a cloud of radioactive gas high into the sky.

Melanie came up behind Carson's chair. "God, you're so tense," she said as she massaged his tired shoulders.

"You're right about that," he said, closing his eyes to better enjoy her ministrations. "Ernie, take us home."

"Aye-aye, Skipper."

Sitting by the helm, Glick smiled. "She's all yours, Ernie. Enjoy it."

"I tell ya, I could really use a nice, long rest," Josh said, stretching his arms out and yawning.

Carson turned to Brooks, wearing a grin that Brooks knew would cost him money. "Admiral, before all this started, you said something about an all-expenses paid vacation."

"Hmm. I do recall that," Melanie said, visions of a tropical paradise dancing in her head.

Brooks began to back himself toward the door. "Did I say that?"

"You certainly did, Admiral Clayton Brooks," Melanie said, quickly following him to the door, "and if you don't make good on *that* promise, you'll be one very sorry admiral indeed. You know what they say about a woman scorned. I'll see to it myself that you won't have a moment's peace. I'll hound you until – "

"Enough!" Brooks finally screamed. "You win. Just pick the place, but do me a favor."

"What?"

"Don't let Griffin see the bill."

Pulsar carried them home, all of them laughing into the cosmos.

THE END

Thank you for reading.
Please review this book. Reviews help others find Absolutely Amazing eBooks and inspire us to keep providing these marvelous tales.

If you would like to be put on our email list to receive updates on new releases, contests, and promotions, please go to AbsolutelyAmazingEbooks.com and sign up.

ACKNOWLEDGEMENTS

I'd like to thank everyone who encouraged me to continue writing when I didn't have the will myself to sit and get it done, as well as the writers and film makers who shaped my talent and love of the genre, with special mention to Stephen King, Joss Whedon, and Gene Roddenberry for making me think out of the box and into places "not of this world". A special thanks to my editor Autumn, and my publisher Absolutely Amazing E-books to know I can be a pain sometimes, but at least a somewhat talented one. Mostly I want to thank my wife Janice, who saw the talent in me, and had the patience to deal with me while I to put these adventures into words, and still stay married to me.

ABOUT THE AUTHOR

The DarkLight represents the first novel in the new Commando, Inc. series from C.J. Daniels, author of *The Coming*. With degrees in marketing and English, C.J. has a passion for all things sci-fi and states, "Nothing is better than an amazing story, a great setting, and characters you care about." Originally from New York and now residing in New Hampshire, C.J. is currently working on sequels to both *The DarkLight* and the second book in *The Coming* trilogy.

ABSOLUTELY AMAZING eBOOKS

AbsolutelyAmazingEbooks.com
or AA-eBooks.com